T0304867

COURT OF SHADOWS: PRELUDE

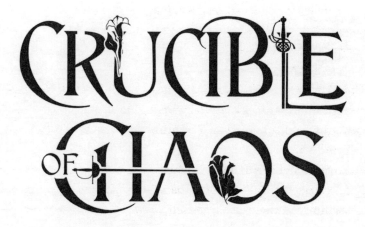

CRUCIBLE OF CHAOS

SEBASTIEN
DE CASTELL

Jo Fletcher
BOOKS

First published in Great Britain in 2023 by

Jo Fletcher
BOOKS

Jo Fletcher Books
an imprint of
Quercus Editions Ltd
Carmelite House
50 Victoria Embankment
London EC4Y 0DZ

An Hachette UK company

A CIP catalogue record for this book is available
from the British Library

HB ISBN 978 1 52943 700 3
TPB ISBN 978 1 52943 701 0
EBOOK ISBN 978 1 52943 703 4

10 9 8 7 6 5 4 3 2 1

Typeset by CC Book Production
Printed and bound in Great Britain by Clays Ltd, Elcograf S.p.A

Papers used by Jo Fletcher Books are from well-managed forests
and other responsible sources.

For all the ghosts who kindly haunted me during my childhood. Whatever happened to you guys, anyway?

CONTENTS

CONTENTS

PART THE FOURTH:

THE SIGILS OF INVITATION

PART THE FIFTH:

THE SIGILS OF WARDING

PART THE SIXTH:

THE SIGILS OF SILENCE

CHAPTER 1

THE WARRING MONKS

MOST EMINENT ARBITER of the King's Laws, Duellist of Well-Deserved Renown and, Perhaps Boldly Stated, My Colleague in the Investigation of Matters Occult and Supernatural Pertaining to the Safety of Our Troubled Nation, I Greet You Thus, Estevar Valejan Duerisi Borros,

Rumours of theological disputes erupting between the monks of my abbey will have reached your notoriously vigilant ears by now. Though not subject to the King's Laws, Isola Sombra nonetheless resides within your judicial circuit, and it is for this reason, as well as for your particular investigative expertise, that I seek out your assistance at this most troubling hour.

Given your often hostile attitude towards religion, you may have already deemed this a mundane ecclesiastical dispute beneath the notice of a Magistrate so highly regarded as to have been dubbed the King's Crucible.

'Bickering among religious zealots can neither be described as unusual or of any great importance,' I imagine you declaring upon receiving the news, no doubt fiddling with the braids of that preposterous beard of yours (I must again remind you, Estevar, that the oiling of one's hair is both a sign of vanity and, given those foreign scents you will insist on employing in this unwise aromatic endeavour, an offence against those downwind of you). 'That silly old Venia,' you will be muttering to yourself as you read this letter, 'forever predicting hurricanes from every stray summer breeze.'

We have never been friends, you and I – indeed, our correspondences on the intersection between religion and the supernatural have often grown so heated as to make me wonder whether you are about to appear at my door with a rapier in one hand and a writ for a duella honoria in the other. Perhaps the disharmony between us is inevitable: I am a priest and you a magistrate; I

1

serve the Gods and you serve a set of laws written by fallible kings and queens. But while I have tried many times to make you a man of faith, it is precisely that lack of faith on which I must now depend.

Something unnatural takes place within the walls of Isola Sombra. Since the murders of the gods two years ago, debates have raged as to which new divinities will take their place. What began as earnest theological enquiry has become a conflagration that will engulf us all. I fear what might ensue, should angry words turn to condemnation, and condemnation to open warfare within the abbey. My efforts to calm my brethren have failed, and my own status as Abbot of Isola Sombra diminished to an empty title and a tower from which I dare not venture.

Estevar, I have asked a trusted emissary to place copies of this letter in the hands of every travelling Bardatti troubadour passing through this duchy in hopes that one of them finds you in whichever courtroom or duelling circle your passion for justice and intemperate nature has brought you. I need a Magistrate, Estevar. I need the only Greatcoat in all of Tristia who understands both the laws of this land and the occult traditions that have both protected and plagued it in the past. My only hope is that the monks of my abbey will place their trust in the King's Crucible to resolve the theological disputes over which my own counsel no longer holds sway.

Ride swiftly to Isola Sombra, Estevar, I beg you. It is from this holy place that religion first spread throughout Tristia. If we fail to purge the divisions between my brethren, something far more dangerous may be coming in its wake.

Venia, Abbot of Isola Sombra

PART THE FIRST

THE SIGILS
OF SEVERING

The first sigils of the rite are not an unlocking, but a separation. Begin by washing and chilling the flesh, then inscribe upon the skin the symbols depicted herein, chanting the words as set forth below, and with every stroke strip away the will from the mind. Once the two are irrevocably severed, then shall the body become a canvas for your intentions.

CHAPTER 2

THE ABBEY IN THE SEA

Out beyond the shore of the Western Sea, a great abbey towers above the waves. Tall as any castle, Isola Sombra's treasures are the envy of princes. Its six colossal spires, armoured in stone walls impervious to the buffeting winds and pelting rains, rise up as if to taunt the gods to which they were once consecrated. The relentless fury of the storms which lately assail the abbey suggests such impertinence has not gone unnoticed. Given those same gods were murdered two years ago, an inquisitive traveller to this once holy site might wonder whose outrage now summons the tempest?

The tiny islet upon which the abbey was built centuries ago is tethered to the mainland by a half-mile-long causeway barely wide enough for two carts to pass each other without one being shoved off the slippery cobbles and into the sea. During the winter months, thick fogs often blanket the causeway, blinding travellers to the unpredictable currents. Anyone foolish enough to attempt the crossing during a squall is likely to find themselves swept away beneath the ocean swells, horses, wagons and all.

Estevar Borros had neither wagon nor horse. He slumped heavily in the saddle somewhat precariously strapped to the mule he'd purchased six months ago at the start of his judicial circuit. He'd named the beast Imperious, though the ostentatious sobriquet wasn't due to any regal bearing evinced by the mule, but rather for the way its rain-drenched muzzle would turn every few plodding steps so it could glare at its rider and remind him precisely who was to blame for their soggy predicament.

'The fault isn't mine,' Estevar grumbled, his words drowned out by the sleet and rain currently hampering their approach to the causeway. 'Bring suit against the First Cantor if you're so aggrieved. It was she who assigned us this gods-be-damned judicial circuit that never ends.'

Imperious offered his own grunt in reply, which Estevar took as agreement that the responsibility did indeed lie some two hundred miles to the northeast with a woman barely nineteen years of age whom fate – and the execrable former First Cantor of the Greatcoats – had placed in charge of the King's Travelling Magistrates.

Estevar's ice-cold fingers reached beneath the dripping black braids of his beard to pull up the collar of his muddy crimson greatcoat in a hopeless attempt to protect his neck from the beating rain. Even this small movement drew a groan from him. *That damned wound* . . . The seven-inch gash just above the bottom rib on his left side showed no sign of healing. This particular ache could not, alas, be blamed on the new First Cantor, but rather on Estevar's own temper.

Staring into the thick fog ahead of them, he could almost picture that suave, conceited duellist standing there: long and lean, his blade swift as a devil's tail, his spirit unburdened by conscience. His employer, a wealthy lord caravanner charged with the murder of his own wife, had demanded an appeal by combat after Estevar had rendered his verdict. There had been no necessity to accept the challenge; the evidence had been incontrovertible, and King's magistrates aren't bound to cross swords with every belligerent who disagrees with the outcome of a trial. And yet . . . there was that smirk on the too-handsome face of the merchant's champion, as if no one so wide of girth as Estevar could possibly score a touch against him.

In fact, Estevar had won first blood. His use of an unusual Gitabrian sword bind – rather clever, he'd thought at the time – had sent his smug opponent hurtling to the courtroom floor. A single clean thrust to the forearm with the tip of Estevar's rapier – hardly more than a scratch – had been precisely the sort of merciful and honourable declaration of victory expected of a Greatcoat. When the clerk of the court struck the bell to end the duel in Estevar's favour, he had even extended a hand to assist the man back to his feet.

Arrogance. Sheer, wanton arrogance.

His enraged opponent had pushed himself off the floor with one hand and delivered a vicious rapier cut with the other. Worse, at the instant of full extension, he'd added injury to insult by turning his wrist to add a vicious puncture to an already deep laceration, the sort of wound that invariably leads to infection and rarely heals properly.

The King's Third Law of Judicial Duelling was unequivocal on the matter: Estevar was the victor. Unfortunately, the local viscount, no admirer of the king's meddling magistrates, had taken advantage of Estevar's public humiliation to overrule his verdict. The lord caravanner had ridden away unpunished. His murdered wife was buried in an unmarked grave the next morning, denied both justice and priestly blessings.

Estevar pressed a hand over the nagging wound. There wasn't so much as a scratch on the leather. The bone plates sewn into the lining would have protected him, had he not been so vain that he'd consented to the duellist's demand that he fight without it.

'Surely so *redoubtable* a physique, one so *voluminous* in vigour, needs no armour to protect the many, many layers of valorous flesh beneath?' the tall, sleek fellow had shouted mockingly before the entire court. 'What use those silly bone plates sewn into the lining of that preposterous garment you "Greatcoats"' – he'd imbued the word with such irony! – 'insist on wearing when compared to the blubber straining its seams?'

Fool of a fool of a fool, Estevar's mother would have chided him – which was nothing compared to the lashing he could expect to receive from the preposterously young First Cantor when this last stop on his judicial circuit was dealt with and he returned to Castle Aramor.

Voluminous, he thought bitterly, pressing even harder against the wound, but failing to ease the sting. Six days and a hundred miles since he'd cleaned and sewn up the cut, but the pain hadn't abated one jot. Worse, it now felt hot to the touch, suggesting infection. *Perhaps if I survive the fever I'll name the scar 'Voluminous' as a reminder to have a thicker skin in future.*

'And now what shall we do, Imperious?' he asked the mule. 'We're under no obligation to heed the abbot's request for judicial arbitration between his unruly monks. As Venia so reliably reminded us in his letter, Isola Sombra does not consider itself subject to the King's Laws. Why should we tarry here when we could already be on our way home?'

Despite his optimistic words, Estevar had no illusions about the welcome awaiting him at Aramor once the First Cantor learned that one of her magistrates had lost a judicial appeal he'd been under no obligation to grant in the first place, only to then take a grievous injury due entirely to his inexcusable pride rather than any skill of his opponent. He would be lucky if she didn't immediately demand he relinquish his coat of office.

Imperious swivelled his sorrel head once again, this time in an attempt to bite his rider's hand as punishment for bringing him to this hellish place. Evidently, it wasn't only the First Cantor to whom Estevar owed profuse apologies.

'Let us away home then,' he declared, tugging gently on the reins to circle his mount back towards the mainland road. 'We'll leave the monks to their quarrels.'

He was about to give the mule's flanks an encouraging nudge when a voice shouted out from the mists, 'Hold where you are!'

Man and mule both turned. The grey haze between the mainland and the causeway had thickened, distorting the voice and making it difficult to locate its source. A less experienced traveller might have heard the command of an angry ghost come to exact revenge for some long-forgotten crime. Estevar, however, had investigated many supposed supernatural apparitions during his tenure as a Greatcoat, and quickly decided this one sounded more man than spectre. He patted Imperious' neck to calm him, but the mule lowered his head and hunched his shoulders, as if determined to leap into battle against their unknown assailant.

'Who approaches the cursed Abbey of Isola Sombra?' the hidden figure demanded.

Estevar closed his eyes a moment, allowing the eerie echoes to surround him. The voice was deep, confident, but that gravitas was trained rather than natural. The accent – most notably the rising inflection on the last vowel of the abbey's name, almost as if he were saying 'Som–brae' – suggested a commoner raised in this duchy, not highborn himself, but accustomed to being in the presence of nobles.

He reached back for the oilcloth bag strapped behind the cantle. He'd wanted to protect his rapier from the rain and hadn't anticipated having to fight his way into an abbey famed almost as much for its hospitality as its wealth. With his fingers chilled to the bone, the knots were proving perniciously difficult to untie. His mind, however, was moving more nimbly, envisioning the unfolding scene from the perspective of the fellow who now sought to block his passage.

He sees only a fat man in a leather greatcoat slouched wearily upon a mule, Estevar thought, *someone too slow to present a genuine threat. Someone he can bully as he pleases.*

This was, regrettably, a common enough conclusion on meeting Estevar Borros. A magistrate's first duty being to the truth, he decided it was incumbent upon him to cure this new acquaintance of a potentially fatal ignorance. He coughed briefly before allowing his own deep baritone to rumble across the sandy shore.

'To you, stranger, is the privilege of greeting Estevar Valejan Duerisi Borros, often called the King's Crucible. As one of His Majesty's Travelling Magistrates, the duty of hearing appeals to the King's Justice throughout the Seventh Circuit of Tristia falls to me. Any fool who stands in the way of that endeavour will soon find himself flat on his back, gazing up at the sky and asking the gods why they cursed him with such poor judgement as to challenge me.'

Not bad, Estevar mused, all thoughts of abandoning the monks to their own devices banished as he drew his rapier. *The cadence was a little off, but melodious eloquence is surely too much to ask of a fellow in my feverish state.*

At last, a tall figure emerged from the mists. First came the glint of steel, the position and angle suggesting a longsword held in a high guard. Next came the shimmer of a chainmail surcoat partly covered by a hooded cloak of pure white trimmed in silver and emblazoned with three azure eyes across the front.

A Knight of the March of Someil, Estevar reasoned, which explained both the accent and commanding tone.

The chainmail was going to be a problem. Estevar's rapier was a duelling weapon meant for courtroom trials and back-alley ambushes, not squaring off on the battlefield against armoured knights. Tristian steel came in varying qualities, however, and a Greatcoat's rapier was as fine a weapon as was ever forged in this benighted little country. Wielded with force and precision, the point could shatter the links of a mail surcoat to find the fragile flesh beneath. That was, of course, assuming its wielder was not already wounded and exhausted.

The wise move would be to fight from atop the mule. The added height afforded a superior position, and Imperious was no shy pony to cower in the face of danger. Should the need arise to flee, being already in the saddle would increase the odds of escape.

But my opponent is a man of war, Estevar reminded himself, *trained to slash the throat of his enemy's mount first to counter his advantage.*

He dismounted, hiding his unsteadiness beneath a show of nonchalance. He patted his mule's reddish-brown mane and whispered into one long, twitching ear, 'No heroics, my friend. When the first blow is struck, turn tail and run. Find yourself a mare and – well, as I don't suppose mules can reproduce, just enjoy yourself and think fondly of your old friend Estevar.'

Imperious ignored him, instead issuing a braying warning to the approaching knight. Running away clearly wasn't the beast's style.

'Damned good mule,' Estevar murmured, bringing his rapier up to a centreline guard suitable for initiating a deceptive flick at the eyes followed by a more powerful – and desperate – thrust to the narrow gap between helm and gorget, which would be his best hope of evading the mail surcoat.

'Borros?' the knight called out, coming into full view at last. A handsome devil, you had to give him that. The very portrait of a young chevalier: broad in the shoulder, narrow in the hips, square-jawed and golden-haired beneath a steel half-helm. Even the broken nose lent his otherwise smooth features a determined dignity. No doubt many a lad and lass had swooned over this one. At his side dangled a curved ivory horn. Estevar had known the blare of such instruments to carry for miles across flat terrain. 'You are truly Estevar Borros, the King's Crucible?' the knight asked.

'The storm is not so deafening that you failed to hear me the first time,' he replied, widening his stance and raising the blade of his rapier. 'Now, stop where you are. Inclement weather and poor soil make for arduous grave-digging, and I have more pressing business at the abbey.'

Without warning, the knight rushed Estevar. The fool might well have impaled himself, had not the combination of a magistrate's quick judgement and a duellist's quick instincts enabled Estevar to tilt his rapier blade off-line in time to stop the point sliding over the steel gorget and into the knight's exposed throat.

'My name is Sir Daven Colraig,' the young knight declared, hugging Estevar with frantic relief. 'I am Sheriff Outrider to His Lordship, Margrave Someil. It was he who commanded me to await you here these past seven days.'

'Seven days?' Estevar had to suppress a groan when the young man's exuberant squeezing aggravated his wound. He shoved the fellow away, not quite as gently as he'd intended. 'You expect me to believe you've been out in this storm for an entire week?'

Sir Daven nodded, water dripping from his helm onto the golden locks plastered to his forehead. 'Indeed, Eminence. The margrave had hoped you would arrive sooner.'

'My pace was perhaps more leisurely than anticipated,' Estevar admitted.

Yet why would the Margrave of Someil be keeping abreast of a magistrate's travels? And why would he make one of his knights camp out in the cold and wet until my arrival?

'The Abbey of Isola Sombra is less than half a mile across the causeway,' Estevar observed. 'The monks are known for their gracious hospitality to all who arrive at their gates. Why await me here? Unless it was to prevent me from reaching them myself?'

Sir Daven slid a gauntleted hand into his cloak and withdrew a cylinder of black leather roughly eight inches long and barely an inch in diameter. The message sheath was banded in azure and bore a silver wax seal of a wasp shattering a shield: the hereditary insignia of the

Margraves of Someil. 'I know the Greatcoats have oft been at odds with the nobles of this duchy, Eminence, but my lord is no enemy to the new king, nor to his magistrates.'

Estevar eyed the black leather tube warily. Bribing magistrates was a common tactic for those with a vested interest in the outcome of a case. The lord caravanner had offered him a small fortune to avoid a trial. Was this some attempt by the Margrave of Someil to secure a ruling against the Abbey of Isola Sombra, whose legendary obstinance in refusing to pay taxes – either to the king or to the local nobility – rested upon the dubious claim that their tiny island was by tradition a sovereign nation unto itself?

'Please,' Sir Daven said, jabbing the message sheath at Estevar's chest, 'read my lord's words and heed them, I beg you.'

Imperious attempted to bite off the knight's hand. When that failed, he snatched the leather cylinder away from him.

'Cease, you avaricious beast,' Estevar growled, yanking the crushed tube from between the mule's teeth. 'Save your appetite for the abbey, where we shall shortly be feasted as befits visiting dignitaries.'

He undid the azure ties, unfurled the parchment and read quickly, before the rain smudged the ink, rendering the missive illegible. He checked the half-seal at the bottom of the parchment, comparing it with its mate on the other side, a security device. The rich purple-black ink he recognised as a rare mixture made of the iron-gall from an oak tree and the crushed seeds of a berry found only in this duchy: a concoction so carefully guarded by the margraves that even the finest forgers found it near-impossible to reproduce. All of which suggested the document was authentic, which made the five lines scrawled upon it all the more troubling.

From his Lordship Alaire, Margrave of Someil,
Warden of the March, Defender of the Faith,
To you, my friend, in earnest warning,
As you love life and value your soul,
you will not set foot on Isola Sombra.

A blaze ignited in Estevar's belly, chasing away the cold and wet, even the ache of his wound. When bribery was deemed unlikely to succeed, the nobility all too often resorted to blackmail and bullying.

'A threat?' he demanded, crushing the parchment in his fist as the rain poured down even harder, the thunder in the sky above punctuating his outburst. 'Your precious margrave would seek to intimidate a Greatcoat into abandoning his lawful mission? Does he so fear what the Abbot of Isola Sombra might reveal to me of his activities that he'd stoop to—?'

'Abbot Venia no longer rules Isola Sombra,' the knight said icily, his countenance darkening. 'He who once defied kings now cowers beneath the covers inside his tower while madness and devilry reigns over that holiest of islands!'

Estevar could barely restrain his laughter. 'Has the cold and damp frozen that helmet to your head, Sir Knight? You speak of two hundred pampered, petulant monks as if they were an army of invading soldiers!'

Sir Daven shook his head, sending splatters of rain onto Estevar's face and beard. 'Not soldiers, sir, but warlocks – heretics who dabble in curses and necromancy, perverting their bodies in unholy orgies—'

Estevar cut him off. 'Enough. I am a Greatcoat, not some backwoods constable to be frightened off with childish tales of witchcraft. As the King's Crucible, it falls to me to investigate cases suspected of supernatural intervention. I have witnessed hundreds of occult rituals all across this country – some genuine, most elaborate trickery, but none the preposterous pantomime you're ascribing to the brethren of Isola Sombra.' He handed the black leather cylinder to Sir Daven. 'You call yourself a sheriff outrider? If the Margrave of Someil truly believes some nefarious demon worship to have taken hold of the abbey, surely he would have sent a contingent of his finest knights to investigate, rather than have you wait out here in the rain like an unwanted pup?'

The knight refused to take back the sheath, saying instead, 'Look inside the cylinder, Eminence; a second document awaits your perusal.'

Estevar cursed himself for failing to notice the smaller piece of parchment tight against the inside of the case. He had to dig it out with his fingernail before unfolding what turned out to be an elaborate sketch of a naked man such as one might find in a medical text. What made it unusual were the strange markings covering the body: esoteric sigils in designs unrecognisable to Estevar despite his years of research into the esoteric traditions of Tristia.

'My Lord *did* send a dozen of my fellow knights to investigate,' Sir Daven said defiantly. 'When they emerged the next morning ...' He paused, visibly shaken by whatever memories plagued him. 'Twelve braver, steadier men and women I have never known, yet not one of them has uttered a word since their return. They sit in separate chambers within the margrave's fortress, attended to by his personal physicians – not clerics, mind you, trained *physicians* – who claim their souls have fled their bodies.'

'There has to be a logical explanation,' Estevar murmured, returning the picture and the margrave's message to the cylinder before placing it in a pocket of his greatcoat. 'There is *always* an explanation.'

Steel returned to the younger man's eyes as they locked on Estevar's. 'Theories and conjectures do not fall within my purview, Eminence, nor was I sent here merely to await your displeasure.' He lifted the ivory horn strapped to his side and jabbed his other hand towards the six stone towers rising from the dense greyness. 'Should anyone or any*thing* come back across that causeway, my orders are to first raise the alarm, then fend off whatever chaos has been spawned in the cloisters of Isola Sombra until help arrives or death takes me!'

Holding the knight's gaze, Estevar sifted through what clues he could discern in the younger man's determined expression. Were the clenched jaw and stiff posture signs of the unyielding devotion to duty so often espoused by Tristian knights, or mere melodrama meant to frighten away one of the King's Magistrates before he could interfere in whatever schemes were unfolding on Isola Sombra?

Estevar's fever-addled brain rebelled against him, alerting him instead to the flush in his cheeks and the burning ache in his side. What business did he have setting foot upon the ill-fated isle at the end of that storm-drenched causeway armed with nothing but a rapier, his arrogance and a cantankerous mule?

'Heed my liege's warning, Eminence, I beg you,' Sir Daven said, no doubt sensing Estevar's wavering intentions.

How strange that only moments before, he'd been ready to abandon this place and ignore Abbot Venia's plea for him to arbitrate the dispute between his contentious monks. Now that this same dispute had exploded into something far more unsettling, Estevar found himself unable to walk away.

He knew himself to be a ludicrous figure in the eyes of many: a foreigner to these shores who dared demand a place among the legendary Greatcoats; a fat, pompous buffoon who insisted on fighting his own duels when younger and fitter men would have refused; an eccentric who alone among the King's Travelling Magistrates investigated crimes attributed to witches, demons and sundry other supernatural forces. In short, Estevar Borros was a silly fool, driven by his innate stubbornness as much as his affinity for the law. But there was yet one more failing to which he was ever subservient – the one that, even more than his arrogance, had led him to accept the most recent duel: the persistent, impossible-to-quiet voice that had brought him from his homeland across the sea to this strange, troubled nation. The addiction was more potent than any drug, a nagging need that could overpower even the pain of a festering wound in his side.

Looking towards the abbey in the sea, contemplating what chaos awaited, he murmured, 'I am curious.'

'What?' asked Sir Daven, grabbing his arm.

Gently, he loosened the younger man's fingers. 'I thank you, Sir Knight. You have delivered your message, fulfilling this part of your mission. No one could fault your courage or your loyalty to your liege.' He slid his rapier into the sheath ingeniously designed into the leather panel on the left side of his greatcoat, wincing at the sudden sting that was surely his stitches coming apart.

Sir Daven gaped at him as he if were mad. 'Look at yourself,' he cried, his frantic voice bubbling over with scorn and unease. 'You can barely stand – yes, I see you, attempting to hide whatever injury ails you. But even after what I've told you, still you insist on crossing the most perilous causeway in the country during a raging storm while the tide rises? I have told you that death and worse await you on the other side – do you presume the rest of us to be gullible dolts deluded by some petty parlour trick?'

'I think nothing of the kind,' Estevar replied, taking the reins and tugging his reluctant mule towards the narrow cobblestone road ahead. 'You claim the monks of Isola Sombra commit unspeakable crimes, dabbling in forbidden occult rituals and desecrating the oldest holy site in the country. Surely that calls for the intervention of a King's Magistrate, no?'

'You're a fool,' Sir Daven spat, no longer pretending at admiration, or even sympathy. 'A mad fool! What will be left of you once the monsters prowling that cursed abbey have peeled away the last layers of your arrogance from your flesh?'

Estevar placed a hand on the mule's neck to steady himself as the two of them began their crossing. Shouting over the wind and rain he replied, 'According to my sainted mother? Only more arrogance.'

CHAPTER 3

THE DRUNKEN PLAGUE

Estevar's boots slid on the slick cobblestones, each step offering the pelting rains and rising currents another chance to sweep him off the causeway and into the sea. Even the sure-footed Imperious struggled to keep his hooves from slipping on the seaweed-coated path to Isola Sombra. Years ago, when last he had come this way, the tides had seemed lower and the road better maintained. Now, it felt as if nature itself was determined to keep them from the abbey. Though unsteady and feverish, Estevar walked alongside Imperious, unwilling to risk the poor beast stumbling and breaking a leg by riding him through the onslaught.

'The last thing either of us desires,' he told the mule, 'is an injured, out-of-shape magistrate, soaked to the bone, carrying *you* on his back.'

Imperious gave no reply, just narrowed big brown eyes against the chill wind, undaunted by the oncoming rain. Estevar felt ignoble by comparison.

A deafening boom of thunder filled his ears, and a second later, a crack of lightning split the grey sky above. The sea on either side of the causeway roiled as if with hideous glee, spraying water over man and mule alike. The tide was rising; the time to cross was running out.

'No wonder Sir Daven and his beloved margrave have fallen to superstition and nightmarish conjectures, eh, Imperious?' Estevar attempted a cheerful tone despite the raging waters increasingly flooding the path ahead.

He could have sworn the margrave's note, now secreted inside one of the many interior pockets of his greatcoat, was pricking his ribs, much like the wound that ached so mercilessly. In this one regard, the storm was his ally, for it reminded him how easily nature's cruel majesty could turn less rational minds to supernatural explanations.

'The Dancing Plague,' he shouted over the roar of the wind. 'You weren't with me on that case, Imperious, but it was not so dissimilar to this one.'

The mule gave a stuttering huff, which Estevar took as an inducement to continue.

'A village called Saltare in the north of Domaris – not far from where you were likely bred, in fact.' He poked the mule in the shoulder for good measure. Imperious promptly turned and tried to bite off his finger, which Estevar found oddly reassuring. 'Don't blame me if your home happens to be in one of the most gullible and blindly religious parts of the country. Now, as I was saying, I received word that a small but prosperous village was suffering from an epidemic of something the locals called "the Dancing Plague". Without warning, men and women would drop their tools and baskets, remove all their clothes and run into the streets, where they pranced and jumped and twirled, apparently quite unable to stop themselves, until they dropped from exhaustion or their hearts gave out.'

A rising wave caught Estevar's attention, leaving barely enough time for him to throw his arms around Imperious to shield the poor beast's head from its impact. Once the wave had receded, the two unhappy companions were left twice as drenched as before.

Estevar returned to his story through chattering teeth. 'This plague of febrile frolicking was at first believed to be a hoax – a scheme concocted by the villagers to justify abandoning their duties because the local viscount whose lands they farmed had refused to lower their taxes. The viscount in question, a cunning enough man in his own right, sent a veritable army of physicians, philosophers and tax collectors to the village. But can you surmise what transpired mere hours after their arrival in the village?'

The suffering mule was entirely too focused on placing one hoof safely in front of the other on the treacherous causeway to reply. Imperious was shivering badly now, and Estevar, whose expertise in animal husbandry was limited to knowing that one should feed their mount frequently and never kick them, feared the poor beast would collapse in terror before they reached the gates of the abbey.

'Quite correct, my friend,' Estevar said jovially, patting the mule's neck as if the animal had indeed ventured a guess. 'That very night, having enjoyed the villagers' hospitality, the viscount's envoys proceeded to strip off all their clothes and join the afflicted in their whirling frenzy!' Estevar began laughing heartily, as much to mask the tumult of thunder overhead and soothe the mule's nerves than from genuine mirth. 'Imagine that, Imperious, an assembly of high-priced physicians, battle-hardened soldiers and keen-eyed clerks, naked as the day they were born, dancing around the village like maniacs!'

He took on a serious air, for this was the part of the tale he most enjoyed recounting – even lacking an audience capable of comprehending his words. 'This, my friend, is when Estevar Valejan Duerisi Borros, better known as the King's Crucible – yes, indeed, it was I – was summoned. Matters of the supernatural *are* my area of expertise, as you know – though I've had precious few opportunities to employ them since that upstart girl Chalmers was named First Cantor and decided that all her Greatcoats must resume their judicial circuits to restore the rule of law to our troubled nation. I suppose I cannot fault her reasoning . . . But you have me digressing now, Imperious, for this case was years ago, before our new monarch took the throne. It was his father, King Paelis, who had commanded me to investigate this diabolically plagued village and determine what manner of witch or demon had taken possession of its citizens.'

Estevar paused a moment, looking up past the fog that not even the rains could dissipate to the glistening towers and mighty stone curtain wall looming high above the tiny island ahead. Two, perhaps three hundred yards to go, not a great distance, but the water was above their ankles now and rising very fast. He knew well how quickly the currents could render such a causeway impassable in a storm. To be trapped between island and shore at such a time in this tempest would mean both of them would drown for certain. He took hold of the mule's reins and urged him to a faster pace. Imperious, already uncertain of his footing, resisted.

'Come now, my friend, think of the feast awaiting us on the island! Succulent roast lamb drenched in juices, spiced with saffron and mint for me, delectable grains for you. In fact, it is grain which brings us back to the conundrum of the Dancing Plague.'

Whether from hunger, curiosity, or simply the desire not to suffer his master's bragging any longer, the mule at last quickened his pace.

'Yes, indeed, the grain,' Estevar continued, so enthralled with the intricacies of the case that he could almost forget the pain in his side and the treacherous path he was treading towards a destination allegedly full of its own dire perils. 'The barley grown in the farms around the village of Saltare had been bred for its ability to prosper in colder climes, which is how it got its name: "winter's gift". But this was summer, you understand, and an unusual hot spell had engulfed the duchy. With the warmer weather came a plague, indeed – but not one of dancing.'

Estevar's boot heel slipped and his grip on Imperious' saddle horn failed him. He came crashing down onto his buttocks and inadvertently swallowed a mouthful of salt water, which set off a fit of coughing. The mule brayed, head swivelling left and right as if searching for some dry place to flee, yet still not keen on the island ahead.

Estevar forced himself back to his feet, ignored a host of new aches and urged the shaking beast onwards. 'No, my friend, the plague that afflicted Saltare was that of the penny locust. Most insects of that genus are foul things which devour crops, but this one is a smaller, less malignant insect. Copper-coloured, much like an actual penny – or at least, the ones in Domaris – the diminutive penny locust nibbles on the stalks rather than the barley itself, leaving the best parts for the farmers. A most miraculous creature, wouldn't you agree? However, their feasting leaves behind traces of their saliva. Under normal conditions, it's mostly harmless, which is why farmers don't concern themselves with the penny locust. But when heated beneath an unseasonable sun, day after day . . . ah, then this peculiar insect's saliva reacts with the chemicals within this particular barley, and when fermented into ale, this unexpected combination produces a potent narcotic. Those who ingest it are soon afflicted with a rather severe case of . . . disinhibition!'

Once again Estevar roared his laughter over the thunder, clapping a reassuring hand on the mule's shoulder. Imperious was now too frightened by the raging storm and sea even to nip at him in retaliation. 'That's right, my friend, neither the villagers nor the viscount's envoys were suffering from any demonic dancing plague – they were merely intoxicated out of their gourds!' Estevar's foot slipped a second time and he felt as if the water itself was trying to drag him down. Managing at last to right himself, he went on, 'In fact, naming the affliction a "dancing" plague was a euphemism if ever there was one. Now, I'm not one for salacious talk, so let me simply say that by the time I uncovered the source of the bizarre behaviour, many an unexpected babe was already on its way in that village!'

Estevar felt a chill around his calves and looked down to see the water had risen above the tops of his boots and was sloshing inside, and they still hadn't reached the island gate.

Time was running out even faster than he'd feared.

'Quickly now, Imperious,' he commanded the mule, tugging harder on the reins until he was half dragging the terrified beast. 'Don't you see my point? This so-called "dancing plague" was nothing but the unfortunate side-effect of fermented barley and insect saliva!' He jabbed a finger at the gate, now barely a hundred yards ahead, and the winding road leading up to the abbey. 'What are the monks of Isola Sombra famous for? The potency of the liquors they brew from crops grown on that very island. Can we not, therefore, deduce that these recent storms may have triggered similar effects, not only on grapes and grains but also on the psyches of the people who live here?'

Imperious brayed again and Estevar held on tightly to the reins with one hand, patting the mule's head repeatedly with the other in hopes of calming him. 'Think, Imperious! Wines rendered mildly toxic by some change in the soil, a few monks too long living in isolation on this tiny islet, muttering their endless prayers to this god or that, and the well-known superstitious nature of ducal knights. The abbot confines himself to his tower, the margrave sends a dozen of his stalwart warriors to investigate, and what do they find? Naught but an abbey filled with frightened – and likely inebriated – quaesti, venerati and deators drunkenly debating theological esoterica. The knights no doubt deride the brothers, bullying them and making sport of their fears, and help themselves to the abbey's legendary liquors. The irate monks decide to take advantage of the knights' stupor by sending them packing – but not before painting upon the skin of the drunk and stupefied knights those hideous markings we saw on the picture that came with the margrave's note. Days pass before the knights recover, and when sobriety returns, do you suppose they confess their drunken behaviour to their lord? No, they claim demonic influence!'

Even amid the battering wind and rain, Estevar found himself grinning as he pulled the mule along. 'Do you see now, Imperious? The scheme is so simple, even a mind far less accustomed to such devious ingenuity than that of your friend Estevar could pierce this fragile veil of ignorance and gullibility!'

He felt the mule's tension ease at last, and his own ebbed along with it. The stairs up to the gate were less than twenty yards away now, and even with the water at his knees, his anxieties began to fade. His tale had been meant only as a distraction for himself and Imperious from the discomfort of their journey across the causeway, but with every step he'd grown more convinced that he'd stumbled upon the truth of it. The incident at Isola Sombra which had so distressed Margrave Someil's knights was nothing more than the effects of those most foul demons that Estevar had battled his entire career: superstition and duplicity. Now he needed only to validate his deductions, free the monks from their supposed supernatural hysteria and induce the easily panicked Abbot Venia to descend at last from his tower and resume his duties.

It was with a lighter heart and a confident smile that he led Imperious along those last few feet to the steps of Isola Sombra – only for a wave higher than all the others before to crash down on them both, dragging man and beast beneath the water and out to sea.

CHAPTER 4

BENEATH THE WAVES

Tumbling and twisting, Estevar was tossed about like a discarded child's toy. What breath he'd been able to take in before the currents had snatched man and mule from the causeway he now held to as firmly as the hilt of his rapier during a duel – for a duel this was, and his opponent a relentless mistress of the disarm.

Already his lungs burned, but he set the pain aside; it was a distraction, a feint, nothing more. His mind, that was the key: he must keep his thoughts clear, precise, sharp as any blade. No battle worth the fight was won on brute force alone, so even as the currents flung him to and fro, he sought to cut through his dilemma. This was a puzzle, after all – a mystery whose solution hinged on a single question: how does a man already weakened by a sword wound, burdened by exhaustion and, let us be honest, a fondness for rich foods exacerbated by a belligerent streak that insisted that so long as he could still win his judicial duels, no evidence supported the proposition that his girth was an impediment, rise from this watery grave before the pounding waves inter him for ever?

A conundrum easier to solve when one is not turned upside down, he admitted, though he was no longer entirely sure which way was up. Briefly, he wondered how poor Imperious was faring. Mules were reputedly strong swimmers, though Estevar had never tested his beast in this regard.

Curse his bleary eyes! On dry land, they saw all, yet here beneath the water, he could barely make out his own hand in front of his face. He'd been a skilled diver in his youth, able to leap from the clifftops of the magnificent city of his birth to land with exquisite precision between the merchant vessels below, never coming back up without having found some lost trinket to bring to his belov—

Stop reminiscing about the past, you fool. It's the present which seeks to kill you! Nostalgia is the trap that promises insight yet offers only the slow, insidious acceptance of failure. You will not outwit your watery nemesis this way. If only I had dry land beneath my feet and not this frenzy of—

Wait . . . That's it!

Fighting the currents was a fool's game, no different than chasing a younger, swifter opponent around the duelling circle. Estevar needed firm soil on which to stand and fight – and there it was, waiting for him below!

Quickly he calculated the relative incline of the shore where first he'd set foot on the half-mile-long causeway. This far out, the seabed would usually be too deep to serve him, but the causeway itself wasn't constructed as a narrow wall but rather a sloped ridge of soil and rock that widened as it descended deeper beneath the surface. The wave that had swept him and Imperious from the causeway couldn't have driven them more than ten or twenty yards away, which meant the bottom shouldn't be more than fifteen feet down.

His lungs ached mercilessly, as did his wound. Once again, he pushed such trivialities away and concentrated on the first step towards survival: figuring out which direction was up. The sky, darkened by grey clouds, sent precious little light this far down, but still, he could make out shadows well enough. He let out a tiny portion of his precious air and watched for the bubbles.

Nothing.

Too dark. Damn those storm clouds!

Unless it *wasn't* too dark after all? He craned his head back as far as it would go and released a bit more air. This time, he saw the bubbles drifting in a line up to the surface; he was, indeed, upside down. Rather than right himself, Estevar swam as hard as he could, straight down until he felt undulating tendrils brush his cheeks, and then his hand touched the sandy seabed below.

Grabbing a handful of the seaweed, he pulled hard, swinging his legs under himself until his feet found the bottom, then, bending his knees, he flexed his thigh muscles and launched himself upwards, kicking his legs furiously to speed his ascent, as fast as he could, until for one brief, beautiful moment, he broke the surface.

He gulped air into his lungs and tried to get his bearings. The chaos of the storm above was as disorienting as the roiling maelstrom below. His gaze swept the waterline, searching for the shore. He could barely make out the rocky cliffs of Isola Sombra – was that someone standing on a stony outcrop? A woman? The seawater stinging his eyes blurred his vision, but he thought he saw a sleeveless white dress and thick curls of red hair dancing in the wind as if waving at him.

Who would venture out in such a storm—?

His rumination was cut short by another wave crashing down upon him, pushing him back beneath the surface.

Already weary from his exertions and unable to swim back to the surface unaided, he was forced to return to the bottom, find purchase and once again launch himself upwards. This time, his nose and mouth broke the surface for only a second, barely time to catch a breath, before he began to sink again. He caught another glimpse of the cliffs, but there was no one there, and all too soon the currents were pulling him deeper under the water.

Despair began to set in. His muscles were tiring quickly and only the insulating warmth of his greatcoat was keeping the chill from his bones.

Saint Zhagev-who-sings-for-tears, his *greatcoat*!

The garment that had protected him through countless judicial duels and ambushes, with its slender bone plates sewed into the lining and its dozens of secret pockets filled with the tricks, traps and potions upon which he relied to survive, was now an anchor dragging him like a shipwrecked vessel to the bottom of the sea.

The thought of removing his coat, of abandoning this most precious of treasures, was almost unthinkable. His fingers fumbled with the damnably sturdy buttons he'd done up to keep out the cold and rain.

Air. He needed air or he'd drown before he could remove the very thing that was weighing him down.

One final attempt then, he thought, allowing his body to drift back to the bottom, then pushing off with every remaining ounce of strength. Even

25

as his legs kicked him towards the surface, he managed to undo a few of the buttons trapping him inside the leather coat. He broke through a third time, but desire was a cruel temptress and she tricked Estevar into breathing in too soon. As much water as air came into his lungs, leaving him coughing and choking and, worst of all, sinking back down, unable to shed his coat or even unscabbard the rapier still belted to his side.

So much for my much-vaunted talent for observation, he thought bitterly, *accounting for every element of the puzzle but the one that's going to kill me.*

Estevar had always assumed death would come in the form of a duellist cannier than himself, or perhaps one of the ghosts or demonic spirits the king had so often sent him to investigate. But to die like this, for no better reason than because he'd grown so accustomed to the comforting fit of his greatcoat that it hadn't occurred to him until too late that the same armour that had protected him all these years had become the casket in which his drowned corpse would be interred in at the bottom of the sea?

Perhaps when the First Cantor writes the letter of condolence to my mother, she'll be kind enough to leave out the actual manner of my death.

He was just about to give in to the frigid waters trying to seep into his lungs when his stiff leather collar dug into his throat, choking him. Something hard, like the pommel of a sword or the butt of a spear, struck him in the back – once, twice, then a third time. Some unseen enemy appeared to be intent on beating him to death before the sea could finish the job. But even as the glancing blows continued, Estevar felt his body rising up through the water. His head broke the surface, and even though his collar was tight against his neck, he was able to open his mouth wide, this time to drink in the blessed life-giving air in great gulps.

Finally, still panting and coughing, he turned his head in search of the source of this simultaneous rescue and pummelling – and bashed his cheek into something covered in matted hair. He found himself staring into the big brown eye of a mule who was frantically kicking under the surface of the water, keeping Estevar from sinking beneath.

'Imperious!' he cried out with joy and relief, 'you dashing, dauntless rogue! You magnificent monarch of mounts, saint of all equines!' A wave washed over them, setting Estevar to coughing again, but his elation

26

could not be contained. 'No mere beast of burden are you, my friend.'
He reached a hand around to grab hold of Imperious' neck so that the
mule could let go of his collar and continue to kick against the ocean's
currents. 'There is many a tale in our Order of legendary steeds of
such indomitable will and superlative intellect that they were named
Greathorses. To this day every magistrate who dons the mantle dreams
of riding such a miraculous creature, but to hells with them, I say! I
name you, good Imperious, *noble* Imperious, first of the Greatmules!'

Estevar was so overcome with gratitude and relief that he had to wipe
the welling tears from his eyes. Only then did he spot the prow of a
small rowboat some twenty feet ahead, with a hooded figure paddling
towards them.

'Do you see that, Imperious? One of the monks has come to liberate
us from this miserably wet hell! Not long now, my friend, not long at—'

The wave that crashed into them wasn't nearly as strong as the one
that had pulled them from the causeway in the first place, but it proved
just as deadly, sweeping man and mule backwards, away from the boat.
Estevar felt something bash against his shoulder. Too late, he saw the
rocks jutting out of the water – the sharp edges would have torn him
to shreds, were it not for the sturdy leather of his greatcoat.

Imperious, however, was not so lucky.

Estevar saw the red gash on the poor beast's head, the blood already
seeping into those big brown eyes. Imperious appeared stupefied by the
stunning blow from the rocks – then a current caught hold of the mule
and began drawing him further out to sea.

'No!' Estevar cried, but separated from the animal's prodigious
strength, he was being pulled below once again – until a hand reached
down to grab hold of his arm and yanked him up until his armpit was
over the edge of the rowboat.

'Quickly now,' his rescuer commanded. Estevar half expected this might
be the red-haired woman he'd spotted earlier, but the figure in the grey
hood was a man twice her size. 'The storm's getting worse,' he said, as if
this were Estevar's fault. 'This boat wasn't made for such weather.'

Estevar hauled himself into the rowboat, then immediately got to his
knees and gazed out at the water in search of Imperious.

'There!' he shouted, spotting the mule's bleeding head a dozen yards away. 'Row that way!'

But the little boat began drifting backwards, towards the island, not towards the struggling mule. Estevar's rescuer was taking him to shore.

'No, damn you!' he cried, turning on the man. He could see now the sturdy face beneath the grey hood, neither young nor old, but weathered by hard living and unyielding in the face of his passenger's distress. 'That way!' Estevar pleaded, thrusting an arm to where poor Imperious fought with ever-feebler kicks to reach the boat.

The wind pulled the hood away from the man's head, revealing the shorn scalp. 'The currents are too strong, you fat fool!' the monk told him. 'I won't risk—' The monk quieted when he felt the tip of Estevar's rapier at his throat.

'I am hesitant to so poorly reward one who braved storm and sea to rescue me, but nor will I abandon the comrade who has saved me once already!'

'Has the storm taken your wits?' the monk demanded, wary of the blade at his neck. 'That's not some comrade-in-arms you ask me to risk my life for, it's a bloody mule!'

'Then it is well that I am not asking,' Estevar told him. 'Now row, damn you, or by every saint and god to ever curse this land, I will see both of us drowned beneath the waves where our deaths will only be ennobled by sharing them with that mule!'

'Madman,' the monk spat, but he began rowing with strong, clean strokes through the swells to where Imperious was losing his battle against the waves.

Estevar removed his rapier from the man's neck, meaning to slide it back in its scabbard, but the hilt slipped from his shaking fingers and the weapon fell clattering to the bottom of the little rowboat. He fumbled with his buttons, finally sliding the coat off his shoulders, pulled off his boots, and picked up the free end of a rope tied to the prow and coiled under the seat. Tying it around himself, he told the monk, 'If you wish to abandon me to the depths, all you need do is sever the rope.'

Estevar didn't wait for a reply but plunged into the water and swam after his mule.

CHAPTER 5

A DUBIOUS RESCUE

Estevar fought the waves as he swam for Imperious, frantically trying to keep his head above the water. Lacking the insulating warmth of his coat, the cold was burrowing beneath his flesh all the way to the bone, numbing extremities even as it sapped the last of the strength from his limbs.

At least the coat isn't dragging me down to the bottom of the sea any more, Estevar thought, forcing his right arm out of the water, reaching as far as he was able and pulling himself forward, then repeating the clumsy stroke with his left arm. He could only hope that his legs were still kicking beneath the surface; he'd lost the feeling in them already. All the while, he sought out Imperious, but the salt spray stung his eyes so badly that he couldn't keep them open for more than a second at a time.

Then he heard it: the braying of a mule, and nearby, too.

'I come, my friend—'

Befuddled fool. He'd nearly sucked water into his lungs again. Fortunately, even those few syllables were enough to reinvigorate the mule's efforts to stay afloat, and soon the two were colliding together.

'Steady, Imperious,' Estevar said, as soothingly as he could manage while shouting over the storm raging above them. 'Deliverance is at hand, I swear it.'

Quickly, he untied his end of the long rope and looped it around both his chest and the mule's neck, binding them together. He began pulling for all he was worth, but he felt only slack.

Damnable monk! he raged silently, ceasing his wasted efforts. *Never trust a man who claims to serve the will of the gods, yet would leave a mule to drown alone in this cruel sea.* Surely any divine being who could countenance such callow disregard was worthy of no man's prayers.

'We will have to make for the shore ourselves,' he told the mule, but the throbbing scarlet gash on the beast's forehead and the glassy-eyed stare suggested Imperious was long past the end of his own rope.

Estevar wrapped his arms around the animal's neck, determined to keep him from sinking into the depths, though all too aware that he lacked the power to save him. He cursed his own pride, his perpetual insistence that a keen mind was a more potent weapon than all the brute strength in the world. Tears began to slide down his cheeks, such a useless manifestation of grief. Oh, what he wouldn't give for a little brute strength now—

Suddenly he was jerked backwards, and Imperious yanked along with him. The rope was taut around them now, crushing them together as they were pulled along, slowly but surely. Estevar turned his head and there, some twenty feet away, was the monk hauling on the rope, dragging them towards the rowboat. Bless every god dead and living, he was an even more towering figure standing than he'd appeared when seated.

'Are you planning to help, you overstuffed buffoon?' the monk shouted at him.

Estevar got as good a grip on the rope as he could, though his hands were so feeble he might as well have been trying to grip the water itself, and pulled with all his might. Inch by inch, he and the monk fought the currents, shrinking the distance between them. A few minutes of teeth-grinding effort later and Estevar was sliding himself up and over the edge of the rowboat. But when he turned to help Imperious come aboard, he felt an open-handed blow to the back of his head.

The monk had slapped him.

'He's too heavy, you idiot! He'll capsize the boat!'

'I told you before, I'll not leave him behind—'

But Estevar had made a terrible mistake: the rapier with which he'd cajoled the monk earlier was now rolling in the bottom of the boat, out of his reach. Worse, his efforts to rescue Imperious had cost him his last ounce of strength.

'Please,' Estevar begged, 'in the name of whichever god you serve, help me—'

'Don't be so quick to invoke the gods,' the grey-hooded man warned. 'Not these days, and not this close to Isola Sombra.' Taking up his oars, he moved back to sit on the very edge of the stern. 'Hold the beast's head above the water,' he instructed. 'Try to shift as much of your own weight back towards me as you can. With luck, I can row us back without the two of you tipping us over!'

Estevar did as he was told, arms wrapped around Imperious' neck, the mule's frantic pulse throbbing against his cheek. He muttered soothing words into the poor beast's ear even as he fought the constant feeling of terror that he was being pulled back into the water himself.

'Sentimental halfwit,' the monk growled, pulling against the current with arms stronger than Estevar would have expected in a man of the cloth. 'Greatcoats, they call you? More like Great*fools*!'

Imperious brayed piteously, trying to get his hooves up over the side himself, and Estevar was forced to prevent him from doing so lest he have them all over. He pleaded with the mule to trust him, whispering promises of the warm hay and hot mash awaiting them onshore, and all the while, the rain pounded mercilessly against his back and lightning crackled menacingly above as if it sought to set the sea aflame.

How easy it had been, back on the causeway, to dismiss the notion that Isola Sombra was under some form of crazed witch attack or demonic infestation. Now, it was taking all of Estevar's commitment to reason and investigative dispassion to keep himself from praying to any god who might heed his plea for salvation. In the back of his mind, though, was the unsettling awareness of the parchment in his coat carrying the Margrave of Someil's scrawled warning:

As you love life and value your soul, do not set foot on Isola Sombra.

Something scraped beneath the hull of the rowboat, and it came to a wrenching halt. He feared the rickety vessel had run aground on a reef, but suddenly Imperious reared up, breaking Estevar's grip on his neck as his front hooves found purchase on the boat's wooden stern thwart and he surged forwards.

The monk stepped out into the water, which Estevar saw was now only up to his knees, and started dragging the boat higher onto the beach. Some fifty yards up the rocky path stood the tall arch of a massive iron gate, and beyond it, stone steps twelve feet wide rising up to the curved cobblestone road that wound around the tiny island like a serpent until, at the very top, it kissed the foot of the abbey towering above them all.

Once the rowboat was beached, Estevar rose unsteadily, every muscle in his body groaning. He surveyed the boat, searching for the dark crimson leather of his greatcoat, but found only the rope that had saved his life, lying in a pool of frigid water sloshing at the bottom.

'Where is my coat?' he demanded.

'How should I know?' the monk replied, tossing his oars in. 'The boat was being tossed about like a leaf in the wind out there – probably fell over the side.'

Estevar's ears, trained to discern the least bit of rehearsal in the testimony from witnesses appearing before him, found the monk's delivery too confident, too smooth. Now that they stood together on the shore, he noted how tall the man was – topping his own six feet by several inches. The fellow's shoulders were broad, and when he bent to tie the boat to its mooring, the sleeves of his robes exposed thick, powerful wrists and hands big as mallets. Most conspicuous of all, the man's straight-backed bearing was far more reminiscent of a soldier accustomed to the weight of armour than the stooped posture of a monk who spent his days kneeling in prayer.

'And what of my rapier?' Estevar asked.

The monk offered him a shrug, paired with a sneer. 'Guess that fell overboard, too.'

'A suspicious person might consider such ill-luck more than coincidence.'

The monk laughed, his back to Estevar as he set off along the rocky path for the gate. 'Welcome to Isola Sombra, *Trattari*,' he said, spitting out the archaic Tristian word for 'tatter-cloak' so often used to denigrate the Greatcoats. 'Hope you survive the experience.'

CHAPTER 6

THE GATE

Estevar's skin was cold and wet beneath his drenched linen shirt and wool trousers. Lacking even his boots now that they – along with his sword and greatcoat – were settling into watery graves somewhere off the coast of this misbegotten island, his progress over the slick rocks and spiny scrub became a slow, endless series of stumbles and scrapes. At least the damnable storm had settled down. In its absence, another fog had begun to blanket the shore.

He kept coughing, his throat and lungs aching from the seawater he'd breathed in during his struggle against the currents. As a boy in his homeland of Gitabria, a thousand miles across the sea from here, he'd heard tales of sailors who'd been pulled from the frigid waters and brought to safety, only to be found dead in their bed hours later, drowned by the water still in their lungs.

'Not us,' he murmured to Imperious, patting the mule's flank. 'We have defeated the sea herself, my friend, outwitted her servants, the mighty ocean currents. Surely Saint Werta-who-walks-the-waves herself blesses our arrival, eh?'

Imperious gave a wheezy neigh that made plain his distinctly less optimistic assessment of their situation. Estevar clung shivering to the mule's side as they shuffled up the path like a pair of miserable drunks, following the grey-robed mountain of a monk who'd saved their lives.

Ahead, the massive gate of Isola Sombra awaited, the downwards curve of its mighty arch like a god frowning at them, warning them away. The iron bars, thick as a man's forearm, were rusted, the lower

CRUCIBLE OF CHAOS

crossbars covered in barnacles, suggesting the water had further still to rise. But beyond were the stone stairs leading up to the winding cobbled streets that promised civilisation: food, shelter and care for their wounds.

He took a last look back the way they'd come before the stormy sea had intervened in their journey, but the causeway was nowhere to be seen.

'This time of year, the road disappears for days at a time,' the monk informed him, making his way with far more ease and grace than his unwanted companions. 'There used to be a ferrywoman who'd sell passage back and forth during the winters, but she hasn't turned up this season.'

'I thought I saw someone,' Estevar said, 'standing on the clifftop. She had long red hair and wore a pale, sleeveless dress or shift of some kind. Might that be—?'

'Sounds as if your mule wasn't the only one to hit his head on the rocks.' The grey-robed man turned briefly, gesturing to the beach as he shot Estevar a smirk. 'But feel free to wait for your mystery woman to ferry you upon her lustrous red locks back to the mainland if it suits you.'

Estevar's eyes locked on to that mocking grin, his gaze following the twisted contours of the monk's disdain and apparent lack of interest, peering deeper until he observed the faint pinching around the man's lips that suggested hidden pain.

No, Estevar thought. *Not merely pain. Anguish.*

He hadn't imagined the woman after all.

'Imperious and I shall be quite content with the well-known hospitality of your abbey, thank you,' he called back.

His guide resumed his march, which Estevar took as assent. The moment they reached the iron gate, the monk took a sharp turn and set off down a barely discernible trail heading away from the stairs.

'Where are you going?' Estevar shouted. Imperious leaned against him and groaned, as if to make it clear that any thoughts of pursuit were futile.

The monk kept walking away from them. 'Ring the bell in the old way,' he called back. 'Whoever sits in the watchtower will come down from the abbey. Assuming there's anyone left.' Then he stepped into the mist rolling along the shore.

34

On a more auspicious day, with a dry shirt on his back and a decent meal in his belly – or at least the prospect of one – Estevar would have clapped his hands together in excitement at the cryptic reply and the possibility of intrigues to untangle and mysteries to solve. But he was wounded, starving and cold, and his poor mule was suffering those very same depravations, with the deep gash on his forehead a jagged bolt of scarlet lightning badly in need of tending. So, far from being enthused by the monk's enigmatic words, Estevar was filled with a sudden rage that overpowered his exhaustion.

'It is well that I owe you my life, Brother,' he shouted, 'else I would trace a duelling circle right in the sand between these gods-forsaken rocks so that I might remonstrate with you most violently!'

The monk's hulking figure became less and less distinct as he stepped deeper into the mist. 'Gods-forsaken?' His deep-throated laughter inter-mingled with the rumble of the rising ocean waves. 'At long last, the Greatfool says something sensible.'

'You think my challenge a jest?' Estevar demanded, although he had indeed meant it as such when first he'd issued it. 'Come here then, you mountainous canker sore! Let us see how an overgrown oaf who hides beneath monk's robes and would leave a brave mule to drown among the waves fares against Estevar Vale—'

'Estevar Valejan Duerisi Borros,' the monk finished for him. 'Some-times called the King's Crucible. The magistrate not one but two silly monarchs have trusted to interfere in matters beyond mortal compre-hension.'

'You know me?'

At last, the monk stopped and turned on his heel, smoothly, assuredly, despite the precarious rocks on which he stood. 'Everyone here knows who you are, *Trattari*. Venia, the old fool, prayed often that your "peerless intellect" would one day set you on the path towards faith and humility – a dream that not even the gods would indulge in, from what I've seen.'

There was something unnerving about the monk's lazy tone, the unflappable confidence with which he spoke. Estevar had dealt with many a braggart in his day, and more than his share of madmen. This fellow was neither.

'Who are you to speak so callously of your own abbot?' he asked. 'What sort of monk spouts such spiteful irreverence?'

'They call me Malezias,' the man replied, then lifted his hood back over his head, casting shadows that hid his face, save for the gleam of white teeth as his lips parted in a feral grin. 'And I never said I was a monk.'

With that, the grey-robed figure spread his arms wide, took three backwards steps and disappeared in the thickening fog.

PART THE SECOND

THE SIGILS
OF BINDING

The sacrifice's spirit will soon seek to flee from the flesh. This, you must not allow, else the vessel becomes porous, a leaky chalice incapable of containing the powers you summon. Inscribe the second set of sigils to bind the spirit eternally to the skin, thus may the rite proceed.

CHAPTER 7

THE BELL CHANT

'*Ring the bell in the old way*,' Malezias had said before abandoning Estevar and Imperious at the abbey's gate. A bronze bell twice the size of a man's head hung precariously from the rusted iron frame of the arch. Estevar yanked on the heavy rope dangling from the iron clapper inside the bell, but when both the rope and his palms proved too slick for his grip to hold, he wrapped the end of the rope tightly around one hand, fighting the exhaustion infecting both mind and body to recall the traditional petitioner's plea.

Any fool could make a bell clang, but pilgrims granted official sanction to call upon the religious houses of Tristia would be trained in the special technique of striking the clapper to the bell, then using the rope to hold it just close enough for it to vibrate against the bronze lip without silencing it entirely. The effect was a sonorous hum the monks called 'the bell chant'.

Alas, that was the easy part.

The real challenge was in manipulating rope and clapper to play a specific pattern of bell chants, the codes memorised by journeying monks to convey specific messages to those inside the abbey walls. One pattern might signal that an arriving wagon was full of supplies in need of unloading; another might warn of an invading army mere minutes away from storming the gates. In times of peace and prosperity, such codes were rarely required, for visitors could simply attract the attention of one of the monks within, assuming the gates were even locked.

Clearly, these aren't peaceful times in Isola Sombra, Estevar thought. *Now, what's the gods-be-damned code for an emissary come on the king's business?*

Trying to recall the details of an obscure language of clangs and hums that he'd rarely employed since learning it at least a dozen years ago, especially while fighting off a raging fever, was proving beyond even Estevar's usually faultless memory. Fortunately, the Greatcoats had their own secret language. In the sword tongue, the interplay of two blades made it possible to exchange vital intelligence under the guise of a friendly fencing match or even a full-on duel. Estevar's first judicial circuit included a number of prominent monasteries along his route; he'd observed then that several patterns from the bell chant were almost identical to ones in the sword tongue.

Which makes one wonder if both languages possess a common ancestor?

Imperious, his flank pressed against Estevar's bulk, was panting sporadically, even though neither of them had moved for several minutes. The jagged gash on the mule's forehead had stopped bleeding, but the wound looked dangerously deep.

Careful not to rile the beast, he retrieved a roll of bandages from one of the saddlebags and was pleased to discover the leather case had kept the linen blessedly clean and dry. He wrapped one length around his belly, where blood from his duelling wound had begun to seep through the stitches to stain the thin fabric of his drenched white shirt a troubling crimson, then fashioned a clumsy dressing for the gash on Imperious' head. With one eye partially covered by the bandage, the poor mule was looking like a confused pirate. With a third piece, Estevar dried off the hilt of the dagger he kept at the back of his belt, to ensure it wouldn't slip from his grasp if he needed to draw it quickly.

'Steady, my friend,' Estevar told the mule, whose head was now swivelling this way and that in search of an enemy to fight. 'The dagger is merely a precaution. Be at ease a moment while I ponder how to solve our current predicament.'

At its root, the bell tongue consisted of four syllables: the clang, which by necessity began every message; the long hum, which was hardest to produce reliably; the short hum, and the silence, which required the greatest physical effort to pull on the rope at a sharp-enough angle that the clapper would press against the swaying bell and silence its ringing.

'Friend' is the easiest word, Estevar suddenly recalled. *Three clangs ending with the long hum.*

Yanking the rope hard to the left, he swung the clapper so it slammed against the side, then immediately swung it to the right, producing the second clang, then again to the left – and this time, holding the rope at an angle, his weary shoulders strained to apply just the right amount of force to elicit the humming sound that made his teeth vibrate.

'What now?' he wondered after several minutes of waiting. When no one appeared, he repeated the 'friend' bell chant twice more, to deafening silence from within.

'Perhaps it is not friends they want here?' he said aloud.

Imperious slumped down on his haunches, gave out a quiet, almost plaintive grunt, and closed his eyes.

I must get him help, Estevar thought, wiping the rain from his eyes. He forced himself to set aside his rising anxiety over the mule's condition. *'Ring the bell in the old way,'* that Malezias fellow had said – but he'd added something else, after, hadn't he? *'Whoever sits in the watchtower will come down to let you in soon enough, assuming there's anyone left.'*

Estevar peered through the rain and mist up beyond the gates to the six towers. The tallest would be the watchtower: from that vantage point, a monk could see for miles and spot a fleet of ships on the horizon hours before they could reach the shore, or a battalion of soldiers hours before they crossed the causeway. Had he still been in possession of his greatcoat, the Gitabrian spyglass would have enabled him to discern whether the watchtower was occupied. But his treasured spyglass, along with the greatcoat itself and all the other tools, tricks and traps that had seen him through every manner of peril, was lost to him.

'So, we make do with what we have, eh, Imperious?' he asked, but the mule made no sound save for his continued panting.

The watchtower was too far for Estevar to see clearly, but still he noted the narrow vertical slits arrayed around the outer wall. On the topmost floor, light leaked out from all of them, save one.

Someone is standing in front of that window, blocking the light as they watch us, he reasoned. *Yet they do not come when I name myself a friend.*

He rang the bell again, but this time followed the pattern for friend with another clang, followed by a short hum and then a stop, which he was fairly sure meant 'succour'.

When the last echoes faded, he stared up at the watchtower. The same window was still blocked.

'A friend of the abbey pleads for assistance!' he yelled, dropping the rope. Barefoot, with no coat and soaked to the bone, not even his fury could fight the chill that had set his teeth to chattering. He doubted the monk could understand his words from this distance, but still he shouted, 'Is the suffering of a benighted traveller and his injured mount no longer sufficient cause to rouse your lazy brothers from their soft beds?'

No one replied. No one came.

And still the window in the room at the top of the watchtower was blocked by whoever was looking down on Estevar.

Malezias' instructions, uttered with scorn and malice, returned to him once more.

'Ring the bell in the old way' – what was older and more fundamental than a pilgrim begging for aid?

Estevar looked through the iron bars to the cobbled street beyond. Two hundred brethren had lived in the abbey when last he'd set foot on Isola Sombra, and nearly four times as many lay people made their homes outside its high walls, some growing crops or working for the monks; some merely beggars, waiting outside for the end-of-day scraps. Surely they couldn't all be gone? But where were the errand-runners, the merchants with their well-laden wagons, the sellers of dubious religious icons, the children playing in the streets?

'Could this entire island have been deserted without anyone noticing?' he asked aloud, one hand stroking Imperious' muzzle as the dazed mule's head lolled back and forth. 'What petty theological dispute would induce so many to abandon such a prosperous abbey?'

A simple if troubling explanation was that those bearing witness to his plight didn't consider a half-drowned wretch and an injured mule worthy of their friendship, and cared not one jot for their need for succour.

'I do not see you,' he said between teeth clenched to keep them from chattering. He gazed at the watchtower with its silent, uncaring sentry. 'I do not see you, but I know you are there, and by the oath I took as a Greatcoat to deliver justice to every corner of this country, I *will* make you open this gate.'

Grimly, he picked up the rope and wrapped it around his hand once again. There was one bell chant taught to every King's Magistrate whose circuit included a fortified religious settlement: a message only a Greatcoat was permitted to use. Estevar sounded it now with ferocious precision.

First, the clang, strong and loud, repeated once more with equal force to signify an outsider come to call. But after these came two short hums separated by a brief silence, followed by a third clang and then, finally, a hum he kept resonating until at last the bell stopped swaying and the sound died away. It was a simple enough code for a magistrate to memorise, and a summons that always unnerved those dwelling within who understood its meaning: *The trial is about to begin.*

He let go of the rope, then looked back up at the watchtower. The light now shone from the top window. His hand trembling from his exertions, Estevar reached around to the back of his belt and wrapped his fumbling fingers around the hilt of his dagger.

'Let us see what greeting we receive now,' he murmured to himself.

CHAPTER 8

THE PORTER

Despite his feverish condition, Estevar had been ready to fight to the death whichever mad monk or demonic apparition descended to the gate where he and Imperious waited.

His fearsome adversary proved to be a diminutive woman of advanced years whose grey-stubbled scalp barely came up to his chest. She was garbed in the three-layered robes of a sectati, a monk who saw to the mundane needs of a religious community. Over the traditional ankle-length grey wool tunic was a thicker, sleeveless one in black with worn honey-oak buttons down the front. The short cape of her faded blue chaperon hood was decorated with six faded pewter coins, one for each of Tristia's gods, dangling from silver chains no longer than a fingernail.

'Forgive me, Eminence,' she said with a cheerfulness that belied any genuine contrition. She descended the stairs in leather-soled sandals with more confidence and nimbleness than her scrawny frame and obvious age suggested. She gave a forlorn sigh as she halted on the other side of the locked gate. 'I was deep in the bowels of the abbey checking the storm drains these past hours. Just as I was climbing back up the ladder, contemplating a nice pot of tea, I heard the bell.'

Estevar presumed it was his use of the judicial summoning code which had revealed him as a magistrate, since his barefoot, shabby state – to say nothing of the loss of his beloved greatcoat – did nothing to evoke his rank. 'You were not in the watchtower?' he asked.

'The watchtower?' The old sectati glanced up towards the abbey.

44

'Did you see someone? Did they appear to—?' She shook her head, a lopsided smile on her thin lips as she turned back to Estevar. 'Forgive me, Eminence, my mind is still down in the storm drains.' Both lenses of her spectacles had cracks near the bottom edges, giving her milky grey eyes a slightly confounded look as she peered at him through the iron bars. 'And here you are, from all appearances having held back the ocean herself with naught but those big, strong arms of yours!' She produced a set of keys from an inside pocket of her outermost robe and set about unlocking the huge gate for him.

Conscious of the dagger loosened in its sheath at the back of his belt, Estevar found himself disarmed by her amiable, business-like chattering. 'You'd begun to say something about the sentry in the watchtower?' he prodded, but the sectati didn't take the bait.

'Oh, now, isn't this a handsome fellow?' she said brightly, ignoring the shrieking squeal as she pushed open the gate; Imperious took great exception to the hideous racket, nearly bowling Estevar back down the stone stairs to the rocky shore below.

She stroked the mule's cheek cautiously before gently folding back the edge of the bandage across his face. 'A nasty scrape,' she said, casting Estevar a disapproving glance. 'This calls for cleaning and stitching, not clumsily wrapping a few lengths of linen around it as if you expect the gods to heal it for you.'

An odd jibe for a holy woman, he thought, noticing a pair of little bone dice dangling beneath her chaperon cowl from a thin leather cord. While there had once been a Saint Gan-who-laughs-with-dice, Estevar had rarely encountered any of his devotees in an abbey. He decided to probe the sectati's religious allegiance further.

'I spoke a seven-fold prayer to Amoria,' he said with almost theatrical piety as he spun a lie so obvious any child could see through it. 'We were bound north for Pertine when my mule Pedar here panicked. I'd been such a fool, taking him up on deck, but he does so hate to be kept down below for days on end. The thunder drove him a little mad and he leaped over the railing and into the water.' Estevar stroked Imperious' mane. 'By the time I got to him, the two of us had washed up on the shore. He stumbled and fell, wounding himself against the rocks.

I prayed as we came up the path, and promised to sacrifice a month's wages to Amoria should she grant Pedar a swift recovery.'

The sectati pulled her cowl up against the rain that was starting up again, then took hold of the mule's reins and urged him through the gate and up the rough-hewn steps. 'A month's wages is a generous opening bid,' she observed drily. 'I wonder, did the Goddess of Love accept immediately, or might she be contemplating a counter-offer? For she has clearly done nothing to help your mule, Eminence.'

Her tone was jovial, devoid of apparent malice: a fine impression of a doddering, elderly monk playfully spouting sacrilege to a pious stranger on a drizzly winter's day.

Estevar was not deceived.

When last he'd come to Isola Sombra, the streets had been bustling with life, with stoop-backed scholars from all across Tristia come to consult the abbey's legendary library of archaic religious tomes and nervous schoolchildren from the mainland sent to learn their letters from stern-voiced monks, not to mention all manner of travellers come to gawk at this holy site so they could return home and claim to have walked upon the soil from which the gods first arose. The tiny shops lining the main road used to display their wares beneath brightly coloured awnings, and everywhere men and women – even the monks – proudly wore the tiny purple roses for which the island was famous pinned to the necklines of their coats or robes.

Today was very different. Though not yet noon, the shops were closed. Many of the awnings had been torn down and broken bits of pottery and shards of wood were strewn around the place. There was no commerce taking place, no humming village life – and there was not a single rose to be seen. No one save Estevar, Imperious and their enigmatic guide walked the streets.

When he made mention of these changes, she was utterly unperturbed. 'Subdued, you say?' she asked as if she couldn't perceive the gloom all around them. 'Did you come in winter, when all but the hardiest of souls make for the mainland? Did you, perchance, arrive during a once-in-a-century storm season, no less?'

'No, it was autumn, yet still—'

46

The sectati spun on her heel to face him. All traces of her charming smiles and disarming chatter vanished. 'Let us not play games with each other, Trattari. We have greeted each other as liars do, with lazy tales meant to test weak minds. That is well, for we have no reason to trust one another and these are not trusting times.' Wrinkled with age and murky with cataracts, still her eyes pierced like iron nails as they locked with his. 'You didn't chance upon Isola Sombra by accident. No captain in his right mind sails these reefs during winter, and never during a storm. Nor would I call the leaky rowboat that dredged you up from the water a ship.'

'Fair enough,' Estevar conceded, settling his hands on his hips in a way that suggested arrogant defiance, but was actually to make drawing his dagger quicker, should this be the place for an ambush. 'And what of *your* deceptions, Sister?'

'Brother,' she corrected with a faint sneer. 'We keep to the old ways here. Some of us, anyway.'

An odd tradition of this country, Estevar had always thought, that those who undertook monastic lives called themselves brothers regardless of sex. He supposed it was meant to remove the false distinctions of gender that separated men and women in the secular world.

'Forgive me, then, Brother . . .'

'Agneta. I am Brother Agneta, the abbey's chief quartermaster.' She paused a moment before adding, 'One of them, anyway.'

How does an abbey have more than one chief quartermaster? Estevar wondered, but set the question aside for more pertinent ones.

Beneath her penetrating gaze, he felt scruffy and oddly oafish in his soaked, filthy, bloodstained clothes and bare feet. The water overflowing from the gutters curving down the street was slithering between his toes, chilling him even more. If only he weren't so tired and feverish. He kept imagining tiny fencers jabbing needles into his wound, over and over, cutting through his stitches. If his mind were clear, he might deduce from the sectati's words and tone, her mannerisms and subtle insinuations, such evidence as would help him uncover what was happening on this island. Instead, he was forced to employ blunter methods, the kind more suited to a brutish village constable than a King's Magistrate.

'Well, Brother Agneta,' he began formally, 'that you saw the row-boat means you were not, as you claimed, inspecting the storm drains beneath the abbey. Nor have you asked who rescued me from the raging currents, so the boatman must be known to you. That you did not come to the gate when I rang the bell as a friend seeking succour exposes an uncharacteristic distrust of strangers. That you reacted as you did when I mentioned seeing someone in the watchtower suggests that distrust extends to your own brethren.'

He took a step closer to loom over the diminutive monk. 'You know me for a Greatcoat, so you also know that I may compel your testimony if I require it, and I surely do now. So, answer me, Brother Agneta, what disharmony plagues Isola Sombra?'

His question drew a sudden smile and a curt, almost barking laugh. '*Disharmony?* Oh, Eminence, your wisdom is indeed a blessed light shining through the fog inside this cobweb-infested old skull of mine. Dishar-mony – *that's* the word I've been racking my brain for these past weeks. Yes, Eminence, *disharmony* is the word that has eluded me until now.'

Estevar's wound had roused again, the freezing rain like tiny claws picking at it. 'Answer me, then,' he urged her. 'Tell me why Abbot Venia, who summoned me here, hides in his tower. Why did the twelve knights who came to investigate the odd goings-on in the abbey return to their fortress suffering from a torpor the margrave's own physicians cannot explain? Who covered their bodies in markings that suggest heretical occult rituals performed inside the walls of Tristia's once-holiest site?'

Brother Agneta opened her mouth to speak, but closed it again as heavy footsteps came clomping down the wet flagstones from the winding road ahead of them. 'Ah,' she said, sounding almost sad. Her shoulders slumped beneath the chaperon cowl of her robes. 'I'd hoped to spare you from the knowledge you seek, Trattari. However, I fear that you are about to discover the answer to all your questions.'

With that, she let go of Imperious' reins and produced from inside the folds of her black outer robe a brass-fitted mahogany wheellock pistol. Aiming it directly at Estevar's chest, she said, 'Forgiveness is more a part of my vocation than yours, Eminence, but I do hope you'll forgive me for what happens next.'

CHAPTER 9

INTRUDERS
AND INTERLOPERS

Two monks, a man and a woman, came striding around the corner. Their combined ages were, he suspected, less than half that of Brother Agneta, while the glares they shot her would have better suited those of enemy infantry charging the battlements than loving brethren.

Both were tall, their dark hair not quite shorn to the scalp. Over rich black wool robes they wore sleeveless surcoats not unlike Brother Agneta's, but these were cut from sturdier leather and dyed a shimmering dark yellow. The traditional dangling pewter coins were absent from their cloaked chaperons, which were trimmed with gold rather than blue. The woman, broad in the body and square of jaw, carried a longsword, the blade resting on one shoulder, the hilt gripped in both hands, ready to strike. The man was slender and sharper-featured. He carried a shortbow, already strung, in one hand, while his other reached for an arrow from the quiver slung to his belt.

'Strange to find religious recluses so well armed,' Estevar observed. He couldn't reach for his own dagger, needing both hands to hold tightly to Imperious' reins. The confused mule strained against his tether as if he wanted to stampede the invaders, neither of whom were looking at all hesitant about using their weapons against him.

'These are, indeed, strange times,' Brother Agneta agreed. The muzzle of her wheellock was still aimed squarely at Estevar's chest. 'Almost makes me wish I hadn't given up liquor.'

Estevar was familiar with her weapon, recognising the theological

49

and military symbols carved into either side of the brass plating in the mahogany barrel. Inscribed in the brass on one side was a phrase in archaic Tristian.

'*Not by my will is judgment rendered,*' he read aloud. The other side he recited from memory. '*By a god's decree is my hand guided.*'

'So nice to meet a Trattari who recalls that not all laws fall under the purview of the Greatcoats,' Brother Agneta said, offering the courtesy of a barely discernible nod.

'Only those laws for which justice is the desired outcome,' Estevar replied, keeping an eye on the other two armed monks, neither of whom were approaching any closer. 'You are no doddering sectati, are you, Brother Agneta?' He didn't do her the insult of waiting for a reply. 'Shall I instead address you as *Cogneri*, or do you prefer *Inquisitor*?'

Agneta allowed him a small smile, but her hand remained steady around her pistol's grip. 'Let us not stand on stodgy formality, Eminence. We are both enforcers of the law, are we not? Besides, my young colleagues here find such antiquated terms offensive to their modern sensibilities.'

'He is ours,' the tall woman in the black and yellow habit declared. Her voice, though stern and unyielding, was more distinctly feminine in tone than Estevar would have expected. She raised the blade of her longsword up to a high diagonal guard well-suited for a quick beheading. 'The interloper belongs to the Trumpeters now. That was the agreement.'

'The agreement,' Agneta repeated, uttering the last word in a slow, disdainful manner. 'Since when do the Trumpeters concern themselves with the honouring of agreements, *Sister* Parietta?'

Trumpeters, Estevar thought. The term was unfamiliar, but so too was the yellow and gold adorning the monks' surcoats and chaperons. He noted the subtle differences between Sister Parietta's cowl and that of her colleague. *A military distinction?* he wondered. *And the use of 'sister' rather than the more customary 'brother'* . . . Agneta looked unduly irritated by the unconventional term. Why? Because it broke with tradition? *No*, he thought, noting the faint curl of her upper lip. *Her dislike is more personal, yet not entirely directed at Sister Parietta. Her leader, then? A different 'sister' who is also, judging by the habits and behaviour of these 'Trumpeters', a kind of general?*

The young man – was he also a 'sister' like Parietta? – was arguing with Agneta, blustering something about pacts and which faction had rights over intruders despoiling holy ground.

'You see what I am forced to contend with of late, Eminence?' Agneta asked Estevar in a theatrically weary tone. 'My days are wasted debating with amateur lawyers unfamiliar with the finer points of laws and contracts.' The muzzle of her pistol hadn't moved an inch from Estevar's heart. 'What Sisters Parietta and Jaffen do not understand is that there is a crucial legal distinction between an intruder and an interloper.'

'They are the same!' Jaffen insisted.

Estevar smiled indulgently, more to see what effect it had on the two Trumpeters than out of any genuine patience. He might be caught in the middle of someone else's battlefield, but there was a limit to how long he would tolerate threats against him while poor Imperious was in dire need of medical care. 'Both the intruder and the interloper might enter your home without permission, but where the first does so without just cause, sometimes the interloper comes bearing royal authority.'

'A most apt distinction,' Agneta said approvingly. 'No doubt one with which our esteemed Eminence is especially familiar, given how often the Greatcoats are greeted as interlopers by those over whom they seek to impose the King's Laws.'

'No king reigns on Isola Sombra,' Jaffen declared. Having nocked his arrow, he raised his bow. 'Nor shall any, so long as the Trumpeters defend it.'

Estevar now had a pistol, a sword and an arrow waiting to settle the debate of which would kill him first, and still had no answer to what had transpired on Isola Sombra to turn its monks into homicidal thugs.

There is a way to do this, he thought, his gaze sweeping over each of the three aggressors, seeking out the flaws in their stances and how far the angle of their weapons would need to shift to diffuse their potential lethality. Agneta's pistol was the first problem, but also the easiest to solve; he needed to distract her just long enough to spin sideways on his heel, jostle her weapon hand off-axis and then wrap his arm around hers to trap her. Doing so would require releasing Imperious' reins, but since the mule would launch himself at the two monks in yellow, that would give more precious seconds for Estevar to gain control of Agneta's weapon. The main problem was Sister Parietta. Her bowman companion would almost certainly shoot wide, given his agitated grip on the bowstring, but she would instinctively cut down with her longsword, missing Estevar but likely decapitating the mule.

We are beset, my friend, he thought, still clutching the reins. *Beset by religious lunatics waging a war whose nature we cannot yet discern.*

'Of course no king rules Isola Sombra, Jaffen,' Brother Agneta said, her eyes fixed on Estevar and her smile suggesting she was all too aware of his hopeless tactical position. 'It's much too cold and wet here for monarchs. Young Filian sits in his warm throne room in Aramor and sends those like our uninvited visitor to interfere in our affairs on his behalf. So, unlike the knights we graciously turned over to your faction, this one' – she gave a slight twitch of her pistol and Estevar found himself imagining the sensation of a lead ball piercing flesh and bone before finally reaching his heart – 'belongs to us.'

'You know full well the Hounds took the knights before we could get to them, you cankerous Bone-Rattler,' Jaffen snarled. He shifted position, now aiming at Brother Agneta. 'Set aside your foul schemes, Inquisitor. The pistol shaking in your hand cannot take both Parietta and me before one of us kills you.'

'Of course not, dear,' Agneta said, her tone exasperated. 'That's why I'm aiming it at our visiting magistrate. Save those calluses on your fingers from a nasty bowstring burn and place that arrow back in its quiver or I'll fire this lead ball right through his Eminence's heart. He'll bleed out right here in front of us, his corpse desecrating this oh-so-holy street. If I understand the edicts of this new god your so-called "general" awaits, this will be cause for considerable consternation from your side of the abbey.'

Trumpeters, Hounds and Bone-Rattlers, Estevar thought, forcing his feverish brain to get to work divining the meaning behind the names of these three factions. *A pact over who gains custody over captives . . . the Trumpeters were meant to have the knights, but the Hounds – whoever and whatever they are – got to them first, which means they're the ones who etched those sigils into the knights' flesh before sending them back across the causeway.*

When a child in Gitabria, Estevar had sat for hours marvelling at his contraptioneer mother's inventions, watching the tiny springs and cogs and gears move so smoothly this way and that. Now it was the gears in his own mind turning, and though their grinding was another ache to add to all the others, he felt more at home in this bizarre battle of wits than he had since coming to this gods-forsaken holy isle.

'Well?' he asked aloud, 'who shall have the pleasure of my company this night, and ease their troubled spirits by confessing their crimes before a true and just magistrate?' He looked first at the two in their militaristic yellow and black habits. 'Will the General of the Trumpeters receive me and share her plans for the protection of this island from whichever god she fears is coming to this troubled place?' Ignoring their shocked expressions, he turned back to Brother Agneta. 'Or the Bone-Rattlers?' He gestured negligently to the front of her habit. 'I presume the sobriquet is in reference to the dice you keep on a chain around your neck – six sides for six gods? A way of deciding who to pray to even when most of those gods are dead?'

Agneta gaped at him, but she hid her anxiety faster than the others. 'Be careful when mocking an old woman,' she warned, pressing the muzzle of her wheellock pistol against his chest. 'We have precious little to live for and vengeance is as good a reason to die as any.'

But Estevar was done playing the helpless victim. He might be held captive by their weapons, but the longer they played this game, the faster his mind would unlock the secrets they were keeping hidden from him – and each other.

'Perhaps I will instead take my supper with the Hounds,' he said somewhat wistfully, for his stomach had finally muzzled his other complaints so that it could protest the lack of food in his belly. Watching their reactions, he added, 'Discussing the purported occult effects achieved through the inscribing of certain esoteric sigils upon human flesh over a nice hot meal and a glass of wine would offer a most diverting beginning to my investigations.'

Jaffen, apparently no longer quite sure where to aim his arrow, spat in outrage, 'You think yourself amusing? You fat foreign bast—'

'Look at my face, *boy*. Does it look as if I'm laughing?' He held Imperious back; the mule might be wounded and exhausted, but it clearly shared his fury, and was looking all too eager to translate it into reckless action. 'I am cold, wet and suffering a fever that grows worse by the hour. My companion has a head wound badly in need of tending.' He turned his gaze towards Agneta. 'They are right, Cogneri; your pistol hand begins to shake. Either shoot me now and put an end to this rank idiocy or shoot the swordswoman. Imperious desires to remonstrate with the bowman himself.'

There was silence then, save for the petulant drumming of rain upon the flagstones of the winding street and the breeze whistling through the torn awnings of the shuttered shops. The quiet was oddly comforting, despite the drawn weapons. But Estevar had no use for quiet or comfort right now – he didn't wish his opponents to have time to hatch some other scheme to take him away.

'You have to the count of three,' he told Agneta, ignoring the inquisitor's defiant stare. 'At that moment, if the three of you have not put down your weapons, I will release Imperious' – the mule did him the exquisite service of straining especially hard at the reins at that moment – 'and then, you self-styled "holy" brethren, we shall find out whose god loves whom the most.' He patted the mule's side. 'Mine gets especially cantankerous at times like these.'

Sister Parietta tightened her grip on the hilt of her longsword. 'You do not issue ultimatums here, Trat—'

'One,' he said, pulling Imperious' reins a fraction to the left while avoiding so sudden a move that Agneta might accidentally shoot him. If he could convince the mule to flank rather than charge their opponents, he could hurl his bulk past Agneta, knocking her pistol arm aside, dropping low enough that Parietta's longsword would slice the empty air above him while he barrelled into her legs. The two would fall in a tangle of limbs, where his dagger would have the advantage over her sword.

'He's bluffing,' Jaffen insisted, his gaze darting to Parietta before returning to Estevar, proving the sister was indeed his superior in the Trumpeters' hierarchy.

'Two,' Estevar said.

54

He wished his plan had some hope of succeeding, but the odds were abysmal. Only the notoriously lucky Falcio val Mond – that same former First Cantor who'd saddled Estevar and his Greatcoat colleagues with his untried nineteen-year-old replacement – could hope to emerge unscathed from a standoff like this one.

'He's not bluffing,' Agneta replied. 'What you mistake for deception is, in fact, the arrogance of a man who'd rather die than allow himself to be under the control of others. I have met many such men in my years.' She gave a wry smile. 'Usually they were strapped to a rack at the time, but still, that's how one learns which ones won't break.'

'Three,' Estevar said.

Agneta's arm swung to the right, the brass and mahogany barrel of her wheellock pistol now aimed at the forehead of Sister Parietta. 'If your general were here, she would point out that sound tactics dictate that I should shoot the bowman before the swordswoman, but if I can only kill one of you before I die, I'd prefer you, my dear.'

'You heretical bitch,' Sister Parietta cursed. 'Even your false gods must be looking down on you in disgust.'

The inquisitor shrugged. 'My gods are a lot less uptight than yours, dear. By the way, that's a bad word you just used. Best run off to your cell so you can slap your blade against your naked buttocks for a few hours in penance.'

'Do not—'

'My turn to give the ultimatums,' Agneta said. 'You have ten seconds. Nine, seven, five—'

'You appear to be skipping a few numbers,' Estevar observed. Now that the lines of attack had changed, he was going to need to find a way to knock down the old Cogneri *after* she'd shot Sister Parietta but *before* Jaffen loosed his arrow.

'I never was good at maths,' Agneta replied. 'Where were we? Oh, right: four, two, o—'

'We'll go,' said Sister Parietta, lowering her sword but keeping it in front of her just in case, 'you dried-up old—'

'Oh, Saint Arcanciel-who-watches-all-pass, here it comes,' Agneta muttered.

Parietta was undeterred. 'The pact will not endure much longer. The time of choosing comes, and once the choice is made, the purification of Isola Sombra will begin. *Haeraticum purgadis anteva deato!*'

Haeraticum purgadis anteva deato, Estevar repeated to himself. *Before come the gods, the heretics will have been purged.* Something about that antiquated phrasing put an itch in the back of his skull. Such axioms were usually rendered in the simple future tense in Tristian, not the future sublime. *So why is that particular phrasing both unknown to me and yet somehow . . . familiar?*

For her part, and for the first time, Brother Agneta sounded genuinely affronted. 'I was a *Cogneri*, girl. An inquisitor! You think I haven't purged more than my share of heretics already? Now get out of here before *my* god, lazy hag that she is, informs me that she's sick and tired of all this posturing and forces my finger to squeeze on the trigger of this thrice-blessed weapon of mine so that by her will I shoot you in the head and put you out of everyone else's misery.'

Slowly, the two yellow-and-black robed monks stepped away, walking backwards up the street so that Jaffen could keep his arrow trained on Agneta. Estevar wondered if the young man would try to shoot her once he was far enough away that his bow was a more accurate weapon than her pistol, but the old woman had already shifted behind him to use his bulk as a shield while keeping her wheellock aimed at the departing Trumpeters. Only when they were gone did she at last face Estevar.

'How tiresome life has become,' she said, her right arm sagging, the pistol dangling from her hand. 'Though you are no holy man, Trattari, I make this confession to you: I will not bemoan my own passing from this melodramatic existence one bit.'

'Would you really have pulled the trigger?' he asked. 'Shot a stranger, a man of the law who has done you no wrong?'

'Of course, I would,' she replied, then raised the weapon to his face and, without warning or apology, squeezed the trigger.

Estevar heard the whir of the winding spring as it expanded, saw the sparks from the striker wheel spinning against the pyrite, but neither flame nor lead ball emerged from the muzzle.

Agneta stared at the weapon a moment. 'Wouldn't you know it? These things cost more than a cottage and they still don't work for shit when you let the powder get wet.'

Though he was sure she'd been fully aware the weapon wouldn't fire, still Estevar felt the familiar outrage rise up in him at being used this way. The challenge he so badly wanted to issue came to his lips as easily as his own name, but he was too tired, too weak from his wounds and too worried about poor Imperious, who was once again leaning heavily against him. Besides, he'd lost one duel already, thanks to his own poor judgement. Neither his pride nor his body could sustain another.

The elderly inquisitor watched him as carefully as he'd been watching her. 'Good,' she said, apparently approving of the resignation no doubt visible in the slumping of his shoulders, and she slid the pistol back into whatever holster she had hidden in her robes. 'Now then, Magistrate Borros, knowing Greatcoats as I do, I suspect that by now you believe you have some sense of what hellish discord afflicts Isola Sombra.'

'I believe I do. Some of it, at any rate.'

'And no doubt that idealistic fool Abbot Venia summoned you here in the hope that you could arbitrate the dispute and bring loving peace back to this troubled yet still hallowed ground?'

Estevar didn't much like the disdain with which those on this island spoke of the abbot. He'd never much liked the man's religious zealotry himself, but nonetheless, it pricked at Estevar's conscience to another's dignity being so casually stripped away. 'The abbot perhaps had more faith in the desire of his gods that their worshippers not suffer needlessly than you do, Inquisitor.'

'Excellent!' Agneta took the mule's reins and resumed their journey up the long, spiralling street towards the abbey. 'Then let us test each other's knowledge of those gods, you and I, and when we are done, I will show why the situation at Isola Sombra is so much worse than you imagine.'

CHAPTER 10

THE MAD
AND THE MIGHTY

'The gods are dead,' Estevar pronounced breathlessly, he and Imperious both struggling to keep up with Brother Agneta, who was setting a merciless pace. It wasn't such a long way to the abbey, Estevar recalled, no more than three-quarters of a mile, but the incline was steep and the streets so slippery with rain and overflowing gutters that Imperious was having trouble finding purchase on the flagstones. The mule was also having trouble focusing on the way ahead, taken by surprise by every new thing that appeared – an empty shop, a dilapidated cottage, broken wooden struts of a barrel or a pile of bricks. Imperious shied away from everything, even the seagulls landing on broken awnings to squawk down at them causing him to recoil in shock.

Estevar quietly reassured the trembling animal every few steps, 'Not long now—' although all too aware that he'd been making that same unfulfilled promise ever since the waves had first dragged them out into the ocean. He wasn't doing much better himself. His breathing was shallow and interspersed with increasingly long fits of coughing. His bare feet were so numb that he couldn't even feel the pain of the cuts, scrapes and bruises accumulated since abandoning his boots to the choppy seas. That privilege was left to the wound in his side, no longer merely aching but instead burning as if even now the pitiless old inquisitor were holding a white-hot brand to his flesh.

'The gods *died*,' Agneta corrected him.

'Hmm?' It was becoming harder to hold onto a single chain of thoughts

58

long enough to make sense of them. When he swiped at the clammy slickness on his forehead, his palm came away with more sweat than rainwater.

If only he hadn't lost his greatcoat! There was a tiny jar of the black salve in the fifth pocket on the left side, nearly empty thanks to that gods-be-damned duel, and what little was left stank worse than any dung heap. Yet he longed for the soothing coolness of that foul paste, for it could have stayed the infection long enough for him to rid himself of this nagging inquisitor and find the abbey's infirmary.

'Focus, Trattari,' Agneta chided him without slackening her pace one jot. The Cogneri, church inquisitors granted jurisdiction over religious crimes, leaving the Greatcoats to investigate and render verdicts on secular ones, had never been known for their soft hearts. 'I asked you what you believed you knew about the discord afflicting Isola Sombra, and you began with, "The gods are dead." This is imprecise. The gods *died*, which is not the same thing at all.'

Had she bothered to notice how pale Estevar knew he must be, how hard he was struggling to keep from collapse, perhaps she might have allowed him a moment's rest? Instead, she reached up a thin, wrinkled hand to snap her fingers in front of his face. 'Quickly now, or we will lose the chance to probe that vaunted intellect of which Abbot Venia spoke so admiringly before you pass out and are no use to me at all. Begin again. What nefarious plague threatens Isola Sombra?'

The remains of a fallen bell tower split the street in front of them. He took the left path, Agneta led Imperious up the right. 'T-two ...' He had to pause to stop himself stammering. 'Two years ago, the gods died – in Domaris, a few hundred miles northeast of here. Not far from where I've just been, in fact, and close to where Imperious' forebears were first—'

'The mule is a handsome fellow, to be sure,' Agneta interrupted, 'but he is not the issue here, nor are the deaths of our nation's six benighted gods, but we must start somewhere, eh, your Eminence?'

Why must she peck at him like a grey-feathered crow feasting on the entrails of his corpse? Was her haranguing meant to keep him from losing consciousness entirely, which would leave her having to drag his substantial bulk to the abbey herself? Perhaps he ought to be grateful for her ministrations, which she probably considered kindly, coming as they were from a former inquisitor no doubt more comfortable torturing those in her presence than caring for them.

'As I was saying,' Estevar began again, 'the gods were killed by—'

'Murdered,' Agneta corrected. 'Are we not finders of facts, you and I? Enforcers of the law? Different laws, I will admit, but precision remains an investigator's first duty and most reliable ally.'

'Saint Zhagev-who-sings-for-tears, woman! Must you—?'

'Also murdered two years ago,' she interjected amiably. 'As were a great many other saints. The seventh year of the interregnum was a rather tragic one for religious figures, wouldn't you agree?'

Estevar took a deep breath to calm himself, but that only set him hacking again, forcing him to lean against Imperious to keep from falling to his knees.

'The gods were *murdered* by a man wh—'

'Specificity, please.'

'Enough!' he bellowed, grabbing at her shoulder even as he fought back the cough that threatened to smother his outrage. 'I am a King's Magistrate, summoned here by your own abbot. It is *I* who holds jurisdiction over such matters on behalf of the Crown, and it is *I* who will conduct the questioning. Do we have an understanding, Cogneri?'

'Feeling better now?'

Never had he wanted so badly to slap an elderly person in the face. Still, he had to confess, at least to himself, that the irritation and indignity she'd provoked in him was a potent elixir, for all the while it was burning in his throat, it was also clearing the fog from his mind.

'The person responsible for the death of Tristia's gods was an Inlaudati,' he went on, and alongside the equally unsteady Imperious, resumed the trek. 'A human being, like us, but one possessed – whether by accident of birth or tragedy so profound it altered the inner workings of his mind – of a strategic, or some might say *spiritual* – intellect far beyond the limits of ordinary genius.'

'Some would also call such individuals perversions of the natural order,' Agneta commented sourly, 'but do go on.'

Estevar found himself eager to do so; this subject tested the bound-aries between the mundane and the supernatural, piquing his curiosity. 'Little is known of the Inlaudati, how they come to be, or the inner workings of their gifts. But among the Greatcoats, it is believed that the Tailor' – out of habit, his thumb and forefinger came up to pinch the leather collar of his own magnificent dark crimson coat, only to wince at the feel of sodden, tattered linen – 'the woman who designed our coats,' he said, trying to recover his excitement, 'who guided her son, King Paelis, in his reforms and helped restore the Order of Travelling Magistrates from little more than legend is believed to be an Inlaudati.'

'Or was,' Agneta retorted. 'I'm told the old buzzard's mind has settled into something approximating sanity now that her grandson sits the throne and the historical tides that gave birth to her unnatural talent have quietened at last.'

Estevar had never heard it put that way. He'd assumed age, or perhaps sorrow at the recent death of her granddaughter, had induced the Tailor to retire from politics and intrigue. Now it was the sixteen-year-old Filian, also of her blood but raised by her most hated enemy, who sat the throne in Aramor. Whether the boy would prove to be a king in the mould of his idealistic father or instead follow in the steps of the coldly brilliant, pragmatic woman who stole him as a baby yet appeared, in her own callous way at least, to love him, remained to be seen.

'Keep up, Trattari,' Agneta urged, still striding ahead of him.

Does the woman never tire?

'Tell me of this other Inlaudati, the one who contrived to murder the gods themselves.'

Estevar licked his lips, tasting salt. Despite being soaked from head to toe, he was thirsty; his fever had stolen every ounce of moisture from the tissues of his mouth and throat. 'The Inlaudati called himself the Blacksmith,' he said, wheezing. Agneta was right, though, he needed to talk – to *think*. 'The Blacksmith chose that sobriquet because he believed that he alone had discerned the secrets of the metals running through the oldest mines in Tristia. By long-forgotten means, those sacred ores once combined with the force of our ancestors' faiths to bring the gods they worshipped to life.'

'You make it all sound so tedious,' snapped Agneta. 'The Blacksmith's *real* achievement was in constructing iron masks made of that same ore and imprisoning the saints he captured within, weakening them enough to steal their spiritual power, which he then used to subdue and slaughter the gods, that he might forge a new one in his own twisted image.'

Estevar had been hundreds of miles away when Falcio val Mond, the former head of his order, had led the enquiry that uncovered the Blacksmith's scheme to destroy the living expressions of faith in Tristia and replace them with a far crueller and more demanding deity. '*A god worthy of this corrupt nation*,' the Inlaudati had said, according to the records of his testimony in defence of his own villainy. '*A god of fear to rule over a craven people.*'

Oh, to have been there when Falcio met the Blacksmith's foul creation in the duelling circle: to test not only one's blade, but the steel of one's will against the ultimate expression of that which the Greatcoats were made to fight against: injustice and tyranny!

Estevar's heel caught on a loose rock and he swore as he lost his footing. His stumble halted by the redoubtable sturdiness of Imperious, he recovered his balance, though the wound in his side screamed as if he were being stabbed all over again.

Then again, he thought bitterly, *seeing that I lost a judicial duel to a petty fencer-for-hire, perhaps it's as well that it was Falcio who crossed swords with the god of fear and not me.*

He sensed Agneta was about to start cajoling him again, so he resumed quickly, 'The slaying of our gods left a void within the country. The spiritual energy of which they were born, some small stolen part of which infuses those we call saints, was lost for a time.'

'Nothing is lost,' the implacable inquisitor corrected, *tut-tutting* him as if he were an errant schoolboy. 'Nothing is created or destroyed. All that exists remains, from my frail old bones and your sorry carcase to the mighty stones upon which Isola Sombra was built and will one day crumble. Given enough time, that which has been obliterated becomes something new. It is the waiting that tests our spirits.'

She stopped suddenly and Estevar, so intent on keeping up, barrelled into her. At first he thought she was staring up at the dark clouds blanketing the sky, then he followed her gaze and saw that they had rounded the last curve and stood at last before the sublime, broken majesty of Isola Sombra.

'It cannot be . . .' Estevar whispered, surveying the calamitous destruction beyond the gate.

Brother Agneta pushed open the gate and took Estevar's arm. 'Oh, it gets much worse, Trattari. Trust me on that.'

CHAPTER 11

BLASPHEMY

Wrought-iron gates spanned the entire width of the street. Estevar had imagined the flagstone path as a long, serpentine tongue: now, at last, he and Imperious were about to enter the snake's mouth. In his fevered mind, the abbey's six towers were fangs rising up to bite the sky until the rain turned to blood. The question was, he wondered, even in his dazed state, what poison dripped from those fangs down onto the earth below?

'Enter ye without faith,' Agneta intoned with mocking solemnity as her key unlocked the gates and she swung them open, 'and faith will enter ye ere ye depart.'

The old Tristian abjuration was meant to instil reverence and righteous fear in schoolchildren, one utterly at odds with the lovingly held principles of science and exploration taught to Gitabrian boys and girls. But even Estevar's finely honed mind could not escape the dread that filled him when he saw what awaited them in the abbey's grand courtyard.

When last he had visited Isola Sombra, the abbot had proudly taken him on a tour along the stone paths that wove through the garden wherein stood six magnificent sculptures of Tristia's gods, each carved from a single block of marble and shaped into a colossus three times the height of the tallest man. The remains of those statues now lay in rubble; they had crushed flower beds and smashed the wrought-iron benches where the abbey's theologians had debated religion, philosophy and even obscene literature with scholars who had travelled from lands as far as even Estevar's distant homeland. Abbot Venia always said he loved this part of the abbey best of all, for here, he claimed, faith was every day tested by cold logic and burning passion, and every day, faith – gentle faith – won. On Estevar's final evening of that visit, Venia had tried to convince him to take holy orders himself – and he had come perilously close to succeeding.

'What do you see?' Agneta asked. The old inquisitor's voice was quiet, genuinely solemn, for the first time since Estevar had met her.

The two of them stood at the edge of the statuary where a thick, swirling fog that had crept unnoticed upon them had begun to settle over the ground, obscuring what lay beneath the shattered remnants. A trick of the unseasonable weather, he tried to tell himself, although Imperious shied away, braying tremulously when Estevar tried to walk closer.

'I see futility,' he replied at last. 'Callous, ignorant destruction committed by men and women unable to find meaning in their faith after learning of the Blacksmith's foul deeds. A wound has festered in this abbey, sowing discord between its brethren. I have observed such rifts forming, theological differences festering into factionalism that tears religious communities apart and sets at each other the lay people whose own lives intertwine with those of the so-called faith, for all they never started the disputes and rarely understand the matters.' He gestured to the ruins, a graveyard not merely of statues but of an ideal that, while he didn't share it, still made him sad to see it destroyed so utterly. 'Rather than retreat into contemplation or doubt, one faction of your brethren took sledgehammer and axe to these beautiful representations of divinity and left history with nothing to remember them by.'

'A pretty speech,' Agneta said, her caustic manner returned. 'A trifle poetic, but a logical deduction nonetheless.'

Estevar recognised her feigned agreement as just another thorn to scratch him. He closed his eyes; the fever was making it increasingly hard to concentrate. There was something he wasn't seeing – something in the pattern of destruction in the statuary?

'Abbot Venia is a deator,' he said, almost smiling at memory of the short, stocky fellow speaking with utmost humility of his calling. 'He's an interpreter of spiritual events.'

Agneta sniffed. 'A rather mundane understanding of the rarest rank of cleric. Many of my more superstitious brethren would insist that the deator speaks with the voice of the gods themselves – although I'll admit that's a difficult claim to disprove.'

'Indeed,' Estevar agreed. 'But unless Abbot Venia has changed much from the person I met years ago, such grandiose assertions are not his way. Perhaps, however, many of your brethren saw the death of the gods as proof that Venia was a charlatan and his teachings a litany of lies.'

Is that why you are hiding in your tower, rather than fencing with me in the duelling circle of ideas as we've done so often over the years? he wondered, looking up to the aptly named Abbot's Tower near the far end of the abbey grounds. *Is it fear that keeps you cowering in your chambers while your monks run amok below? Or is it instead . . . shame?*

'You've grown quiet, Eminence,' Agneta observed. 'Am I to assume you have solved the case?'

'There is nothing to solve, merely the matter of shaking your abbot from his spiritual somnambulism and—' Estevar's eyes grew unfocused; the courtyard undulated before him. For a moment, he thought perhaps an earthquake was adding to the abbey's misfortunes, but it was only his own unsteady legs causing him to rock back and forth.

'I've kept you at this too long,' Agneta said without apology. 'Your wound needs tending, as does that of your noble mule. Yet I must hold you here a moment more.'

'Why?' he asked.

'I said before that your explanation of events was entirely logical, but you'll have noted I did not agree that it was correct. You make the mistake that all Greatcoats do by presuming that people control their own destinies.'

He arched an eyebrow at the diminutive woman. 'Forgive me, Brother Agneta, but I find it hard to believe that one as cynical as you is about to deliver a sermon on the guiding hand of the divine.'

She ignored his jibe, taking his arm and leading him into the ruins. 'Look closer at the rubble, Trattari. Let the clues left behind by the instigators of this vandalism awaken that legendary clockwork mind of yours.'

Estevar wasn't interested in pursuing vandals. What he wanted was a hot meal, a cool glass of water, a warm bed and a vial of alcohol with which to burn away the infection in his wound, followed by a needle and thread to sew it back together. Besides, with this bedevilling mist everywhere, how was he supposed to—?

'Impossible,' he said, as some of the fog was swept away by the afternoon breeze, revealing more of the ground beneath the ruins. 'How can this be?'

Shattered stone spread out from each broken statue like the scorched rays of a sun that had burned itself black. Some was in fist-sized chunks, but most of the remains were shards and splinters. At the centre of every circle of ruin, the ground was charred and covered in ashes.

'Still imagining hysterical monks wielding sledgehammers and axes?' Agneta asked.

Estevar didn't respond, too busy focusing what little attention his fever allowed him on the evidence before him. His initial hypothesis was that oil had been poured over the destroyed sculptures by a mob, who'd then tossed holy texts and scriptures onto the pile and set fire to the whole lot. That, however, failed to take into account for the island's near-constant winter storms. The winds and rains would surely have washed or blown away any ashes left behind by books and paper, which meant the charring at the centre of each ruin was caused by something hotter and more potent than any bonfire.

'Explosives?' he wondered aloud, but then shook his head. 'No, they would have had to have somehow been placed *inside* the statues to produce this exact pattern of destructions. But how then could six individual explosions be made to occur with such intens—?'

Overhead, the clouds rumbled; the rains would be back soon, and once more Isola Sombra would be assaulted by—

'Lightning,' Estevar murmured just as the first crack of distant thunder reached his ears, almost as if it were whispering agreement with his inescapable conclusion. 'Six statues, each struck from the sky by a bolt of lightning that shattered it and sent the ruins radiating away from a central point, charring the remains black.'

He turned where he stood, his gaze sweeping over the rest of the abbey grounds: the cloister, the chapter house, all the other buildings and towers, even the curtain wall. There was not a single sign of similar damage anywhere else.

'The gods died,' Agneta said, then repeated her earlier admonition, 'but that is not the same thing as saying they are dead.' She placed her hands on Estevar's arms and turned him back towards the ruins of the courtyard. 'When my brethren woke after the first winter storm seventeen days ago to discover the portrayals of their gods obliterated this way, they were forced to ask the inevitable question.'

Seventeen days ago. Had it been this that had induced the abbot to send copies of his letter for Estevar off with every travelling Bardatti his unnamed 'trusted emissary' could find?

Oh, Venia, you silly fool. What manner of faith led you to expect a Greatcoat could arbitrate the riots that envelop an abbey when it appears the skies themselves wage war upon your beliefs?

'You understand now?' Agneta asked, suddenly eager as her fingers squeezed Estevar's arms painfully. 'You see the futility – the danger – of a secular magistrate seeking to impose his will upon the monks of this abbey at a time like this? Flee this madhouse, Trattari. I will provide you with clothes and food and medical supplies so that you can return to the shore with your mule and await the lowering of the tide when the causeway will be passable again. Leave the sickness afflicting my brethren to one who understands both its cause and its cure!'

Estevar Borros had never been so tempted to abandon a case. Brother Agneta was right: this was no business of his. Whatever intellectual fascination he might have with the improbabilities of six bolts of lightning so perfectly striking six statues – perhaps they had been reinforced with iron rods and their towering height was the cause? – still, that was a poor reason to insinuate himself into a situation which he could not in good conscience hope to ameliorate.

'Where is Abbot Venia?' he asked, once again gazing up towards the tower at the far side of the abbey grounds. 'Was it the destruction of the statues that led him to hide up there all this time?'

When she failed to answer, he looked at her, guessing from the tightness of her features that she was formulating a response that would divert him from something she was hiding from him. She saw his stare, and appeared to respect him enough that she cast off whatever attempt at deception she'd been concocting.

'No, Eminence, it was not the statues that sent him into hiding inside his tower. He had already sent his missive summoning you before this happened. The destruction of the statues is what caused him to descend from his tower for the last time.'

'What? Then where is he? Why has Venia not come to meet me?'

Agneta dropped the mule's reins and walked across the ruins to a mound Estevar had not noticed before. The low pile of upturned dirt was a mundane sight compared to the rest of the destruction.

'What – or who – lies beneath that soil?' he asked warily.

'Come,' she said, gesturing for him to join her. 'It's almost time.'

Leaving Imperious outside the statuary, they stepped across the field of charred stone shards.

'Time for what?' Estevar asked.

She pointed to the dark earth at their feet. The mound was roughly the length of a man, not a tall one, but of comparable girth to Estevar.

'We keep burying him,' she said, her voice oddly sorrowful, 'but he refuses to lie where he should. Perhaps it is because he still hears his name called so often, in grief or in disdain.'

'Brother Agneta, what is this madness that overtakes you? If Venia has been killed, then—'

'Ah, there, you see?' she asked, jabbing a forefinger at the mound. 'It's as if we keep summoning him.'

Estevar was about to urge her away from the grave when he thought he saw the ground shifting as if thousands of earthworms were burrowing their way out of it. He would have assumed it was simply his fever overtaking him again, but now Brother Agneta was murmuring something, almost chanting.

'Venia,' she said quietly. 'Venia, Venia, Venia.'

The dirt shifted again, and Estevar reached to the back of his belt for his dagger. He'd investigated cases involving the so-called 'living dead' before. Tristia's flora was rich in plants that caused unusual effects in the human body, including several which could make a person appear dead, only to waken in a stupor hours or even days later.

More of the soil fell away, revealing the first glimpses of pale yellowish skin.

'Impossible,' Estevar whispered, for no concoction he had ever encountered could induce a cadaver whose head had been severed from its body to move itself out of the earth.

'Impossible, indeed,' Agneta agreed, also staring down at the prone corpse of Abbot Venia, his naked flesh inscribed with the same foul sigils drawn in the sketch placed in Estevar's hands by Sir Daven Colraig on behalf of the Margrave of Someil. 'And yet, no matter how many times his remains are reburied, still he returns to remind us that some crimes refuse to remain unpunished.'

'Who did this?' Estevar demanded. 'Who beheaded Abbot Venia and desecrated his corpse in this fashion?'

Agneta chuckled, a deeply disturbing sound given what lay at their feet. 'I show you statues blasted by lightning and a beheaded cadaver that won't stay buried, and yet you seek an answer to the most prosaic question imaginable?'

Estevar felt a fire rising in his belly raging hotter than his fever. 'You mocked me earlier for being a Greatcoat: a magistrate whose jurisdiction you Cogneri deem trivial because we deal only with secular matters.' He knelt down and began examining the pale corpse in earnest. 'Well, here lies the victim of a murder. The means, whether mundane or magical, are far less important to me than the identity of the murderer. And that, Inquisitor, lies squarely in my jurisdiction.'

'He was a deeply spiritual man,' Agneta said, as if she hadn't heard him at all. Her voice was filled with an evident fondness for the dead abbot. 'But in matters of canon law, he was guided by his reason as much as his faith. Given the circumstances, he too would no doubt deem you the logical choice to investigate his murder and bring the guilty to justice.'

Estevar reached out a hand to tentatively touch the abbot's corpse. The skin was cold and lifeless, yet showed no signs of decomposition or the gnawing of the flesh by worms or insects. He rose to his feet. Before he could investigate properly, he needed to tend to his wounds and those of Imperious, as well as establish a place within the abbey from where to work, most likely the infirmary. Then he noticed the way Brother Agneta was looking at him. 'I would have been Venia's choice to pursue his murderer, but not yours, Inquisitor?'

The lines of her face looked deeper, her body more frail. 'Faith is not a matter of choice, Eminence.' She gestured one by one to the six towers rising above the abbey. 'It is no more my business deciding who should or should not investigate Venia's murder than is the business of monks to debate which gods they will believe in and which ones they won't. Religion is not built on compromise. It is a matter of conviction.'

'Then you will not seek to impede my investigation? For I will see the killer face justice, and this, I believe, will aid us in uncovering the deeper sickness festering at the heart of this abbey.'

She smiled back at him, weary and ... something else – pitying, perhaps? He'd never seen a Cogneri – even one as old as Agneta – so meek before a secular magistrate. With great gentleness, she reached out and placed her palm over the wound at his side. He realised it was bleeding freely once again. 'You Greatcoats, with your idealism and your grand swordplay, you see the law as the means not only to punish the guilty, but to bring peace. It is a noble thought.'

'You speak as if we were dreamers.'

'Forgive me, then, Eminence. I was an inquisitor, not a magistrate, and my sword-fighting days are long behind me. All that remains ...'

Estevar saw for the briefest instant the old woman's hand close into a fist, and the short, sharp blow she delivered to his wound that banished his consciousness like a puff of air to a faltering candle flame.

As he fell backwards, slumping against the braying, confused mule that had braved its fear of the statuary to try and save him, he thought he heard Agneta say, '... are my convictions.'

PART THE THIRD

THE SIGILS
OF TESTAMENT

Bring forth the sinners of the community and compel the testimony of their transgressions. Inscribe upon the flesh of the sacrifice a sigil to represent each offence, being careful not to draw the sigils too large, else the sacrifice's skin may prove too small a canvas for them all.

CHAPTER 12

THE ONLY QUESTION THAT MATTERS

'Is your mind clear?'

The voice echoed from somewhere in the darkness, suggesting that Estevar was in a large chamber or cavern with stone walls. The skin on his back hurt, as if he'd been stung dozens of— No, not stung: *scraped*. There were scrapes and cuts down his back – new ones. Someone must have dragged him a long way, and judging from the painful bruises accompanying the scrapes, dragged him up or down steps as well.

'Is your mind clear?'

The question was a fair one, Estevar judged, and set about answering it by first devoting his muddled thoughts to deducing who had asked it.

The pitch was deep, somewhere just below the second open string of a bazatia. The heavy, lute-like instrument was played with the bottom of its belly resting on the floor, giving it a sonorous drone. Bazatias were favoured by the minstrels of his homeland as bass accompaniment for more melodic flutes and guitars. Not one in twenty adult men had voices so deep, and fewer than one in a thousand women.

Estevar had made a study of the particularities of the human voice years ago when he'd theorised that verbal deception could be detected by an attentive ear trained to alterations in pitch, tremulousness of the tongue, tightening of the throat and various intermittent hesitancies masked through the use of 'hems', 'ahs' and, of course, that old plodding clod, 'umm'.

Alas, extensive experimentation on known charlatans had failed to confirm any of Estevar's hypotheses, and he'd been forced to accept that most people *sounded* like they were lying most of the time, whether or not they spoke the truth. The most skilled deceivers were, in fact, the least likely to reveal themselves through their voices, any more than by their facial expressions.

'Is your mind clear?'

The accent was Tristian, but there was something underneath, possibly a foreign tongue dulled by years of disuse. The choice of words was odd, yet also familiar somehow, almost as if—

Estevar reined in his wandering thoughts, returning to the voice, for there were more clues there, as yet unexamined. The deep tone suggested a big man, the hint of a rumble possibly indicating someone of substantial girth. There was something else there, too: a faint wheezing threading through the syllables.

An old man, then? No, too much vitality in the vowels, something that typically faded with age. Perhaps what Estevar had heard was the exhaustion of someone who'd run a long way to reach him? But no, that too was unlikely due to the absence of the rapid 'huh-huh-huh' inhalations that signified the lungs trying to recover from exertion. This wheezing was slower, accompanied by a brief rattle cut off with each consonant, like the sound of someone in pain trying to mask their infirmity.

Try all you wish, my friend, Estevar thought, perhaps a trifle arrogantly, *I will discern your nature and intent soon enough.*

'Is your mind clear?'

That same question again, but this time Estevar recalled why it was familiar to him. Years ago, Kest Murrowson, one of his fellow Greatcoats, had asked him to consider delivering a seminar on investigative reasoning for newly recruited members of their order. Estevar's travels at the time – along with his often less than cordial relationships with his fellow magistrates, who had got into the habit of calling him 'The King's Spook Hunter' – had inclined him to refuse. Still, he'd spent a great deal of time during subsequent journeys contemplating how best he would impart the investigative arts to others, should he ever decide to do so.

None of his ideas had proven fruitful, at least in his own estimation, as each one relied on bits and pieces of knowledge that could only be acquired after years of focused study. Few Greatcoats, their heads filled with visions of riding a fast steed, sword in hand, to storm a corrupt noble's palace and rescue some unfortunate – often very attractive – soul from injustice, displayed such patience.

In the end, Estevar had settled on a compromise: the best he could do would be to distil his methods down to core principles – elemental questions that would enable an investigator to properly focus, thus enabling them to better utilise what intellect they did possess. And the first question was:

'*Is your mind clear?*'

This was the keystone – the foundation upon which every other aspect of an investigator's subsequent reasoning depended. It was the first question they must ask themselves when stepping into a situation in which their case – or perhaps their very lives – would depend upon whether or not they could outwit the perpetrators.

That was how Estevar divined the identity of the deep-voiced foreigner hiding his ill-health and speaking into the darkness.

'*Is your mind clear?*'

He had been talking to himself.

'No,' he replied as he slipped back into unconsciousness.

This time, however, he could have sworn the voice asking belonged to someone else.

CHAPTER 13

IS YOUR MIND CLEAR?

The next time Estevar heard that question, he was certain someone other than himself was doing the asking.

'Wh-what?' he mumbled groggily. He was flat on his back, but this time lying on something that made the scrapes on his skin itch – a woollen blanket or a rug, protecting him from the rough rock underneath. The air was musty, suggesting a cave, or perhaps a prison cell.

When he tried to prop himself up on his elbows, his head swam and he fell back with a thump that very nearly knocked him out again. Feeling an unexpected coolness over his skin, his hands went to his chest and then his legs in dismay. His shirt and trousers were gone, leaving him naked save for a pair of breeches that he was fairly sure did not belong to him. Running his fingers over the braids of his beard, he found the bristles were dry, suggesting considerable time had passed since the elderly inquisitor half his size had bested him so easily.

I seem to be losing all my duels lately, he thought, *even those I was unaware had already begun.*

He kept his eyes closed to avoid the nausea that threatened his tenuous hold on consciousness. Time was what was needed now: time to allow his beleaguered body to contend with the multitude of abuses it had recently suffered before facing whatever onslaught awaited him next. His mind, however, was eager to begin.

He didn't need to inhale that deeply to detect the pungent scent of hay and fresh manure in the dank air.

Someone brought Imperious down here with me. An act of compassion? Or just to get us both out of sight to prevent our deaths being witnessed?

'Imperious?' he called out.

An unexpected reply shocked Estevar to an even more acute wakefulness. 'The mule was very sick,' said a woman's voice – thankfully, not Brother Agneta.

Estevar tried to locate the source of the speaker, who sounded neither near nor especially far. His ears picked up the faint hint of an echo that he recognised as reverberations off stone walls. *Whoever she is, she is skulking at the far end of a long, cavernous chamber*, he reasoned. *Out of fear? Unlikely, given my present infirmity. No, she doesn't want me to see her. Not yet.*

'Where is my mule?' Estevar asked, the tremulous tone revealing more anxiety than he wanted. 'Why don't I hear him breathing?'

'He's asleep,' came the reply. 'The wound troubles him, and he kept trying to kick through the door. I couldn't risk him running through the tunnels, braying and attracting attention from those above. That would have been very bad for both of you.'

Which confirms we are still within the abbey's walls, he thought, not entirely pleased with that discovery, *surrounded by armies of fractious monks and at least one cunning and ruthless inquisitor.*

'Who are you?' he asked, more to make himself sound confused and helpless than out of any expectation of an honest answer. His throat was sore, but not as dry and painful as it ought to be, given his fever. The woman must have given him water. 'Why do you hide in the shadows?'

When she failed to reply, he rolled onto his right side, reawakening the agony of the wound below his left ribs. He clamped his teeth shut to stop himself screaming but couldn't keep a groan from escaping his lips. Probing the wound with his fingertips, he found it covered in a thick, gooey substance not unlike tree sap, and beneath that, stitches that were not his own.

'You sewed up my wound?' he asked.

Again, he was greeted with silence. Chancing the nausea, he opened his eyes and glanced around what was indeed a dimly lit cavernous room. He took note of the rough-hewn rock slanting inwards towards a curved ceiling, and the crude, archaic engravings depicting Tristia's six gods adorning the walls. Shadows pooled at the far end of the chamber, where his rescuer no doubt hid from him. The source of illumination came from a single wide-based candle on the floor nearby, set inside a chalk circle surrounded by esoteric symbols, some of which Estevar recognised.

'Witchcraft?' he asked. 'Inside Isola Sombra's ancient prayer chamber?'

The feminine voice – young, perhaps early twenties, her tone light, almost musical, as if she were amused rather than afraid – mockingly repeated her earlier question. 'Is your mind clear, Estevar Borros?'

'Stop asking that!' he shouted, which set off a fit of coughing and retching.

'You're not doing very well,' she observed. 'Don't you think you should answer my question?'

'Why?'

A breeze of teasing laughter. 'Because you've been mumbling it ever since my man brought you down here, so surely it must be important?'

Estevar felt a stab of embarrassment that something so personal had become a source of amusement for a stranger. 'Of course my mind is—'

'Ah, ah, ah,' she interrupted. 'A question so vital that it has haunted your sleep, pierced even the shroud of fever that nearly burned the life right out of you, surely deserves a more considered response.'

That voice was steadily becoming ever more irritating, not least because she was definitely mimicking his own vocal mannerisms. Yet, she was also correct: his wound might be stitched, the worst of the fever passed, but he was still on abbey grounds so the danger was far from over. Worse, his rescuer said Imperious was sick and now sedated, which meant he couldn't flee without abandoning the mule who'd saved his life.

I will not depart this place without you, my friend, he swore silently. *Not that there's anywhere for either of us to go, not with the causeway flooded.*

'Are you concentrating?' the woman asked. 'Because I can't tell if you're deep in contemplation or merely constipated. I'm starting to get bored. It's probably best for you that I not grow weary of your company.'

Still on his side, Estevar placed his palms on the woollen horse blanket and pressed carefully against the stone floor to assess how weak his ordeals had left him and whether he dared rise. Everything ached, especially his wound, but nothing so badly it warranted the greater risk of just lying here until either someone discovered him or his apparently fickle rescuer decided to amuse herself in other ways. Slowly, he pushed himself up. The sensation of his stitches being tugged was jarring, but he endured the discomfort until he'd managed to get himself sitting upright, cross-legged.

'My, you're a big fellow, aren't you, *Eminence*?'

Rather than taking offence at the familiar joke, he was grateful. Buried beneath her apparent ridicule were clues that might give him deeper insight into the mysterious woman, although despite what she might hope, she had, already provided Estevar with a great deal of evidence to work with.

My, you're a big fellow.

That wasn't the sort of jab one makes when the butt of the joke is dying. She'd done an admirable job of stitching his wound, itself a rare skill. Add to that the use of the salve that was likely intended to stave off further infection and he would be justified in deducing that she possessed medical knowledge, which in turn gave him some confidence in her assessment that he wasn't in any danger of imminent demise.

Her tone hadn't been mocking, either. In fact, her earlier reference to the person who'd dragged Estevar here from the courtyard as '*my man*' had been almost flirtatious – although probably neither husband nor lover, given the way she was playing with Estevar. A servant of some kind, then.

'Ugh,' she groaned theatrically from the dark. 'Am I to stand here all night, waiting?'

All night. He'd been here many hours, but not an extra day, else his stomach would be raging rather than merely grumbling at its emptiness. He peered past the candle and into the shadows, but still couldn't make out the figure lurking there.

'I'll make you a deal,' she said with sudden enthusiasm. 'Prove to me that your mind truly is clear. Apply your investigative abilities to me, and with every correct guess, I will take a step forward until you can see who I am.' He heard her clap her hands together. 'Oh, I do like this idea. Come now, oh dauntless paragon of reason, impress me.'

Estevar rubbed at his temples. He had a fierce headache, but what she asked for was little more than a parlour trick. It would help him regain his focus while he planned his next move.

'I have no need to see you,' he answered back. 'You are the woman from the clifftop: the one with the wild red hair and the immodest taste in winter clothing.'

'A lazy guess,' she chided him reprovingly.

'Given how few people are left on this island and the religious vocation of those who remain, I would call it a logical deduction. But perhaps this will amuse you more . . .' He gestured to the chalk circle of symbols prominently lit by the candle at their centre. 'You are not a witch.'

'What?' she asked, her tone suddenly sharp as a knife's edge. 'I save your miserable life with my precious spells and you demean my ancient traditions?'

'I demean nothing, I merely state the obvious.'

'How so?'

He placed a hand over his wound. It still felt hot, but the sticky salve was doing its work. 'First, because you placed your trust in medicinal compounds and stitching thread rather than incantations and hexes.'

'A witch can't know herbs and healing? Perhaps the spell was in aid of the medicines?'

He ignored the feint meant to distract him. 'Second, I am familiar with a wide range of the more genuine mystical traditions of this country.' He reached out and traced one of the chalk symbols. 'You've made a beggar's stew of your sigils here, mixing ones for divination with others for summoning good luck at cards. Most of the rest are made up.'

'I never said I was an especially *good* witch.'

'Last, and this is the most relevant fact: only a fool would sneak into an abbey and leave the remains of a genuine witchcraft ritual in plain view of any monks who might walk in here.' He swept away some of the chalk with his hand. 'Not only did you fail to hide your work, you placed a candle at the centre so that your counterfeit symbols would be the first thing I saw when I roused myself.'

'Why would I go to such bother?'

'Because you heard Brother Agneta and me talking earlier about my particular role among the Greatcoats, which indicates that you followed us up the road to the abbey, which is how you knew she had struck me.'

Did the Cogneri truly leave me in the courtyard to die? Would the ancient tensions between inquisitors and travelling magistrates extend to outright murder? Or is there something larger at stake in this monkish feud than I yet comprehend?

'The old bird did take you rather easily.' The woman interrupted his rumination with an air of disappointment. 'She may be a bitter old vulture clinging to the past, but she took you down as easily as a mule's tail swatting away a fly. Could it be, Eminence, that your worship of reason and the law in a country where the gods themselves were murdered might be tragically misplaced?'

Estevar ignored the jibe. His lack of religiosity – even among his fellow magistrates – had often been the subject of disbelief. His answer now was the same as it had been then. 'One needn't doubt the existence of gods to deny that they are worthy of one's faith.'

But you have revealed something to me, my mysterious kidnapper, he thought to himself. *'A bitter old vulture clinging to the past' means Agneta is known to you. And that bit about a mule's tail is you seeking to remind me that something I care about remains at risk and depends on your assistance.*

Estevar tried to stand, until a bout of sudden dizziness made him think twice of the endeavour. Sitting back down, stroking his wobbling legs, he said, 'You asked how I knew you weren't a witch and I have provided you the answer. As to why you should pretend? You've shown yourself to be someone who enjoys playing games and is easily bored. After treating my wounds, you grew weary of waiting for me to rouse by myself and decided to see if you might trick me when I awoke.'

She took a step forward from the other side of the stable, and now he could make out her silhouette. Slender, as she'd looked on that clifftop, not tall, but a grown woman nonetheless. She adopted a sly pose, but not a coquettish one, which meant she wasn't relying on seduction as a principal tool for getting what she wanted. An opponent to be wary of, Estevar concluded.

'I do like games,' she admitted. He couldn't see the smile on her face yet, but he heard it in her voice. 'A rather tedious tournament has been taking over the abbey for quite a while now: roving bands of half-crazed monks are looking for ways to chop each other up so they can claim this abbey for whichever god they've decided to worship.' She sighed. 'Dull. Inconsequential.'

'I'm sure those whose lives have already been lost do not share your opinion.'

'Ah, but see, now that *you're* here ... The vaunted Estevar Valejan Duerisi Borros, pitted against the machinations of those who see themselves as savants as attempt to manoeuvre you around the board? *This* game intrigues me!'

Estevar thought back to every conversation he'd had since crossing the causeway. He'd never used his full name in front of Brother Agneta or Sister Parietta or Jaffen, but he *had* with the boatman. Malezias had said he wasn't a monk, although he had been dressed as one – was he this mysterious trickster's servant? Had she, seeing Estevar drowning, ordered Malezias – who clearly hadn't been keen on rescuing him – to go out in the rowboat? Then, after Agneta had left him for dead, had she summoned Malezias again, this time to drag him from the courtyard down to the relative safety of this ancient prayer cave?

Saint Anlas-who-remembers-the-world, how many times over do I owe this woman for saving my life?

'Come, unraveller of hidden truths,' she chided him from the shadows. 'Tell me more about myself. I begin to fear I'll forget who I am entirely at this rate.'

Growing weary of her theatrics and feeling somewhat more himself, Estevar looked around until he saw a pile of folded clothes on the floor behind him. Even in the dim light he could see they weren't what he'd been wearing earlier, nor were these the drenched set from his saddlebags. She assumed they would fit him, which suggested they belonged to Malezias, further confirmation that the big brute was beholden to her in some way. With renewed determination, he rose and shakily began dressing himself. His plethora of aches and pains made it slow, clumsy work, but that didn't prevent him from continuing the game, especially since he'd likely need this enigmatic woman's help at least once more.

'You were born on this island,' he said, trying to step into the trousers and very nearly toppling over, 'possibly in this very abbey.'

That did pique her curiosity. 'How could you know that?'

'A simple deduction, given most – if not all – of the residents have fled the island. Only someone with a deep personal attachment to this place would remain when both storm and mayhem are threatening Isola Sombra. Furthermore, you were comfortable sneaking onto the grounds, which demonstrates knowledge of places to hide and avenues of escape, should the need arise.'

'Perhaps I'm one of the monks myself. Have you considered that?'

He had, but quickly rejected the possibility. 'A monk's life is one of solitude and quiet devotion.'

'I would surely die from such tedium.'

Estevar nearly laughed at that, for he'd said much the same thing to Venia when the monk had tried to recruit him for the abbey. Once more, his balance failed him and his trousers slipped from his grasp, forcing him to bend down and pick them up again.

'They do possess a great number of books, though,' the woman said wistfully.

So, she comes here on occasion to pilfer – or 'borrow' – from the abbey's libraries. Was that what brought her here earlier? Then when she saw Brother Agneta leave me for dead, decided to play a prank on the monks? How far might such impulses take her?

With painstaking care, Estevar finally managed to tug the trousers up over his hips. They were too long in the leg and a trifle tight in the waist, but he could roll them up easily enough, and there was a belt, which would avoid the necessity of having to do up the top button. Boots and socks were next – the boots were a trifle too big at first, but there was an extra pair of socks which solved that problem. He walked unsteadily back to the fake ritual circle.

'You desecrate a holy site as a practical joke,' he said, rubbing away the remaining chalk with the toe of his borrowed boot. 'Furthermore, you do so with impunity. Not only do you feel at home in this abbey, you resent those who live here. The simplest explanation is that you were born to one of the brethren who violated their vow of chastity.'

'An antiquated rule,' she said, but took another step forward. Her face was still in shadow, but the red curls hanging down to her shoulders gleamed in the candle's wavering light.

'Most of Tristia's churches have abolished the tradition,' Estevar reminded her as he slid the shirt over his head. Like the trousers, it was too long, but he stuffed the excess length under his belt and it worked perfectly well. 'Isola Sombra is one of the only remaining holy places where chastity is required.' He paused a moment, then decided it might be useful to probe her resentment deeper. 'I believe Abbot Venia wished to eliminate the rule, but realising it would cause unrest among his brethren, abandoned his reforms.'

Several seconds passed before she spoke again, and when she did, her tone was suitably unimpressed. 'A feeble attempt from so renowned an investigator. You wanted to see how I'd react to the use of the abbot's name to determine whether perhaps I was the one who killed him.'

'And did you?'

'What do you think?'

Estevar looked around the dimly lit cavern, hoping to find either his dagger or some other weapon. He feared he would be needing one soon. 'Given the patterns of speech you've employed thus far, I believe that if you despised him, you would have called him "Venia" or referenced him with a diminishing slur. Instead, you called him, "the abbot", which suggests a modicum of respect, if not admiration.'

'Wrong again,' she said, although she took another step closer. Now he could see her face. Derision twisted her lips into a smirk, above the sharp nose, between grey-blue eyes that almost matched the stormy waves, he noted a faint pinching of the skin. She was sad about Abbot Venia's death – sad, and angry.

'Well, then?' she asked.

'What?'

She rolled her eyes. 'My question. *Your* question. What is the answer?'

'My mind is clear,' he said without hesitation.

'Good.'

She disappeared back into the shadows at the far end of the cavern, returning a moment later with something long and thin wrapped in a blanket. When she was standing before him, he observed that she was pretty, in the way of Tristian women, which was to say, not entirely to his taste. The delicate cleft in her chin added to the mischievousness in her expression. She was also, he was quite certain, dangerous to anyone who crossed her path. Nonetheless, she'd proven herself to be clever and she knew details of this abbey that Estevar did not, which made her a useful ally. At least, for now.

'Call me Caeda,' she said, and handed him the bundle. 'If you hope to survive what comes next, you'll be wanting this.'

He unwrapped the blanket and found a scabbarded rapier underneath. It had a cup-hilt, unlike his own swept-hilt weapon now lying at the bottom of the ocean. Drawing the sword from its sheath, he found the balance not too bad and the length well-suited to his height. Malezias hadn't struck him as the sort of fighter who would choose to wield so precise an instrument, which meant Caeda had almost certainly filched this one from somewhere in the abbey.

'An inauspicious gift for a man who recently lost a sword fight,' Estevar said. 'What is it you predict is going to occur?'

She grinned at him, tapping the flat of the blade with a fingertip. 'The three things that always happens when a Greatcoat sticks his nose in other people's murders, Eminence. An enquiry, a trial and, inevitably . . .'

Estevar belted the rapier to his side, trying not to wince when even that small effort made his wound flare with pain. 'A duel,' he finished for her, then asked, 'Why did you bring me down here rather than to the abbey's infirmary? Has it been taken over by one of the factions?'

Her tone was icy. 'I will not go to that place.'

'Why?'

'I don't . . .' A curious uncertainty revealed itself in the brief furrowing of her brow, quickly banished. 'That crazy inquisitor who tried to kill you might have found you there and finished the job.'

Before Estevar could press her further, Caeda knelt and picked up the candle, then strode to the other side of the chamber, banishing enough of the shadows to reveal the dark silhouette of Imperious, kneeling on a small pile of horse blankets and swaying as if groggy. Roused by the candlelight, he gave a confused bray and rose unsteadily to his hooves. Caeda stroked his neck before walking to the far end, where she opened the wooden door set in an arch carved into the rock, peeked outside, then motioned for Estevar to join her. He first went to check on Imperious, whose jagged wound had been cleaned, stitched and smothered in the same sticky gunk as his own. The mule didn't look too happy about it.

'Patience, my friend,' Estevar said quietly, rubbing the mule's neck affectionately. 'The enemy struck the first blow, but they will not take us so easily next time.'

Caeda beckoned him with a curled forefinger. 'If you would accompany me, Eminence?' She winked.

Estevar took hold of the reins and guided the weary mule towards the door. *Unless they've already taken us.*

CHAPTER 14

OF HOUNDS, TRUMPETERS AND BONE-RATTLERS

The candle in Caeda's hand was fighting a losing battle against the darkness outside the ancient prayer chamber. Carved into the walls on either side of the narrow tunnels were centuries-old ossuaries. Dank, musty air filled the maze of passages, reminding Estevar of mist rolling across a moor.

Is there no part of this cursed island free of dampness and fog? he wondered.

Caeda moved with an easy grace, her slender figure navigating the cramped, winding passages with ease, while Estevar's shoulders grazed the encroaching stone and the low rounded ceiling forced him to stoop like a crook-backed old man. Imperious, still only half-roused from whatever sedative Caeda had administered, kept shying away from the mouldy, fungus-covered bones jutting from the walls.

Estevar tugged gently on the reins, urging the poor beast onwards.

'The storm drains,' he asked, his deep baritone echoing through the tunnels in a most unsettling fashion. 'What happens if they fill, or if the grates get clogged?'

Caeda paused at a junction before choosing the path to the right. 'The storm drains are above us. *This* is where the water comes.'

'The monks allow this ancient holy site to flood?'

'It wasn't *their* holy site. It belonged to whatever cult or religious sect previously occupied Isola Sombra.' Caeda took a few more steps, then held up the candle to an iron grate above their heads. 'Water from the courtyard flows down here,' she whispered, evidently concerned someone walking the grounds above might hear. Then she held the candle close to an identical grate at their feet. 'Which, when all goes well and the sewers underneath us don't flood, keeps both levels reasonably safe.'

'And what happens when the sewers do overflow?'

She grimaced. 'A great many dead rats – and occasionally, unlucky monks – float to the top.'

A potential point of sabotage, Estevar noted, filing away that knowledge for future use.

Fortified abbeys like this one were easy to protect against the outside world. The causeway ensured a narrow passage for enemy infantry, and then only when the tides were low; the abbey's position at the island's summit lent it a superior vantage point for fighting off invaders, and the massive curtain wall itself could repel a siege for weeks or months if needed.

But once inside, the abbey was entirely vulnerable. Shared food and water supplies meant a single saboteur could poison hundreds. Without a standing constabulary, any attempt to incarcerate a well-liked rabble-rouser could incite rebellion if his friends or followers considered him innocent. But no vulnerability was as dangerous as the weakened bonds of fellowship and faith: two virtues which had apparently proven insufficient in maintaining order during these troublesome times.

'The factions,' Estevar asked, tugging Imperious' reins to keep the mule moving. 'How many are there?'

'Ah,' Caeda said, making no effort to hide the glee in her reply, 'I could tell you one for every monk living within these walls and you'd have a hard time convicting me of perjury, Magistrate.'

Estevar bit back a retort. He'd never been fond of cynicism as a form of wit, but he was a stranger here, with precious little knowledge of the terrain or the monks themselves. If he hoped to bring Abbot Venia's killers to justice – to say nothing of restoring peace to Isola Sombra – he needed a guide.

'The theocratic coalitions are unstable, I presume?' he asked, hoping for a more useful answer to his question.

'As if we all stood on quicksand, Eminence.'

Her refusal to speak plainly revealed part of her desire: to have him be reliant on her expertise, and to be fully aware of that dependence.

Very well, Estevar decided, *let us presume you have reasons beyond bitterness and malice for remaining here and see where you lead me.*

'Have you a theory, then, Madam?' he asked. 'Which faction presents the greatest threat to the abbey's future and which seek to live in harmony within these walls?'

She turned and smiled up at him. She enjoyed being referred to as 'madam' or 'lady', he'd noticed. Perhaps she was accustomed only to spiteful looks and mean-spirited gossip from the monks. Had Abbot Venia, despite his claims of humility and open-mindedness, failed to protect Caeda from the callousness of his brethren, or had he hoped their cruelty would induce her to abandon this place and begin a life elsewhere, free from the shadows of whichever parentage had left her held in such low esteem?

'Have you ranks within the Greatcoats?' Caeda asked abruptly, halting their progress once again.

Estevar was glad for the chance to catch his breath. The fever, though somewhat abated, still bothered him, and he'd yet to recover from the additional injuries he'd accumulated.

Saint Eloria-whose-screams-draw-blood! What am I going to do if upholding my ruling over the governance of the abbey requires me to fight another duel?

His red-headed guide was staring at him with a curious expression and he realised he'd forgotten to answer her question.

'Ranks, my Lady? Not really. When a trial requires the attentions of several magistrates, the whole is referred to as a "choir", and the Greatcoat charged with leading that choir is called a "cantor".'

Caeda sighed wistfully. 'How lovely. It's almost as if the law were a kind of music and all of you players seeking to compose a more harmonious song together.'

Another deflection from Estevar's enquiry. Clearly, she wanted something from him, though she hadn't demanded any kind of promise or assurance about who he'd side with or what sentence he might impose. Which meant the young woman wanted something more personal – something for herself.

Is that such an unreasonable expectation in exchange for her assistance? He set aside for a moment his own predilection for ignoring all considerations save those that dealt with the facts of the case. *Whatever life she has lived here, it isn't one I would wish on my own daughters.*

An idea took him – a whimsical impulse, but one that might aid his investigations. 'Among my people, who live across the ocean,' he began with great solemnity, 'we have an instrument called a *tonalto*. It is a type of flute, made from silver and tin. In Tristia you have something similar – a *piccolo*, you call it.'

Caeda suddenly stepped back into him, turned to place a finger to his lips and hide the light of her candle. Before long, his ears picked up what she'd heard much sooner: the patter of sandals on the floor above them, carried down through a grating in the roof not three feet from where they stood.

Torches in the passageways above suggested they must now be beneath one of the abbey interiors; there was certainly more light in this part of the tunnels. Estevar leaned forward to glance up at the drain and saw a man in monk's robes squatting over the iron grate. A moment later, the first trickles of urine drip-drip-dripped onto the rough stone floor in front of them, soon turning into a rather torrential stream. In the confines of the tunnel, the acrid stench invaded their nostrils. Caeda's face pinched with disgust when something even more off-putting slithered down between the grate's iron bars to plop down on the tunnel floor.

For his part, Estevar was intrigued by such blatantly disrespectful behaviour in the heart of the abbey. *So at least some of the monks here no longer fear reprisals for desecrating their holy place.*

After the monk had slunk away from the scene of his crime, Caeda unshielded her candle and stepped gingerly over the evidence of his malfeasance. 'Pigs,' she spat, picking up her pace to get away from the stench. 'Now, what were you saying about these tolanos ... tonaldi ...' She gave up mangling his native tongue and asked, 'You mentioned something about piccolos?'

'Lovely instruments,' Estevar continued. 'Their tone is light and delicate, but can rise to be heard over an entire orchestra.'

'I suppose,' she said without conviction, sounding annoyed by the obscure direction he'd taken their conversation. 'I've never heard a piccolo. I suppose it makes a pretty noise?'

'Not merely pretty, but *potent*, as well – especially when one seeks to pierce the smothering din of ignorant louts who would otherwise talk or shout over the music. Often it is the piccolo which commands the silence of an audience and compels their attention.'

They were halfway up a slope now, and Estevar could see a narrow door waiting at the end of the passage. Caeda stopped, her expression excited, almost childlike, having finally understood his reason for discussing musical instruments. 'This piccolo does indeed sound like a most potent device. A vital one, would you say?'

Estevar placed his hands lightly on her shoulders. 'Caeda, you are not under my command, nor can I compel your service in this matter. Nonetheless, my investigation will be lost without your knowledge and insight. If we are to be partners, I must count on both your discretion and your willingness to comport yourself within the ethical boundaries of a magistrate. Might you, therefore, consider taking the part of the piccolo in this song we are to compose together?'

Delight blossomed across the young woman's face. She took two steps back and gave Estevar the most preposterously flamboyant obeisance he'd ever seen, beginning as a curtsey, drifting into an elaborate bow and ending in a chaotic series of gestures that he presumed was meant to be a salute.

'Greatcoat Piccolo Caeda reporting for duty, my Cantor!'

Estevar couldn't keep himself from laughing, until Imperious found all this sudden amusement unsettling and gave a low, anxious neigh. Careful to avoid the stitches that marched from the top of the mule's head to just above his muzzle, Estevar stroked his cheek reassuringly.

'And now, Greatcoat Piccolo,' he said to Caeda, who grinned even wider, hearing him address her thus, 'which of the many factions threatening this abbey do you propose we interrogate first?'

She tapped a fingertip against the delicate cleft in her chin. 'Well, of the three main ones . . .'

Three factions, Estevar thought, recalling the debate between Brother Agneta and the two Trumpeters earlier. *Would it have been so difficult for the girl to have confirmed that simple fact half an hour ago?*

'The Bone-Rattlers – that's what everyone calls the traditionalists who were closest to Abbot Venia. They wear those silly dice around their necks to choose which deities to worship at any given time, even though most of those gods are probably still dead and the ones reborn too feeble to matter. Don't expect them to be of much use; they scurry around in the dark like mice, hiding from everyone else. On the other hand, they'll probably be the most agreeable to your presence, since your connection to Abbot Venia will lead them to assume you'll take their side.'

Brother Agneta had not appeared to share that reasoning, he noted. 'No doubt this will set the other two factions against us?' he asked. 'And they are?'

Caeda nodded agreement. 'The Trumpeters – that's a type of flower that grows on the island in summer. Poisonous, of course, which suits those yellow-robed goons marching around the abbey in perfectly formed squads. They believe the six old gods are gone for good and that the abbey needs a new deator to speak for whichever one comes to take their place. In the meantime, they're keen to practise their smiting of heretics – which is anyone *not* wearing a yellow robe.'

Certainly, Sister Parietta and her comrade Jaffen had been eager for an opportunity to smite Brother Agneta, along with taking Estevar himself prisoner. He wondered why it had been so important to the inquisitor to keep him out of their clutches, given she'd left him for dead in the courtyard minutes later. Perhaps Agneta feared whoever led these 'Trumpeters' might have persuaded him to join their cause?

'And what of the Hounds?' he asked Caeda. 'Do their drunken attempts to channel the spiritual energies of Isola Sombra into themselves make them as feared as the Trumpeters? Or does their devotion to ritualistic self-indulgence lead to ridicule?'

She tilted her head, looking much like a cat. 'Who said anything about the Hounds being self-indulgent?'

'Perhaps I was mistaken. I assumed that if one faction, the Bone-Rattlers, were devoted to the old gods, and another, the Trumpeters, portrayed themselves as the apostles of some new one – both outwardly theological perspectives – then the third faction had likely abandoned formal religion altogether and chosen a path of occult hedonism.'

Caeda frowned. 'Forgive me, Cantor, but that sounds more like speculation than deduction.'

'*Induction*, actually,' he told her. 'Deduction reveals what must be true when all else is eliminated, whereas *induction* enables us to develop hypotheses based on known facts.'

'In other words, induction is just another name for speculation,' she insisted.

'Speculation bound by—' He stopped himself. 'Forgive me, Piccolo. I have a bad habit of lecturing others about my methods whether asked or not.'

She put her hands on her hips. 'If I'm to be a proper Greatcoat, then I suppose I'll need to learn a few investigative techniques, don't you think?'

He couldn't help but smile at her use of mockery to mask her eagerness. Estevar had had many *actual* magistrates-in-training foisted on him. They were often keen to ride into the fray, delivering justice at the end of a sword. Rarely were they as interested in the less heroic yet far more intricate and vital process of uncovering the facts of a case. This made a nice change.

'Imagine a village,' he began, 'peaceful, until one day a messenger comes to warn of an invading army marching towards them.'

'A bedtime story?' Caeda asked, gesturing to the door at the top of the sloping passageway. 'Deadly schemes and monstrous intrigues await beyond that door, oh wise Cantor. Do you really want to pass the time telling me bedtime stories?'

'Hush, Piccolo. You asked that I explain my reasoning; allow me to do so in the fashion I believe most conducive to your training.'

'All right. I'm imagining a village. It's very peaceful – except for the whole invading army thing.'

'Good,' he said. 'Now, let us begin with the premise that, when presented with such a dilemma, most people fall into three camps.' Estevar put up a hand before she could interrupt. 'There are more than three ways to react to such dire tidings, of course, but if I asked you to describe the three most common ones, how would you answer?'

Caeda shrugged. 'Some would cower, hoping that either the messenger was lying or that someone would come to save them. Others would take up arms, vying for control and believing that only *they* were brave enough or smart enough to save the village.'

'Excellent,' he said approvingly. 'And the third . . . shall we say, *faction*? What would you expect them to do?'

'Probably decide that death was inevitable and start drinking and fu—' Her mouth split into a wide grin. 'That's exactly what the Hounds – well, "Wolves" is what they call themselves – have been doing ever since the storm destroyed the statuary and someone killed the abbot. They think that if the gods really are returning to Isola Sombra, it's only to dish out some righteous vengeance, so they holed up inside the Venerance Tower – that's where noble guests stay, where the best food and booze is kept – and started performing these occult rituals their leader found in some book in the abbot's private library. He claims it's ceremonial magic to imbue himself and his followers with godly powers, but his so-called rites mostly involve drunken orgies.' She poked Estevar in the chest to accentuate her words. 'So. Very. Clever! Oh, you are going to be excellent fun, my Cantor.'

'I saw the markings on Abbot Venia's body,' Estevar said, stepping back and combing his fingers through the beaded braids of his beard as a way to avoid any further poking, 'and the knights who came here days ago had similar inflictions. These "Wolves" must have sharp teeth indeed to have captured and then had their way with a dozen of the Margrave of Someil's finest chevaliers before sending them home in a stupor.'

Caeda's smile disappeared. In a whisper, she said, 'Make no mistake, my Cantor, the Wolves *are* dangerous. I wonder, will you brave their lair? You know how it is with wild dogs; if they sense even a hint of fear' – she clacked her teeth together menacingly – 'their fangs will soon find your throat.'

Estevar had rarely known actual fear during his tenure among the Greatcoats. When he arrived in a town or village, there would usually be constables or soldiers whose assistance he could conscript on behalf of the king. When that failed, twelve ordinary citizens could be formed into a jury, paid with the gold coins hidden as leather-covered buttons on his coat to help ensure his verdict held once the trial was over. Now he was alone on an island, far from his fellow Greatcoats and even further from the king's influence. All he had was this mysterious young woman whose origins and intentions remained unclear to him. He felt like an imposter, standing there with no coat, wearing another man's ill-fitting clothes, a rapier belted to his side that he could barely draw without tearing out the stitches resulting from his last duel – the one that had nearly killed him.

Caeda stared up at him. She looked concerned, though whether for his future or her own, he couldn't be sure. Favouring her with a broad smile, he resorted to the bluster that had carried him through so many other perils. 'Well, my Piccolo, you recall how one commands a hound, don't you?'

She folded her arms across her chest. 'How?'

This time he poked *her* in the shoulder. 'You teach the silly beasts to obey your whistles!'

Caeda laughed at that and stood up on her tiptoes to kiss his bearded cheek. 'Oh, Estevar, we are going to be such good friends!' With that, she turned on her heel and strode up to the door, which he knew now must lead into the Venerance Tower, the kennel these 'Hounds' had taken for themselves. She placed one hand on the door handle, then looked back at him, her expression disquietingly wistful. 'I do hope you won't die too quickly, my Cantor.'

CHAPTER 15

THE KING OF HOUNDS

'Caeda, my lovely,' proclaimed the tall, rakish figure lounging half-naked against the blue velvet back of a beautifully gilded oak throne that had once been occupied by the gentle, softly spoken Abbot Venia. 'What a delight to see you! I'd presumed you'd fled the island with the rest of the common cattle. Had I known otherwise, I would have unleashed a few of my boys to scour the island for you that I might at last bed you. But here you are, delivering yourself to me as if fate herself demands that you be good and properly fucked.'

Laughter erupted from the three dozen men and women sprawled around the austere circular chamber, nestled together on priceless silk tapestries of gold and silver thread depicting ancient Tristian religious scenes. Like their leader, whom Caeda had named Strigan but who styled himself 'the Wolf-King of Isola Sombra', their state of undress revealed bare flesh inked with heretical black sigils that would doubtless have seen the lot of them incarcerated, if Brother Agneta had had her way. In this one instance, Estevar rather hoped she would.

Why these particular symbols? he wondered, *and why do I find them so familiar, yet cannot recall any occult codex in which I've seen them before?* Most of the sigils had been inscribed on the margrave's twelve listless knights, as pictured on the illustration in the leather tube. He regretted the loss of the message, now with his greatcoat at the bottom of the sea.

I've seen them once before, in other circumstances, I'm certain of it. He tried and failed to summon anything more from his tired brain. *If only this wretched fever would abate long enough for me to remember . . .*

Although the laughter had died down, one fellow couldn't stop giggling: a heavyset man almost his own size sitting cross-legged in front of the large curved hearth set into the tower wall. The Venerance was usually the part of Tristian abbeys where momentous questions of faith were researched and debated – and this half-naked fellow, surrounded by a fortune's worth of books dragged down from the now-empty shelves, was presently tearing pages from one of the volumes, bunching each gorgeously illuminated piece of parchment in his huge fist – and then tossing it into the flames.

Estevar handed Imperious' reins to Caeda before crossing the floor to loom over the giddy monk burning the abbey's literary treasures. 'Did you know,' he began, staring down at the fellow whose unshaven jaw and sweating, malodorous body suggested he hadn't bathed in weeks, 'that in Tristia it is a crime to burn a book?'

The monk gazed up at him. His confused, inebriated smile and a brownish-green paste clinging to his teeth suggested his extreme intoxication was the result of more than mere alcohol. Estevar suspected the abuse of the abbey's herbarium.

'I do not speak merely of the crime against another's property, you understand,' Estevar continued, 'although that would be troubling enough. No, the law in this civilised nation decrees that the burning of *any* book is publishable by several months in prison.'

He turned to the rest of the Hounds, who were witnessing his performance in disbelief, doubtless anticipating the price their leader would extract from him for his brazenness. 'You are all educated men and women – do you know the manner in which the sentence for book burning is assessed?'

He gave them time, but no one spoke, though Strigan the Wolf-King watched with a keener intensity than his followers. Caeda shot him a warning glance, perhaps to remind him that it wasn't only his safety at risk here.

'No one knows?' Estevar asked. 'Then allow me to explain, for it is, I think, a remarkable example of what we call *equajudia*, or balanced justice. The sentence for burning a book is commensurate with the number of months required for a scribe to produce a new copy of that same book. Most equitable, no?'

The monk who'd been burning pages attempted a threatening scowl, as if he were debating whether to challenge Estevar. He seemed to think better of that, however, and cast a questioning gaze at his liege.

'Careful now,' warned Strigan. 'The Venerance Tower is my domain, Greatcoat, as the abbey will be soon enough, and the entire island not long after.' He leaned forward, resting one elbow on his thigh, the ropy muscles exposed by torn grey robes. With a forefinger, he traced one of the black sigils covering his muscular chest and shoulders. 'The sheep have fled Isola Sombra; it is the laws of wolves which govern here.'

Estevar silently reached down and took the book from the monk's hands before returning to where Caeda and Imperious waited. He stuffed the tome into the mule's saddlebag.

'What do you propose to do with a half-ruined book?' Strigan asked. 'Assuming I allow you to leave with it?'

'I propose to make a gift for you, Mighty Strigan.'

'A gift?'

Estevar said solemnly, 'In recompense for your cooperation with my investigation into the murder of Abbot Venia, I promise that on my return to Aramor, I will speak with the royal scribes on your behalf. They may be able to find a second copy of this book within the castle library and thus reproduce the pages torn from this one. Once fully repaired, I will have whichever of my fellow magistrates is next travelling this circuit return the book to the abbey, and the sentence for your complicity in its destruction will be commuted.'

Strigan laughed, the rich, carefree laughter of one who knows he holds all the power and can afford to appear amused by blatant challenges to his rule. 'Alas, your Eminence, we have burned very, very many books already.'

Estevar's forehead was slick with sweat, from both the fire and his own fever. He locked eyes with the taller, leaner, younger man. 'Then I suggest you be very, *very* cooperative.'

Jeers erupted from the Hounds – some even barked. The Wolf-King rose from his throne and held out his right arm, palm flat. His unspoken command was instantly obeyed as one of his followers placed a rapier in his hand. The hilt was an A-cup, much like the one hanging from Estevar's belt, and of identical length.

Estevar walked to Caeda, waiting with Imperious. 'The sword you gave me was stolen from this tower?' he asked quietly.

'Technically, he stole them from the old armoury, which is a crime. Me being your Piccolo and all, which is halfway to being a Greatcoat, it was my duty to administer *equajudia* – isn't that what you called it?'

'I feel I must observe that you pilfered the weapon *before* we discussed you assisting my investigation.'

'Whatever. He's got so many rapiers, I doubt he even noticed one was missing until you walked in here wearing it.'

'Kneel before me, Magistrate,' Strigan commanded, the rumbling voice from deep in his chest conveying his intention to take control of the situation and administer his own justice. 'Kneel, and I will have my wolves strip the clothes from your body. Upon the ample canvas of your flesh will the symbols of my reign be inscribed so that when we send you naked from this place, back to your broken castle with its brittle boy-king, all will know you as my property. In appreciation of this service, after we slaughter that ugly donkey of yours and cook him over the fire, I will leave you a haunch of his meat so that you do not go hungry on your journey home. That will be *my* gift to *you*.'

Estevar appraised the smug scoundrel as a prospective duellist. Strigan was likely faster, and had a longer reach. *Whereas I am exhausted, injured and barely in my right mind*, he reminded himself. The only sensible course of action would be to soothe this self-proclaimed 'Wolf-King' before the conflict escalated any further, especially as the stab wound in Estevar's side was mocking him relentlessly for his recent defeat. What his magistrate's prudence judged a calamity to be averted, however, his duellist's heart took as a challenge.

'A generous offer, your Majesty,' Estevar said. 'Allow me to ponder it a moment.' He began to turn away, then paused. 'Although I must first correct you. Imperious is a mule, not a donkey.'

'I'm certain he'll be equally tasty as a mule.'

Estevar let that one pass, as he was quietly asking Caeda, 'How adept would you say this Strigan is with a sword? He was a monk until recently, no? Surely Abbot Venia did not tolerate swordplay among his flock?'

'A group of them practised in secret,' Caeda whispered back. 'Strigan and a few others would often challenge sailors visiting the island for sport. I used to watch the fights. I never saw him bested.'

'Kneel,' the Wolf-King commanded a second time, and from the edge of his eye, Estevar watched the tip of the rapier blade rise like the head of a snake.

'A moment, your Majesty.' Estevar again turned to Caeda. 'But how able were these sailors of whom you speak? A drunken brute is hardly a challenging opponent for an adequately trained fencer.'

'Strigan killed the captain of a war galleon once. The woman who'd been his second-in-command told me he'd fought dozens of judicial duels at court and never lost one – until Strigan challenged him.'

'Kneel!' the Wolf-King shouted.

Several of his followers were rousing themselves, preparing to drag Estevar to the throne.

'Yes, your Majesty,' Estevar acquiesced politely. 'Forgive the rudeness of my delay. As my accent no doubt betrays, I am a foreigner, and so needed to consult with my colleague regarding certain regional customs which eluded my training as a Greatcoat. I shall attend you presently.'

He started towards the throne, his left hand loosening the rapier in its scabbard. Caeda grabbed his arm and hissed into his ear, 'Do not risk it, you fool. Anger him and you'll end up dead – and me his prisoner!'

'Ah, little Caeda,' Strigan said, as if he'd forgotten she was there. 'I'd not dreamed I would find you still lurking on the island. Give me a moment to deal with this oily bearded oaf. Then I can give that luscious body of yours the attention it deserves.'

Estevar patted Caeda's hand gently, then started his slow approach to the throne. He noted the hawkish way Strigan was watching him move.

He possesses a duellist's eye, he realised, despair beginning to seep through the crevices left behind by his crumbling arrogance. 'Might I plead for your Majesty's wisdom and compassion, after all?' he asked.

'It is my *mercy* for which you should beg, Greatcoat.' Strigan extended his rapier and rested the blade on Estevar's shoulder, then pressed down with the flat. 'You may do so on your knees.'

'Greatcoats don't kneel to anyone,' Caeda declared loudly. 'Everyone knows that.'

A pity her admiration for the Greatcoats exceeds her concern for my wellbeing, Estevar thought, bending the knee to his enemy.

The tower exploded with laughter as Strigan's drunken followers roared their approval at the sight of one of the Greatcoats – those supposedly indomitable sword-fighting magistrates famed for refusing to kneel even before their own monarch – doing so now for the Wolf-King of Isola Sombra.

Falcio would kill me himself if he saw me, Estevar thought.

'Good,' Strigan cooed at him as if he were a child. 'That's good. Now, plead for my benevolence.' The rapier's tip lifted the collar of Estevar's borrowed shirt and slipped underneath. 'But I warn you, Caeda is mine. I've had dreams about that little lass, my friend, dreams that would rouse a dead man's cock.' He chuckled. 'Perhaps even Abbot Venia's, eh?'

Estevar's shoulders tensed, the shift in his muscles passing along the steel blade in Strigan's hand.

'Does that thought offend you, Eminence?' Strigan sat back down on the edge of the throne. He lifted the hilt of his rapier higher, allowing the tip to caress Estevar's spine while his other hand gripped Estevar's jaw and tilted it upwards at a painful angle. 'You want to know who murdered the abbot?' The Wolf-King bared his teeth. 'Here sits your killer.'

CHAPTER 16

THE GAMBIT

Kneeling before an enemy who'd just confessed to murder, Estevar's impotent outrage warred with his investigator's instincts. Strigan's fingers were still holding his head, as if at any moment the Wolf-King of Isola Sombra might rip out his throat with his teeth. And yet . . . was that murderous intent Estevar saw in the younger man's eyes, or bluster?

Strigan was clearly observant, for his own anger boiled over. 'You *doubt* me?' he demanded, spittle drooling from the corners of his mouth like a rabid dog. 'I cut Venia's head from his shoulders with the same blade resting on yours. I inscribed my sigils upon his flesh, branding him as one does cattle.' He released Estevar's jaw and turned to gaze upon his pack of slavish supporters. 'Every night, the Bone-Rattlers bury his corpse. Each time, they dig deeper – why? Because I do not choose to allow Venia his rest. The magic that flows through me, stronger every day, forces his cadaver to rise up through the dirt so that all may witness the price of defying . . . *the Sorcerer Sovereign of Tristia!*'

Chaos rose like a tide: the lapsed monks started dancing wildly across the chamber, their howling approval a chilling, animalistic cry that sent a shiver through Estevar's bones. Caeda was holding Imperious' reins tightly to keep him from either bolting in terror or attacking the monks – either of which would result in the mule's swift execution and roasting.

'Well?' Strigan asked Estevar, the tip of his rapier once again tracing his spine, 'should you not be begging me for mercy now, Eminence?' He leaned closer. 'What's that, Eminence? I'm afraid your piteous mewling escapes me.'

The carnival of wanton madness all around him had the unexpected effect of calming Estevar's nerves. His fever faded and his thoughts settled, so he could weigh his options with cold, dispassionate reasoning.

Death – his own and those of Caeda and Imperious – hung upon his next move.

He waited until the clamour from Strigan's followers died down, then lifted his head and whispered in his captor's ear, 'Listen closely then, you vain, pathetic child, for it is indeed of mercy we will now speak, you and I. Ah, ah, no – do not attempt to raise that blade of yours to strike me. Look down instead at my right hand, you pustulated canker, you preening toad in tattered rags. See how, when you so graciously bade me kneel, you made it possible for me to bring my right hand across my body to where it now rests upon the hilt of my rapier – actually, I believe the weapon belongs to you, but I will need to borrow it a while longer. Rest assured, I will pay a reasonable fee for its loan, especially if I decide to stain this blade by carving your worthless hide, you pitiful, prancing popinjay, you crust of defecation stuck to the heel of better men's boots, so lacking in substance that you cannot even stink with distinction.'

The harsh intake of Strigan's breath and the increased pressure of his own rapier blade hinted that he was formulating a violent response, but Estevar was not nearly done.

'I understand you count yourself a skilled fencer,' he continued. 'No doubt, within the voluminous library of this abbey, even Abbot Venia, a peaceable man, allowed a book or two on the subject. Perhaps one of your more literate brethren took sufficient pity on you to read them out loud to you – slowly, I would imagine. Assuming a vessel as tiny as your unremarkable mind could hold onto even a sip of that knowledge, you will, I assume, have studied the famed Cressi Manoeuvre?'

Estevar gave the tiniest shake of his head to keep Strigan from responding. He had given many stirring speeches while delivering verdicts. This one would need to make all the others pale by comparison.

'No, no, don't answer me, *Wolf-King*, or you die as ignorant as you were born. Allow me to educate you, first with words, and then, if you are so foolish as to test my earnestness, with steel and blood. The Cressi Manoeuvre is counted as one of only three ways a swordsman whose weapon is in its scabbard may kill on the first strike an opponent whose blade is already bared. The trick, you see, is to lure the enemy into either a high thrust under which the fencer must duck, or a diagonal slash aimed at the neck which, by bending over, is taken on the back instead. Now, such a cut would normally cause merely a significant, albeit debilitating, wound, but you have done me the courtesy of already placing your blade over my back, so we may safely come to the second part of the Cressi Manoeuvre with me unharmed. My hand – see the fingers wrapped lightly around the hilt?'

He paused there, just long enough to give Strigan's eyes the chance to drift downwards.

'Perhaps you noticed me loosening the blade before I came to kneel before you, *Majesty*? All I need do now is perform the quick-draw – a manoeuvre I have practised not hundreds, but *thousands* of times. The top third of my blade – the sharpest, as you well know – will slice your belly open before you can so much as exhale the last foul breath that will ever leave your worthless body. The shock will slow down your reflexive attempt to bring your own weapon back for a thrust to my face or throat. By the time you are halfway there, my own blade will be buried to the hilt in your craven, odious heart.'

A final pause, to let the enemy visualise that outcome, before the performance's finalé, delivered with a hiss filled with all the contempt and condemnation Estevar could muster, which at this moment was a great deal indeed.

'Do you understand at last, *your Majesty*, why I consented to kneel before a noxious piece of refuse whose continued existence I tolerate only because inside your witless skull may reside some scrap of information that might assist in my investigations? Your pitiable, self-aggrandising confession of having slain Abbot Venia rings as hollow as your claims of mystical powers. So I give you leave to answer me now, *Sorcerer Sovereign*, but only to acknowledge what I have told you. One word more – *one word* – and you and I will demonstrate for those half-dressed hyenas of yours – many of whom I suspect secretly long to witness your fall – whether the vaunted Cressi Manoeuvre is deserving of the years of study and practise I have devoted to its mastery.'

There, when Estevar could not have uttered a single word more without gasping for breath, he allowed his threat to hang in the air between them . . .

. . . and waited for the Wolf-King's reply.

CHAPTER 17

THE CRESSI MANOEUVRE

The silence that had descended over the Venerance Tower was absolute. It had substance, took up space, swallowing every inch of the circular chamber from the once-spotless marble floor, now stained with shallow pools of spilt wine, to the glorious painted ceiling that depicted a sky full of stars and six pairs of heavenly eyes gazing down at those fools bound to the grim absurdity and inevitable end of their earthly existence.

The silence among Strigan's followers, those three dozen lapsed monks he called his hounds, remained absolute, tolerating no raucous jeering, no anxious whispers or shuffling of feet as they awaited an answer that would either bring about a truce or spark bloodshed. Even the fire in the hearth had ceased its crackling, the last page torn from the book Estevar had recovered from the gleeful arsonist now nothing but ashes.

No one but Caeda had been close enough to overhear him threaten the Wolf-King. Estevar now wondered if that had perhaps been a mistake.

Why wouldn't his gods-be-damned opponent answer? Why did Strigan sit there on the edge of his stolen throne, leaning cheek to cheek with Estevar, his warm breath tickling Estevar's neck as if they were a pair of hesitant lovers, each waiting for the other to initiate the first kiss? The flat of Strigan's rapier blade still rested against Estevar's back. A quarter-turn to the sharp edge followed by a quick draw backwards would be the prelude to a thrust that would end Estevar's life. The only thing staying the glib, grinning Wolf-King's hand was a hastily concocted tale of a mythical fencing manoeuvre. Neither could truly know who would prevail, should blades clash. Death, if he happened to be one of the gods who'd returned to Tristia, must surely be standing over the two men, an expectant smile lingering on his pale lips.

The waiting was unbearable. Estevar felt as if he were trapped once more beneath the waves, not knowing if he would reach the surface again. Worse, the knee supporting his weight on the marble floor was aching more and more with each passing second.

Perhaps this is the real reason why Falcio val Mond insisted the Greatcoats never kneel, Estevar thought bitterly. *Perhaps he suffers less from excessive dignity than from a pair of bad knees.*

If only he could have shifted his posture even a fraction without revealing his discomfort and therefore his weakness, but this had become a test of resolve now: a war of attrition. The Wolf-King no doubt suspected the Greatcoat's boast of having mastered the quick-draw was a ruse ... but he couldn't be sure.

He has every reason to believe I'm lying, Estevar thought despairingly. *A man ten years older and a hundred pounds heavier, displaying no particular swiftness of reflexes or unusual skill with a sword – who would imagine a fat old goat could hope to gore a young wolf?*

The stand-off couldn't continue much longer. Strigan's followers probably assumed Estevar was still whispering pleas for mercy and soon they would wonder why their mercurial leader wasn't getting bored and simply slaying this foreigner Greatcoat who'd dared speak of laws and trials in the presence of wolves.

Say you understand. Estevar tried to will his obstinate partner in this odious dance between life and death to speak. *Tell me you understand and no one need die. I'll let you laugh and mock me in front of your fawning sycophants. You can gloat that my begging has become so embarrassing that you can't be bothered to kill me. Then you and I will take a walk so that you may answer my questions before returning to your drunken revels and proclaiming yourself the Sovereign Sorcerer of Isola Sombra to all who will listen.*

Another breath sent the stench of soured wine and bitter herbs slithering into Estevar's nostrils, yet still the Wolf-King neither snarled his defiance nor whined in submission.

I must draw soon, Estevar realised, *else he'll doubt my determination and initiate the first attack himself.*

The arrogance of his reckless gambit had become an even sharper weight than that of the blade resting against his back. Hadn't he made this same mistake just a week ago, accepting a challenge that—?

The fingers wrapped around the hilt of the rapier at his side began to tremble – and Estevar forced them to be still before they caused the blade to clatter inside its scabbard and mistakenly signal Strigan that he was about to attack.

Perhaps I should make the attempt, he thought. *Now, before my damned knee does give out and I lose my nerve.*

Never before had he been so bedevilled with doubts over his own abilities. The King's Crucible had crossed swords with dozens of men and women who'd considered themselves his superiors, who'd mocked his girth, convinced a body such as his could never produce the speed to best them. What had changed? A single lost duel in some backwoods courtroom in Domaris? Every Greatcoat had suffered defeat at one time or another. Why was he so filled with trepidation now?

'*Say you understand,*' he whispered, so quietly he doubted Strigan had even heard him. Better if he hadn't – otherwise Estevar would have revealed himself as nothing but a reckless gambler who'd wagered all he possessed on a single hand and only now remembered to look at the cards he'd drawn.

Then it happened: his hand began to shake again, and this time, he failed to halt it before he heard – and knew instantly that Strigan had heard as well – the clack of his blade's steel ricasso on the bronze lip of the rapier's scabbard.

Too late, he thought.

The sharp intake of Strigan's breath preceded his blade shifting against his opponent's back. Cursing himself for having waited too long, Estevar began to draw his own weapon, knowing he'd already given away the initiative to his enemy. Imperious was going to be killed and eaten, Caeda captured and abused, Venia's murder unavenged, and all of it – *all* of it – would be his fault.

I'm sorry my friends, he had time to think just as his blade began to slip free from the scabbard.

'I . . . I understand!' the Wolf-King cried out.

CHAPTER 18

THE HOUND'S TESTIMONY

'Were you really going to kill me?' Strigan asked plaintively. The tall, tattooed figure trudged up the stone steps spiralling around the inner wall of the Venerance Tower. 'And do you bring that donkey everywhere you go? It's a tad eccentric, if you ask me – even for a Greatcoat who goes around threatening to slice open people's innards.'

'Imperious is a mule,' Estevar corrected.

Truth be told, he would have preferred to have left his befuddled mount in some warm, snug stable rather than forcing the poor beast up this awkward climb. The 'Cressi Manoeuvre' gambit might have transformed the Wolf-King from snarling predator to affronted lamb, but there remained the danger of his followers. Admittedly, Strigan had put on an impressive performance, granting his captive the rank of court jester and promising to hear in private his questions before deciding whether to cut off his head and sew it to the body of the donkey or vice versa. Estevar wasn't about to leave his mule to the dubious self-restraint of a pack of lapsed monks already grown accustomed to satisfying their every cruel and lustful appetite. Besides, Imperious appeared to be unwilling to be parted from him, so for now, Estevar would do whatever he must to calm his faithful companion's nerves.

'Mule, right.' Strigan leaped up the last two steps to the second-floor landing, pivoted on his bare heel and disappeared through an arched doorway. A moment later, he poked his head back out and beckoned them with a curled finger and a lecherous grin.

'Why, Caeda, there you are! Always meant to bed you when the chance availed itself. No time like the present, eh?'

'He was less annoying when he was threatening to kill us,' the young woman muttered through gritted teeth as she followed him inside.

Estevar wasn't so sure. He would need to be careful now, his every word and facial expression designed to maintain Strigan's fear of his skill with a blade. The moment those abilities came into doubt, the Wolf-King would no doubt seek to impose his authority over his 'guests' once more.

Then again, the way the drugged, drunken fool keeps forgetting Caeda's here, perhaps he won't recall that we're enemies.

The second floor of the Venerance Tower was taken up by another large circular room, this one a magnificent bedchamber. Curved divans upholstered in rose-coloured velvet lined the outer wall, set beneath tall glass windows that overlooked the abbey's cloister on one side and the still raging sea on the other. The subtle curvature of the ceiling created a shallow dome at the centre, beneath which the gold curtains of a large canopied bed opened to reveal pillows of white and silver silk resting atop a lushly embroidered crimson coverlet. The mosaic floor was softened with thick fur rugs in front of a generous hearth. Twelve gold-framed portraits were, alternately, past abbots and abbesses and erstwhile Dukes and Duchesses of Baern.

There were other luxuries, too: a huge mahogany armoire on one side, a rosewood writing desk with bone inlay on the other. The grandest feature of the bedchamber, however, was the cast-iron tube set into the floor next to the bed pouring water into a large brass wash-tub. Estevar noted steam rising from the water, and rose petals floating on the surface.

'Delightful, isn't it?' Strigan asked, sauntering towards the tub like the lord of the manor returning home from the hunt. 'Even with the abbot dead, the Bone-Rattlers assigned to service this room keep coming, day after day. It's all I can do to persuade my hounds not to kill them. He dangled his fingertips in the rose-scented water. 'I do enjoy a hot bath, though. As a matter of fact, I'd been planning on a nice soak when the two of you showed up.' He grinned sheepishly. 'I suppose that's why I was so cheeky with you.'

'*Cheeky?*' Caeda repeated.

Estevar gave her a subtle shake of his head, trying to convey that this was the wrong time to press the point. This opportunity to interrogate Strigan over the death of the abbot was a brief interlude before his capricious temperament took over once more.

'Have you ever spent the night in an abbot's bedchamber, little Caeda?' the apostate asked, his disdainful tone suggesting these opulent surroundings were evidence of Venia's hypocrisy and thus proof that he deserved whatever fate had befallen him.

A poor ruse, Estevar thought. 'This is no abbot's bedchamber,' he said as he led Imperious to the rugs by the fire so the mule could warm himself. *Would that you were in finer form, my friend. I wouldn't be nearly so fretful.*

'You sound awfully sure of yourself, for an outsider,' Strigan observed. 'Maybe you were as easily fooled by Venia's false piety as everyone else.'

'My assertion was not based on any intimate knowledge of the abbot's humility or frugality. All that required was a pair of eyes and a modicum of intellect.' He turned to Caeda. 'Would you care to enlighten him?'

'Ah, there's my red-furred pussycat,' Strigan cooed. 'You know, I've always wanted t—'

'A moment, if you please,' Estevar said, cutting him off. 'Proceed, Piccolo.'

The sharp-featured young woman looked pleased to be offered so simple a test – as well as the opportunity to make it clear to Strigan that she was a participant in his interrogation, not some plaything for him to taunt. 'Anyone with half a brain who met Abbot Venia would know within two minutes that he – unlike the dissolute weasels he inherited from his avaricious predecessor' – she cast a scathing glance at Strigan, who was now sitting on the edge of the tub, picking at his toenails – 'would have drenched himself in lantern oil and set himself on fire before spending a single night indulging in all this gaudy excess.'

Estevar held back a sigh of disappointment. She'd seemed so quick and perceptive during their first meeting. 'Yes, Piccolo, but more importantly, th—'

Now it was her turn to cut him off as she adopted a pompous tone suspiciously reminiscent of his own. 'Nonetheless, such an obvious conclusion leaves open the presumption that this chamber belonged to Venia's predecessor, and that after his death, the new abbot simply left it unused.'

'Which is precisely what he did,' Strigan insisted petulantly, dipping a toe into the steaming water before pulling it back out again. His tattered loincloth was proving inadequate to the task of keeping his private parts hidden. He seemed entirely at ease with his own nudity, though visibly troubled by Caeda's apparent indifference to what he no doubt thought of as his feral sensuality. Estevar wondered how Malezias might react to this brash libertine's repeated propositioning of the woman he either loved, served or both.

Caeda walked over to the foot of the huge bed, turned back towards the other two men and promptly flopped backwards onto the velvet cover. 'Were I an abbot, would I choose to fill my sanctuary with the portraits of my dead predecessors? Would I want to wake up surrounded by paintings of snooty dukes and duchesses looking down their noses at me?' She propped herself up on her elbows. 'No, you decorate a room like this for the benefit of visiting dignitaries. You want the first thing they see each morning to be all those abbots displayed as prominently as aristocrats and royalty – a reminder that many in this country hold the clergy in equal regard as the nobility.' She winked at Estevar. 'Not a bad piece of propaganda, eh, my Cantor?'

He couldn't help but be impressed, both by her acumen and by how she'd been testing him as much as he was testing her. Still, he gave no sign of his favour, instead attenuating his approval – after all, he'd expected no less from her.

He turned to Strigan. 'Are we done with your little feints, Wolf-King? Are you ready to answer my questions, or have these attempts at deception become so second nature already that you can't help yourself?'

Too far, Estevar realised before he could hold his own tongue. *I've pushed the hound too far.* Damn this belligerent arrogance that had consumed him of late. He'd worried about Caeda's sharp tongue, but it was his own that would likely draw steel.

'You still haven't answered *my* question,' Strigan said, his tone low again, the prelude to a growl.

'Which is?'

114

The Wolf-King stood taller, placed one bare foot in front of the other as if preparing to stalk his prey. 'Would you really have killed me? Are you as fast with a blade as you pretend?'

The shift in Strigan's mood was odd. Sometimes, he was just like any brash young man in his twenties, blessed with good looks, a warrior's physique and just enough charm to cover his lascivious nature, pushed, no doubt, by some wealthy father into a religious life to which he was unsuited. The allusions to practising dark magic, the sexual aggression and displays of dominance added a layer of pompous showmanship over the base impulses that drove so many men in this barely civilised country. At other times, though, Estevar could see a violent hunger flaring beneath that vain, pretty exterior. In those moments, Strigan was indeed a wolf in man's clothing.

After so many years riding the long roads of Tristia, hearing cases over which lords and commoners alike would kill, Estevar understood the ways of wolves.

Rather than make a show of readying himself for a fight, he walked up to the other man casually, neither slowly nor quickly, his movements devoid of either impetuous anger or excess caution. 'You wonder now whether I am as dangerous as I led you to believe?'

Strigan's nostrils flared as he locked eyes with him. 'I begin to doubt.'

'Wolves are creatures of instinct, are they not?'

'I suppose.'

'In the chamber below this one, while I was on one knee, my rapier scabbarded and yours already drawn with your blade upon me and you occupying the more advantageous position, your instincts warned you not to test me.'

'So?'

Estevar didn't smile, didn't preen or posture. 'My advice is to trust those instincts.'

Strigan abandoned his posture so quickly it was as if he'd entirely forgotten that he and Estevar weren't simply two old friends sharing a jest. 'Fine, fine,' he said, throwing up his hands. 'Who knew the King's Magistrates were so homicidal?'

He will seek to reassert himself through other means, Estevar thought. *To shock or surprise.*

His prediction was proved correct only a moment later. Strigan strode back to the water, stripped off his tatters right in front of them and stepped into the brass vessel, splashing hot water and rose petals over the side. Leaning back, he rested his arms atop the curved rim. 'After Venia died, I reconsidered his teachings on the spiritual decay brought about by excess luxury.' Strigan gestured towards the paintings of past abbots, abbesses, dukes and duchesses on the wall. 'Let those dead fools gaze down at me with disapproval. I feel no shame.'

Likely the truest words Strigan had ever uttered.

Estevar was about to seize on the opening he'd provided, but Caeda beat him to it. 'Speaking of dead fools, when did you last see the abbot?'

'What a delight to find you there, sweet Caeda, and me here . . .' Strigan slid his hands over his tattooed chest, stroking those unusual esoteric sigils, and down further into the water. 'Why not join me? Surely the Greatcoat doesn't need someone like you to ask his questions for him?'

'The Lady Caeda is my partner in this enquiry,' Estevar replied without hesitation. 'When she speaks, it is with my voice, which is that of the King's Order of Travelling Magistrates.'

'How dreary you are,' Strigan said, exasperated. 'I would've thought such a big fellow would be more jolly.' He sighed theatrically. 'Fine, let's get this over with. I last saw Venia a little over a week ago, the morning his body turned up in the courtyard statuary.'

Already he concedes the lie about having killed him. Is there nothing constant about this preening peacock? 'Where, precisely did you first see the corpse?' Estevar asked.

'Like I told you, in the statuary.' Strigan brought one hand out of the water to gesture lazily at nowhere in particular. 'The body was between the shattered remains of Fabrida and Lutrizo.'

Fabrida and Lutrizo, the names given the gods of Craft and War here in the Duchy of Baern. Falcio val Mond claimed in the reports he left in Aramor that he'd witnessed the return of three gods: Love, Death, and a new one, Valour. Was there some meaning then, that the abbot's corpse should be found between the statues of two gods *not* to have been reborn?

'Why did you move the body?' Estevar asked next.

Strigan cocked an eyebrow at him. 'What makes you think we moved it?'

'Piccolo?'

Caeda leaped up from the bed and began to pace around the room like one of those bombastic investigators in the old plays so often staged in the Duchy of Pertine – *Between Two Midnight Murders* and the like. 'When the knights stormed across the causeway eight days ago, they declared that the abbot's corpse had been defiled and decapitated, his flesh covered in mystical symbols.' Without turning from her examination of an ivory wall sconce, she swung one hand negligently towards Strigan. 'Symbols like those adorning your own body.'

The Sorcerer Sovereign chuckled at her, making a show of playing with himself beneath the water. Estevar badly wanted to remonstrate with the foul lecher, but held his temper in check. Imperious, however, whether sensing his rider's disapproval or simply from his own instinctive dislike of wolves, wandered over from the comfort of the hearth to raise one leg and send a bucketload of urine streaming against the side of the tub. When he was done, he craned his neck over the rim and chewed on a rose petal.

'Damned beast!' Strigan swore, but stopped splashing about when the mule raised his muzzle to show his teeth.

'You admit to finding the body nine days ago,' Caeda snarled, as if urinating mules were a standard part of any Greatcoat's interrogation technique. 'No doubt you sought to take advantage of his death to intimidate the other factions. You and the Trumpeters have both been vying to see who can terrify the Bone-Rattlers into joining your side. You cut off Abbot Venia's head and tattooed his body in a pathetic display of power, hoping to scare the other monks into submission. That would have taken time, though, a day at least for all those sigils. Then you had to wait for the opportunity to sneak him back out to the statuary for one of the other factions to discover, knowing they, in turn, would throw the body into the ocean rather than leave it there as a testimony to your viciousness.'

Good, Estevar thought. *She intuits the language and by-play of posturing between the factions, even if she is a trifle too keen to show off her intellect. She should not have attributed the beheading and tattooing to the Hounds without evidence.*

'You make me sound like a very dangerous man,' Strigan said, smiling.

'How did you remove the head?' Estevar asked.

'Hmm?'

'The abbot's head. Did you cut it off with a slice of your rapier, or use your bare hands?'

Caeda stared at him questioningly, wondering, no doubt, why he would suggest that a beheading could have been accomplished with so unwieldy an instrument as a slender rapier blade or – even more prepos-terously – that a man's head could be removed without any blade at all.

Strigan took the bait, giving them a feral grin as he lifted his hands out of the water. 'These were all I required to separate Venia's fool head from his shoulders.' The grin widened as he bared his own teeth. 'Are you still so certain you could take me with your "Cressi Manoeuvre", Greatcoat?'

'You're lyin—' Caeda began, but Estevar cut her off. The thrust needed to be delivered with precision, driven deep enough to make him anxious, but not so far as to make him stop talking.

'You are a petty showman.' Estevar began his own pacing, but around the brass tub, forcing Strigan to swivel his head to keep an eye on him. 'You call yourself the "Sorcerer Sovereign", yet you appear to know little of the mystical traditions of this nation. You claim every outrageous crime we lay at your feet, even those you could not have committed yourself – which is why, when my associate tested you a moment ago by suggesting you beheaded and tattooed Venia's corpse, you went along, hoping to make yourself appear even more frightening to us.'

Out of the corner of his eye, he saw Caeda stiffen, then resume her own perambulation of the chamber, nonchalantly studying the room's décor.

'Oh, *fine*.' Strigan leaned one elbow on the rim and rested his head against his fist. 'Yes, yes, we found the body,' he confessed. 'Yes, the head was already removed. Obviously, whoever drew the symbols on Venia did so to implicate me in his murder.' He perked up now, and tracing one of the sigils on his chest, said, 'But these aren't just for show, you know? Unlike those scurrying Bone-Rattlers who await the return of the old gods, or the Yellow Bitch and her Trumpeters who somehow think they can coax new ones to arise, *we* understand the true nature of faith. My Wolves have been studying religious fervour, how it can be transmuted into magical potential. That's why we imprinted these runes on ourselves; there's as much power in rituals of desecration as consecration, you know, especially in a place invested with the country's spiritual belief. Our experiments in harnessing that essence are close to bearing fruit.'

Caeda snorted, which annoyed Estevar; why did she insist on revealing as much about her own thoughts as she discerned from the subject of their interrogation? But he would not undermine her before Strigan.

'My colleague happens to be an expert in Tristian occult lore. There is a language to symbols, to ritual, and you are far from achieving your aims, Strigan.'

The monk leaped up, splashing water over the side, the phallus of which he was unduly proud dangling for all to see. He stared at Caeda with an altogether different form of desire than before. 'You could help us then – both of you! Join us!'

'We are otherwise employed,' Estevar said, taking a plush scarlet towel with gold trim from a wicker basket and tossing it at the naked man.

Strigan snatched it neatly out of the air. Estevar would have been happier if his reflexes were not so sharp. He stepped out, dripping water and rose petals and the physical evidence of his excitement. 'I'm not suggesting you become part of the order, of course,' he said, doing a haphazard job of drying, 'but you'll have to side with one of the factions sooner or later. This state of siege can't continue much longer, each of us occupying part of the abbey, arming ourselves for the inevitable war to come. Those yellow morons are bloodthirsty lunatics, you know – chanting and muttering and flagellating themselves in hopes of winning the attention of some new deity they've conjured up.'

'Yes, how silly they are, these superstitious monks,' Estevar observed drily.

'At least *we're* approaching the matter scientifically,' Strigan insisted. He finally wrapped the scarlet towel around his waist. 'What do you think's going to happen if the Trumpeters gain control of Isola Sombra and then decide one of their new gods favours human sacrifice? You think it's a coincidence that they named themselves for a poisonous flower? How about when Mother Leogado commands her "troops" to rile up the people of the March of Someil against their margrave? He's weak, you know, Someil is. Those knights of his – sauntering up here with their swords and axes like they owned the place – were so ill-disciplined that the first thing they did when they came to the abbey was start drinking our holy wine.'

'Axes?' Estevar asked. That was the second time Strigan had mentioned an unusual choice of weapon. 'What sort of axes?'

'The regular kind,' he replied, and with a shrug, 'What of it?'

The regular kind, Estevar repeated to himself. Strigan was a swordsman, but not a soldier. What he saw as 'the regular kind' of axe would likely be the sort meant for chopping wood, not a throwing or mêlée weapon.

'So you poisoned the wine they drank?' Caeda pounced before Estevar could signal to her to keep silent on the subject.

'Ha!' Strigan exclaimed, delighted, as if he'd just scored a touch in a fencing match. 'Shows what you know. We had nothing to do with the wine. Probably Venia's old followers slipped herbs into the knights' cups. They're like that, the Bone-Rattlers: sly and sneaking. We didn't find the knights until hours later in the statuary, drugged out of their minds.' He smirked at his own cleverness. 'So we marked them up, too, mounted them up on their horses in a stupor and sent them packing back to their margrave as a warning.'

All this the young man had said with a kind of dazed merriment – almost as if he were making up events as he went along, yet was instantly convinced by his own fabrications.

'If any of that is true, you make a poor case for seeking the support of a King's Magistrate,' Estevar said.

But Strigan was not so easily dissuaded. 'Don't you see? We were protecting the abbey.' He spread his arms wide. 'This whole island, it's important – and not just because of all the wealth amassed by its abbots over the centuries. People all over the country look to us for spiritual guidance. That boy-king you serve? He's weak. His castle is half in ruins, his treasury hollowed out before he's even paid for a truce with Avares that he can barely afford. The new First Cantor of the Greatcoats is rumoured to be some girl who can barely swing a sword – I'll bet she'd like to have a strong ally here in the Duchy of Baern!'

Strigan walked over to the room's writing desk and reached for a small bronze ink pot. 'Agree to support my faction as the rightful rulers of Isola Sombra and I'll sign a pact here and now, swearing our fealty to King Filian and promising to obey the rulings of his magistrates.'

'You are already subjects of the king, and while I'm sure he appreciates your loyalty, I doubt he expects to pay for it. Similarly, you and your fellow "Wolves", along with these "Trumpeters" and "Bone-Rattlers" and all the other lapsed monks wandering this abbey, remain bound by the laws of this land.'

Strigan chuckled. 'Go and try that speech out on Mother Leogado after you've climbed to the top of her vigilia. She'll hurl you from the watchtower window herself.'

The watchtower, Estevar thought. *Was it this General of the Trumpeters who'd stood there blocking the light of the window while I rang the bell in vain? Why then did she wait for Brother Agneta to open the gate before sending two of her yellow-habited brethren to take me prisoner?*

He stopped his meandering to pat Imperious' neck. 'We shall test your theory, Wolf-King.'

'Hmm?' Strigan asked, still fiddling with the ink pot.

Estevar took the reins and began leading the mule towards the door. 'I will visit this Queen of Trumpeters and allow her the opportunity to make her case for control of the abbey, just as you have. In the meantime, I suggest you remain in this tower with your own supporters. When I am ready to begin the trial into the death of Abbot Venia and determine the future of Isola Sombra, I will summon you all in the old way.'

Strigan abandoned his pretence at composing some grand treaty, sweeping paper, pen and ink across the floor in petulant fury. 'You seriously think you'll ever discover who killed Venia?' he demanded, rounding on Estevar. 'Nobody wants you here, Greatcoat. Nobody trusts you, either, and the moment you try to impose your "verdict" on the monks of this abbey, somebody's going to slip a blade into that big belly of yours.'

'Perhaps you are right,' Estevar conceded, leading Imperious to the door and handing the reins to Caeda before turning back to face the Wolf-King one last time. 'Perhaps justice has no purchase on the treacherous soil of this island. But you asked earlier whether I had the stomach to kill you, so I will answer honestly and without guile. Cross me once more, *Brother Strigan*, threaten my colleague or my mule, and the next faction you'll join will be the one filled with men and women far more skilled, far more vicious than you pretend to be, who tried the patience of Estevar Valejan Duerisi Borros once too often.'

He turned on his heel and abandoned the tattooed monk standing there in his towel, surrounded by borrowed opulence and well-deserved unease. When he caught up with Caeda halfway down the stairs, she paused to look up at him curiously. 'Just how dangerous are you really, my Cantor?'

Estevar gave no reply, just took back the reins to lead Imperious down the stone stairs and out of the tower. He'd learned long ago that some questions were best left unanswered, especially when the answer was, *Not nearly dangerous enough for what lies ahead.*

PART THE FOURTH

THE SIGILS
OF INVITATION

Steady your hands before inscribing the sigils which follow these words, for such symbols are no mere testament or abjuration, but rather, a coaxing for sin to swallow sin, for darkness to devour shadow. Only when evil has had its due will the sacrifice of the purest among us redeem the wickedness of all.

CHAPTER 19

A MATTER OF FAITH

The rains had died down again by the time they left the Venerance Tower. The last few sparkling stars were disappearing from the sky, dispersed along with the darkness by the first glimmer of dawn. Estevar paused before an iron-gated arch in the curtain wall looking out over the sea. In the eerie morning light, it looked as if a gargantuan oil painting were suspended over the water, awaiting only the artist's finishing touches – a few birds in the sky, perhaps, and a sail on the horizon.

The abbey's solitude won't long outlast the storm, Estevar thought. The urgency of solving Venia's murder and restoring the rule of law to Isola Sombra was a weight hanging round his neck. *Unwitting merchant ships will stop to trade with the monks; scholars whose journeys began weeks or months ago will arrive expecting to find ancient wisdom within these walls. When turned away, those peaceful pilgrims will be replaced by the Margrave of Someil's troops bearing some dusty tome of ducal law to justify the use of force in re-establishing order.* Had he time, he might cross the causeway and find a messenger to take word to King Filian, along with an entreaty to send as many Greatcoats as could be summoned to protect the abbey from within and without. *And what would they find when they arrived?* he wondered, a sense of helplessness pricking at him like a fencer waiting to begin the match. *A spiritual community at peace with its contradictions, or a blood-soaked battlefield?*

'What do you make of Strigan's claims?' Caeda asked.

Estevar turned away from the serene vista beyond the wall. 'Which one? There were so many.'

125

'When he said there was no more need for gods in Tristia, silly.' She poked him playfully and painfully in the ribs, a suspiciously intimate gesture, but her eyes, he noted, were focusing somewhere past him to the other side of the cloister.

So, she's noticed our clumsy stalker, he thought approvingly. Three times since they'd left the Venerance Tower, his ears had caught the faint rustle of leaves; when he'd turned, he'd seen furtive movements in the shadows beyond the bushes and silver-barked trees growing either side of a path in the cloister. He had no idea who this fretful spy might be, but for now, feigned obliviousness suited his purposes better than some futile chase through the abbey grounds.

'Faith has always shaped the lives of the Tristian people,' he said in answer to Caeda's question and, resuming their walk towards the Vigilance Tower overlooking both the sea and the flooded causeway, continued, 'That the Tristian people can, in turn, shape the gods with their faith is a more complex phenomenon rumoured to involve the veins of mystical ore deep beneath the rocky ground of this island and a few other holy sites across the country. Whether in theory those same forces can be harnessed for personal power as Strigan and the Hounds intend, I cannot say, only that he is unlikely to succeed.'

'You mean because he's such a prat?'

Estevar stopped when Imperious dropped his head, tugging on the reins, to crop a patch of long grass surrounding one of the columns holding up the cloister's stone roof. He made a show of examining a carving of the face of Amoria, Goddess of Love, on the column. Across the open gardens, a figure in the grey robes of a traditionalist – one of the so-called 'Bone-Rattlers' – ducked down behind an iron-banded oak bench. Was this some frightened novice following them, or one of Brother Agneta's fellow inquisitors? Estevar had no particular use for either right now.

'How well do you know the brethren of Isola Sombra?' he asked Caeda quietly.

She was tracing Amoria's lips, apparently entranced. 'Only a little. I'm not allowed in the grounds, officially speaking. You might say I'm a bit notorious around here. They all think they know me, which is why that pustule Strigan was so free with his attentions, but in truth, I hardly know them at all.

Notorious. An interesting choice of word, but not pertinent to Estevar's current line of enquiry. 'Have you no allies here at all? Not even—?'

'Abbot Venia was kind enough to me, I suppose. He always spoke a word or two when we ran into each other at the village market. Malezias says it was he who forbade the Council of Brethren from banishing me from the island due to my blasphemous behaviour.'

Again, Estevar refused to take the bait. 'Malezias – he is your friend?'

Caeda looked up at him, head tilted. 'That's a queer formulation of the question, isn't it?'

'What do you mean?' he asked, acceding to Imperious' tug – he'd finished demolishing the patch of grass and was apparently keen to resume their walk.

Caeda ran a few steps to catch up with them. 'Why not ask if he is my husband or my brother or my landlord, for that matter? "Friend" is a term so ambiguous that it might contain any, none or all of those more specific relationships.'

'Ah, yes, but when someone seeks to withhold information from you, they prepare for the questions they anticipated. "Were you here on the night of the murder?" or "Had you argued with the victim in the days before his death?" These linear interrogatories play into the rhythms of the suspect's rehearsed responses.'

'Whereas if you ask something non-threatening . . .'

Estevar ran his fingers along Imperious' flank. The mule was in great need of grooming. Worse, he was still unsteady on his hooves. 'A skilled investigator plays with the rhythm of the interrogation, forcing the witness to either answer plainly or seek to delay while they concoct what they believe you wish to hear.'

'Look, I'm not hiding my relationship with him. Malezias and me, we're more like—'

'You needn't go on.'

'Why? You don't believe me?'

'I already know the answer.'

She moved ahead of him, then turned to walk backwards so she could see his face. 'Tell me.'

Estevar resisted the temptation to have her work out the answer herself. He needed to keep reminding himself that, however enjoyable a companion she might be, like everyone else on this cursed island, she was keeping secrets from him. 'That Malezias is a former monk is obvious by his robes, irrespective of his denials. He is a man of unusual size, yet they fitted him perfectly, which meant they were made for him. That he is in love with you is evidenced by his rescue of me at the risk of his own life, despite having demonstrated no personal inclination to do so. Any doubt as to his subservience to you was eliminated when he brought me – at your behest – down to the abbey's prayer caves after Brother Agneta had left me for dead.'

'Except we're not lov—'

'Forgive me the interruption, Piccolo, but our admirer on the other side of the cloister may seek to close the distance soon, so we must complete this particular discussion before it can be overheard.' He hastened them onwards, wishing he had even a handful of spiked caltrops to drop behind him, or any of the dozens of tools and traps hidden inside the pockets of his beloved greatcoat, lost for ever at the bottom of the ocean. 'I already know that Malezias is not your lover, nor does he hold any claim of kinship over you, otherwise he would not so meekly allow you to risk your life as brazenly as you do now, traipsing about with a Greatcoat whose enemies within this abbey are likely innumerable.'

He could have told her more – of her conflicted attachment to Isola Sombra, of the paradox that she remained here despite an obvious longing to experience a different life, evidenced by her excited participation in his investigation. For now, he was prepared to let her broach those more intimate topics when it suited her, especially when there was a witness whose testimony was far more urgently needed.

Looking at the Vigilance Tower ahead, his vision suddenly grew hazy. He worried his infected wound was bringing on another fever, until Caeda said, 'Look – the fog's rolling in off the shore. It happens at strange times here, often without warning. That's one of the reasons why it's such a dangerous place for ships.' She gestured at their feet – she and Estevar appeared to be standing on clouds. 'It comes all the way up to the top of the hill. Soon you won't be able to see your hand in front of your face.'

'Will you do me a favour?' Estevar asked.

She stopped, suspicion playing across her features.

She has excellent instincts, he thought, holding out Imperious' reins. 'Will you take him somewhere safe for me? Somewhere he can eat and stay warm? I think he trusts you now, and it is vital that he rest.'

Caeda stared down at the leather reins in his hand as if he'd slapped her with them. 'You don't want me there when you question Mother Leogado?'

'It is better that I speak to her myself.'

'Because, unlike your mule, *you* don't trust me at all, do you?'

Estevar held back a sigh. He'd never enjoyed the performative quarrels that too often occupied the people of his adopted country. They argued as if reciting lines memorised from a play, rehearsing the same scenes over and over again. He would insist that she was wrong, that he valued her greatly. She would take umbrage, accusing him of being like all the others – whoever 'the others' were supposed to be – and that this was proof he viewed her as little more than an ignorant fishwife with nothing to offer so great a detective. Back and forth they would go until the dramatic climax of the scene when she would storm off. Estevar had, inevitably, come to learn both parts of the script, but he had no intention of delivering his expected lines.

'Is that what you believe?' he asked instead.

She tried to force him back to the play, retorting, 'It's obvious that's all y—'

'Ah, ah, ah,' he interrupted, employing her chosen rebuke from earlier, 'you seek the role of investigator? Investigate *me*, then.'

She took a step back. 'What that's supposed to mean?'

Estevar stroked Imperious' muzzle to allay the mule's restlessness. 'Based on what you have learned of me thus far, what is your analysis of both my situation and my intentions?'

There was a rustle nearby: their hidden admirer was getting closer. Estevar resumed their walk, picking up the pace. No need to make it easy for their pursuer.

'Well?' he asked when Caeda still hadn't spoken.

She gazed up at him appraisingly as they walked. 'You look like shit.'

'From which you concl—'

She cut him off with a dismissive wave of her hand. 'The waves banged you up badly, but those bags under your eyes show you were tired long before you reached this island. The wound I stitched up means you either lost a duel or came close enough to almost die. That *might* explain the nervous twitch in your sword hand that you don't appear to notice. Mother Leogado *will* notice that, however, and the trick you used on Strigan won't work on her. Before she joined the abbey, she was a proper captain in the ducal army – she led men twice her size into battle and not one of them would speak a bad word about her.'

Ah, but how would you know that? Estevar wondered. The answer came to him quickly. *Because Malezias, almost certainly a former soldier himself, served under Captain Leogado and followed her here. He probably bragged to you about his service under so legendary a military commander.*

Caeda continued her dissection of Estevar's ruinous odds. 'The moment you step inside the Vigilance Tower, you'll be in the clutches of her Trumpeters. You give a pretty speech about being a Greatcoat and all that, but without your coat and the ability to back up your words with a blade, you're just a fat man with funny braids in his beard.'

She was testing his vanity now, probing whether it would impede his judgement. Good. Vanity, he had aplenty, but he'd been at this game of secrets and lies too long to fall into such traps. He gestured for her to continue.

She flicked the reins dangling from his hand. 'You're right not to take Imperious. If the Trumpeters demand that you lend judicial blessing to their faction, slitting your mule's neck would be an easy way to show they're serious without having to risk killing a King's Magistrate. Instead, they'll take you prisoner, at which point you'll be helpless and friendless.'

'Will I be?' he asked.

'What?'

'Friendless.'

This time, when she glared at him, the hurt and irritation were replaced by a fierce pride. 'You'll be helpless, Estevar Valejan Duerisi

Borros. You'll need someone to rescue you – someone who knows all the ways in and out of this abbey.'

'Someone brave,' he added.

'Someone *fearless*, more like.'

Estevar felt an unfamiliar stirring in his heart. He'd never wanted children, never even contemplated marriage after he'd fled his homeland, leaving the love of his life to the far better man she'd chosen over him. Yet now, seeing the fierceness in Caeda's grin and the cunning in her eyes, he knew what it was to wish for just such a daughter. Alas, some dreams are best left undreamt. 'I am all the things you say, Piccolo,' he conceded. 'I am injured, tired and no longer sure of my sword arm. The causeway is flooded, the Margrave of Someil either terrified, as he wrote to me, or merely biding his time until the bloodshed begins so that he can step in and take the island for himself.'

'I'd bet on the latter.'

Estevar risked impropriety to put his hands on her arms. 'You asked earlier whether I believed the old gods have returned or new ones have taken their place, or if this nation is done with deities. I tell you now, Caeda, I do not care about such things – gods, magic, witches, ghosts, they are all the same to me.'

She shook off his hands. 'You're supposed to be the "King's Crucible" – the Greatcoat who goes around investigating supernatural phenomena!'

'A crucible is a pot in which ores are melted so that the dross – that which is false – can be separated from the true metal. I investigate these matters not to determine which magic spell was real or which demon a hoax, but to uncover the facts of the case and bring justice to the perpetrators regardless of the means by which the crime was committed. *That* is my *devozia*, my devotion. My faith lies not with gods, but in laws written by mortal hands to ensure the dignity of us all.'

'And what will you do if it turns out the gods don't much care for your laws? The Trumpeters certainly won't!'

Estevar felt uneasy – and not solely from having ignited Caeda's ire. They were standing next to the mound where Venia's corpse had risen yesterday, and where it might well rise again today. The spy following them was nearer now, but it hardly mattered who among the living or the dead heard Estevar's next words. 'There is only me here, Caeda. The rest of the Greatcoats are too few and too far away, and somehow I must bring justice to the murdered Abbot Venia and peace to his abbey.'

'You're wrong,' she said, and before he could argue, reached up to pinch his chin through the rough hair of his braided beard. 'You have me. I may not be some king-appointed Greatcoat, but I care what happens to this place. You need me, whether you know it or not, my Cantor. When the time comes to sing the verdict, you'll need a piccolo to pierce through the clamour!'

That brought an unexpected smile to his face. What a wondrous Greatcoat she might have been. 'Your reasoning is beyond dispute, Lady Caeda. Indeed, logic dictates that I now leave the decision to you.' He gestured to the imposing watchtower looming over the northwest corner of the abbey grounds. 'Do you wish to lead the questioning of Mother Leogado? I would be happy to act as your assistant.'

Caeda gave him a shove that despite their difference in size, nearly sent him stumbling onto the mound of earth that served as Venia's grave. 'You know perfectly well she won't see me, you manipulative blowhard. I've nothing to offer her, whereas you *might* lend legitimacy to her claim over Isola Sombra.' She turned and tugged Imperious' reins. 'There's a stable on the way back to the village. I'll wait until Malezias returns from his fishing and have him watch over Imperious. Expect to find me outside the Vigilance Tower at nightfall.'

'What if I'm otherwise detained?'

Without turning, she swung one arm back and made a rude gesture with two upturned fingers. 'Then I'll come and rescue you, you pompous arsehole!'

CHAPTER 20

THE OLD DEBATE

Estevar sat down heavily upon a toppled marble section of what had once been the rather seductive legs of Amoria, Goddess of Love, alone among the ruins save for the grey-robed spy, who must not have been aware that his panting breaths could be clearly heard across the deserted courtyard. The sun was still peeking out over the mainland to the east and Caeda would not return until it had set. Estevar found he wasn't ready yet to face the faction of militaristic monks calling themselves the Trumpeters.

'What a preposterous name,' he said to the earthen mound covering the body of the man who'd summoned him here. 'Trumpeters?' He glanced around the place, nearly catching his unwanted companion as the fellow ducked behind a row of shrubs in a flurry of grey wool. 'There are none of that particular species of poisonous yellow flower to be found in this abbey, nor anywhere, I suspect, on the entire island.' He kicked the mound. 'Was that not a clue you should have acted sooner to prevent the faction from forming in the first place, you silly fool?'

No response came from the interred abbot, but the sudden slap of sandalled feet on the flagstones, as quickly halted, told Estevar a great deal about his stalker.

A slight limp on the left foot, he thought, *presuming he starts with his right, as most people do.* More illuminating, however, was the way the spy had set off so quickly when Estevar had kicked the dirt, only to then stop again. *The desecration of the abbot's resting place troubles you, does it, my friend? And yet you're too cautious to challenge me directly.*

Estevar suspected he'd found Venia's gravedigger, the one who reinterred the cadaver each night after it mysteriously rose from the ground during the day.

Why do you not remain at your rest? he wondered. Even now, he could see particles of dirt trickling down the unquiet mound as if something were burrowing slowly beneath.

'Oh, will you rise up to remonstrate with me now, Venia?' he asked aloud. 'Have I ever struck you as someone impressed by cheap parlour tricks – whether supernatural or not? Perhaps you intend to resume our debate over whether humanity's place is to follow the will of the gods or whether the gods, those arrogant reflections of our own faith, serve us best by pointing out the hollowness of our intentions?'

Still no answer came from the dead abbot's grave, and Estevar was surprised by how deeply he missed the squat, thin-haired fellow, the strident tone that rose and fell in pitch as he illustrated his argument with extravagant gesticulations. A rapier blade too often drawn becomes nicked and dulled, requiring a whetstone to sharpen, but a mind is honed only through the vigorous clash and clang of incompatible ideas.

'Why were you killed, Venia?' he asked quietly. 'The who, I will uncover by one means or another. The motive will be, as always, greed or jealousy or spurned love or mindless fury, but the reason – the *true* reason – why you lie unquiet in this mound of dirt surrounded by the dust of dead gods? That is the knot I must untie if there is to be any hope for this abbey you so loved.'

Estevar stood, only for dizziness to overtake him. He pressed his palm to his forehead, gauging the degree of heat and clamminess of his skin, then looked about and saw on the opposite side of the courtyard an open door. If he recalled aright, it led to the chandler's workshop, which had a small cot in the corner. Estevar liked candles. They were both a reminder of his duty and a metaphor for his vocation.

Cast a light upon the things that hide in the shadows, he told himself as his tired legs carried him resentfully over the debris towards the workshop, *for there can be no justice in darkness.*

'I am going to rest a while,' he said, loud enough for his silent companion to hear, then patted the rapier belted to his side so the hilt rung

134

against the brass rim of the scabbard. 'You may try to kill me if you wish, but others have found it an onerous endeavour, and should you succeed, there will be no one to find your beloved abbot's killer.' As he was about to step into the chandlery, he added, 'Oh, and do something about your left heel. The awkwardness of your footsteps suggests the limp is recent.' He felt at the wound beneath his ribs. 'Best not to let these things fester.'

CHAPTER 21

THE TOWER
OF VIGILANCE

Noon had come and gone before Estevar woke inside the abandoned chandlery. The cot had proved more comfortable than he'd anticipated, the pair of brass candlesticks with which he'd barred the door a sufficiently reassuring means of both delaying and warning against any potential intruders. Alas, slumber had failed to provide any new insights into the death of Abbot Venia. There would be no avoiding his visit to what he felt sure would be a garden whose flowers had more thorns than petals.

When at last he made his way across the courtyard to ascend the stone steps of the Vigilance Tower, the doors swung open before he had a chance to knock. His arrival had evidently been expected.

Two hooded monks wearing sleeveless yellow surcoats over their black robes dashed out and grabbed him by the arms. Neither of his would-be captors was of any great size, but Estevar offered no resistance when they hauled him inside. A great thump behind him signalled a pair of similarly garbed brethren placing a heavy wooden bar across barricade brackets mounted into the stone walls on either side. The iron was so free of rust that the brackets fairly gleamed, in spite of the dampness permeating the tower.

A recent addition meant to withstand battering rams, not a few swords wielded by Strigan and his drunken hounds, Estevar observed to himself.

'Watch for the witch or her traitor,' bellowed one of Estevar's captors as she stripped the borrowed rapier from him. She drew back her hood and Estevar recognised her as Sister Parietta, the swordswoman who'd attempted to wrest him from Brother Agneta's clutches – was it only the day before?

'*The witch or her traitor,*' Estevar repeated silently to himself. *So Caeda's relationship with Malezias is well known, and his loyalty to her considered treachery to Mother Leogado, which is further proof of my theory that he was once a soldier under the captain's command.*

The interior of the vigilia, the abbey's watchtower, was as unlike that of the Venerance Tower as Sister Parietta was from Strigan the Wolf-King. This vigilia was more fortress than palace, the stone walls bare of tapestries or portraits, the main floor a single massive room filled with yellow-garbed monks standing over rough-hewn wooden tables performing tasks as varied as chopping potatoes and grinding millet to oiling the rust off old swords and trimming feathers for fletching. There was no sign of excessive opulence and revelry in this place.

'Upstairs with you,' Parietta ordered him brusquely.

'A pleasure to once again make your acquaintance, Madam,' he said, and set off up the stairs spiralling around the tower to its upper levels.

On each floor there were more yellow-robed monks hard at work, though not all at siege preparations. On the third level, a dozen were busily wrapping gold-framed paintings, porcelain sculptures and what at a glance looked to be musical instruments in woollen blankets before packing them carefully into wooden boxes.

'Keep moving,' Parietta said, pairing the instruction with a jab in the small of his back from the pommel of her longsword.

The pain was noteworthy, triggering a sharp-tongued response. 'Offer such romantic attentions without my consent again, Sister, and you will find me—' Estevar caught himself. What was he doing building up to another of his customary long-winded challenges? He'd barely bluffed his way out of the last one.

'What did you say to me?' she demanded. The hiss of a blade drawn from its sheath preceded a sharper prodding against his back.

'Forgive me Sister,' he said, raising his hands in surrender. 'I was recalling a most inappropriate invitation I received from a woman of noble birth but less than noble intentions.'

Parietta shoved him from behind to make it clear his pace was inadequate for one she considered her prisoner. 'Can't imagine any woman wanting you in her bed – not unless she can afford to replace it once you've done breaking it.'

A different approach then, Estevar decided, and turned briefly to wink at the stern, yet not unhandsome woman. 'Your faith in my sexual prowess is most flattering. Perhaps I was too hasty in my reproach of you finding so many ways to touch me.'

'*What?* I wasn't—'

Despite being a little short of breath already, Estevar forced himself to trot up the remaining stairs, leaving Parietta to chase after him. 'No time for flirtations now, my dear,' he called. 'My next assignation awaits!'

When he finally reached the top of the tower, Estevar, noting the absence of any guards, opened the door, slipped inside and turned to close it in Parietta's face. 'Alas, *mea amadore*, we must be parted a while. Your would-be abbess and I have business to discuss.'

Sliding the bolt into its iron brace, Estevar remained at the door a moment longer, allowing himself a small measure of enjoyment at the remarkable string of curses accompanying Parietta's footsteps back down the winding staircase.

'That was foolish,' said a voice behind him, this one deep, mature – strong without relinquishing its femininity. This was a voice accustomed to command, neither brutish nor bullying, merely certain of itself. 'Sister Parietta has a temper sharper than her sword. A wise person would not fence with either.'

Estevar hadn't turned yet. He'd always preferred to study a suspect with his ears before his eyes, and this one bore close listening. However, he couldn't stand staring at the door for ever. This particular conversation – no, this *interrogation*, he reminded himself – would take place face-to-face, with neither of them afforded the opportunity to retreat before he had his answers.

'With regards to tempers and swords, Madam, from the moment I set foot upon this supposedly holy isle, I have noted with regret that far too many of your brethren have forgotten their manners.' He turned to stand before the woman who had transformed at least a third of the abbey's faithful from humble monks into fearsome soldiers. 'Far too few of you ask yourselves what price you might pay for making an enemy of me.'

'Let us begin, then,' said the General of the Trumpeters, 'and decide whether either of us can afford to make one more.'

CHAPTER 22

THE QUEEN OF SWORDS

She was close to Estevar's age, which was to say past, though not long past, her fighting years. The hem of her long black wool robe was a touch more frayed; her yellow and gold surcoat lay discarded on the floor by the door, beneath the hook from which it had doubtless fallen. In one hand she held a short, curved knife, and in the other, a piece of wooden dowelling she was carving into what appeared to be the shape of a knight standing at attention.

'Helps me think,' she said in response to Estevar's questioning gaze.

Her skin was a shade darker than his own Gitabrian colouring, but where his hair and beard were a rich, pure black, the short, tight curls clinging close to her scalp were a lighter brown, sprinkled with grey. Despite being a full head shorter than he was, still her presence dominated the observance chamber atop the Vigilance Tower.

'You are Mother Leogado, I presume?' Estevar asked, though he had no doubts about whom he was addressing. 'Or do you prefer *General* Leogado?'

She turned her head, casting him a smile he found both genuine and surprisingly charming, and stepped towards the sole piece of furniture in the otherwise empty chamber: a huge wooden table constructed from rough planks. It must have been built inside this room, for it was too large to have fitted through the door. It was littered with maps, charts and scraps of parchment bearing scrawled diagrams that could have been military formations. The largest of these, the yellowing paper curling at the ends, was a sketch of the island upon which figurines like the

140

one she was now carving were assembled into several wooden armies, knights, archers and ships amassed against a handful of helpless-looking wooden monks.

Mother Leogado placed her latest creation on the map, then walked to one of the tall windows, this one facing southwest towards the causeway and the mainland beyond.

The same window from which she no doubt watched me ringing the bell, Estevar observed. He could see her attention was far away, miles from the abbey.

'The first assault will come by land,' she said as if resuming a prior conversation with a trusted lieutenant rather than sharing military intelligence with an outsider, 'after the tides have subsided and the causeway is passable again. Three days, perhaps four.'

Estevar said nothing. She still hadn't met his eyes.

She left that window and moved to the one facing due west, overlooking the water. Even from where he stood near the door, Estevar could see the tumultuous waves, higher than they'd been this morning. He had to force himself not to hold his breath at the memory of his near-drowning.

'After we repulse them at the causeway,' Mother Leogado went on, still with that quiet, distracted voice, as if speaking only to herself, 'they will attack by sea. He hasn't many ships of his own, but he has influence and will make whatever promises he pleases to those who can provide them.' She squeezed the handle of the carving knife still in her hand. 'With the help of his knights, he'll beg, borrow and bully his way to a modest fleet – perhaps a dozen ships – along with enough mercenaries to overwhelm us when they storm the beaches.'

'Of whom do you speak, my Lady?' Estevar asked, feeling it prudent to remind her that there was someone else in the room with her.

She crossed her arms, still gazing out to sea. The blade of her knife jutted upwards from her hand as she leaned against the rough wooden window frame. 'Forgive me, Eminence. The tales I'd heard of the King's Crucible spoke of a sharp wit that detested the plodding pace of idle conversation. I assumed you'd prefer we skip over the usual pleasantries and posturing and instead get to the matter at hand.'

'That being your prediction of an invasion by the Margrave of Someil?'

'Prediction,' she repeated slowly, making clear her disappointment in his choice of words. 'The invasion is a matter of time, not intention. Someil craves Isola Sombra as a new and loftier seat of power from which to achieve his ambitions. This abbey shoulders a great history – greater, some might argue, than Castle Aramor itself. Where the latter serves as little more than an ostentatious country house for kings and queens, Isola Sombra is where the people of this nation turn for spiritual guidance.' She reached up with her free hand to pull a slender brass lever, then pushed the window open. The wind that rushed in brought the smell of seawater, and something else, too: the strange, not-quite-burning scent of air before the lightning strikes.

'I've read the *Canon Dei* cover to cover, Madam,' Estevar said. 'I can quote you the passages that claim the gods were born when lightning struck the ores deep beneath Tristian soil where slaves penned up by foreign conquerors had prayed and carved their prayers into the rocks, though they had no religion of their own, no priests, no holy books.'

'The gods never asked us for scriptures or rituals,' Leogado countered. 'They awaited only our faith to give them form, *here*, on Isola Sombra. Love. War. Death. Craft. Coin. The Mys—'

'The map of holy sites across this country whose clerics make that same claim would be crowded indeed.'

'And that's what a Greatcoat must fear most, isn't it, Estevar Borros? Some charismatic zealot concocting their own pantheon, enshrining a God of *This* and a God of *That* – along with a new set of commandments to take precedence over your precious King's Laws?'

'They are laws written by human beings, Madam: laws meant to serve the men, women and children of this nation, not the whims of supernatural beings conjured from mystical rocks and poor weather. *That* is what makes them precious.'

Mother Leogado laughed, and Estevar found himself laughing as well. He doubted either of them had expected this meeting to devolve into the kind of theological dispute Abbot Venia had so adored. The leader of the Trumpeters was correct in one regard, however: Isola Sombra held tremendous value, even beyond its accumulated riches and strategic positioning. History is replete with minor nobles whose cunning conquest of a revered holy site was the first step to anointing themselves as chosen by the gods to rule over all.

So, was Someil's warning meant to curry favour with King Filian by protecting his beloved Greatcoats from the supposed 'demon plague' awaiting them on the island, or to ensure no magistrate would be present to witness the invasion that might be the prelude to taking his throne?

A crack of thunder out over the water drew Estevar's gaze to the darkening sky beyond, then a sudden flare of lightning returned his attention to the table, for the wooden figurines had taken on an eerie glow. For an instant, it almost looked as if the pieces had come to life and were marching across the map.

A trick of the light, he knew, but he still bent to examine the carvings and their positioning. Estevar was no military strategist, but he'd once made a thorough study of warfare in the hope of applying it to the investigation of certain criminal organisations. He need only memorise the tactics laid bare upon this table and share them with the margrave for all of Mother Leogado's preparations to come to naught.

A ruse, then? he wondered. *False plans left here for my benefit so that, if I am a spy for the margrave, I will lead him into a disastrous campaign? Or does the general seek to persuade me that she is the only one capable of defending the abbey's religious freedoms, thus, I must rule in favour of her faction against the others?*

Thunder boomed, louder this time, and the wind began to whistle a haunting tune through the window. Estevar feared for what new destruction this approaching storm would bring.

'You wasted your time meeting with the Wolves,' Mother Leogado said, the hem of her black under-robes swirling around her. 'Strigan is an apostate – and worse than that, he's a fool.'

'A fool who commands almost as many monks as you do, and has a greater share of the abbey's old armoury.'

Still not meeting his gaze, she returned to her table, picked up another piece of wooden dowel and began carving again. 'You are best known for investigating matters of the occult on behalf of the king, are you not?'

Another twist in the conversation, he thought. *She seeks to lead me down a path, but what is its destination?*

'You accused me of divination earlier,' she continued, her knife making quick, deft cuts into the wood. 'When I spoke of the margrave's impending invasion, you called it a prediction. That's as good as charging a woman with witchcraft in so devout a place of worship as this abbey.'

'I believe you are aware that was not my intention, Madam. Furthermore, I will remind you that it is not the King's Magistrates who imprison his citizens for witchcraft. Such cruel and superstitious prosecutions are the province of your own Cogneri.'

Little shards of wood fell at her sandalled feet as she continued working her knife. 'You've met Brother Agneta, then?'

'You know I have.' He pointed to the window she had earlier abandoned. 'It was you I saw watching me as I rang the bell for entry. You ignored my plea until I used the pattern of a magistrate. Only then did you send two of your "Trumpeters" – to take me prisoner.'

More flashes of light blossomed in the north-facing windows, the booming thunder that followed behind so deafening it might've been mistaken for cannon-fire.

'You should have begged to go with them,' Mother Leogado told him, 'given the state in which Brother Agneta left you. But let us return to the matter of witchcraft.' The curved blade of her knife was tearing chunks from the wood almost as quickly as she changed subjects. 'What is your opinion of divination?'

'Divination?'

'Soothsaying. Prophecy. Crook-backed crones casting cards, rattling bones and imbibing hallucinogens to trigger mystical visions. In all your travels, have you ever encountered evidence supporting the belief that one can predict the future?'

'No,' he answered simply.

In his various supernatural enquiries on behalf of the Crown, he'd witnessed many forms of magic. Some had proven genuine, others merely intricate fakery. When it came to divination and soothsaying, however, the results had always been the same.

Mother Leogado resumed her clockwise perambulation around the room, her rhythm so steady she might have been a wind-up toy. She stopped at a third window, this one overlooking the courtyard and the ruins of the statuary. 'You claim no one can foretell the future, yet I am willing to wager all I hold dear that you, Estevar Borros, possess the ability to predict with near-perfect accuracy the fate awaiting the self-styled "Wolf-King and Sorcerer Sovereign" of Isola Sombra. Is that not a kind of divination?'

Wary of the knife in Leogado's hand, yet more at ease with this peripatetic warrior woman than he'd felt in a long time, Estevar joined her at the window. She didn't shy away, and her confidence was as attractive to him as her incisiveness. He could almost imagine the two of them seated by a fire in some little cottage somewhere, debating philo-sophical conundrums and the finer points of logic, without rancour or competitiveness, for days at a time. A shame, then, that their respective roles all but guaranteed they would soon be at odds with one another. 'What you speak of is not Strigan's destiny, Madam, but the inexorable destination to which his choices will lead him.'

She leaned ever so slightly closer to him. He liked the way she smelled, reminiscent of the spicy fragrances of his homeland. It would be a pity if the first time she met his eyes was while stabbing him through his sword wound with her whittling knife.

'And what destination might that be?' she asked.

Estevar risked extending an arm over her shoulder to point towards the Venerance Tower on the other side of the cloister. 'Days from now – possibly hours, depending on how quickly they run out of wine and what little food they thought to gather after the abbot's death – his followers will grow anxious over their own futures. Worry will turn to resentment. These lapsed monks will begin to doubt Strigan's claims of being on the verge of harnessing the island's power to their own ends. They will see themselves in the mirror, feel the discomfort of those silly tattoos he convinced them to inscribe upon their own skin, and wonder whether perhaps – just perhaps – the only miracles conjured up by his nonsensical sexual escapades masquerading as demonic rituals will be a few unintended pregnancies.'

Rain began to patter upon the open glass, softly at first, but within seconds, it was coming down in torrents outside. Leogado laughed at Estevar's joke, untroubled by the worsening storm outside. 'You

Greatcoats *do* have a way with words, don't you, Eminence? Allow me to complete the tale.' The playfulness disappeared from her voice, her tone now imbued with the grim certainty of a magistrate rendering a verdict. With her knife, she pointed to the lightning-struck statuary below. 'They will drag Strigan to this last, terrible centre of genuine godly power to perform a final ritual that will complete their apostasy. They will slit the Wolf-King's throat, his wrists and ankles, desecrating the abbey grounds with his spurting blood as punishment both for Strigan's lies and the ones they blame on the rest of us.'

'A dark prediction indeed,' Estevar said, taken aback, but Mother Leogado wasn't done.

'Chaos and bloodshed will ensue as his feral apostles run wild through the abbey, slaughtering everyone they encounter, providing the perfect moral and legal justification for the Margrave of Someil to invade Isola Sombra and—'

Her ominous prognostication was interrupted by more thunder. The crack of flagstones outside being fractured suggested lightning had struck. Estevar wondered where Caeda had taken Imperious, and hoped the poor mule wouldn't be driven to panic by this gods-be-damned storm.

'Would you condemn us to madness and mayhem?' Leogado asked, turning to place a hand on his arm, her gaze down at her feet. 'Or will you take action and save not only the lives of Abbot Venia's flock but also the religious freedoms for which he fought so long?'

'You make an excellent case, General,' he conceded, gently removing her hand. 'I encourage you to act as chief advocate for your faction after I have completed my investigation into the abbot's murder and hold a hearing into who should govern the abbey.'

She retreated a few steps, then tossed her latest carving at him. 'You fail to live up to your reputation, Eminence.'

Estevar caught the figurine in his hand and held it up to the dying light.

It can't be more than an hour or two after noon – why is the sky so dark? he wondered. When next the lightning flashed, he studied Leogado's gift. The work was rough but already he could make out the contours of a heavy-set man whose braided beard came down to his broad chest. There was a sword in his hand and a blindfold over his eyes.

'I am not quite so unseeing as you imagine, General,' he said, pocketing the figurine. 'You speak of the Margrave of Someil using the chaos in the abbey as justification for taking control, yet you do the same by stoking fear of him conquering the island. The frantic military preparations I witnessed downstairs serve a purpose little different to that of Strigan's revels: they keep your followers too busy to question your decisions over which gods the abbey should serve.'

There was no ire in her reply, but plenty of condemnation. 'Only a fool would believe all the dead gods will return. The mechanism of their creation derives from the faith and desires of the people of this nation. Tristia has changed; so too must its deities.'

She went silent, as if waiting for some proof of her assertion to emerge from the blackening sky outside – and sure enough, it came in the form of blinding lightning accompanied by thunder so devastatingly loud it left Estevar's ears ringing.

'You think these storms are natural? The entire island will be shattered like the statues in the courtyard and sink into the sea before your vaunted intellect perceives that which would be obvious to any child. The gods aren't coming, Estevar, for *they are already here!* The storms are their heralds, commanding that we divine the natures of our new deities so that we can bring the people closer to them. *That* is the only path to salvation, Eminence, not your trials and your laws.'

Her fury was beginning to match that of the storm and Estevar knew he ought to be cautious, yet he'd never allowed deception – however subtle – to go unchallenged in his courtroom and nor would he do so now. 'I couldn't help but notice your monks below, packing up the abbey's treasures, General. Perhaps it is not only by the gods' will that you seek to prosper?'

Accompanied by the almost military drumming of the rain echoing against the stone walls of the tower, Leogado marched back to her map table. She snatched up a handful of her carvings of knights and archers and for a moment, Estevar thought she might hurl them at him. Instead, she brought them closer. 'Each of these represents a troop of ten soldiers. Someil commands a hundred and fifty knights, ten times that in infantry and archers. He has siege-engines, Estevar! I cannot defend this place with rusting duelling swords and poorly made arrows!' She tossed the figurines back onto the map table. 'Can the simple calculus of our situation escape you? We are all as doomed as Strigan, even those of us who have stayed true to our vows! Either you help me unite the brethren of this abbey under my leadership, or Someil *will* take this island.' She wrapped her arms around herself, as if suddenly aware of the cold. 'He threatened Venia, you know.'

She let that last piece of testimony hang in the air. Even the thunder remained quiet, the longest gap since the storm had begun.

'The margrave?'

Leogado nodded. 'Time and again, Someil sent his envoys to the abbey. Sometimes they brought gifts, other times, letters signed by legal scholars and even other clerics, all claiming that Isola Sombra was part of the hereditary lands belonging to the March of Someil.'

'An argument King Filian would not be likely to find persuasive,' Estevar noted.

The general shook her head as though frustrated that he, Estevar Borros, was too slow-witted to comprehend her analysis. 'I took up carving only recently,' she said, returning to the map table and fumbling among the papers until she produced another wooden figurine. This one was far more refined than the others, the lines more detailed, the wood stained and polished to perfection. She tossed it to Estevar.

It was carved in the form of a monk, smiling beatifically, with a noose around the neck.

'This was my inspiration for taking up my new hobby,' Leogado said. When Estevar held it out to return it, she shook her head. 'Keep it. There are plenty more sitting idle in the abbot's private study. The margrave had taken to sending one of these on the first of each month.'

Estevar stared at the deceptively simple wooden sculpture in his palm. A master's work, without question. What had Sir Daven said when he'd met Estevar at the causeway? '*My lord is no enemy to the new king, nor to his magistrates.*' It appeared the same could not be said of the margrave's intentions towards the brethren of Isola Sombra.

Estevar turned to go. The pace of his investigation would need to quicken. He must chase down the Bone-Rattlers, those traditionalist monks who'd stayed true to Venia's teachings. He would have to search Venia's rooms, uncover whatever clues hadn't already been trodden into dust by monks searching for any small treasures they could snatch up before their brethren beat them to it.

'You still intend to waste your time searching for Venia's killer?' Leogado called after him. 'To what end? A trial? Followed by some preposterous arbitration in which each of us is forced to plead our cases so that you might bless us with your final verdict? Perhaps Strigan isn't the only one obsessed with false rituals.'

Estevar placed his hand on the doorframe. He felt an odd loss, as if he was leaving something unexpectedly precious behind in this lonely watchtower. 'That is what Venia asked of me. I am a magistrate. My duty is not to any god but to uphold the peace.'

He heard her surefooted steps across the floor. Despite her shorter stature, three strides were all it took to bridge the distance between them. He felt her hand grab hold of his wrist and was surprised at how easily she spun him to face her. 'Then *uphold* the peace! You speak of factions as if there was some choice to be made, but you've admitted yourself that the Wolves will abandon their pack. The Bone-Rattlers scurry about the abbey, rolling their dice and praying to whomever the pips command, not out of principled belief but because they know not what else—'

More thunder threatened to shatter their eardrums, more flashes of lightning split a sky far too dark for so early an hour – and all of it was striking too close to the abbey to be attributed to the fickleness of nature. No wonder the villagers had fled and the monks retreated to whatever dark corners they could find.

Leogado caught the concern in Estevar's expression and sneered in disgust. She let go of his wrist and strode back to the window, jabbing her finger outside as if accusing the entire world of treachery. By chance, her gesture was accompanied by yet another bolt of lightning, this one so bright, the thunder so deafening, that it must have struck right in the heart of the abbey courtyard. Estevar's ears felt as if they were plugged with wax, forcing him to read Leogado's lips to make out what she said next.

'What you see as divisions are little more than the petulance of children refusing to clean their room because Daddy has gone away and Mummy refuses to give them . . . give them—'

'My Lady?' he asked, his own voice sounding muffled and distant. He saw, rather than heard, the breathless gasp escape Mother Leogado's gaping mouth as she looked down at the ruins of the statuary below. Only her silhouette was visible now; the tower was shrouded in darkness. A chill seeped into Estevar's bones when he noticed that the rains had stopped and the storm was passing the island, because it meant that what he heard next could not be confused with the shrieking of the wind or the crashing of thunder. Screams were rising up from the courtyard like ghostly hands coming to drag someone back to hell with them – screams that evoked more horror inside him than he'd ever known before.

'By all the gods,' he swore, an uncharacteristic oath that felt like the only one worth uttering in that terrifying moment.

'There are no gods,' Leogado said, her tone flat, stripped of pride, of courage, of hope itself. Hands that had held steady a sword in the most brutal of battles now shook uncontrollably. 'How could there be gods in a world where such things as those are allowed to exist?'

Estevar didn't want to join her at the window, where his gaze would be inexorably drawn to whatever it was that could fill so battle-hardened a warrior with dread. It wasn't any courage of his own that compelled him, but instead, that more potent impulse that had always been both his bane and his saving grace: the fathomless curiosity of one who had to know the truth of things, no matter the cost.

Here on this island, though, where he would never have set foot if he'd listened to the wound in his side warning him he was too weak and slow to face another enemy so soon, the price of knowledge was too high.

He raced for the door and down the stairs as fast as his legs could carry him, convinced he would be too late, while equally certain the oath he'd taken years ago when he'd first donned the leather greatcoat now at the bottom of the sea demanded from him a greater duty than to watch the victim die alone and unaided.

Estevar Valejan Duerisi Borros had travelled across his adopted homeland dozens of times, investigated wonders and horrors aplenty, but until that moment, not even the King's Crucible could claim to have witnessed a man being torn apart by demons.

CHAPTER 23

DEMONS

Estevar took the stairs two at a time, heedless of the exhaustion and injury that threatened to send him hurtling down the spiralling staircase, breaking an arm or a leg or perhaps even his skull. Though he clung to a faint hope that some trick of the storm had deceived him, the memory was a white-hot cattle brand burning itself forever onto his eyes, and a creeping intuition was warning him that if he failed to reach the statuary before Strigan was slain, more than just the Wolf-King's life would be lost.

The tormented monk's screams followed him down the winding stairs, rising and then fading in volume each time he passed one of the narrow windows. New sounds began to drown them out: the disbelieving shouts of Trumpeters spreading word of the attack; the unsheathing of swords; the winding of crossbows in preparation to repel an assault for which such weapons would surely prove as inadequate as Estevar's own rapier.

Too slow, he thought, his mind racing far faster than his body could manage. He imagined himself watching from above, staring down at this lumbering fool whose arrogance in believing he had any role to play in what was unfolding outside was worthy only of derision. What propelled him onwards – what *haunted* him – was a vision that refused to be banished: a vision of hell made real.

Five of them, he'd counted, shaped like parodies of men but with short horns of varying shapes adorning hairless white skulls. Their limbs were equally pale, and stretched too long, looking too slender for the fearsome strength they displayed. Four of the assailants had been holding Strigan's wrists and ankles, effortlessly resisting his mad writhing. The fifth . . . Saint Eloria-whose-screams-draw-blood, the fifth was flaying him with fingernails long as knives, slicing sigils into his flesh with the same casual adroitness as Mother Leogado carved her wooden figurines. The eyes were the worst, though: narrow slits of the brightest blue Estevar had ever seen, cutting through the fog like the beams of mirror-backed lanterns.

At long last, Estevar reached the bottom of the stairs, where it took every ounce of his not inconsiderable strength to heave the massive wooden bar from its brackets across the tower entrance. His confiscated rapier was leaning against the wall and he grabbed it as he burst out the door, nearly tripping down the smaller steps he'd forgotten were there. In the unnatural darkness and haze it took him a moment to find his bearings. He was facing the abbey gates – the opposite direction from the statuary. Turning so swiftly that he nearly twisted his ankle, he took off at a run towards the path to the statuary.

He could see nothing at first. The rains might have stopped, but the cursed, unpredictable fog had not yet lifted. As he ran, he heard the thumping of sandalled feet, swords and crossbows rattling and clanking. A squad of Trumpeters were close on his heels.

'Keep your fingers off those triggers until I tell you otherwise,' he shouted in the most commanding tone his breathless lungs could deliver. The last thing he needed now was to be shot in the arse by a monk with a twitchy finger.

The haze was so thick that he ran headlong into the closed iron gate blocking his path. Cursing, he swung it open, the screech of the hinges no match for the terrified shrieks of poor Strigan being tortured just a few paces ahead.

As Estevar stalked forward, his rapier blade out in front of him, he saw first the glinting of sapphire-blue eyes. A few more steps brought him inside the ruins, where desecration and cruelty had become a gleeful dance performed in defiance of all that could once have been called holy.

The five creatures moved in sickening harmony: one would let go of a limb, only to grab the next, as they rotated the body, sending it round and round so that each got their turn to slice open the black-ink tattoos with their sharpened claws, the same sigils now written in their victim's blood. The first, fleeting tableau he'd witnessed from the watchtower had failed to capture their manic grins, but grin the creatures did, even nodding happily to Estevar as if inviting him to partake of their mischief. Now that he was closer, he could hear their chanting, a whispered song of hisses and hideous slurps, as they bent their heads so they could lap at Strigan's wounds.

They're cutting into the tattoos with their claws to turn what had before been mere ink into bloody inscriptions – why?

'Gods, save us!' one of the Trumpeters called out behind him.

To which god do you plead, he wondered, *and would even they dare intervene against monstrosities such as these?*

Strigan's head came up, his eyes wide with terror. When he saw Estevar, he screamed, 'Eminence, *please!* Please save me!'

A few of the Trumpeters fired their crossbows, ignoring Estevar's previous admonition. One of the bolts nearly took out his left ear before flying off into the mists. The other two were better aimed, yet the shafts split apart before they touched the leathery white skin of Strigan's tormentors.

From atop the tower, a forceful voice shouted to her troops, 'Retreat! Back inside the tower, all of you. Whatever fate the heretic has brought upon himself, we cannot risk the defence of the abbey for one man!'

The yellow-garbed monks required no further urging. Their footsteps quickly faded to silence as they withdrew from the field of battle. When Estevar looked down at his own feet, he saw that he too had – quite without his own volition – begun to retreat.

'Eminence, *please!*' Strigan cried, in between petrified gasps.

Eminence, Estevar repeated to himself. Never before had he heard the title spoken with such desperate reverence. *There's nothing I can do for him,* he told himself, still staring at the ground, unable to meet the eyes of the man he was abandoning. *Let this all be a fever-dream from which I'll soon awake, Caeda shaking her head in disapproval and pointing out that a cantor of the Greatcoats has no business wetting his bed.*

Strangely, when he imagined himself looking up at Caeda, it was the face of another he saw there: a face a few years younger, not nearly as pretty. A short woman, plain and utterly unimpressive, reputed to lack even modest skill with a blade. Chalmers was no one's vision of a duelling magistrate, let alone the First Cantor of the Greatcoats. Many of his fellows had threatened to leave the order upon hearing of her elevation – the undeserved gift of an even younger and less deserving King Filian the First at the behest of the former First Cantor, Falcio val Mond.

'How did you do it?' Estevar had asked her on being summoned to receive his orders from her. He'd come to Castle Aramor fully intending to turn in his coat, knowing she meant to force him to resume his judicial circuits, thus curtailing his passion for investigating the supernatural. But when he'd come face to face with her in the Greatcoats' wardroom, he could think only of the stories he'd heard of the war with Avares, how Chalmers had been selected by Falcio himself to perform the dreaded Scorn Ride. Alone astride her horse, this bare slip of a woman had ridden the enemy's front line as thousands of bloodthirsty warriors had grabbed for her, driven half mad by the insult of a girl being sent, bellowing their vows to tear her apart. Tristia had won great respect – and perhaps been saved from an invasion it could not withstand – when Chalmers had not only ridden the entire line, but then turned back to do so a second time.

'How did I do it?' she'd asked, repeating his question as if at first she couldn't fathom the answer herself. Her hands began to shake and her bottom lip quivered at the memory. Estevar recognised such signs; he knew that not a night could have gone by since that fateful ride when she hadn't shuddered awake, still feeling those hands grabbing at her.

Somehow, though, she managed to still herself, to meet his eyes and answer, 'I remembered what it is we claim to be.'

'Which is?' he'd asked dubiously.

Once again her gaze was drawn far away, yet she was calm now, and he sensed he was seeing her just as the Avarean warriors had on that fateful day. 'The Greatcoats have to be more than judges, Estevar. We have to embody the law itself. The verdicts aren't enough. We have to be the proof that some ideals – *human* ideals, like justice and decency – are more powerful than armies, more righteous than gods.' She'd laughed then, awkwardly, the way she did everything. 'It's terribly arrogant of us, don't you think? But if we claim to represent the law, only to allow ourselves to be cowed through fear and intimidation, then there's really no law at all, is there?'

Those words had echoed in his thoughts after he'd relented and set off to ride his gods-be-damned judicial circuit. It was those words that now gave him the strength to draw his rapier, stride into the ruins where the statues of dead gods lay at the feet of those foul creatures presently inscribing their atrocities into the lapsed monk's flesh, and declare in a voice as deep and steady as had ever been heard within that abbey, 'Be you demons, devils or the gods reborn, my name is Estevar Valejan Duerisi Borros, the King's Crucible, summoned here to restore justice to this troubled place. Release that man now, damn you, or form a line so that one by one you may pit your foul magic against my steel!'

CHAPTER 24

SOME THINGS CANNOT BE FOUGHT

Estevar's crusade against the ivory-skinned demons infesting the abbey grounds was doomed from the start. He opened with a slash of his rapier as fast as any he'd delivered in all his years of judicial duelling – only for the creature nearest him to dance effortlessly out of the way, all while suspending one of Strigan's legs in the air.

Estevar's next attack was a double-feint to the left, then to the right, this one against the ram-horned demon closest to him, before pivoting on his back foot to lunge at a different target entirely, this one sporting three curved goat horns. Again, his efforts were foiled so utterly that the monster he'd missed let go of Strigan's arm long enough to applaud the sincerity of his efforts before once again grabbing the screaming monk's wrist and yanking it with such force that Estevar feared the limb would be torn away.

'Please!' Strigan screamed. 'Save me, Eminence! *You must save me!*'

His confidence in Estevar's abilities was admirable, especially given the lack of success thus far. But he'd faced apparently superior opponents before, and he knew that creating the impression of being untouchable was itself a kind of ruse.

Speed, he thought, preparing his next move. *Along with their unnatural strength, they move with such speed and grace as to make fighting them like trying to stab raindrops out of the air.*

The analogy proved useful, as it reminded Estevar that if you know where the raindrop will fall, you need only place the tip of your blade in the way.

Let us see how well you handle this little concoction, he thought, and hurled himself into the fray once more.

A diagonal downwards cut prompted one of the demons, whose long, narrow jaw displayed double rows of curved fangs dripping with something green and vile, to tilt its entire body backwards at a sharp angle that should have sent it sprawling to the ground. Instead, the monster's spindly legs remained perfectly balanced. This latest violation of physical laws might have been unfathomable; nonetheless, it wasn't unexpected. Even before his blade was halfway down its trajectory, Estevar shot his own rear leg back into a reverse lunge so deep his left palm went to the flagstones to support him while his rapier blade swung back to slash at the demon's leg. With a giggle, the creature hopped up in the air, easily evading the cut. Estevar smiled right back, remained in his low position and lifted his point straight up in the air. As the demon came back down, the forearm holding Strigan's ankle descended right onto the point of Estevar's rapier.

The shriek the creature emitted wasn't one of pain or fear, more outrage, as if Estevar had broken the rules of whatever game it thought they were playing together. This struck him as an important clue about the creatures, but right then, he had more pressing business to attend to. Twisting his blade as he yanked it out of the demon's forearm, he rose up to grab for Strigan's momentarily freed ankle. His hope had been that he might now force the other creatures to release their captive, or else he could use their intransigence against them by stabbing freely with his sword.

Seven Hells! he swore silently as he fell back, Strigan once again under their control and Estevar's right arm and leg both gashed by claws so long and sharp he counted himself lucky his limbs hadn't been severed entirely.

If only he had his damned coat! The bone plates would have offered him a modicum of protection, enough that he could risk more elaborate swordplay without the prospect of sudden amputation. With the hidden tricks and traps, he might have given the unholy creatures more trouble – tiny spiked caltrops to hurl at their feet, amberlight to spark sudden flashes of light to disorient them, hells, even a pinch of rusting powder to give that leathery white skin of theirs a decent itch.

If only, if only, he told himself, mocking the impulse to blame defeat on some minuscule disadvantage rather than cold hard reality. On his best day, armoured in his greatcoat and wielding his own rapier, Estevar was an excellent swordsman and a formidable tactician, but even among the Greatcoats, he'd never been the most skilled duellist. And here he was, wearing borrowed, ill-fitting garb, gripping a rapier that lacked the familiar heft and balance of his own, and fighting gods-be-damned *actual* demons? This was very far from Estevar's best day.

'Face me, damn you!' he shouted as the monsters began to lead him on a distinctly un-merry chase through the statuary. They never laughed, though, merely grinned at him as they paraded the helpless Strigan among the lightning-blasted ruins of the statues of dead gods. He chased after them like the unwanted child in a game of keep-away. Sometimes they'd let him catch up to them for a moment, only to hoist their victim effortlessly above his head before running past him in the opposite direction. Other times two would break away and watch poor Strigan as their foul brethren hurled him through the air in a hideous game of jester's juggle. Estevar began to despair, though not nearly so badly as the man he was trying in vain to rescue.

'Kill me,' Strigan began to beg. All the while this hideous game had unfolded, the role of scribe had shifted from one demon to another as they took turns tracing the sigils tattooed onto his skin with their claws, leaving bloody tracks all over his flesh. The oozing of his blood lent the sigils a twisted, distorted aspect as if they were coming alive. 'Please,' he pleaded again, 'please, kill me!'

Even had Estevar been so inclined, the demons would never let him reach their captive. Perhaps if a dozen of the Trumpeters armed with crossbows had taken up his cause they might have put up a decent fight, but the yellow of their habits had proven to be a disheartening metaphor for their lack of courage as they'd fled back inside the Vigilance Tower. Estevar could almost feel their eyes on him from the safety of their fortress.

Suddenly, a shot rang out – and Strigan screamed. A bright red gash had appeared from nowhere across his ribs. A woman's voice swore somewhere in the shadows to Estevar's right and he turned to see the grey-stubbled head of Brother Agneta bent over her wheellock pistol, pouring powder into the flash pan in preparation for reloading.

'Damn thing hasn't shot straight in years,' she complained.

There would be no time for a second shot. Whatever obscene formula the demons had been inscribing into Strigan's skin must now be complete, for they were laying him down amid the ruined statues.

Venia's grave, Estevar realised, watching in horror as the demons placed taloned feet on Strigan's limbs, pinning him to the ground, then raising their arms up high, the six-inch-long nails of their fingers aimed at his chest as they prepared to drive them like daggers into his heart. Most perversely of all, the fifth demon stood over the screaming Strigan, palms pressed together as it—

By every saint cruel or kind, Estevar swore silently, *the creature is . . . praying! Why do they pray whilst shedding blood over the grave of a dead abbot?*

Estevar was about to rush the demons once more, though it would be a fool's errand. No amount of amateur heroics could save Strigan now. The lapsed monk was convulsing beneath the feet of his tormentors. Was this the result of blood loss, or fear? Or was something far more malignant happening inside him?

Leave the investigation for later, he reminded himself, furious with his own reckless lack of strategy. He hurled his rapier aside – what good was a sword against demons? He might as well have sinned his way to hell and challenged every devil there to a duel!

No, he told himself, focusing his mind once more. *Don't be distracted by supernatural mummery, however powerful it might seem.*

There were other magistrates and lawmen across this country who, whether by choice or by chance, found themselves involved with mysteries that delved into the occult. What had always made Estevar different was that he treated such cases the same way as he did the mundane ones. He was neither a believer nor a sceptic; all that concerned him were the facts, not if magic was or was not involved. Murder was murder, whether committed by a warlock's spell or a poison any cook could brew in their kitchen. The only thing that mattered was bringing the killer to justice.

Furthermore, as his encounter with the irritatingly precocious Chalmers had reminded him, a Greatcoat's job wasn't to prove themself the best duellist, but to see their verdicts enforced by whatever means were at their disposal.

A bluff is as good as a blade when you can guess your opponent's fears, he thought. He had neither the means nor the time to investigate what struck fear in the heart – assuming they had them – of a demon, and yet, he wasn't without clues to work with.

He strode up to them, standing barely six paces away from their unholy ritual. 'Desist!' he commanded, letting his voice rumble deep within his belly. He raised his fist high in the air as if he were holding a magistrate's sceptre and was about to bring it crashing down upon the bell to bring the trial to order.

The creatures paused, their unspeakable chanting suddenly quiet. They swivelled their heads in unison towards the source of the outburst. One by one, their mouths twisted into even more hideous grins. Estevar felt as if those fangs were already tearing at the stitches in his side. His throat tightened, unable to keep from imagining those long, distended fingers wrapped around his neck.

It took every bit of his will to unclench his jaw and summon forth all the sternness he could muster. 'Gaze not impertinently upon he who judges you!' he said, imbuing his words with a smouldering rage.

Years ago, when Estevar was given his coat of office and sent out on his first judicial circuit, he'd wondered what power a magistrate had over those who refused to accept his authority. No decree – not even one issued by a king – is worth more than the parchment on which it's written to people who cannot read it and do not fear the consequences of disobedience. But Estevar had soon discovered something unusual about the peculiar role of the magistrate. There was a strange sort of . . . compulsion to allow a trial to be held. In their own way, trials were rituals, as potent as a prayer service or wedding, or even the coronation of a king. A verdict might be ignored, the sentence evaded, and yet a judge's ruling could make the air itself inside a courtroom thrum with condemnation.

Let us see, then, if there is yet something in this paltry world of weak humanity that you fear.

He took another step towards the demons, invading the ground of their ritual, but before they could begin to show their disdain for him, he started pacing around them in a circle, as he often did when sorting through the tangled details of a case. All the while, his tongue sought out weaknesses in their defences that his rapier had been unable to pierce.

'You have violated a holy place,' he began. 'For that crime you must now await the punishment of this court.'

Their arms were still raised up high, poised to strike the near-unconscious Strigan with their claws. Yet they hadn't moved, which gave Estevar the beginnings of a theory.

They may be unnatural in form, yet by their rituals they reveal themselves to be creatures governed by traditions, rules, perhaps even laws. I need only discern what those laws might be and convince them they've violated them.

A new sound emerged from their mouths: a kind of hush mixed with a buzzing that was like fingernails scraping the inside of his skull.

'The defendants will speak in the language of this court!' Estevar shouted. This time, he did bring his fist down as if to strike a bell. He was both surprised and pleased when the demons flinched.

One of the creatures' obscenely wide mouths contorted painfully. 'We . . .' he began, only to clamp his jaws shut as if even uttering that single word had been agony.

A second assailed the apparently arduous task. 'We were . . .' but he, too, failed to say more.

'Summoned,' offered the next, gurgling the two syllables as if he were choking on a handful of slithering worms.

'*We were summoned,*' Estevar repeated silently to himself. *Magic then – real magic, conjured here in this abbey. So what Strigan attempted so clumsily has been achieved by another.*

'By whom?' he asked.

A third demon stretched out a distended milky-white limb. The movement was at once awkward and yet almost formal, as if the jerky contortions were the opening of a ceremonial curtsey. A long, stiletto-like fingernail traced the air a fraction of an inch above Strigan's chest, following the line of one of the now-bloody sigils carved there.

'*We were summoned*,' the creature repeated.

Estevar's curiosity flared inside him – an almost overpowering urge to question these apparitions, to uncover who had brought them here and by what means, but this gambit could carry him only so far. Brother Agneta was staring at him, and in her dubious expression he saw that she both understood what he was attempting and had little confidence in its success.

Turning his attention back to the demons who could – at any moment and with barely any effort – disprove all his blustering by tearing him to pieces and devouring him at their leisure, Estevar Borros laughed. He laughed long and hard, then stepped even closer to clap a hand down on one of the creatures' shoulders. The skin felt slick and scaly, like that of a fish, yet there was some far more discomfiting sensation in that touch: a kind of . . . *itch* settled on his palm, like the first sting of acid before it burns the flesh away for ever. With his fingertips, he felt something else as well: subtle variations in the texture of the creature's skin forming patterns of curved lines. He'd missed them before because the markings were as pale as the skin underneath, but these were, unmistakeably, the same sigils as those Strigan had tattooed on his own body.

Another clue, he thought, *insufficient to determine the esoteric workings of this ritual and little use in determining the culprit behind it all. Still, the discovery might be turned to good use.*

'The one who summoned you has tricked you,' he told the creatures with the assuredness of a verdict. 'Nothing awaits you in this place but your own doom. You were deceived into believing the gods who ruled this place are no more, but look!' He pointed to the storm clouds drifting closer.

'Are your ears so dulled that you do not hear the rumblings of their displeasure? The gods of Tristia, birthed by a magic deeper and more potent than your own, arm themselves with lightning and thunder. Tarry here and they will strike you down.'

The creatures tilted their heads this way and that, as if trying to hear something far, far away, then repeated in their glottal murmurs, 'We . . . were . . . summoned.'

Good, he thought. *They are not mocking my assertion, which suggests they know no more about gods than I do, save that they fear them.*

'You were deceived,' he repeated. 'You allowed yourselves to be ensnared by one who had no right to command your service, and in so doing, have set yourselves in greater peril than you can fathom.'

'We . . .'

'We were . . .'

'Sum—'

'Enough!' Estevar roared. 'The evidence has been heard and it weighs against you. As magistrate of this trial, I am prepared to render my judgment.' He raised his fist high once more. 'Are the accused ready to hear the verdict?'

It was a risk, of course – what if these demonic beings politely declined to allow him to pass sentence? And yet all his instincts, those of a magistrate *and* those of a duellist, told him that something he was saying, something he'd chanced upon, was the key to their banishment.

The five creatures abandoned Strigan's unconscious form to surround Estevar. As one, they brought their claws to his neck, a ring of daggers barely a hair's breadth from his throat.

If there were any saints inclined to beg the gods to grant miracles to magistrates, one surely spoke up then, because a rumble of thunder emerged from the clouds overhead. The distended fingers of the demons twitched, and Estevar felt the faintest of scratches against his neck.

'We . . .'

'Await . . .'

'Verdict . . .'

Estevar forced himself to take in a breath and said, 'By the laws that bind *all* who tread upon this land, I judge you guilty of violating the sanctity of this abbey. You are trespassers. Unwelcome. Unsanctioned. Mercy is a gift granted only once to the ignorant, and so I give you this one chance: depart this place now, or by the authority vested in me will I rule that by lightning and fire will the foul flesh stretched over

164

your bones be immolated, and by the will of the gods whose voices you begin to hear, your spirits will be torn apart, the scraps of your being tossed into the sea to drown beneath the waves for ever.'

Estevar said no more. There was nothing else to say, after all. He had no more power to enforce his verdict than a butterfly's wings had to wear down a mountain. He stared into those eyes that were surely windows into hell, and saw hell staring back at him. He refused to flinch, even when the claws at the end of their fingertips quivered in anticipation of inscribing their evils on his flesh.

'Well?' he asked.

'We . . .'

The necklace of sharpened fingernails around his throat touched his skin, pressed, ever so gently at first. Estevar heard the click of Agneta's pistol and prayed her aim would be truer this time.

'. . . depart,' the creatures finished in unison.

Estevar might have breathed a sigh of relief then, but he heard one of the demons speak a final time – a whisper so quiet it might well have been a trick of the breeze.

'For now.'

That parting warning echoed in his thoughts. He hadn't even realised he'd closed his eyes until they opened of their own accord and he watched the creatures walking into the fog, fading away until at last he could see them no more. He stayed where he was, though, mostly because his legs would not respond even to his urging to let him collapse to the ground.

Agneta's footsteps preceded the unexpectedly gentle touch of her hand on his arm. 'Did you . . . did you know that would work?' the inquisitor asked.

It took him a moment to answer, mostly because he didn't want his teeth to chatter. At last he said, 'Of course I knew it would work! I'm a Greatcoat. Such daring gambits are second nature to us.'

But when he looked down at the blood-soaked, unconscious body of Strigan, saw the gleaming scarlet sigils carved by unnatural fingernails into his flesh, two incontrovertible deductions tore at his confidence. First, Sir Daven Colraig's warnings on behalf of the Margrave of Someil had proved to be more than mere hysteria: demons did walk the earth.

Monsters from the depths of some unimaginable hell had violated this sacred abbey. Only a brazen bluff, mixed with whatever superstitions beings such as them might believe, had forced them into this temporary retreat.

The second deduction?

The demons would be returning, and there was always a price for playing tricks on the Devil.

PART THE FIFTH

THE SIGILS
OF WARDING

The next sigils must be placed with great speed upon the skin of the arms and legs, lest those who come to devour the spirit take the body as well, and the entire ritual must begin again with a new sacrifice. What you seek is a pure vessel, stripped of every sin as well as of any will of its own. Only then can the great work truly begin . . .

CHAPTER 25

THE INFIRMARY

'We were summoned . . .'

Those words haunted Estevar as he carried the blood-soaked and unconscious Strigan from the ruins of the statuary through the cloister's endless colonnades, past the cathedral-like chapter house and finally into a vast building of dressed stone which Brother Agneta claimed was the infirmary.

'It's more of a hospital for the entire island,' the inquisitor informed him, leading the way while Estevar struggled beneath the Wolf-King's weight – a more slender figure than himself, to be sure, but solidly built of lean muscle and bone, and a greater burden than his own injuries could bear. There was so much blood drenching the man's naked skin, it was like holding on to a hundred and sixty-pound eel. Worse, every stuttering breath was a warning that it might be the lapsed monk's last.

'Not far now,' Agneta promised, turning down an unlit passageway where every shifting shadow set Estevar's frayed nerves on edge. 'We've had to conserve lantern oil,' she explained. 'Most of the supplies and food are in the Sustenacum Tower and we've yet to wrest that one from those delusional Trumpeters. I swear, they've renamed the Vigilance Tower three times in the past week, always for some new god they insist is about to arise from the ruins of the statuary like a babe ejected from the womb.'

'You don't place much stock in the prospect of a new divine pantheon for Tristia?' Estevar stopped, leaning against the arched wooden frame supporting the passageway in the hope of catching his breath. The darkness was so absolute that he couldn't make out his guide properly and was left to imagine the pistol that was surely still in her right hand, reloaded with powder and lead ball, the wheel spring wound and ready to fire. Were they to be allies now that demons stalked the abbey grounds? Or was the old inquisitor merely using him as a packhorse to get Strigan – the only person who might be able to shed light on how such monstrous creatures were made to manifest in this once holy sanctuary – to the safety of the infirmary before she put an end to the meddling magistrate once and for all?

'I am unconcerned either way,' she said, gesturing for him to get a move on before continuing, 'Should the old gods return, or new ones take their place, I will happily serve them – with *humility*. What I *won't* do is claim to know their will and raise up an army to rain chaos down on a nation already weakened from the last war.'

Estevar grunted, his whole body aching from the strain and soaked in sweat, not only from his most recent exertions but from the way his heart wouldn't stop pounding in his chest. Had he truly faced down infernal monstrosities using the sort of bluff he more commonly employed against ignorant venal noblemen and tavern drunks looking for a fight?

'I take it you disapprove of Mother Leogado's militant appetites?' he asked between gasping breaths.

'Just because a Cogneri must occasionally act with decisive force to ensure the spiritual laws of this country remain intact, that does not mean I approve of monks being turned into soldiers under the boot heel of a despot.'

Estevar wouldn't have judged the woman he'd met in the Vigilance Tower to be a tyrant, would-be or otherwise. Right or wrong, her belief that Isola Sombra was under threat of invasion by the Margrave of Someil and his knights would have appeared genuine – even sensible – were it not for the events of an hour ago and the far more unsettling conquerors who'd clearly set their sights on this abbey.

'Why are you laughing?' Agneta demanded from the darkness ahead.

'Nothing,' he said. 'Gallows humour is an unavoidable pastime for a magistrate.'

Now he heard her chuckling in the darkness ahead. 'Something we have in common, then. Come, it's this way.'

He followed the sound of her voice and at the next corner, saw a sliver of light leaking out beneath a door a few paces away to their left. Agneta took a key from inside her robes, opened the lock and ushered him into a massive room. Beyond a dozen beds arranged in two rows were three large wooden tables, each the length of a man. The shelves beneath each one were filled with wax-stoppered bottles, rolls of linen bandages and surgical instruments. *The inquisitor might not approve of the soldierly mentality of Mother Leogado's Trumpeters,* thought Estevar, *but this abbey could very easily serve as a military fortress.*

'Bring him here,' Agneta ordered, removing the brass oil lantern by the door to hang it from a hook attached to a six-foot-tall wooden pole mounted to the corner of one of the three tables.

The moment he'd laid down the shivering, unconscious monk, Estevar slumped against the table himself. It was all he could do to keep from collapsing to the floor.

'There's a chair behind you,' Agneta informed him as she set about collecting several bottles and metal instruments from one of the shelves beneath the table. 'If you pass out on the floor, that's where you'll stay, for I'll not torment my own back trying to lift you.'

Too weary to trade barbs with the irascible inquisitor, Estevar stumbled to the chair, flopped down clumsily into it and had to readjust himself to keep one of the arms from pressing against his ribs. Almost immediately, he had to fight to keep his eyes from closing, a fight he was keen not to lose.

'It wasn't my intention to kill you,' Agneta said matter-of-factly, pouring what looked like silvery milk over Strigan's chest and wiping away the diluted blood to reveal the damage caused by the demon's claws.

Those symbols, Estevar thought, seeing the intricate sigils clearly for the first time. *I must make a record of them.* He reached for the stylus and notebook he kept handy in his top pocket for capturing such details, only to feel the sweat-soaked wool of his borrowed shirt. *Focus, you fool,* he warned himself. *Your coat lies drowned at the bottom of the sea, and your own situation is not much better.*

Wanting to hide his exhaustion as best he could, he forced himself to his feet and began searching the shelves around the room for writing implements.

'Had I wanted you dead,' Agneta went on chattily, 'you would already be in the ground.'

For once, fortune favoured him. He found some scraps of paper sitting beside a pot of ink and a small basket of ready-sharpened quills. Now armed, he decided not to allow Agneta's verbal apologia to continue unchallenged.

'You struck my wound with your fist,' he reminded her, 'split open my stitches and left me to bleed out next to Abbot Venia's corpse.'

The nonchalance of the inquisitor's shrug was maddening. 'Those stitches needed to come out one way or another,' she said, holding up as if evidence a glass bottle filled with a thick amber liquid before pouring liberal quantities over Strigan's wounds. 'I would have returned with another pair of hands to help carry you, had you not disappeared before I got there.'

'Hmm?' Estevar asked, unable to suppress a yarn. One of the beds nearby was calling to him. He would have resisted, but its position opposite the table where Strigan was lying would make an excellent vantage point from which to make a study of the sigils carved into the monk's skin.

'I said, you were too damned fat for me to carry myself, and it turned out, you had other allies lurking inside the abbey already, so my ministrations weren't needed after all.'

Casting an eye over the canvas of Strigan's flesh, Estevar was struck by the meticulous precision with which the demons had followed the inked lines of the tattoos. When he'd seen those same markings on the drawing delivered by Sir Daven, the convoluted sequence had struck him as nonsense, just an unrelated hodgepodge of pseudo-esoteric symbolism. Why, then, did some of the runes look so familiar?

So much for your vaunted memory, he chided himself. *A decade spent studying every occult text in Tristia and you can't recall where these symbols appear?*

'Remarkable,' Agneta said, her awestruck voice jolting Estevar from his ruminations. She was bent over Strigan, peering through a magnifying-glass.

172

'What do you see?' Estevar asked, trying and failing to rise to his feet and join her. His body had apparently determined that his conscious mind could no longer be trusted to make decisions for it.

'The incisions,' Agneta replied, moving her glass to another of the wounds. 'They're so precise – so perfect – they would put a master sculptor to shame. Had the tips of the creatures' nails not been so sharp, the skin would be in ribbons, but see here, the way the flesh holds together. The scars left behind will look almost beautiful, in a way.'

'*Beautiful?*'

She shot him a scathing glance, as if he'd tried to catch her in a lie. 'Evil things can still be beautiful, even transcendent.' Absently, she traced the air above one of the wounds. 'This one reminds me of the old illuminated manuscripts in the *Canon Dei*.'

'No!' Estevar said, suddenly on his feet as the excitement brought on by Agneta's tiny mistake banished his weariness. He quickly set a piece of paper on his abandoned bed, balanced the pot of ink precariously next to it and picked up one of the quills.

'What's got you flapping about like a chicken?'

'Not the *Canon Dei*,' Estevar replied, dipping the quill, 'for that text comprises the *accepted* writings of earlier Tristian theologians.'

'*Accepted?*' she repeated. From the tone of her voice, she had evidently found some cause for insult in his use of the term.

Estevar began scrawling names of various obsolete religious texts, along with the titles of even more obscure theological tracts banned from inclusion in the official *Canon Dei*. When he couldn't think of any more, he began crossing out those which he knew had no mention of anything occult in nature. After whittling down the list, he underlined the ones known as *sacrificia*, those religious rituals excluded because of their use of human beings in the rites.

'Not that one,' Agneta said, coming to loom over his shoulder. 'The *Sacrificia Humilita* wasn't actually a ritual – it was more of a flowery homily about the ecstasy of servitude. It was adapted into a less sexualised version in the *Canon Dei*.'

She was right. He struck that one too.

'Get rid of that one as well,' she said, pointing to his barely legible reference to the *Sacrificia Daemolo*.

'Why?' Estevar asked, suddenly suspicious. In archaic Tristian, daemolo could mean either 'misfortune' or 'diabolical'. Moreover, he had a faint recollection that it contained a number of ornate sigils that might be related to the ones on Strigan's skin.

'Because, as any Cogneri would tell you, the *Daemolo* was a fake,' Agneta replied. Snorting with laughter, she added, 'If you remove every second word from the text, the whole thing becomes a rather unsavoury condemnation of the clergy.'

'What of the accompanying sigils?' Estevar asked.

The old inquisitor snatched the quill from his hand, found a tiny blank section and drew a pair of elaborate sigils, each contained within a half-circle. The first looked like a sun rising over the horizon with a seated female figure depicted inside, arms spread as if rejoicing in the coming of the day, mouth open in song. The second half circle Agneta had drawn upside down, like a bowl, save that it clearly represented a half-moon and inside was the figure of a man on a bed, eyes closed in happiness at the end of his working day. After handing Estevar the quill back, she folded the page carefully so that the two half-circles combined.

'Still think the *Daemolo* might contain a dastardly ritual to summon demons?' she asked.

Tired as he was, and urgent though his need was to figure out which text he was looking for, he laughed at what was clearly an image of a man and woman coupling, he, smugly self-satisfied at his performance, she, crying out in ecstasy.

'Heretics had better senses of humour back then,' Agneta observed.

Estevar retrieved the paper and laid it alongside the first two pages, studying the eight remaining texts. Any of those banned *sacrificia* might be the source of the sigils inscribed onto Strigan's skin.

The Sacrificia Expiadis, the Absolvio, the Purgadis, the Liebernum, the Mortadis, the Solno, the Vividum, the Penito: ponderous theological ramblings, one and all. How am I to remember which one contained the markings?

'Which of these tracts are to be found in the abbey libraries?' he asked Agneta.

'None of them.'

'Are you certain?'

'I'm an inquisitor, you oaf. Do you really suppose I'd allow heretical treatises banned by canon law inside the holiest site in the entire country?'

You might not, Estevar thought, *but the abbot was curious about the origins of faith, not only its tenets.* In fact, he was now all but certain that it was during his last visit to Isola Sombra that he'd seen the sigils which now bedevilled him – and it was Venia who'd been rifling through the clutter of crumbling parchment scrolls on his desk at the time, searching for one meant to bolster his argument about the supremacy of religion over the state!

Too bad you left me with no clue as to which one that was, you proselytising zealot! Instead, you tricked me here with that silly letter complaining about the factions in your abbey, ending with that absurd demand that I somehow 'purge the divisions' between your brethren!

And there it was.

Purge the divisions.

'You're wrong,' Estevar told Brother Agneta. 'Some heretical texts have escaped the ignorant fires of your inquisitor's torch.' He tapped a finger on the third scrawled title. 'Abbot Venia kept a copy of the *Sacrificia Purgadis* here in the abbey.'

'Impossible,' the Cogneri murmured.

Estevar guessed it was her faith in the abbot which was being challenged, not his ability to hide an old text from her.

'The *Purgadis* requires a human sacrifice. Venia would never—'

'He might,' Estevar said gently, placing a hand on her arm. She felt suddenly frailer to him, somehow. 'If he was convinced that new gods were coming to Isola Sombra, forged from the esoteric ores beneath its rocky ground and shaped by the faith of those who tread upon it . . .'

Finally, the image which had been lurking at the back of his mind became clear, though he'd glanced at the parchment for only a few seconds before Venia had rolled it back up and hidden it away. The *Purgadis* described a series of rituals which purported to map upon the flesh of one sinner the spiritual misdeeds of an entire village. The sinner would then be 'given over to the darkness', whereupon their spirit would be devoured – and the sins of their community purged.

'What does it mean?' Brother Agneta asked, the first time she'd shown any sign of valuing Estevar's opinion. 'The *Purgadis* was more folk superstition than religious ceremony – meant to bring the loving gaze of the gods back to a place where crops wouldn't grow or children failed to thrive. How could it bring *actual* demons to life?'

He closed the ink pot, replaced the quills in the basket and stacked his three pages, then placed the lot on the floor next to his bed. 'That, I do not yet know.'

'Then why are you smiling like an idiot?'

Estevar sat back heavily on the bed. 'Because now I have a piece of the puzzle, and from that one piece, a motive for whoever instigated this foul conjuration. Someone is attempting to purify Isola Sombra to protect the world from gods arising out of the madness of warring monks who cannot agree on who those gods should be.'

A dozen more questions were now dancing through his addled brain. Was the perpetrator of this crime the same individual or group who murdered Abbot Venia? Had they condemned Strigan as punishment for his own experiments into the occult, or were they perhaps the ones who'd tricked him into engaging in such efforts in the first place? Did the lightning strikes which destroyed the statues of the gods incite them to set off on this dark path, or was that part of a plan begun long before the fracturing of the abbey's brethren?

The heady, almost drunken sensation filling Estevar made him wonder for a moment if he'd somehow been drugged – but no, he knew this feeling. This was the intoxication of discovering previously hidden connections between contrary facts, of clues becoming deductions which would, in turn, become the evidence with which he would conduct his trial against those who had brought murder and desecration to this holy place.

'Will Strigan live?' he asked. He felt he needed to stay in the infirmary, to be the first to speak to the Wolf-King, should he awaken.

'I can't be sure,' Agneta replied. She returned to her patient's bed and picked up a needle and thread she'd cleaned with her viscous amber fluid. 'The boy has lost a lot of blood, but the wounds themselves aren't so deep. The shock and trauma are what may kill him now. Better that you be here when he wakes.'

'Why?' Estevar asked, distrustful of the fact that something he'd assumed would require skilful negotiation was now being offered to him so freely.

She pinched together the skin on either side of an incision and slid the needle through. 'He called out your name when he saw you coming from the Vigilance Tower. It was you he begged for help. Perhaps your presence will calm him, maybe even help his recovery.'

She added another stitch, and then a third, precise and neat, working along the line of the wound.

Her expertise and patience were relaxing. Estevar had always found the methodical application of skill to be soothing, almost hypnotic. He carefully folded his hastily scrawled diagrams of Strigan's markings and placed them in his pocket before allowing himself to lie back on the bed.

'I must warn you, Madam,' he mumbled, 'I have a friend in this abbey who will be searching for me. She may not seem like much of a threat to an inquisitor on first meeting, but should you attempt to harm me, you will find in her a most formidable opponent.'

'Oh, I wouldn't count on Leogado venturing out of the Vigilance Tower to rescue you, Eminence,' Agneta said. 'She hasn't left that crow's nest of hers in weeks, and this part of the abbey is traditionalist territory.'

Estevar was so unduly pleased by her poor guess that he said more than he ought. 'I speak not of Mother Leogado, but of my assistant in the enquiry into Abbot Venia's murder.'

Agneta paused in her needlework. 'I saw no one with you when you arrived at the abbey, and the causeway has been impassable since.'

'Caeda,' Estevar said, his head sinking deeper into the pillow, his eyelids growing heavy. 'My piccolo.'

Though his eyes had closed and consciousness was giving way to exhaustion put off too long, part of him wondered why Agneta hadn't yet resumed her ministrations. She said something to him, but the words sounded far away now, and he couldn't ask her to repeat them because by then he was all but asleep. If asked to testify, however, he would have sworn the inquisitor had said, 'Caeda Branwen died two weeks ago. Abbot Venia killed her.'

CHAPTER 26

THE WOLF'S SCARS

The infirmary had no windows, leaving Estevar without the means to distinguish day from night. He awoke in darkness, unsure whether the lantern had run out of oil or someone had stolen it. He could hear uneasy breathing; apart from his own, he thought at first there might be two others. When he listened more carefully, it turned out to be just Strigan's restless wheezing.

When Estevar tried to rise, wanting to find what had become of Brother Agneta, he quickly fell back down. He wasn't shackled to the bed – no ropes or chains tugged at him – only a litany of aches old and new, warning him of dire consequences should he venture forth into the pitch-black depths of the infirmary.

The duelling wound was the worst, emanating heat across his abdomen, whispering of fever and renewed infection. When he prodded gingerly beneath the bandage with his fingertips, he discovered that Caeda's stitches were gone, replaced by new ones, presumably Brother Agneta's. He wasn't surprised – he'd felt them tear during his encounter with the demons – but how had the pain of a needle and thread passing back and forth through his inflamed flesh not awakened him?

Did she drug me? It would have been easy enough to slip me something after I fell asleep.

He set the questions aside for now, while his fingers traced the lines of other new lacerations on his shoulders and forearms, all courtesy of demonic claws. Several of these sported stitches too, and were itching as if wasps had taken up residence all over his body.

The case, he reminded himself. *Mere irritations of the flesh cannot be allowed to impede the investigation – especially when Brother Agneta's absence provides an opportunity to question the witness.*

Presuming, of course, that Estevar could convince his limbs to get him moving, and that the traumatised monk could be roused.

Determination was something Estevar Borros understood. With a groan from somewhere deep in his belly, he forced himself to a seated position on the bed. He was still wearing his borrowed trousers and boots, but his tattered shirt, now much the worse for wear, was on the floor. The effort of bending over to find it strained his resolve, though not nearly as much as the dizziness that washed over him when he rose to his feet.

How long can I keep fighting my own body's demands for rest and proper medical care? he wondered, shivering. *Am I to die here on this accursed island before I can bring Venia's murderer to justice and his abbey back to sanity?*

Slowly, tentatively, he set forth into the dark room, following the sounds of Strigan's breathing – and in only ten steps, he found himself at the surgical table where he'd deposited the bleeding body. Now that he was on his feet, Estevar felt sure several hours had passed since then.

So Agneta hasn't been able to find someone to help move her patient to one of the beds. Or maybe she no longer cares whether he survives.

He could not yet make sense of the inquisitor's behaviour. For all she'd displayed an ease with violence, even brutality, he sensed in her a moral code as strong as his own, if perhaps twisted to a purpose he couldn't fathom.

A quickening of the young monk's breathing told Estevar he was waking.

'It's all right,' he said, leaning against the edge of the table for support. 'You are in the abbey infirmary.'

'I thought . . .' Strigan sounded hesitant, confused and on the edge of tears. 'The wood beneath me . . . I thought I'd woken inside a coffin.'

Hearing the hoarse voice, Estevar asked, 'Would you like some water?'

'Please.'

It took a while to find the jug of fresh water Agneta had used earlier. Cursing the impenetrable darkness, Estevar carefully balanced the vessel on the table, leaning it against his own belly for safety. 'I must touch your face to find your lips,' he warned Strigan. 'I will try to pour the water slowly, but we may be in for a drenching, you and I.'

The endeavour required several attempts, and more than once Estevar feared he was drowning his patient, but some time later, the monk's hand rested on his arm. 'Thank you,' Strigan murmured. 'I think I'd like to sleep now.'

Estevar set the jug back down on a shelf beneath the table. 'There are questions I must ask you first. Those demons will surely return, and the horrors inflicted on you could be performed on others.' He reached out a tentative forefinger, found one of the sigils carved into Strigan's chest. 'Who inscribed the *Sacrificia Purgadis* upon you?'

'Sleep,' Strigan repeated, plaintively.

'The symbols – who first painted them on your skin?'

'No one. It was me. Wanted the power ... wanted to ... but the demons!' He squeezed Estevar's arm tighter, his own nails digging through the loose fabric of the linen shirt. 'Don't let them have me again – don't leave me here in the dark!'

'I won't, but you must answer me. How did you know about those specific symbols? You don't strike me as a scholar, so who—?'

'Venia,' Strigan muttered, bitterness rising in his voice like bile. 'Venia tricked me. Showed me his scribblings, taught me the patterns to draw on my skin, the words, the rituals ... He said they would give me powers to protect the abbey, that I was the bravest of the brethren. I was to be "the wolf who guards the sheep". Why did he lie to me?'

Those words fell upon Estevar like an icy cloak. Why would so devout an abbot resort to such cruel deception? And yet ... hadn't their long correspondence and occasional visits begun when Venia had written to Estevar seeking his opinion on the authenticity of certain mystical texts in the abbey's library? What if these ongoing, apparently innocent enquiries had been carefully crafted to validate some of the occult underpinnings of the *Purgadis* ritual without revealing his intentions?

'Did Venia show the symbols to your followers as well?' he asked.

Strigan tilted his head slowly to the left, then the right, like a dreaming child. 'Trumpeters were taking over. Leogado ... damn her. Knew how to recruit ... inspire. Someone had to stand against her ... someone *had to . . .* I drew the symbols on those who'd follow my leadership, promised them . . . promised . . .'

'Power,' Estevar finished for him.

The *Sacrificia Purgadis* was meant for purification, for the transmutation of sin – something it had clearly failed to achieve in this instance. But why would the result of that failure be the conjuration of demonic beings? And at that time? Why had they not appeared when the symbols had first been inscribed, or anytime thereafter?

The storm, Estevar thought. *Leogado was right: the magic is awakened when the storms envelop the island and the lightning strikes the ores beneath its surface.*

He traced the lines of one of the symbols on the self-styled 'Sorcerer Sovereign's' chest. *With the unity of the storm and the stone, faith is transmuted to power.*

Strigan's breathing was slowing, becoming more regular. He was starting to fall back asleep, leaving Estevar with questions still to be answered.

'*Purely for academic purposes,*' Venia had insisted years ago when Estevar had jokingly pointed out that for a religious zealot who renounced violence and heresy, he owned a goodly number of swords and supernatural texts. But had those tools of violence and sorcery, amassed over decades, been intended solely for preservation and study, as the abbot had always insisted?

What if he wasn't the man I believed him to be? What if the quiet, modest Abbot Venia hid his darker inclinations from all of us?

Estevar prodded the slumbering patient as gently as he could. 'Strigan, why does Brother Agneta claim that Caeda is dead? Why does she believe the abbot killed her?'

A sleepy smile came over the young monk's face. 'Caeda, poor Caeda. I always wanted to fu—'

'Yes, yes – so you made clear several times when the two of us came to the Venerance Tower. But why does Agneta believe her to be dead?'

'Alone . . .' Strigan muttered.

'What?'

But there was no answer. Estevar shook the monk more vigorously. 'Answer me, damn you! Your foolishness, engineered no doubt by someone with a greater and even more malicious nature than your own, has brought hell itself to this abbey. I cannot protect any of you if I do not understand what's going on!'

'Alone,' Strigan repeated as if already lost in a dream. 'One fat, loud-mouthed magistrate walks into my tower with his donkey and tricks me with some nonsense about a "Cressi Manoeuvre" I'd never heard of. Tricked me just like Abbot Ven—'

'Forget the damned Cressi Manoeuvre,' Estevar shouted, shaking him again. 'You *spoke* to Caeda – you spouted your despicable lechery right in front of her!'

Strigan was weeping now in abject misery, able to abide the torment of wakefulness no longer. 'You were alone – please, I'm so tired. Can't you let me . . . ?' The wounded monk's words tailed off into snores.

How was any of this possible? Strigan and his followers had been drinking and drugging themselves into a stupor for days; were they all suffering from similar delusions? He badly wanted to beat Strigan into answering him, but the damned monk's breathing had fallen into a mad-deningly slow and steady rhythm, so unlike his own exhalations, which were becoming ever more agitated. Almost as if Estevar weren't alo—

'Who's there?' he called out, certain this time that he had heard the breathing of a third person. 'Brother Agneta?'

No answer came, only that soft, gentle movement of air, almost like a breeze through an open window – but there were no windows in the infirmary.

He cursed himself for having forgotten to search for his rapier, for he was now unarmed and helpless. 'I warn you,' he called out to the intruder as he knelt down and began fumbling through the shelves beneath the table in search of something sharp. 'If it's my life you seek, others have tried and failed to take it before. Shall I send you to meet them so that you may learn how they fared in the exchange?'

Bluster, he thought, unable to find anything suitable as a weapon. *In the end, all I have left is bluster.*

'Don't be silly, my Cantor,' the intruder said, her voice an eerie melody against the drumbeat of Estevar's heart. 'Won't you need your Piccolo to help you compose the song of justice that will for ever be sung about Isola Sombra?'

CHAPTER 27

PATIENT SECRETS

'Caeda?' Estevar peered into the darkness of the infirmary, no longer merely blinded but smothered beneath its numbing, all-consuming shroud. No answer came from the young woman who'd been both his ally and his deceiver. In fact, he could hear nothing at all in the vast room. So fixated was he on Caeda's presence – and the many dangers she might represent – that he imagined himself trapped inside a coffin, just as Strigan had when he'd wakened for those brief minutes before drifting back into restless slumber. Estevar was suddenly grateful for the Wolf-King's proximity, the unsteady breathing proving the monk was still alive. Estevar was equally sure that his own heart was thumping as precariously within his chest, even if he couldn't hear it right now.

'Caeda?' he asked again, and was again met with silence.

She is no spectre, he told himself. *You stood next to her, listened to her voice, felt her touch, even held the scent of her hair in your nostrils.*

That fragrance came back to him now: fresh, salty, with a hint of brine conjuring images of the sea the morning after a storm. Witnesses claiming to have encountered ghosts spoke of odours lingering from the place where they'd died. Among his own handful of encounters with genuine apparitions, some had evidenced such traits, others not. Like the living, the dead were disturbingly eclectic in their natures.

He was about to call out Caeda's name again when she spoke at last.

'Piccolo,' she said. 'Call me Piccolo.'

Estevar held on to the sound of that brief command. One of the few consistencies he'd found when conversing with apparitions was a strange narrowness in their inflections, as if the dead could express only a single sentiment. Oh, they might be able to shade it a touch here or there: rage might be tamped down to mere irritation, despair diminished to anxious curiosity, but always the voices betrayed a shallowness in their underlying tonality.

Caeda's voice was different. Even those four words had carried a jumble of emotions: annoyance at the way Estevar was behaving as if she might present some danger to him, yet also fearful that he no longer saw her as his partner in this investigation. She'd tried to sound smugly mischievous because he couldn't see her, but something else lurked just under the surface of her words, something he'd never heard in the voice of a ghost.

Shame.

'What have you done, Caeda?'

'Nothing!' she shouted, and he would have sworn he felt her breath against the braided whiskers of his beard. 'That is . . . there are things about me which I haven't told you, but I *haven't* lied to you. I would *never* lie to you.'

'A lie of omission is still a lie.'

'Not if there was no intention to mislead, and I haven't misled you, Estevar. I swear it.'

A difficult oath to credit, he thought, but she hadn't finished.

'Interrogate me,' she demanded. 'Ask me anything you want. That terribly clever mind of yours will tell you if I'm lying, won't it?'

'It's not that simp—'

'Ask me,' she insisted. 'If you decide I'm lying, I'll leave here and you'll never have to see me again. You'll miss me, though, and it'll be your own fault because you should've trusted that your piccolo would never lie to her cantor.'

Why is she speaking this way? he wondered. *Almost like a child, rather than a woman grown?* His hands gripped the edge of the table, wanting to feel the solidity of the wood and reassure himself that he was indeed awake and not under the influence of some raging fever-dream.

'*Ask me anything you wish*,' she'd challenged him. Very well then, that suited him perfectly. Living witnesses were neither entirely trustworthy nor inherently deceptive, and this, he felt sure, was equally true of the dead. So, he would proceed as with any other interrogation.

'Why did you not bring a lantern with you?' he asked.

She hesitated, then replied peevishly, 'Why would you begin with something so trivial? It's not as if—'

'What did I tell you yesterday as we walked through the cloister?'

'"A skilled investigator plays with the rhythm of the interrogation." Is that what you're doing? *Playing* with me?'

'I asked why you hadn't brought a lantern. It's not a difficult question to answer.'

The padding of bare feet echoed across the stone floor: soft, light, but present. Estevar found the sound unexpectedly reassuring.

'I told you before, I was born in this abbey. I know every inch of it. Had I bothered with a lantern, I might have been spotted by one of the Bone-Rattlers scurrying around the halls – or worse, that foul inquisitor might have seen me.'

'*That foul inquisitor.*' She had offered him an opening, which meant she would be entirely too prepared for the question that would follow. *My song, Piccolo. My rhythm.*

'Where is Imperious?' he asked.

Her tone made it clear she took insult at Estevar's implied concern. 'Your mule is fine. He's in the stable I told you about, making himself fat on hay and the carrots Malezias and I found for him. He let me brush him a while. *He* likes me.'

There, Estevar thought. *There's my true opening.*

'Stop playing the petulant child,' he snapped. 'Peevish complaints make poor arguments for a grown woman. You demean yourself and me in the same breath.'

He waited, aware that he'd employed a dangerous tactic: those few spirits he'd dealt with in the past had been easily spooked, some reacting like cornered animals when challenged unexpectedly, responding with whatever means of violence were available to them. However, if he were to give Caeda the benefit of the doubt, treat her as a person and *not*, in fact, like some creature born of ill design, he had to take that risk.

Her footsteps slowed. 'I'm sorry,' she said at last. 'Abbot Venia always treated me like a silly child. Sometimes I found it useful to act that way to get favours from him.'

Estevar longed to see her face, to search her expressions for more revealing details. Alas, he would have to rely on his ears as his sole instrument of detection. 'Tell me about those favours,' he said. 'What did Abbot Venia do for you?'

The question felt like a betrayal; Venia had been the victim of a brutal, unconscionable murder, but Estevar could no longer be sure he knew what kind of man the abbot had been in life.

'There were things I wanted to learn,' Caeda replied. 'About religion and mysticism, about the gods and saints. I wanted to study monasticism.' There was a yearning in her voice now. 'It seems such a beautiful way to go through life, don't you think? Spending your days in quiet contemplation, your hands ever reaching towards the divine.'

'Why not become a monk yourself, then? There are many women among the brethren of Isola Sombra.'

'The others would never allow it. That's what the abbot said, anyway. He always told me I was meant for other things.'

'What "other things"?'

She gave no reply, and without the sound of her footsteps, he couldn't even be sure she was still in the room. He closed his mouth and inhaled deeply through his nostril, catching the odours emanating from the medicine on the shelves; the dried sweat covering both him and the sleeping Strigan; the cloying stench of urine – one or both of them had pissed themselves, probably during the demonic encounter.

Beneath those mundane scents, however, remained the fragrance of sea air.

'Caeda, you must answer me. Why would the monks refuse you admission into their order?'

'They disliked me. Most ignored me, the rest, like that pig Strigan, would have used me as their plaything given half a chance.'

Estevar knew he was venturing into dangerous territory now. With all interrogations, the questions were like a set of cards in your hand. The trick was playing each one at the right moment. *This*, he prayed, was the right moment. 'But Venia cared for you? Loved you, perhaps?'

'I thought so.'

'What changed?'

'Three weeks ago he invited me to the monastery. He was very formal about it, leaving a note at my cottage. I felt like a proper lady then – no, not a lady, a *scholar*. I thought . . . I *hoped* he was going to offer me a permanent position as a lay monk and allow me to study alongside him.'

Alongside him. Her tone had shifted on those last two words, sweet wistfulness turning sour.

'What happened then?'

'He brought me here, to the infirmary. He had these leather straps, like reins, and before I understood what was happening, he'd tied me to that same table where Strigan's sleeping. He didn't let me sleep, though.' She began to rush through her account, her words tumbling over one another with the desperation of one who doesn't want to recount the events because doing so means reliving them. 'I tried to reason with him – I begged him to release me, but he refused. It was like . . . I wasn't a person to him any more, just a thing . . . a . . .'

Estevar never liked to complete the sentences of a witness; doing so risked twisting their memories to match his speculations. But there was an ache in Caeda's voice that could only be soothed by the word she was struggling to find.

'A sacrifice,' he finished for her.

'Yes . . . yes, that's what I was to him – not a friend, not a fellow human being, but a frightened animal to be sacrificed as quickly as possible to minimise its suffering.'

The first step of any murder, Estevar had sensed when dealing with those accused of such heinous crimes, *is to deny the victim's humanity.*

'He stripped off my clothes,' Caeda went on, shame turning to anger. 'He started inscribing all those symbols on my body.'

'Like those on Strigan and his hounds?'

'No, not exactly.'

Hearing her approaching the table, he stepped back, not wanting to spook her.

CRUCIBLE OF CHAOS

'Some were almost the same,' she said. 'I don't remember exactly because they must have washed off in the—' She stopped herself, then resumed quickly, 'The abbot kept me here for days. He never spoke to me, and when I pleaded with him to let me go, he acted like he couldn't hear me. He wouldn't even give me water to drink! All he did was keep drawing those symbols all over my body, while I wept and screamed and threatened him with every punishment I could imagine.'

'How did it end?' Estevar asked.

She was quiet for a long time before answering, 'I don't remember how long he kept me tied up, but one morning, when I was too tired and weak to fight back, even to beg for mercy one more time, he untied my bonds.' A dangerous edge came to her voice. 'Do you want to know what your noble friend Venia did with me then? What the man whose killer you *keep* risking your life – and Imperious' life – to bring to justice did to *me*?'

'Yes,' Estevar answered. 'I want to know.'

Her voice was a scream carried on a wave across an ocean, cresting louder and louder until at last it crashed on the shore. 'He carried me up to the clifftop and hurled me into the sea!'

Estevar clamped his hands over his ears. She couldn't have been as loud as he'd imagined, else Strigan would surely have awakened, but her words echoed over and over in his mind. How could Venia have committed such a heinous crime? And why? To sanctify his abbey from the sins of his own monks? Had he sought to protect them from their own transgressions by first inscribing them on the flesh of an outsider – someone he didn't deem as worthy as his own flock?

'There is a final question I must put to you,' Estevar said quietly. 'You will not want to answer, but our bargain demands your response.'

'Maybe you don't have to ask,' she countered. 'Maybe you just care more about the truth than you do about those forced to live with the consequences.'

Estevar ignored the deflection. 'Did Abbot Venia end your life?'

'He certainly tried.'

'Trying is not the same as succeeding. You know the secret cannot be kept much longer. Why do you persist in hiding it from me?'

188

'Don't,' she warned him. 'Don't make me say it.'

'I'm sorry, but I must. Caeda . . . Piccolo, are you a gh—?'

'Never ask me that!' she screamed, her fury and despair so overwhelming that Estevar felt as if he were back in the water by the causeway, drowning beneath her sorrow. Reflexively, his hand reached for the rapier that was no longer at his side.

'Please,' Caeda said, calmer now, but no less insistent. 'You must never ask me that, Estevar. Never, never, never.'

She had given him plenty of chances to heed her warning, but her secret presented too great a peril, and ignorance was a luxury he could no longer afford.

'Why?' he asked.

'Because you'll ruin everything. I don't *want* to be dead, Estevar. I don't want you to prove to me that I'm some stupid girl who trusted one man too many and ended up dying of thirst or from drowning or both. Can't we . . . ?'

Now it was her turn to leave the question unasked. She wept instead.

'Can't we *what*, Piccolo?' Estevar asked, and repeated the question when she refused to answer.

'Can't we go back to the way things were?' she blurted out at last. 'You can be the brilliant investigator with me, your clever assistant, ever at your side as the two of us delve deeper and deeper into an unsolvable case?'

No one, least of all a young woman of such wondrous vitality, should have to beg for the pretence of a life. And yet, there are some gifts that cannot be given, no matter how well deserved.

'What I do isn't a game, Caeda. I came to this island to uncover who murdered Abbot Venia.'

'Why? What difference does it make? Venia won't be any less dead.'

'But his killer would go free.'

There was another pause, then the sound of her footsteps – not towards him this time, but pacing around the infirmary as she'd done in the bedroom atop the Vigilance Tower. 'What if I told you, my Cantor, that finding the murderer would make no difference to the world? That the person who killed Venia would never harm another?'

The question was so familiar that Estevar almost smiled. How many times had he been asked this by a mother pleading for her son, a husband begging on behalf of his wife? *'It was an accident, Eminence, a tragedy, a singular crime of passion— No, madness! Yes, that's it, madness! But the madness is gone now, and all will be well. Can't you leave it alone, just this one time? Depart this place without bringing further strife to those of us who must remain?'*

Estevar answered the way he had all those before her. 'Justice isn't recompense for the dead, Caeda. It's not retribution against the perpe- trator. It is an ... act of faith: a belief that the truth matters, and that the fairness of a society – as much of it as we can shape together from the poor clay of our natures – matters to all of us. I have been to cities, towns and villages where the laws have failed their citizens. Those who dwell in such places lose their trust in their own neighbours. They become cold, cruel, feral. A Greatcoat does not enforce the law for the sake of the dead, Caeda, but because when the law fails us, the spirits of the living are made fragile by its absence.'

A pretty speech, prettily spoken, he thought, *and no more convincing now than at any other times.* He half expected Caeda to laugh at him. Saints knew, others had before.

'What if ... what if I promised you that I *can* help you find Venia's killer and restore justice to Isola Sombra? No, more than that, if I swore to you that without my help, you'll never catch the murderer and this abbey will never heal? Would you let me be your piccolo again? Allow me by your side as you pursue the investigation?'

The offer took him by surprise – for all the bizarre cases he'd inves- tigated, he'd never imagined himself negotiating with one such as her. There was a truth to Caeda's words that rang deeper than even she understood – and he knew he was too weakened by his wounds to finish this case. Without her help, someone – whether the inquisitor with her pistol or the general with her soldiers or whoever among the Wolf-King's followers had betrayed him – would decide that Estevar was getting too close and put the sharp end of a blade in his back.

That, of course, was if the demons didn't get him first.

'I have a condition,' he said abruptly. 'Since you require that I never ask you whether you are a ghost, you must do something in return for me.'

'What is it?' Her voice was full of tentative hope.

'You may never demand nor even request that I bend the knee to you. *Never*. I am not Malezias or any other servant to genuflect before you.'

The silence stretched out between them once more. This, he knew, would be a hard thing for her to accept.

'Because you think me unworthy?' she asked.

'Because I am a Greatcoat,' he replied, 'and Greatcoats kneel before no one.'

'Except when it comes to lecherous apostate monks with delusions of grandeur?'

'Except then,' Estevar conceded, then raised a finger, 'but only as a ruse and only when absolutely necessary. At such times, a Greatcoat plays whatever role the investigation demands of him . . . or her.'

Even in the brief quiet before she answered, with nothing to go on but the soft sound of her inhalation, Estevar sensed that his answer delighted her.

'Marked,' she said, in the Tristian way of sealing a bargain.

Estevar felt a profound sense of relief then – not only because the immediate danger to his life was past, but because he had grown terribly fond of this strange woman and all her playful enthusiasm for the investigator's art.

He heard a short, sharp scratching sound, then saw the flash of a spark become a tiny flame. The squeak of a brass lid being unscrewed followed, and soon that flame danced in the air before a second, larger one was ignited, which at last banished the darkness from the infirmary.

Caeda was standing a few feet away on the other side of the table, holding the lantern she'd just lit. The red curls of her hair were wet and limp against her cheeks and throat, the white shift she wore soaked through to skin made even paler by the freezing seawater. In her other hand, she held out a long crimson coat, as drenched as she was, the smooth leather marred by a few strands of seaweed stuck to it.

'Greatcoats should look the part, don't you think?' she asked.

Solemnly – with as much reverence as on the first day it had been offered to him by an idealistic king who now, oddly, reminded him of Caeda – Estevar accepted the greatcoat. He placed it over his shoulders and slid his arms into the sleeves, caring not one bit how cold and wet they were.

She ran barefoot from the room, only to return a moment later with one more gift. 'Nobody's going to trust a magistrate who walks around with a stolen sword,' she said, grinning.

Estevar examined his rapier, delighted to find no new nicks or even a trace of rust on the blade. After drying it thoroughly with a length of bandage, he slid it into the sheath in the left side of his coat and walked around the table. He held out his hand and waited for Caeda to take it.

'Come then, Piccolo,' he said. 'Let us sing a song of justice for this sad little island, and perhaps – just perhaps – you and I will save it from damnation.'

CHAPTER 28

THE DORMITORY

Estevar set a quick pace, forcing Caeda to jog every few steps to keep up. The brass lantern in her hand swung back and forth, casting dancing shadows upon the walls of the narrow passage.

'Why are we wasting time here?' she asked. 'You said there were demons roaming the abbey grounds – so who cares where the monks have go—?'

'Three hundred monks once occupied this abbey,' Estevar said, bowing his head to step beneath a door and into yet another empty cell. He beckoned for Caeda to bring the lantern inside. 'The towers serving as lairs for the Hounds and the Trumpeters couldn't hold half that number. So where are the rest?'

Like the other sleeping chambers they'd examined, this one was austere, yet cosy. There was just enough room for a cot on one side and a small oak writing desk on the other. Three shelves stuck out above the cot, presumably for clothing, and a chamber-pot sat in the corner. A single window not much bigger than a man's hand was set in the outer stone wall, allowing the faint blush of moonlight into the room. The desk, shelves and chamber-pot were all empty, the bed scrupulously made, all of which cast doubt on the possibility of its former occupant having fled in the night. The departure had been planned.

'Most of the brethren abandoned the abbey eight days ago, after the statues were destroyed,' Caeda said. 'They interpreted the destruction as an omen that the gods were about to bring vengeance down on Isola Sombra. That's what the Margrave of Someil's knights told the villagers when they rode through the streets, waving their axes in the air and warning everyone to flee, anyway.'

'How many would you say did abandon the island?'

'All the villagers but for Malezias and me, though many had already cleared out for the winter before the storms came. I wasn't exactly counting the monks, but there was a long line – maybe a hundred and fifty? – trudging across the causeway, with whatever possessions they had. That was the day after the statuary was destroyed.'

Half the brethren, Estevar thought. *Were you really so distracted, Venia, that you couldn't sense something terrible was amiss?*

'What is it?' Caeda asked, looking up at him. 'What does it matter if some skittish monks took off rather than clean up the mess left behind by the storm? How will that help us cast out the demons if they return?'

'It won't.'

'Then what are we doing in an empty dormitory cell?'

Estevar walked over to the cot, bent down and, out of habit, lifted the thin mattress in case the previous occupant might have left something behind. There was nothing there. Not that he'd expected to find anything.

'Do you see this cot, the mattress, the bedding?'

'I'm not blind.'

Estevar let the mattress fall back into place, pulled the covers down and patted the pillow. 'Lie down.'

'What?'

'Lie down on the bed.'

She cast him a suspicious glance. 'Three weeks ago, I followed similar instructions from a man I'd trusted my entire life, only for him to strap me down to a table, inscribe sigils on my body and then toss me off a cliff.'

'I suppose the sea water washed away the markings?'

Her hand went to the collar of her shift, closing it tighter around her neck. 'What?'

'Forgive me, my mind was wandering,' Estevar said, moving to the doorway so as not to block her passage. 'Please, lay down on the bed for me. I will stay outside the room.'

She set the lantern down on the desk. The light made the grey of her eyes appear to roil as if they were windows looking out on a storm. 'I'd *prefer* that you give me a reason for why you're asking me to lie down on some flea-ridden monk's cot.'

'Because it is *not* flea-ridden. You claimed a moment ago not to be blind, but I believe both of us have missed the obvious.' He gestured once more towards the cot.

Caeda did as he asked, but not before first checking to make sure the door couldn't be locked from the outside.

She does not entirely trust me, he thought. *Good. We have that in common.*

After flopping down onto the bed with a huff, Caeda lay on her back and stared up at the ceiling. 'There's nothing there,' she said. 'So if this was supposed to be som—'

'Investigations are rarely about deciphering secret codes. What I need you to do is awaken your other senses, Piccolo. I am going to step away from the door, but I promise not to try to lock the door or leave you here. I ask only that you take a moment to experience this room as one of the brethren might.'

'And afterwards you're going to explain the point of all this?'

'It is night-time,' he began, his voice low, 'when—'

Caeda's arm swung up to point at the tiny window. 'I can see that it's night-time.'

Estevar stifled a groan, recalling why, years ago, he'd refused to mentor new Greatcoats in the art of investigation. 'It is night-time,' he repeated patiently, 'and you have reached the end of your day's labours, completed your studies and said whatever prayers to the gods best soothe your spirit. You've had your supper in the refectory, bathed in the lavorium and at last returned to your room. Tell me, young monk, what is it like, this life of yours?'

Caeda was quiet at first, but soon he heard her head nestling onto the pillow and the soft sound of blankets being pulled over her. With a contented sigh, she said, 'I'm very comfortable.'

'Oh? On such a cold, hard cot, in this cramped stone cell?'

She snorted. 'This "cramped stone cell" is a palace compared to where most people live. And this "cold, hard cot" is a lot softer and warmer than a pile of reeds on the floor. I have my privacy, which is a luxury few commoners ever experience. There are thick stone walls around me to keep me safe. My belly is full, my skin is dry. My bones don't ache because even if tending crops or making wine is arduous, it's never back-breaking. There's an infirmary, so if I get sick, I'll get decent care. My mind is alive with the subjects of my studies and conversations with my fellow monks, my spirit lifted by the hours I'm allowed to devote to contemplate the gods and worship as I please.'

'And tomorrow?' Estevar asked.

'Tomorrow . . .' She sounded sleepy now. Her eyes closed and she tugged the blankets up to her chin. 'Tomorrow I get to do it all again. No scrounging for my next meal, no pleading with some merchant or lord not to cut my wages or beat me for no reason. I am . . . at peace.'

'Good,' Estevar said. 'Very good.'

'Can I rest a while?'

'Alas, my dear, you cannot. In fact, you can't sleep at all. You're tossing and turning because this very morning, you and your fellow monks discovered the six statues of your gods struck by lightning. What do you make of that?'

'Hmm?'

'Piccolo, I did not bring you here to nap! I have just informed you of a terrible discovery. A crisis of faith. The gods are dead, their monuments lie in ruins! Tell me, why have you not fled this place already?'

'What? Give up this sheltered existence because a few old sculptures happened to get hit by lightning during a storm? Of course I'm not leaving.'

'Ah, so instead you lie beneath your blanket, seething with resentment towards your fellow monks, convinced they're worshipping the wrong gods, so now you must decide which faction to join in opposition to the others?'

'No, I'm enjoying my lovely cot. *Trying to*, anyway.'

'Why? Are you not furious that—?'

'I'm a monk, not some would-be soldier or zealot!' Her fingernails clacked against the stone wall. 'I chose *this* life because it freed me from violence and deprivation.' Throwing off her blanket and sitting up on the cot, she turned to him. 'Are we done with this, Estevar? Because it feels like a terrible waste of time, given the island's about to be invaded by some petty aristocrat's troops or overrun with demons – unless, of course, the monks massacre each other first and save them both the trouble.'

'One final question.'

She groaned. 'You really take the fun out of investigating brutal beheadings and demonic onslaughts, you know that?'

'Just one more.'

'Oh, fine. Go on.'

'You have told me that the existence of a monk in this abbey is, if not idyllic, then certainly more comfortable than what they might expect in the world beyond these walls. Furthermore, you consider the lightning-struck statues, though troubling, to be insufficient cause to flee Isola Sombra, or to justify the fracturing of the brethren.'

'So?'

'So, my young monk, answer me this: why are you planning to run away in the morning?'

'I'm not! That's what I keep telling you!'

Estevar stepped back into the room with her, gestured to the empty writing desk and the bare shelves. 'But you *did* run away, Piccolo. You and half your brethren. Those who remained either banded together like soldiers awaiting an attack or lost themselves in revels as if death was already certain. If the statues weren't sufficient cause for panic, then why are you leaving?'

'Because . . .'

Estevar placed his hands in front of the lantern on the desk, shaping his hands so that the shadows cast on the wall grew more menacing.

'Because I was already scared!' Caeda exclaimed, leaping up from the bed. 'The troubles among the brethren didn't *start* with the ruined statues – something was already wrong with the abbey, and the monks sensed it. The destroyed statuary was the *last* straw, not the first!' She began pacing around the tiny cell. 'Some of the monks fled the island. Some joined Mother Leogado and walled themselves up in the Vigilance Tower, paranoid about the margrave launching an invasion. Others, like Strigan and his idiot followers, debauched themselves with endless drunken revels.' She rubbed at her wrists, as if at old wounds. 'Is that why Abbot Venia tied me down in the infirmary and inscribed those awful, awful markings all over me and threw me from the clifftop? Because he and the other monks had already gone mad?'

Estevar seldom ascribed madness as an explanation for a crime. Most of those condemned as 'lunatics' or 'deviants' tended to be ordinary men and women cursed not with a defect of the mind but simply of failing to fit in with the ways of their neighbours. That, added to the effects of injury, near-drowning and subsequent fever, were all the excuses he could find for having so utterly failed to recognise that the behaviour he'd witnessed here could not be dismissed as eccentric, or even erratic. Neither theological panic nor the threat of invasion could account for the chaos unfolding on Isola Sombra. The monks had quite simply – and precisely as Caeda had suggested – gone mad.

The question now was *what* or *who* had driven them to that madness?

'Come,' he said, taking the lantern from the desk and handing it to Caeda. 'We have learned everything this empty cell can teach us.'

'Where are we going next?' she asked.

He stepped out into the passageway. 'You and I must follow Venia's footsteps into those dark places his fractured mind led him before his death. *That* is the means by which we will uncover how demons came to tread upon sacred soil.'

CHAPTER 29

THE WRECKAGE

'You're talking in riddles again,' Caeda complained, the brass lantern swinging back and forth as she chased after Estevar. 'Why start here, of all places?'

Their journey had taken them past the refectory, where dozens of broken plates – smashed, no doubt, by those who'd come seeking food after the pantries in the Sustenacum Tower had already been laid bare – had turned the floor into a treacherous terrain of clay shards. From there, an equally harrowing trip through the abandoned East Gardens, where every glint of moonlight brought visions of pale, leathery demon-flesh and claws eager to appeal Estevar's earlier verdict. The faint slap of sandals a discreet distance behind them would have added to their disquiet, were it not for the tell-tale heaviness on the left foot.

Estevar had taken to referring to their unwanted companion as 'the Mouse' for the way he scurried off every time Caeda – who had limited tolerance for being spied on – would suddenly spin around and go chasing after him. To the Mouse's credit, he made great haste on such occasions, disappearing into the darkness while Estevar called out to remind Caeda that they had more *pressing* concerns.

'*Pressing*,' she repeated. 'Why are we visiting the winery?'

'Not the winery itself,' Estevar said, leading the way down some narrow stone steps. 'The wine cellar.'

'Oh, well that explains *everything*.'

A pity her talents for investigation did not include patience, Estevar thought. *And a greater pity that yours lack heeding your own advice!*

On the perilous journey across the causeway, Estevar had recounted to Imperious his old case of the Dancing Plague, which had been attributed to everything from demonic sorcery to divine retribution. Estevar had been intent on soothing his mule's frayed nerves, not really considering he might be dealing with something similar in the Abbey of Isola Sombra.

'*What are the monks of Isola Sombra famous for?*' he had asked Imperious rhetorically, trying to distract him from the storm raging overhead. '*The potency of the liquors they brew from crops grown on that very island.*'

Distracted by his ruminations, Estevar failed to notice a damp patch on the step and lost his footing – only by painfully slamming his palms against the next step did he keep himself from sliding the rest of the way down on his arse.

'Perhaps you should pay more attention to your feet,' Caeda suggested as she helped him up, 'and spend less time mumbling to yourself.'

'I was not mumbling,' he insisted, trudging carefully down the last few stairs. 'I was merely . . . wordlessly vocalising my contemplations.'

'Well, the rest of us call it mumbling, and you can stop now since we've arrived.' She held out the lantern as they stepped through the arched doorway and into cavernous cellars – and nearly dropped their only source of illumination.

'Seven Hells! What happened here?' Her question reverberated against the granite walls rising twenty feet into darkness.

Estevar worked out his bearings: the underground wine cellars were directly beneath the main keep, just inside the northern curtain wall. Unlike the rough-hewn prayer caves below the courtyard and the narrow, confining storm tunnels, the spectacular architecture housing the abbey's wines and ales evoked the majesty of a cathedral.

Vaulted ceilings ascended high above a clay-tiled central walkway between six main chambers, each lined with sturdy iron racks meant to hold the weight of huge oak barrels – the shattered remains of which lay strewn across the floor like a field of corpses after a battle, their blood the shallow pools of spilled wine.

'How many barrels should we expect to find here at this time of the season?' Estevar asked.

Caeda swung the lantern round to illuminate the damage. 'The harvest was three months ago, the wine-making completed seven weeks after that. The new barrels are supposed to be kept down here for at least two years before being sold. When they are ready, they are shipped in the spring ... so now, every rack should be full.' She pointed to the empty alcove near the entrance, where a sign written in archaic Tristian warned, *Quo moderatio festivas, qui exedio calamitas.*

'With moderation comes joy, from excess, calamity,' Estevar said quietly.

'That's where the barrels for the brethren would usually be,' Caeda said. 'The abbot was very strict about how much his monks were allowed to indulge.'

There were no barrels in the house section, nor any detritus beneath those particular racks. Estevar glanced around the other sections of the magnificent cavern, calculating in his head.

Five hundred, he decided at last. *At least five hundred barrels. Yet there do not appear to be that many amid these smashed remains.*

'Why would anyone destroy the abbey's entire supply of wine?' Caeda asked, sloshing her bare foot in one of the shallow pools of red wine, then kicking a small chunk of wood across the chamber.

Estevar took the lantern from her before kneeling to investigate a piece of barrel that held some of the purplish-red liquid. He lifted the improvised wooden cup to his lips and drank.

Notes of blackberry and peach blended amiably with the earthier flavour that was a characteristic of the island's legendary grapes. The full-bodied wine soothed his throat as he drank, leaving a velvety sensation on his tongue.

Outstanding, he judged, discarding his improvised ladle before going in search of another.

'What are you doing?' Caeda asked, watching him curiously.

He grinned at her as he found another helpful shard still retaining a mouthful of wine and brought it to his lips. 'Experimenting.'

'Well, if you get drunk and pass out, don't expect me to drag your fat arse back up the stairs to the abbey.'

'No need for concern, my dear. I am possessed of a redoubtable constitution. Legendary imbibers from every corner of this country have faced me across the drinking table, only to fall before my incomparable resilience to intoxication.'

Despite his boasting, he took smaller sips of what remaining clean samples he could find of half a dozen vintages, each one delightful, which made their wanton destruction even more offensive. Wine lovers across the world would weep when they heard of this carnage of claret. Would it not have been a crime against the art of wine-making, he might have tried to combine what thimblefuls of the remaining vintages into a bottle to take with him.

'Had your fill?' Caeda asked archly when he joined her beneath the central vaulted ceiling once more. 'If you're right about someone having tampered with the wine, you do realise that you may have just poisoned yourself with whatever it is that's driven the monks mad?'

Estevar gestured to the field of broken barrels all around him. 'Survey the evidence, Piccolo. Tell me what you see.'

She turned slowly, her eyes seeking out some clue amid the wreckage that she assumed he'd kept from her during his own examination. Her expression soured with every passing second. 'Not that I particularly care about a drink that leaves men stumbling, half-insensate and looking to paw every woman they come across on their way to whichever ditch they plan to spend the night in, but all this destruction is terribly wasteful. The abbey coffers will be considerably the poorer next year for the lack of revenues that come from our wine sales, and the monks even more irritable than usual.'

'And whom shall we blame for this callous crime?' Estevar asked. 'Strigan's Hounds? Leogado's Trumpeters – the flower for which they're named *is* poisonous, is it not? Or perhaps the Bone-Rattlers scurrying about in the shadows, evading our questions as they avoid the many dangers afflicting the abbey?'

'Clearly you don't think any of them did it,' Caeda said, folding her arms across her chest. 'Are you accusing me? Just because I don't care to have inebriated monks trying to have their way with me, that doesn't make me a poisoner!'

'I know it wasn't you, Piccolo.'

She uncrossed her arms and began to step carefully among the wreckage of the barrels. 'If it wasn't any of the brethren, and the rest of the islanders had already fled, that just leaves Abbot Venia himself.' She opened her arms wide as if to encompass all the destruction around them. 'Do you really think one man could have done all this?'

'No.'

'Then who—?' Again, he saw that sudden excitement lighting up her face as the puzzle pieces finally formed the correct picture. 'The knights! Twelve big men and women – more than enough to destroy all the barrels.' She jabbed Estevar in the chest, hard enough that he was glad for the return of his greatcoat. 'They brought *axes* with them – when Strigan said the knights had come armed with swords and axes, you asked him *what kind*.'

'Do you recall his reply?'

She bit her lower lip a moment. 'I think he said "the regular kind".'

Estevar nodded. 'The military battle axes wielded by ducal knights tend to be double-headed and short-hafted – something a monk would consider noteworthy. The "regular" kind would almost certainly have a single edge and a long haft, the sort used for chopping wood. This suggests that the knights brought with them not weapons, but tools.'

Caeda frowned. 'But the timeline doesn't make any sense – the chaos began weeks before the knights arrived. Venia had already been killed and the brethren split into factions – which means they'd already been poisoned by then.' She gestured to the shattered barrels at their feet. 'Why bother destroying the abbey's entire supply of wine? Unless . . .'

Estevar waited as she strode purposefully towards the part of the chamber which was free of debris. 'The knights *didn't* break all the barrels!' she declared triumphantly. 'They left those meant for the monks untouched – so someone tampered with the wine meant for the brethren, then two weeks later sent the knights to smash the other barrels to make sure the monks would keep drinking the poison!' From across the room she caught his eye. 'That means Mother Leogado is right about the Margrave of Someil being behind this.'

'There was never any question of the Margrave's lust for Isola Sombra's economic and political advantages,' Estevar agreed. 'What he lacked was credible legal grounds for invasion. By having one of his agents meddle with the wine and drive the monks to behave in bizarre fashion – something the villagers would surely have noticed before the knights arrived to usher them to the safety of the mainland – he engineered a pretext for conquest *and* ensured there would be minimal resistance to his troops.'

'But why bother ruining the unspoiled wine? The monks had already gone nuts by then, and Venia's murder should be more than enough excuse for the margrave to intervene. Unless you think he's shaking in his boots at the prospect of facing Mother Leogado's Trumpeters with their silly yellow habits and sour expressions?'

'Do not scoff, Piccolo. A hundred monks, accustomed to hard work and armed with the abbey's weapons, shielded by a curtain wall on all sides, could easily defend the front gates for days, even weeks. All the while, the margrave's own soldiers would be wondering why they were attacking such a holy site, and at what cost to their souls.'

Caeda resumed her wandering about the cavern, swinging the lantern as she turned this way and that. 'So the knights weren't sent to investigate Venia's murder at all but instead to make sure the only wine left came from the poisoned barrels?'

'Precisely. Their role was to ensure the madness spread unabated, setting the brethren against each other so that when the storms abate, the margrave can simply walk across the causeway and claim his prize.'

Sir Daven's frantic tale of twelve knights returned soulless from their journey to the island had been nothing more than a ruse meant to set Estevar down the wrong path. He wondered how the deceitful knight would react when he learned that his fanciful tales of monstrous demons infiltrating the abbey had proven so unexpectedly accurate.

Caeda picked up one of the wine-soaked pieces of oak. 'You asked me yesterday about the three different ways people might react to an impending invasion. Some would want to fight, like the Trumpeters, others hide, like the Bone-Rattlers, and still others loot whatever they can for their own benefit before everything falls apart.' She sniffed at the damp wood and wrinkled her nose. 'Add a little delusion-inducing poison to the mix, and you've got the perfect recipe for what's happened to the monks of Isola Sombra, haven't you?'

But it's not enough. Estevar was frustrated at his inability to bridge the chasm between a few dozen barrels of poisoned wine and a quintet of horned demons prowling the grounds. There were hundreds of herbs, venoms, crushed seeds, insect stings, fermented alcohols and other toxins that flourished in Tristia, each with the potential to transform wine into something far deadlier – with someone's help.

Estevar silently interrogated his unknown suspect. *'Tampering with the wine to drive the monks mad was the first step in your plan, but how did the unleashing of their inner demons give rise to the summoning of actual ones?'*

Caeda, scuffing her foot along the bare floor, was asking the same question. 'What if the monsters you saw came from . . . ? No, that's probably not it.'

'Speak, Piccolo. What are you thinking?'

In the gloom of the wine cellar, the shifting light of the brass lantern swaying in Caeda's hand lent an ominous, almost sinister gleam to her face. 'Abbot Venia always said the first gods were created when the storms over Isola Sombra struck the ores beneath the ground and the mystical forces released were then bound by the faith of the original Tristian slaves penned up in the caves under what's now the abbey. Their prayers gave us the gods – of War, Love, Craft, Coin. But now those gods are dead, or maybe returning but not fully formed yet, so all that spiritual essence is still out there, waiting to be shaped.' She stopped and looked over at Estevar, nervous that he'd find her conjectures silly.

'Proceed, Piccolo. Your thoughts echo mine.'

She smiled, gratitude in those storm-grey eyes. 'The three factions. The Bone-Rattlers are traditionalists, insisting the old gods will return. Leogado's Trumpeters want new ones better suited to our times. And then there's Strigan with his Hounds wanting to steal the spiritual powers of this place for themselves. The brethren were already pulling in different directions before any of this happened, but then someone poisoned them, and they all became wilder – more fervent in their beliefs and desires.' The smile left her face entirely as she came to the same conclusion he had. 'Estevar, what if the spiritual essence left behind by the death of the gods really *is* returning to Isola Sombra, only now it's not being guided by faith. It's being shaped by . . .'

She stopped, as if not wanting to say the word out loud, but a magistrate's first duty was to the truth, so Estevar uttered the unspeakable word for her. 'Madness,' he said, taking her hand to lead her out of the cellar and up the stairs. 'The alchemy of those mystical forces that once gave Tristia its gods is being transmuted by the delusional zealotry of monks who have abandoned their faith, leading inexorably to the birth of a pantheon devoted to chaos!'

PART THE SIXTH

THE SIGILS OF SILENCE

Once those who come in darkness and to darkness transport the sin-infused spirit of the sacrifice, the flesh that remains must be quieted. Terror, horror and despair leave their own imprints upon the body even after the will that once gave it life is gone. Thus by these three sigils will the screams that still reside beneath the skin be forever silenced.

CHAPTER 30

SILENT WISDOM

'Oh,' Estevar added, wagging his finger in the air, 'and I forgot to mention that after Venia's murder, the margrave sent a dozen knights to the island with orders to destroy the untainted barrels of wine.' He looked into the eyes of his audience. 'So there was indeed a lot in common with the case of the Dancing Plague. What do you think, my friend?'

'You're even more of an ass than he is, you know that?' Caeda asked.

Estevar reached out a hand to stroke Imperious' muzzle. The bandage had come off, but the skin around the stitched gash was still glowing an angry red. 'A mule is not an ass, if that was meant to be a joke.'

'Perhaps *I'm* the ass, then, for thinking you valued my opinion,' Caeda said, trudging angrily to the stable doors. The rains had returned, which, Estevar supposed, was probably the only reason she didn't walk off and leave him there.

'I value no one's *opinion* when the fate of my adopted country is at stake,' he reminded her. 'What I need is *insight*, which neither you nor I have been able to summon on our own.'

She strode back as quickly as she'd left. Jabbing a finger at Imperious, she asked, 'And you think *he's* going to provide it?'

Estevar pushed himself back to his feet and reached into the sack of carrots that Malezias, former soldier and failed monk, had managed to scrounge or steal at Caeda's behest.

It is a hard thing to love, is it not, my big friend? he thought, though he doubted Malezias considered him in such generous terms. *And yet,*

209

devotion simplifies our lives, too. You would do anything she asks and it matters not one whit that she will never return that love.

With a lot of urging, Imperious grudgingly took a few nibbles from the carrot, leaving Estevar even more fearful that the once-dauntless beast had lost his spirit.

'He listens,' Estevar said, as much to himself as Caeda. 'Does he understand my words? Probably not. But there is more to wisdom than knowledge.' He placed his hand on the mule's neck, taking comfort from the thick hair tickling his palm. 'He reacts to my tone of voice. He brays and rumbles, clacks his teeth and stamps his hooves. This is how he responds to my troubled and scattered emotions. It is a language I cannot speak, one whose workings I may never comprehend, and yet he steadies me, bringing me back to those deeper truths too often lost in the tangle of facts and clues.'

Caeda came closer, trying not to admit to any curiosity. 'And what does he tell you now? Has the great Imperious solved the case?'

Outside, the distant rumble of thunder warned that the soft patter of rain outside the stable was only a precursor to the return of the storm. Estevar was about to reassure the mule, but for once, the noise wasn't panicking him as it had before.

He smiled, removing his hand from Imperious' neck and bending down to allow himself the perhaps embarrassing comfort of resting his cheek against the big sorrel head. 'Having heard the account of my investigation thus far, the great and wise Imperious reproaches me.'

'Reproaches you? How? For what?'

A second rumble of thunder, closer this time, and still the mule was unmoved.

'You are indeed correct, my friend,' he said quietly, then to Caeda, 'He reminds me that ever since I set foot upon this island, my attention has been diverted by the loudest voices. Strigan's boasting set off my own belligerence. Mother Leogado's unshakeable convictions appealed to my sense of honour. Even Brother Agneta's cynicism sparked my love of debating the finer points between clerical laws and those I serve. And, of course, the demons distracted me by turning all my thoughts to the supernatural elements of this case.'

'And me?' Caeda asked, the edge in her voice betraying her fears. 'Have I been a "distraction" from your investigation?'

Estevar considered his words carefully. She was brittle, this one, and deserving of more kindness than he could give her. 'You, my Piccolo, have been the greatest distraction of them all.' He stood back up so she could see his face and, hopefully, sense his sincerity. 'But not all distractions are bad, nor are they all born of deceit. You have been the finest detective's assistant I have ever known.'

Imperious' belly made a noise that sounded suspiciously like the prelude to the unleashing of noxious gases in protest.

'The *second* finest detective's assistant,' Estevar clarified, but the gurgling intestinal noise repeated. 'The second finest *senior* detective,' he conceded at last, then waited to see what verdict the mule would impose on him.

After a few moments, the mule's stomach settled.

Caeda laughed. 'At last we see who wears the spurs in this relationship.'

Imperious let out a low growl uncharacteristic of his species, yet familiar to Estevar, who drew his rapier from the sheath in his coat. 'Piccolo, to me.'

'Why? what's wr—?'

Heavy stomping outside heralded the arrival of a huge, hooded figure whose modest grey robes were at odds with the massive sword strapped to his back. 'Having fun?' he asked.

Beneath the disdain and menace of his tone, Estevar heard a note of rising fear. He said nothing.

Malezias crossed the stable floor to loom over Estevar like a tower about to fall on top of him. 'What's the matter, Trattari?' he asked, noticing the rapier in Estevar's hand. 'Afraid I've come to slaughter your mule for food?'

Estevar glanced at Imperious, who was unperturbed by the intruder. 'No,' he answered. 'I am not.'

Malezias slid the scabbard's leather loop off his shoulder and drew a two-handed warsword longer than any Estevar had seen before. 'Why not? You think this place has made me too soft for killing?' He barked a laugh. 'You shouldn't. I've seen a dozen battlefields and never found one so bloody as this.'

'Malezias!' Caeda said, coming to separate the two men, but Estevar waved her off.

'I have no doubt such a weapon could easily take my head,' he said carefully, and noting the dark stains on the blade, added, 'It appears I owe you a debt of gratitude.'

'Why would you want to thank *me*?'

Estevar hesitated, unsure if his answer might somehow bring shame to the big man. 'Because my mule has *not* been slaughtered, and that blood dripping from the tip of your sword is fresh, which tells me that others have tried.'

Malezias looked at Caeda, whose expression of surprise faded to a smile of fondness, although not as fond as the giant might have wished. 'Damned Hounds,' he swore, sliding the sword back in its scabbard. He gestured to a corner of the stable where the absence of hay and dirt revealed that something large had been dragged away. 'Didn't want 'em both to bleed out here. Mules are stupid beasts – get spooked by the smell.'

Estevar took his forearm in a soldier's clasp. 'Twice you have saved this particular mule and for this, I owe you a debt that I fear I'll never be able to fully repay.'

The hard lines of the warrior's face softened as he muttered, 'Hard to imagine a sentimental milksop like you goes around duelling trained killers.'

'Demons, too,' Caeda said, running over to throw her arms around Malezias. She looked like a child next to him, barely coming up to his ribs. 'Storms, oceans and demonic invasions. It's only people he can't fight worth a damn.'

'Speaking of fighting,' Estevar interjected, loath to interrupt a tender moment, yet aware that time was slipping away from him, 'how much longer will the causeway remain flooded?'

Malezias pushed Caeda away, a sudden fury turning his cheeks red. 'Why? So you can run off back to the mainland? Now that your mule is safe and you've got some fine stories to tell your Trattari friends, you're going to abandon the abbey?'

'Malezias!' Caeda snapped. 'How dare you? Estevar would never walk away from a case. He just wants to make sure no one else can flee before he's caught the killer!'

'Actually, it's neither of those things,' Estevar told her.

'Then what?' Caeda asked.

He turned back to Malezias. 'You showed remarkable skill navigating the treacherous currents off the shore and you are far more knowledge-able about the tides than anyone else. How soon until the causeway will be passable?'

The big man shrugged. 'Hard to say with any certainty.' He gestured to the far side of the stable. 'Lot of black clouds nearby, but fewer on the western horizon. We'll have another storm tonight – a bad one – but by tomorrow, assuming the currents stop misbehaving, it should be possible to get off the island.'

Or to come here, Estevar thought, but kept that to himself. There would be time enough for those ill tidings to make themselves known, and he couldn't risk Malezias deciding to take Caeda's safety into his own hands.

Glancing back at Imperious, he asked, 'Can you protect him one more night, Malezias? I know it is a great favour t—'

'Of course he can,' Caeda said, patting the giant's arm. 'Ignore his sour temper. He loves horses.'

'That's not a horse,' Malezias corrected, and shot Estevar a glare that promised a brutal reckoning should any harm come to Caeda, confirming that his was the kind of love that made it impossible for him to refuse her anything. 'Fine. I'll sit here all day and night like an idiot watching over a stupid beast who should be roasting over an open fire rather than turning his nose up at every piece of food I put in front of him.' Almost as an afterthought, he asked Estevar, 'And what's in it for me, anyway?'

Again, he had to choose his answer carefully. 'All the gratitude I can offer,' he said.

Malezias and Imperious snorted simultaneously, evidently sharing opinions on the worth of Estevar's gratitude.

Caeda laughed with delight, as if she were still the bright young village girl with her whole life ahead of her, and the world a far kinder place than it had turned out to be.

'Come, Piccolo,' Estevar said, seeing the agony in Malezias' stare and unwilling to risk the man falling to his knees and blurting out tales that for now must remain secret.

'Where are we going?' she asked, following him onto the winding street leading back up to the abbey. Despite the rumbling earlier, neither the wind nor the rain had picked up. If he didn't know better, he'd have thought the storm was biding its time.

It was silly to continue Caeda's lessons, but he couldn't deny her this paltry gift. Perhaps, like Malezias, he was struck by the woman she'd been and felt a debt to the one she could have become. He paused to point back to the stable. 'Are you telling me that after I shared one of my most prized and secretive investigative techniques, you forgot so soon?'

She stared at him quizzically. 'What? You mean that nonsense about Imperious and him "listening" to you in his way and his various brays and grunts and farts somehow help you solve a case?'

'Precisely.'

She turned back to the rundown wooden stable, looking thoughtful. 'When he didn't react to the thunder, you said he was telling you that you'd allowed your investigation to be diverted by the loudest voices.'

'And?'

Her grin of satisfaction when she turned back to him would have broken the heart of any parent who'd hoped for a sensible, sedentary life for their daughter. 'Imperious is right, my Cantor. We've been distracted by the howls of Hounds and the trumpets of Trumpeters, the acid tongue of an old inquisitor and the diabolical doings of demons.' She bent down and picked up a pair of little stones, which she rolled along the flagstones. 'Now we must follow the quiet rattle of bones.'

What a Greatcoat I could have made of her, Estevar thought again, then buried his rage so she wouldn't see it. *Damn you, Venia. Damn you to whichever of the Seven Hells has taken your soul.*

'But how do we find one?' Caeda asked, standing back up to peer through the abbey gates ahead. 'Other than your inquisitor friend, every traditionalist we've encountered went scurrying off into the shadows like a frightened mouse when we approached, shutting their eyes and moaning to whichever god their last dice roll told them to pray to. Even that one who kept spying on us hasn't returned since your encounter with those demons. How do you expect to get anything out of the Bone-Rattlers?'

Estevar forced a reassuring grin to his lips as he set off through the gates towards the one part of the abbey he felt sure would serve their purpose. The familiar ache in his side reappeared and he reached inside his coat to press a hand over the wound, wanting to make sure the stitches were still sound and he hadn't started bleeding again. 'Not all mice are quite so timid, Piccolo. The one we seek will come to us, so long as we set the right trap.'

CHAPTER 31

THE MOUSE TRAP

Estevar crouched behind the wide mahogany base of the lectern at the centre of the chapter house. His knees were complaining bitterly, as if to remind him that, contrary to his frequent assertions that the Greatcoats knelt for no one, he was doing rather a lot of it lately, so perhaps he should do some praying while he was down here and hope the gods took pity on his aching bones.

Tristians typically conducted their prayers in caverns and basements, a tradition born in the underground slave pens where they'd first been housed before being sold off as indentured servants to Avarean warlords in the west. Prayer was a quiet, solitary form of worship in this country, even when performed in large groups. Sermons and theological debates, however, were activities that had been brought above ground and into magnificent chapter houses like this one.

Seventeen marble pillars bore the weight of a domed roof that rose so high the stars in the night sky looked as if they'd been painted upon the curved glass. This chapter house was far less cold and rigid than the abbey's towers and keeps. Bright rosewood-panelled walls complemented polished oak floors inlaid with bronze. There was gold too, elaborate gilding accentuating carvings on the walls depicting scenes of Tristia's liberation: the good God War rallying slaves to overthrow their masters; Craft teaching them to forge weapons with which to fight; Death embracing those who fell; Coin rewarding the victorious with well-deserved riches. Then came the myth that gave Estevar hope for the people of this troubled nation: a scene of Love herself uniting her people at the end of the battle, urging mercy towards their defeated foes and reminding the victors that to enslave an enemy's body is to corrupt one's own soul. The final tableau, perhaps the most profound of all, was the space left empty for the sixth god of Tristia: the missing story, the absence of understanding.

Estevar wasn't a praying man, but if he had been, it would be this unnamed, unknown and unspoken-of deity to whom he would kneel. The world needed reminders that no cleric, no scholar, no magistrate, not even the other five gods themselves, knew all there was to know about the mysteries of life. Crouching here behind this lectern, he couldn't help but ponder what the will of that absent god might be.

'How long do we have to hide here like idiots?' Caeda whispered.

Estevar stifled his irritation. Patience wasn't one of her virtues, he'd seen that, but patience was their sharpest weapon now. He turned his head and tried to pair a reassuring smile with a silencing glare. Neither was successful.

'Oh, fine,' she muttered. 'This is the part where you usually give some long lecture about how a proper investigator listens more than she speaks and accepts that the pace of an enquiry isn't always hers to set. Only instead of your typical bloviating, you're waiting for me to work it out for myself so I can show you I'm one-tenth as clever as you are and thus marginally worthy of your instruction.'

That sounded like a more reasonable explanation for this interminable waiting, so Estevar nodded solemnly. 'Yes, and if there were some way for you to do so without talking out loud, we might actually find the individual we need to interrogate.'

'Assuming such a person exists,' she hissed back at him. Caeda had been of a mind to hunt down as many of the traditionalist monks as necessary, and with soothing words or a firm slap – she was happy to try both – calm them down long enough for them to reveal what they knew about Abbot Venia's last days. But cruelty employed against those who'd committed no crimes themselves in pursuit of the facts was a brute's methodology, something Estevar would not tolerate.

A second – and, if he was being honest with himself, more pernicious – impediment was that most of these monks were so skittish they became hysterical with fear when cornered, which meant their answers would be worse than useless. Terror and torture were ineffective methods of getting to the truth; diligence and persistence were far more reliable tools of investigation, especially when raising questions no one else thought to ask.

Paranoia, elation, paralysing fear – the monks of Isola Sombra had shown all these emotions, but it surely could not be possible that multiple variations of the toxic hallucinogens had been introduced into the wine. It was likelier that the supposed theological differences between the three factions were merely intellectual justifications masking the monks' far more primal responses to the fear brought on by the deaths of the gods two years ago.

An unnerving thought. He had always preferred to believe that one's philosophical position was a matter of reasoning and moral dedication rather than an unthinking response to baser instincts. Abbot Venia had always struck him as a man almost as driven by logic and enquiry as Estevar himself.

What effect did the poison have on your beliefs, my friend? How did it twist that magnificent mind of yours? His gaze went briefly to Caeda, who was tapping her fingertips against each other in a silent rhythm to distract herself from the boredom. *What could possibly have brought you so low as to bind and torment this innocent girl, Venia?*

The answer to that question was hidden somewhere in this abbey, but to trace the abbot's last footsteps, Estevar needed a guide whose mind hadn't been addled. Unfortunately, the only monks who'd remained with Venia had been the traditionalists – the Bone-Rattlers – and from what he'd seen, almost all of them were terrified to the point of catatonia.

It was only when recalling something the perpetually calm and collected Brother Agneta had said during their first meeting that Estevar was able to devise a plan.

'*Almost makes me wish I hadn't given up liquor,*' the old inquisitor had said while Sister Parietta and Brother Jaffen had been demanding to take Estevar prisoner.

Agneta had not imbibed the wine, so she had not been afflicted by the hallucinogen. Her obsessions, her madness, belonged to her alone.

Caeda had asked why they weren't rushing off to arrest her as the obvious suspect, but Estevar had spent enough time with the relentlessly pragmatic Cogneri to recognise that such a reckless and unpredictable gambit wouldn't suit her. A far more likely explanation was that she'd witnessed with growing concern the affliction of her brethren and was now awaiting their recovery before she set about imposing her own vision of the abbey's future. This interpretation better explained why she'd reverted to her old profession of Inquisitor, approaching every dilemma with the same methodical, merciless conviction with which she'd once interrogated apostates.

Since it was unlikely Venia had ever confided his heretical plans to Brother Agneta, Estevar was in need of a different guide to help him trace the abbot's steps during his final hours.

'*In an abbey which housed three hundred monks,*' he'd explained to Caeda before they'd snuck into the chapter house, '*there must be more than one who doesn't drink.*'

Her own experiences, she'd countered, suggested that such a hypothesis relied on an unreasonably high regard for monks.

'Ah, but this is not a question of virtue,' Estevar had pointed out. 'There are any number of ailments that make alcohol untenable for the liver, so we can reliably infer that one or two others among the brethren at least remain in their right minds and have chosen to lurk in the shadows, biding their time, perhaps even haunting the footsteps of a Greatcoat whose intentions they cannot divine.'

While the fretful spy had kept his distance since the advent of the demons, Estevar was sure the fellow would resume his watchful pursuit, especially if the interloping magistrate were to invade so sacred a place as the abbey's chapter house.

At least, that was my theory.

'No one's coming,' Caeda whispered, blowing a strand of hair from her forehead.

Estevar's legs had grown numb and his back felt as if it might seize at any moment. He massaged his thighs to wakefulness, all the while fearing he'd overestimated his quarry's eagerness.

'Come on,' she said, beginning to rise. 'Let's g—'

Estevar grabbed her arm and pulled her back down, still unnerved at how solid – how *alive* – she felt. Ignoring her outraged glare, he held a finger to his lips.

The quiet creak he'd heard seconds before was soon followed by the slow, barely audible padding of bare feet on the oak floor, approaching from one of the chapter house's six doors.

Those doors had been the problem with trying to capture their spy. Tristian holy buildings always had six entrances, one for each of the gods. Worshippers arrived and departed through whichever one was affiliated with the god to whom they were most devoted. A common boast among clerics who sought converts to their own faiths was to declare to their colleagues, 'They may have walked in through your god's door, but they left through mine.'

Hiding behind one of the entrances would have been no different than rolling dice, for if Estevar guessed wrong, his prey would race back out of the door they'd come in, fleeing before he and Caeda could catch them. The lectern, however, was set on a circular wooden dais several feet above the chapter house floor. A wooden railing ran all around it to protect the preacher from accidentally falling during a particularly impassioned sermon. The sole gate onto the dais had been constructed to swing closed and latch on its own, delaying anyone who entered from running back down the stairs.

Come now, my little mouse, Estevar urged silently, listening to the quiet patter of those tentative footsteps. *You saw us enter this holy place, defiling it with our presence. But where are we lurking among the endless rows of pews? Where better to spot us from than atop this sanctified perch?*

Sure enough, a few minutes later he heard the soft squeak of the gate's hinges, followed by the gentle *clack* of the latch falling shut. Estevar counted three more breaths before he made a grab for the intruder. The stubble-headed young monk was quick, though, and without even a cry of surprise, spun on his heel and took two steps towards the gate before leaping up to jump over the railing.

Alas, my friend, Estevar thought, reaching out to grab hold of a handful of grey woollen hem, *here is why coats are superior to robes: coats don't fall all the way to the ankles, thus providing a helpful tether.*

The garment tore free from Estevar's grip, but not before blunting the monk's momentum and causing his ankle to catch on the railing. The young man's arms flapped wildly as he fell forward, ending in a rather hard landing and a great deal of groaning.

'I'd take a moment to catch your breath if I were you,' Estevar advised, opening the gate and ushering Caeda through in a leisurely fashion before descending the stairs behind her. The grimacing monk was attempting to simultaneously cradle one arm while rubbing the opposite knee. 'Please allow us to ensure you've not broken any bones before you escort us on a brief tour of this abbey's less-visited attractions.'

CHAPTER 32

THE GOOSE CHASE

In spite of his newly bruised knee and sprained elbow, Brother Syme limped with impressive speed up the rough-hewn wooden stairs of the suitably named Tower of Humility, resentfully mumbling 'ouch' with every step. That was only to be expected, as apart from the injuries he'd suffered tumbling over the railing of the dais in the chapter house, Syme was also afflicted with a bad case of gout.

'Which means he can't drink wine, can he?' Caeda whispered as they climbed the stairs behind the spy who'd been dogging Estevar's footsteps since his arrival at the abbey.

'Further confirmation of our hypothesis,' Estevar agreed. There could be no more doubt that the already fractured brethren of Isola Sombra had been driven to the brink of madness by the poisoned wine. *Neither can there be any doubt as to who committed the deed*, Estevar reminded himself.

He'd already crossed Brother Agneta off the list of likely perpetrators. There were few depths to which the Cogneri would not sink to achieve their ends, but Estevar had long ago trained himself to set aside his biases in these matters. However dark their predilections, the inquisitors were, in their own fashion, as devoted as the Greatcoats to the laws they enforced. True, religious doctrines did make for an unforgiving brand of justice, but to poison the sinful along with the innocent would not, he was certain, have suited Brother Agneta's nature.

Mother Leogado possessed both the strategic abilities to plan such a gambit in a way that would favour her followers, and she was quite capable of justifying such an act as a necessary evil in service to the abbey. However, her manic carving of her little figurines had absolved her of the crime. That obsession had been at such odds with her demeanour that it was obvious, in retrospect, that she too was under the wine's toxic influence.

No doubt Strigan would have happily perpetrated the crime, and he was quite stupid enough to have accidentally imbibed the tainted wine himself. Furthermore, his arrogance and delusions of grandeur might easily have convinced him that the hallucinogenic properties would enhance the occult rituals in which he and his followers were engaged. But the act required careful planning and flawless execution – hardly characteristics of the self-styled Wolf-King of Isola Sombra.

And then, of course, there was another possessed of both motive and means.

Was it you, Venia? Did you seek to bring your monks closer to the gods by setting free their minds from worldly concerns, only to drive them to lunacy and mayhem?

He banished that suspicion along with the others. Recalling all that had transpired since his arrival at the causeway, Estevar was certain he'd deduced the culprit responsible.

Which will make for a dangerous reunion when next we meet, he thought, reflexively pressing the sword wound in his side, all too aware that it would hamper survival of the duel that was, he was sure, inevitable. *But first, I need one more piece of evidence*, he reminded himself.

Unlike the more ostentatious Venerance and Vigilance, the stone walls of the Tower of Humility were rough and unadorned, stained by water leaking through the wooden roof. Judging by Brother Syme's frequent affronted glares as he led them up the dangerously rotting wooden stairs to the top floor, the novice considered the abbot's private tower to be grander than any palace.

'It's not right that you should force me to bring you here,' Syme said for the fifth time since they'd left the chapter house. He'd been privileged – as he reminded them with equal frequency – to serve as Venia's libatiger, the monastic equivalent of a cup-bearer or page. Since the abbot's death, Syme had been sneaking into the courtyard every night to re-bury his body, hoping every time it would finally stay put. 'I gave up my inheritance to my sisters, praying that through spiritual service to the abbey, the gods might grant me relief from my bodily afflictions,' he muttered as they at last reached the top floor. 'Instead, I am surrounded by desecrators whose only devotion is to their own profane desires. *And* my foot hurts worse than ever.'

Estevar would have shown more sympathy for his guide's discomfort had the young man not made quite so much of a fuss during their search of the tower.

'Look,' the monk said irritably, shoving open the door to a tiny cluttered library barely big enough to be worthy of the name, 'I've shown you his bedroom, his audience chamber, his private dining room, even his lavorium – this is all that's left, I swear to every god living.'

'I wouldn't make a habit of that,' Caeda said cheerfully as she squeezed by the two men to enter the cramped chamber.

Estevar caught the sneer Brother Syme gave her as she passed him, but like Strigan, his gaze lingered on her slender body, clearly visible through the thin fabric of her white shift, but then he appeared to forget her every time she was out of his sight. That was the only thing that saved him from the beating his leering would otherwise have earned him.

'Are we investigating or gawking?' Caeda asked, and Estevar returned his attention to the small windowless room. Books were strewn all over the small desk and stacked haphazardly on the floor; some of those piles had served as impromptu tables for unwashed crockery. The deeply unpleasant smell permeating the room was soon explained by the presence of two chamber-pots left in the corner, filled almost to overflowing. All of which provided ample evidence that someone had indeed locked themselves inside this room every night – and that the occupant had been someone other than the abbot.

Not wanting to embarrass the boy, Estevar skipped over a book of erotic poems and instead picked up a ragged, leather-bound volume of adventure tales. 'In the midst of a crisis in which his fractured flock were turning against one another, you expect us to believe that Abbot Venia whiled away his evenings reading sword romances?'

'Everyone's entitled to a break now and then,' Syme mumbled by way of confession. 'Besides, you're acting like there's some mysterious secret lair I'm keeping from you, which is a lie. You have no proof, so you can stop giving me those looks!'

Estevar turned to Caeda. 'Perhaps the boy is right, Piccolo. We have no evidence that such a location must exist, do we?'

She grinned up at him before taking her cue and wandering over to the shelves. 'Might the absence of evidence be its own evidence, my Cantor?'

With quick pale fingers, she traced a line along the shelves of books. There were fewer than a hundred here, but that was still a goodly number from which to extrapolate what was missing.

Brother Syme, presuming that a clue he could not find himself must therefore be beyond some village girl, loomed over her as he drummed his fingers on one of the shelves. 'Have you ever even read a book, you illiterate street whor—'

Syme froze when he felt Estevar's hand around the back of his neck. 'There are altogether too many ways for a monk to die in this abbey, my young friend. Might I suggest you avoid death by rampant stupidity?'

Prudence warred with indignation and lost the battle. 'How *dare* you?' the novice demanded, shoulders tensing. 'I was Abbot Venia's chosen libatiger from among *all* the other novices – yet you would threaten me *here*, in *his* tower?'

Estevar knew Syme was about to raise his right arm in an attempt to drive an elbow into his throat. Were it not for Caeda having retrieved his coat, he'd be forced to either back away or deliver a crippling blow to the man's kidneys, neither option conducive to advancing his investigation. Now, however, he had more and better tools at his disposal.

'That rather musky aroma of brine your nostrils detect comes from the pinch of aeltheca powder I'm about to toss into your face,' he whispered in the monk's ear. 'The paralysis will be temporary, the short-term memory loss . . . well, soon forgotten. But rather than leave you at the mercy of whoever should enter this tower once Piccolo and I depart, might I instead offer a question for you to ponder?'

'Which is?' Syme asked defiantly – but that defiance was itself a sign of impending surrender.

Estevar removed his hand from the back of the monk's throat, wiped away the slimy bit of entirely unremarkable seaweed he'd pulled from his pocket and turned Brother Syme to face him. 'You were a nobleman's son who gave up title and inheritance to serve a man whom you believed to be humble and righteous. Unlike your brethren, you haven't ingested the hallucinogens that have been driving them mad.'

'So what?'

Estevar said nothing. The young man had unwittingly revealed he already knew the answer to his own question – and that his beloved abbot would surely have banished him for his callous behaviour.

There are many paths to madness that do not require drinking poisoned wine, Estevar thought, as troubled by that realisation as by any of the other ugly truths they'd uncovered in this abbey. *Cruelty breeds cruelty, and chaos breeds—*

'Ah!' Caeda said, so entranced by her investigation that she appeared to have missed the entire exchange. 'Of course!'

'Go on, Piccolo,' Estevar said, grabbing the collar of Syme's robe and yanking him out of the way.

She started pulling books from the shelves, one book after another, only to slide each one back in just as quickly. 'Mathematics, astronomy, history, literature . . . just about every subject one could imagine.'

'See?' Syme demanded. 'I told you the abbot never left the tow—'

Caeda spun on him, pointing an accusatory finger, just like the detective in the final act of *Between Two Midnight Murders*. 'Ah, but there it is, don't you see? The missing clue is not the evidence, but the *absence* of evidence.' She swept her hand back along the row of books. 'Show me any another abbot's library that holds not a single volume of . . . theology!'

A trifle melodramatic, Estevar thought, but he was hardly one to talk. 'Venia's monks were defiling his abbey, embroiled in acts of violence, debauchery and the very desecrations that so offend you, Brother Syme. One might assume a spiritual leader would seek wisdom in religious texts and occult treatises – which Venia was known to collect and yet are absent from his private library.' Syme was slouching away from him towards the door, but Estevar blocked his escape. 'Unless, of course, he feared the looting of his most prized possessions and instructed his trusted clerk to help him secrete them away somewhere safe – some- where the monks running rampant across the abbey would not search for them. *That*, my young friend, is where you are going to lead us.'

CHAPTER 33

THE LAST DOOR

Estevar soon had cause to regret his persistence in seeking out the location where Abbot Venia had spent his final, frantic days. The murky water inside the storm tunnels rose ever higher as Brother Syme led them down the slope. It was already up to Estevar's calves and his heart was beating dangerously fast, sweat beading on his forehead at the memory of his near-drowning three days ago. Caeda, sensing his disquiet, took his hand. Her palm felt warm, reassuring – and a reminder that nothing on this accursed island was as it seemed.

'No one comes down here,' Brother Syme told them, taking a right turn at the next junction. The stone ceiling was even lower here, with jagged deformations that threatened to part Estevar's hair should he stand up straight. 'The other factions fight like animals over storerooms and who gets to occupy which towers. Even before the abbot's murder, I'd been searching for places to hide in case things got even worse.'

'When did you last see Abbot Venia?' Estevar asked, sloshing through the water to keep up.

'The day of the storm. The big one, I mean – when all that crazy lightning destroyed the statues. He hadn't been talking much lately; I was barely able to convince him to eat or drink. But that day ... he was so excited, so ... happy.' Brother Syme's shoulders shuddered as he tried and failed to suppress a sob. 'The next morning I found his body in the statuary. His head had been left six feet away.'

'You buried him in the statuary,' Estevar said gently, careful not to make it an accusation.

Syme kept walking along the narrow passage. 'The cemetery is on the other side of the abbey, past the curtain wall. I couldn't bring myself to drag his headless . . . I dug a grave for him among the remains of the statues of the gods. I thought maybe that would be . . . I don't know – fitting, somehow? But the next day, his body was lying right where I'd found it before, so I buried him again, like I've had to do every night since.'

The novice stopped and turned to face them, misery etched into his features. Estevar would have had no difficulty imagining Syme as a lord, a viscount, a margrave . . . Now, though, he just looked like a lost little boy. 'Was it my fault?'

'What?' Estevar asked.

'Those monstrous creatures with their leathery white skin and those awful blue eyes – did they come because I buried my master somewhere I shouldn't have?'

The sorrow and wretchedness in Syme's voice testified even more to his devotion for the dead abbot. Estevar could feel Caeda's barely restrained outrage through the tightening of her grip on his hand.

And yet she does not shout or scream at this glorification of the man who bound and tortured her for days before throwing her into the sea. I could learn much from her restraint, if only we had more time.

'You did not fail the abbot,' he told Brother Syme. 'What has unfolded in this once-sacred isle is a tangle of supernatural theology and mur-derous intrigue that can only be unravelled by tugging on the threads of Venia's last actions before he died.'

'By defiling his memory – that's what you really mean, isn't it?'

Estevar glanced past the young monk to a small arched wooden door a few yards away at the end of the tunnel. He took a step forward, but his way was blocked.

'Promise me you'll speak well of him,' Brother Syme said, refusing to let them pass. 'Whatever stupid trial you hold when all this is done, whatever verdict you pass on the rest of us, promise me you'll see to it that no one sullies Abbot Venia's reputation.'

This last proved to be too much for Caeda, who shook off Estevar's grip and would have launched herself at the man twice her size had Estevar not stepped in front of her.

Perhaps we could both teach each other a little restraint, he thought, staying there until she backed off. The look in her eyes was one of bitter accusation for a betrayal he was about to commit in service to his investigation.

He surprised her by saying, 'I will make no promises, save to uncover the truth and pay any price I must to end the madness consuming this abbey.'

'Then you're not going inside that room,' Syme said, his tone a warning that, despite his chosen vocation, he knew how to handle himself in a fight and wouldn't be taken off guard again.

Do not take the bait, Estevar admonished himself when his hand reached for his rapier. *If Caeda can suffer the injustice of this moment, you can surely keep your belligerence in check this once.*

Facing the defiant monk, he said, 'I will neither give you the assurances you seek nor bully you into giving way. Instead, I will simply ask you this, Brother Syme: if the abbot you so faithfully served was here, right now, knowing all that awaits us beyond that door and what it might mean for his legacy, what would he tell his trusted libatiger to do?'

The subsequent storm of conflicting emotions was predictable from someone who'd been raised to believe himself above others, and to never take insults lightly, but Estevar felt some admiration for him when, without further threat or complaint, he stepped aside.

Caeda went first, and as Estevar passed Brother Syme he placed a hand on the disheartened monk's shoulder. 'I met with Abbot Venia many times, shared innumerable correspondences with him. Always, I found him to be a kind, decent and profoundly spiritual person. Whatever became of him during his last hours, let us agree to withhold judgement, and remember that what transpired was a tragedy of which he too was a victim.'

Syme made no reply, only wept quietly, staring down at the brackish water flooding the ground.

'The door's locked,' Caeda said from the end of the passage, pushing in vain on the rotting but still sturdy wood that was banded with iron.

'The key, if you please?' said Estevar. 'Venia wouldn't have left his priceless texts somewhere that could be easily breached, so I don't blame you for taking steps to ensure no one else could enter after his death.'

He reached a hand into his greatcoat. 'I can pick the lock myself, but that feels disrespectful to your master's memory.'

At last, Syme produced the key from inside his robes and pushed past Caeda to unlock the door before stepping away so that she and Estevar could enter by themselves. The water to their calves made it hard to push the door open, but their joint efforts soon had it moving. The two of them entered the chamber, and Estevar bore witness to the Abbot of Isola Sombra's final testimony.

Oh, Venia, he thought despairingly, *what have you done?*

CHAPTER 34

THE LAST TESTAMENT

The cell was barely eight feet long and only half as wide. The floor was lower than the tunnel outside, forcing Estevar to wade knee-deep even as he stooped like an old man to keep his head from hitting the rough-hewn rock of the low ceiling.

A sleeping pallet barely wide enough for Caeda – never mind someone of Venia's girth – floated atop the murky water alongside sodden pages which upon examination, proved to be from the missing religious treatises. Estevar reached down to snatch up several sheets he recognised, ripped from the *Sacrificia Purgadis*. Folding them carefully, he slid the wet bundle into one of the lined pockets meant to protect legal documents. Only three copies of that banned text had remained in Tristia. Now there were two.

A familiar fury rose inside him. Every blotch of smudged ink was another desecration that would have broken the heart of the scholarly, inquisitive cleric who'd been drawn to knowledge almost as deeply as faith.

Now, it appeared, the only words Venia had cared to preserve were his own – for scrawled all over the walls was a manic, haphazard last testament and unwitting confession of a man lost to his own madness. Words, phrases, even whole sentences were often at odd angles, sometimes even overlapping. The same word kept appearing, written over and over, until the excess ink had dripped down the wall like a bloody arrow pointing to the water.

There were drawings, too, of creatures wondrous and foul. Some

231

frolicked together, some fornicated, but most were tearing each other apart with monstrous teeth, horns and twisted claws. Estevar produced a small notebook and a slender, leather-wrapped charcoal stylus from a breast pocket and began copying the designs as best he could on the still-damp pages. Two figures stood out among Venia's bizarre bestiary: a man and woman, covered in sigils similar but not identical to the ones Strigan and his followers had inked into their flesh.

'Estevar?' Caeda said quietly. She rarely used his name.

He turned to see her pointing to the wall nearest the door, where five words, larger and more precisely written than the rest, had surely been meant to be the last thing Estevar would see before leaving the room.

Judge me without mercy, Eminence.

'What does it mean?' Caeda asked.

A simple question – the obvious one, in fact. And yet it revealed an innocence that might well destroy her when the time came that Estevar could no longer allow their game of intrepid detectives to continue.

But not now, not yet, he swore silently. *I will not steal one minute of life from you, Piccolo, not until the very end.*

He answered her question truthfully, which would serve them both far better than if he'd done so honestly.

'We are witness to a battlefield, Piccolo.' He turned, gesturing to the scrawls covering the walls. 'A war between madness and reason waged within the mind of one man. A war, I fear, over which we can have little doubt about which side won.'

'It's all nonsense,' Brother Syme insisted angrily. 'I've examined every line written on these walls, searched for scriptural quotations, word patterns, even anagrams. It's nothing but gibberish.'

'*Gibberish*,' Estevar repeated to himself. The novice had employed that word like an advocate demanding absolution for his client, though he was wrong; he merely lacked the mental discipline to navigate the long, twisted path Venia's broken mind had blazed during his final hours.

Estevar reached out to trace one of the scrawls with his fingertips. *You left your footprints for us to follow, didn't you, my friend?*

'Tell me, Piccolo,' he said, turning to Caeda, 'what do you see inside this room?'

She was standing closer to him than usual, as if she, too, feared some-thing swimming beneath the torpid waters of the cramped chamber. 'I see madness. Incoherent babble and ugly images, strung together without purpose, without . . .' She looked up at him. 'Without music, my Cantor.'

'See?' Brother Syme pounced on Caeda's confusion. 'Even *she* sees it's all nonsense.' He backed out of the chamber as if nervous that at any moment something in the water might snap at his heels. 'I've done what you asked, shown you things no one should ever have seen. Now, will you please leave so that I can lock this room and throw the damned key into the ocean?'

Estevar waded towards the door, only to stop suddenly. Staring down at the muddy water, he asked, 'Tell me, Brother, do eels often get past the gratings in the storm drains?'

Syme practically jumped out of his robes and very nearly bashed his head against the low ceiling. 'Why would you ask that? Did you see one? Where is it?'

Estevar bent at the waist, making a show of trying to peer through the murk. 'I thought I saw— There!' he shouted, his finger following the path of something moving under the dark water towards them.

'Saints protect me!' Brother Syme cried.

As the panicking novice kicked at imaginary eels, Estevar reached into one of the pockets of his greatcoat before discreetly passing his hand over the lock on their side of the door.

'That's not an eel!' Syme declared angrily, still kicking at the water. 'Nothing but a crooked stick floating under the surface.'

'Ah, what a relief!' Estevar said, placing a hand on his own chest as if on the verge of fainting. Turning back to Caeda, he went on as if nothing had happened, 'And you, Piccolo, what do you feel?'

'What do I *feel*?'

He gestured at the incoherent scribbles all over the walls. 'When reason fails to reveal the clues, logic dictates we must turn to our emotions. Let us listen closely to where our feelings guide us.'

Caeda took the lantern and sloshed through the water until her nose was a hand's breadth from one of the walls. The writing covering every inch of stone would have required days to transcribe, never mind interpret. And as much again of Venia's scribblings were already below the water line.

Choosing one of the passages, perhaps drawn by the jagged, angry lettering, Caeda read aloud, '*Where have gone the days when prayers charged forth like knights to battle? Faithful voices go unheard, as above, so below, and now our curses hold no sway against their schemes and steel.*' She paused, tapping a finger against the cleft in her chin. 'The abbot bemoans that the gods no longer pay heed to mortal pleas. And this mention of schemes and steel – that could be a reference to the Margrave of Someil plotting to take over the abbey by force.'

'A logical interpretation,' Estevar acknowledged.

'But you don't agree?'

'Madness begets madness, and it does so by cloaking itself in rationality. I did not ask you to analyse the words he left behind but to tell me how it makes you feel.'

Her gaze followed the twisting, zigzagging lines. 'I feel . . . uneasy. I wouldn't want to be near the person who'd written these words. Look here, how the ink at the end of "unheard" suddenly veers off – and there's a tiny pit in the stone.' She turned to look up at Estevar. 'He broke the tip of his quill, didn't he?'

'I believe so. What happened next?'

'What do you mean?' Brother Syme demanded, still lurking outside the open door. 'He went back and finished the sentence. That's obvious.'

Estevar joined Caeda by the wall. 'Tell me the part that is less obvious, Piccolo. Interpret from Venia's actions that of which even he was unaware.'

She stared at the wall a while longer, then turned to look around the room. 'There's no desk here, no shelves, not even a box. Even if the abbot had brought spare quills, he would have had to stop to retrieve one from whatever container he was using to keep them off the wet floor. He would have needed to trim it and dip it into the inkpot before returning to finish the sentence.'

'A few minutes, no more,' Estevar reminded her.

'Yes, but even a few minutes should have calmed him down, especially since he'd just broken the previous one by pressing too hard against the stone. Yet here' – she pointed to the following section – 'as above, so below is written just as jaggedly as the rest. It's a wonder he didn't break a second point.' Again she looked to Estevar with a questioning gaze. 'He would have had to have been feral with rage to write like this.'

'Good,' he said. 'By listening to your own feelings of disquiet, you have found a footstep in the desert buried after a sandstorm. By opening yourself to the feelings of the suspect, you begin to follow his trail.'

Caeda nodded, but she didn't smile at his praise as she usually did. Instead, she began to work more quickly, sloshing about the tiny cell as she found other passages scrawled with an equally unsteady hand, yet revealing entirely different emotions.

'Here,' she said, kneeling to point at a section low down near the water. 'Everything's small here, like the writer is frightened. The angles of the letters are all tilting on a diagonal. And see this dark patch on the wall?' When she ran her finger along it, the tip came back stained. 'That's soot from a candle held too close for a long time. I think he wrote this as he was lying on his sleeping pallet.'

'What does it say?'

'They will come now. I have seen to it. There's a relief in knowing I've failed in every way conceivable, like falling into a well so deep you'll never be able to climb out, yet still there's reassurance in the solidity of the bottom. Let those who wish to fight over this island do battle with sword and claw until it sinks into the sea. Even then, my own sins will never be washed clean, yet in my thousand damnations, still the vilest of my crimes will go unpunished.'

'Who are "they" supposed to be?' Brother Syme asked. 'The Hounds and the Trumpeters? The margrave's soldiers? The demons?'

'It didn't matter,' Caeda replied, 'not to Abbot Venia, anyway.' Her voice softened, the hatred she rightfully felt for Venia now tinged with pity. 'He despised himself at the end.'

Estevar took her by the arm and helped her up. 'Was it the end, though?'

'What do you mean?'

He gestured at the other walls. 'We do not know in which order he wrote these passages, therefore, we do not know which came first and which last.'

'Then what was the point of all this?' she asked, scowling in irritation. 'How are we supposed to decide if any of this matters?'

Estevar reached down and dipped his hand in the brackish water, holding it in his palm as if it were a cup of wine. 'Three ways have we seen the poison affect those who drank it. Paranoia, fear and—'

'Debauchery,' Caeda finished for him. 'You want me to search the walls for erotic poems?'

Estevar let the putrid water slip between his fingers. '*Feelings*, remember? Debauchery is an activity, not an emotion. When we met the Hounds, what fuelled their revels?'

Caeda returned to the walls, running her hands along the scrawled passages as if her fingertips could touch the sentiments fused into the inks. At last, she came to one written in a style different from the others, buried among all the darker testaments. 'This passage is lighter,' she murmured, 'languorous, almost winsome.'

'Read it,' Estevar urged her.

'*Every drop of rain from the storm is a blessing that washes away my guilt and drowns my sorrows. What was once lost is found again, for she has returned.*' Caeda glanced around at the other walls. 'There are no other passages like this one. What does it mean?'

Estevar allowed himself to smile. 'It means many things, Piccolo, but the one that pleases me is that Venia knew a moment's happiness before he died. Amid all his suffering, all his doubt, your presence brought him solace before the end.'

Caeda glanced back at the passage. 'You mean, because I didn't die when he threw me off the cliff? Malezias told me he'd seen me from the shore and rowed out in his boat to pull me from the sea, but I was already unconscious from days of being deprived of food and water.' She turned back to Estevar, confusion and anger warring on her face. 'Why did Malezias even bother? Why do you let me follow you around like a puppy? What does the life of one village girl matter to any—?'

The clang of the iron-banded door slamming shut behind them was immediately followed by the creak of the key turning in the lock. Caeda dashed through the water to the door and hauled on the handle, but it wouldn't budge. 'The coward must have been closing it gradually while we were distracted with Venia's writings so we wouldn't hear him pulling against the water.'

'Forgive me,' Brother Syme called out from the other side. 'She . . . she told me to tell you that yours is not the only legal authority here, and by laws more ancient than those of any king, you are hereby placed in the custody of the Cogneri until a trial for heresy may be convened.'

Estevar walked leisurely to the door that was confining them within a low-ceilinged cell slowly filling with water from the overflowing storm drains that would shortly be flooding the lower passages of the abbey. The wooden door had begun to rot long ago, but it was at least four inches thick and banded with iron strong enough to withstand a war hammer, never mind Estevar's rapier.

He leaned in close and said, 'You're forgiven.'

Apparently Brother Syme had not yet run off to inform Brother Agneta that he'd completed his mission. 'What did you say?'

'A moment ago, as you locked us inside this waterlogged chamber, you begged our forgiveness. Are you no longer desirous of a pardon?'

'I . . . Don't try to fool me with your Greatcoat ruses. She warned me that you might have some trick up your sleeve!'

'Pocket, actually,' Estevar mumbled inaudibly.

'What?'

'I said, run along now, Novice. Inform Brother Agneta that I am most eager to accommodate her in the matter of a trial for heresy. Give her my forgiveness as well, if you're of a mind.' He smiled at Caeda. 'That will irritate her no end.'

Estevar waited until the sound of the monk's feet splashing in the water receded. 'I confess to being at once irritated at his betrayal and disappointed in the lack of originality.'

Caeda snorted in disgust. 'I couldn't believe the way he fell for your silly "Are those eels in the water?" ploy.'

'You saw?' Estevar asked, somewhat crestfallen that his attempt at legerdemain had been so easily spotted.

She knelt down to peer through the keyhole. 'What did you stick in there, anyway? It didn't stop him from turning the lock.'

'Had I blocked the mechanism, Brother Syme would have known his attempt to incarcerate us had failed. We would have lost the advantage of Brother Agneta being deceived into believing we were her captives.' Estevar removed the thumb-sized leather pouch from his coat pocket. 'The powder I pushed inside the lock has no effect on skin or hide, but it rusts metal with remarkable speed. The famed Tailor of the Greatcoats concocted it for burning through iron bars. Some among the nobility make a nasty habit of imprisoning magistrates when they disagree with our verdicts.'

Caeda grinned up at him. 'Oh, I do adore all your little Greatcoat tricks, my Cantor.'

Estevar knelt to listen at the keyhole. The iron inside the lock was definitely hissing. It wouldn't be long now. 'Would you say your fondness for mischief defines you?' he asked.

'Defines me?'

Estevar shrugged as if it had been nothing but an idle question to pass the time. 'Many of us are driven by a singular passion – a focal point – from which all our other tendencies flow.'

She didn't answer at first, and when he looked back at her, she was paler than before. 'You make me uncomfortable when you talk like that, Estevar. It's very rude of you. I wish you'd stop.'

He put up his hands in surrender. 'Forgive me, my dear. I've been wounded, drowned, beaten, threatened with any number of unpleasant deaths and now forced to read the rantings of someone I – grudgingly, I will admit – respected. My mind is perhaps a trifle addled.'

He went back to listening at the keyhole. Hearing nothing now, he grabbed the handle with both hands, placed his heel against the wall and pulled with all his strength. The iron piece holding the bolt in place crumbled and the door slowly opened, splashing even more water over his already soaked legs.

'See?' Caeda asked as if this had all been her plan. 'You're so much more fun to be around when you leave the philosophising to others.' She stepped past him, holding the lantern aloft to illuminate the tunnel. 'Where do we go now? I doubt either the Trumpeters or the Hounds will offer you sanctuary from Brother Agneta.'

Estevar massaged his palms, which now bore the sharp imprint of the door handle. 'It is not we who require sanctuary, believe me.' He glanced either way down the winding passageway, trying to get his bearings, then chose left. 'We must go to the bell gate near the shore on this side of the causeway.'

'Why?' she asked, following behind. 'It can't be more than an hour after nightfall. Malezias said the causeway wouldn't be passable until morning at the soonest.'

'Perhaps, but by now the Margrave of Someil will have assembled his forces on the other side, so I'll need to shout across the channel to inform him that he's in violation of the King's Law against forceful annexation of religious lands. Also, I have reason to believe someone will be coming to meet me by the shore.'

Caeda grabbed the back of his coat to make him slow down. 'Who's coming for you?'

'A dead man,' Estevar replied. 'Though he doesn't know it yet.'

PART THE SEVENTH

THE SIGILS
OF SELECTION

What is recorded hereafter is meant neither for use in the ritual nor for idle study but rather as a warning. Those who first devised the Sacrificia Purgadis noticed an unusual phenomenon: the sacrifice, emptied of both will and sin, becomes a vessel whose spiritual emptiness demands to be filled. The temptation to inscribe sigils from other rituals and thus instil divinity into the sacrifice led some to attempt the creation of their own gods. The results of such heresy led to the first law of the Cogneri: the execution of any who perform such blasphemous experiments, all who bore witness, and above all else, the abominations they spawned.

CHAPTER 35

PRIDE

Late that afternoon, an eerie quiet settled over the shore. When Estevar had first crossed from the mainland three days ago, fiendish grey clouds roiled, thunder boomed and lightning flashed. Now there was nothing, no rain to drip down the back of his neck nor fog to prevent him seeing the tents and pavilions topped by the white, azure and silver flags of Someil half a mile away, across the drowned causeway.

'How did you know they would come?' Caeda asked, peering into the distance. It was too far for the naked eye to make out individual figures, but Estevar fancied he could envision the preparations well enough. Knight-commanders would be arguing with their counterparts among the infantry and archers to settle the lofty question of who should lead the charge once the tides had finally receded enough to make passage across the causeway possible. Engineers would be fighting to be heard over the din as they tried to warn of the dangers of sending too many horses at once over the slippery cobblestones – especially when the piers supporting the causeway beneath the water had likely been weakened by decades of neglect, let alone winter storms more savage than could ever have been anticipated by the original builders.

But the voices Estevar imagined most vividly were those of the priests. Invading the territory of a spiritual community, even in a nation with as dubious a view of religious privileges as Tristia, would surely be sitting uneasily with superstitious soldiers accustomed to praying to their favourite god before every battle. The Margrave of Someil would doubtless have recruited hand-picked clerics sympathetic to his cause:

men and women who aspired to rule Isola Sombra once the heretics befouling its once-sacred soil had been rooted out.

'*They consort with demons!*' one of the clerics would surely be shouting, drumming up a feverish anger within the troops.

Another would suggest, '*And they plot against the margrave!*'

'*They intend to take up arms against us!*' a third would surely venture.

If only all those things weren't true.

'My Cantor?' Caeda asked.

'Hmm?'

'You didn't answer my question. How did you—?'

'Do you agree with Malezias' assessment that by morning the flooding will have receded enough to make the causeway passable?'

She knelt down on the rocky shore to peer beneath the surface of the water at the drowned cobbles beneath. 'The currents are unpredictable in winter, especially during storm season, but I see no reason to doubt him.'

'Nor I – *that* is how I knew the margrave's army would be massing on the other side this afternoon. Someil will want to deny any resistance forces time to prepare, but he also needs his soldiers rested after the long march from his lands.'

Caeda stood up again. 'Have you fought in many battles?'

'Hundreds. I'm fighting one now.'

'I mean real ones, like in a war where it ends in victory or defeat.'

He sighed, wishing Imperious were here with him. As much as he admired Caeda's quick mind and insatiable curiosity, what he needed now was to steady himself for the duel ahead. Sullen as the mule could be, his was a soothing presence better suited to girding oneself for battle. 'An investigator is always at war,' he replied at last. 'Victory occurs when the truth is revealed, defeat when the lie stands.'

Caeda tried to poke him in the chest again, but this time she yelped when her finger struck one of the bone plates sewn into the lining of his coat. 'Ouch, damn it. You know what I meant – why must you be so obtuse?'

'Forgive me,' he said, both for the grievance of which she rightly accused him and of his unspoken but nonetheless ill-mannered comparison of her to a mule. 'I do not like to speak of war, Piccolo. There are many who believe wars to be righteous, even glorious. Others argue for their necessity even if terrible suffering inevitably ensues. But to a magistrate, war means one thing above all others.'

'What does it—?' she began, but immediately held up her throbbing finger to forestall his answer. 'Wait. I'll bet I can guess.'

She began to circle Estevar, studying him as if he were a suspect caught fleeing the scene of a crime. She appeared oblivious to the rocky beach, though her feet were bare. 'A pompous fellow we have here, my Cantor. A man who never fails to show off his superior intellect.' She prodded him in the stomach, more carefully this time. 'Yet, despite his disciplined mind, he eats to excess.'

'Piccolo, this is hardly a matter for jest.' He gestured at the crevices in the rocky slope behind them. 'The final witness will be here soon. I need you to hide before the boat arrives.'

She ignored his protest, continuing her contemplative perambulation around him. 'Because he lacks the will or fortitude to do otherwise? Unlikely. Because his girth is no impediment to good health? Perhaps . . . but a man who duels with such frequency knows he places his life in jeopardy with every fraction of a second in speed lost due to his greater weight.'

'Piccolo, please, take cover in the shad—'

'Ah ah ah,' she said, cutting him off. She stroked the sleeve of his coat. 'He values a garment almost more than his own life. Shall we convict him of vanity? We cannot, for while he *is* unquestionably vain' – she shot him a sideways grin – 'and arrogant, dismissive, prone to pontification, ill-humoured, braids his beard—'

'Mocking me will not produce an answer to your question.'

She frowned now, pursing her lips as if wrestling with a complex mathematical equation. 'One must therefore conclude that these are merely symptoms of the suspect's underlying disease, and his real crime is masked by these lesser sins.'

'And for what crime am I to be convicted?'

'The most heinous of all,' she replied easily. 'Pride.'

'Pride?'

She finally ceased her circling and came to a stop in front of him. 'You love what you do, and you do it exceedingly well. To fail to appreciate the fruits of life' – she stared meaningfully at his belly – 'would be to deny yourself the pleasure of your accomplishments. You seek always to educate those around you on principles of the law and the search for veracity because you hope doing so will make the world a fairer place.' She wagged an accusing finger in his face. 'You pretend to an obsession with the truth, Estevar Borros, but your true ladylove is justice. It is she for whom you risk your life, and it is to her you drink in celebration when her cause is triumphant.'

Estevar couldn't keep the smile from his lips. Pride, indeed, was what filled him then, seeing how magnificently Caeda had dissected him – not that he would let her off the hook any more easily than she would him. 'A pretty speech, Piccolo, but I await the answer to the question you posed earlier. What is war to a magistrate?'

She frowned, but without the hint of mockery this time. There was pity in her eyes; she was sad for him. Sad, and afraid. 'War is the death of justice, Estevar.'

She'd surprised him, and he found he could no longer hold her gaze, so he turned back towards the channel, where, half a mile away, plotting generals and priests were busy justifying the slaughter of monks. 'Sometimes, a single act of justice can prevent war. That is the battle we wage, you and I.'

He felt her lean against him as if for warmth, and her closeness made him painfully aware that yet again he lacked a daughter of his own. He wondered whether she really was cold, or whether that, too, was a stolen memory. 'Why do we wait here then, my Cantor?' she asked, sounding sleepy.

'I await a boat. *You* need to take cover before it gets here.'

'How do you know they'll send one?'

Estevar reached into the small tubular pocket on the left side of his coat and removed a compact brass spyglass. He extended it, then offered it to her.

She took it and held it out towards the mainland, squinting one eye shut as she stared through the glass. 'I see them, but what does that—?'

'If we can see them, it means *they* can also see *me*.'

She handed him back the brass instrument. 'If the margrave was planning on sending an envoy, why would he not have already done so? Why wait for you in particular?'

'There is something he will need from me, just as there is something I will need from his envoy.'

'So you're going to bargain with the Margrave of Someil? Plead for some forbearance before his invasion, or negotiate terms for preserving the abbey?' She'd kept her tone even, yet the very precision of her words betrayed her sense of disappointment and resignation – as if his impending parley was proof that justice was, like all things in this world, for sale.

'I am a Magistrate of the Greatcoats,' he reminded her. 'I distil the facts from the evidence, preside over a trial and render my verdicts. I do not *negotiate* with suspects.'

She grinned up at him, a delighted gratitude in her eyes that made him sad.

'Besides,' he went on, 'Mother Leogado testified to me that the margrave came here several times in recent months, attempting to cajole Venia into some sort of accommodation regarding the island. When that failed, he sent his all-too-cunning lackey to poison the abbey's wine stocks, driving the monks to madness and mayhem – all to concoct the justification for an invasion. Having committed such an unconscionable crime, I doubt he's of a mind to compromise his ambitions when victory is so near.'

'Old news, my Cantor,' Caeda said, feigning a yawn. 'You still haven't explained what it is the margrave wants from you.'

Estevar reached into his greatcoat and retrieved the little leather message case. 'When first I arrived at the causeway, one of the margrave's knights, a Sir Daven Colraig, had waited three nights in the storm to give me this.'

He untied the azure cords securing the cylinder and protecting it from water damage, unfolded the letter inside and handed it to Caeda.

'*From his Lordship Alaire, Margrave of Someil,*' she read aloud. '*Warden of the March, Defender of the Faith, to you, my friend, in earnest warning. As you love life and value your soul, do not set foot on Isola Sombra.*' She stared at the letter a moment longer. 'This Sir Daven told you the message was meant for you?'

'He went to great pains to leave me with the impression that I was the intended recipient.'

Caeda examined the note once more. 'Except it's not addressed to anyone in particular, and surely a King's Magistrate receives a more formal honorific than "my friend"?'

'Indeed – especially since even *that* turned out to be a lie.'

'So, this Sir Daven was under orders to challenge *any* magistrate or other official who approached the island, get their name, then pretend that was who he'd been waiting for all along.' Caeda whistled through her teeth. 'So, the margrave intends to kidnap you and force you to publicly declare to his generals and nobles and whoever else he needs to support his invasion that you, a king's magistrate, have observed the chaos within the abbey and invalidate the monks' claim to the island. *You're* the justification for invasion.' She rolled the note back up and poked him with it. 'This envoy must think you're either gullible or easily bribed, my Cantor.'

Estevar took the note from her and put it away before raising the spyglass to his eye. He could make out the little rowboat sailing towards them, and a familiar broad-shouldered, blond-haired paragon piloting it. 'Sir Daven was perhaps better suited to a career in the theatre than as a sheriff outrider. I should have wondered more at the unaddressed note, but before I could, he distracted me with his tale of twelve knights and their supposedly absent souls. That, too, was a trick – part of the broader plot to justify the margrave's annexation of the island.'

'But when we asked Strigan about the knights, he claimed the Bone-Rattlers had spiked their wine and confessed to marking the knights' naked bodies with those sigils as a prank before putting them back on their horses and sending them home.'

'The Wolf-King also claimed to have beheaded Abbot Venia's corpse when you suggested it, and I suspect he would have confessed proudly to any number of crimes if he'd thought they'd make him look more dangerous.'

'Are you engaging in speculation, my Cantor?'

Estevar collapsed the spyglass and replaced it. 'You heard the Wolf-King's endless boasts. Half the time they made no sense. How would he have got twelve naked and supposedly stupefied knights on their saddles, never mind convinced their horses to ride down a winding road, along a treacherous causeway and all the way back to Someil without their riders falling off?'

Caeda's storm-grey eyes were suddenly alight with excitement. 'Of course! Strigan couldn't do all that; he's an idiot! And isn't it odd that he so easily bought *our* lies? Your gambit – the "Cressi Manoeuvre" – why didn't he attack you later when we were in the dignitary's suite at the top of the tower, or on the stairs? He saw how exhausted and in pain you were, yet he believed you every time you bluffed him.'

Estevar puffed himself up a bit. 'I'm not entirely unskilled at—'

Caeda patted his chest absently. 'Yes, dear Cantor, you're very persuasive. You and this Sir Daven should consider putting on a travelling show together. But every time one of us made some inference or insinuation, Strigan went along with it, embellishing here and there. It's almost as if he believed anything anyone told him.'

'Saint Ethalia-who-shares-all-sorrows,' Estevar swore, suddenly understanding why Caeda had been belabouring the point. 'This also explains why the factions are so unquestioning, following whoever leads them – the poison in the wine has not simply inspired paranoia or fear, but it has rendered them highly suggestible. Clever, my girl. Damned clever!'

Caeda beamed at his praise. 'What better way to make an entire abbey full of monks act like lunatics than to expose them to a drug that makes them believe almost any insane story you feed them?'

Estevar turned back to the water. Sir Daven's rowboat, aided by the tides, was making good progress. Soon, there would be a reckoning.

'Go now, Piccolo. I dislike giving orders, but if you are truly my assistant in this investigation, you will allow me to issue this one final command.' Before she could protest, he patted his left side where his greatcoat covered his sword wound. 'Do not fear for me. I am not quite so unprepared for this duel as I was my last.'

He thought she might argue, but the same keen perceptions that made her so quick a study in the art of investigation also told her when the debate was over.

Caeda walked back towards the rocks, where she could observe unseen what transpired next.

She was almost there when she stopped and turned to him. 'Estevar?' she asked tentatively.

'Yes, Piccolo?'

'Everything we've deduced about the margrave and his conspiracy to drive the monks mad so he'd have an excuse to conquer the island makes perfect sense, but how does any of it explain the creatures you saw? Could you have been drugged, too? Because if you hallucinated the demons, then our hypothesis about the margrave's scheme would explain everything.'

If only that were so, Estevar thought, watching the little boat getting closer and preparing himself for what he must do next. *By every saint living and dead, how I wish the truth were half so benign.*

CHAPTER 36

CIVILITY

Sir Daven Colraig smiled as he stepped off the boat, sweeping his arms wide as if he and Estevar were two old friends reuniting after a long absence. The young knight's lustrous blond hair was suitably wind-swept, the white and azure surcoat over his gleaming silver chainmail shirt favourably accented by the sunset behind him.

'Estevar, so good to see you alive and well!' he called, dragging his rowboat onto the shore.

'I regret that I am less enthusiastic at our reunion,' Estevar said, noting the absence of the longsword the knight had worn during their previous encounter. Arriving unarmed to a peace parley was standard diplomatic protocol, yet entirely suspicious in this particular case. 'Your demeanour is considerably changed since our first encounter.'

Sir Daven gave an elaborate bow. 'I was born in Jereste, a city famed for its actors. I was so good at pretending to be other people, I managed to get myself knighted!' He laughed at his own joke. Leaning casually against the boat's prow, he added, 'Forgive my impertinent familiarity, Eminence. It's only that I feel as if we are kindred souls, given our respective professions.'

'You mean because I am a magistrate sworn to investigate wrongdoing in service of the law while you are a nobleman's lackey who covers up his master's crimes for personal reward?'

'These days, I prefer the title sheriff outrider. But I've not rowed across that miserable, stomach-churning stretch of water to quibble with you.' He glanced around at the beach. 'What happened to that woman who was standing with you? The one in the white gown with the red hair?

251

Damned rowboats work better when you're going backwards, but I managed a glance at her and she struck me as quite lovely.'

'There was no woman with me.'

A flash of irritation crossed Sir Daven's handsome features. 'I saw her in the spyglass from the other side of the causeway, and again while I was rowing here. Forgive me, Eminence, but this seems an odd thing to lie about.'

'Then it is fortunate I have not lied to you.'

'As you will, then, though I don't know why you're bothering to hide her. It's you I've come to see anyway.'

'Then perhaps you would like to get to the point of your visit?'

Sir Daven slapped his own forehead in feigned remembrance. 'You know, you had me so flustered with this nonsensical denial about your lovely companion that I almost forgot why I'd come in the first place. A moment, if you please.' He walked back around to the port side of the little rowboat and reached down beneath the seat. When he turned back, he was aiming a pair of flintlock pistols at Estevar's chest. 'Good news! I've come to rescue you from this foul island of madness.'

'A kind gesture, but unnecessary.'

Sir Daven looked down at his pistols. 'I suppose I could shoot you instead. Do you have a preference?'

Estevar gestured to the path along the rocky beach, away from the crevices in the slope where Caeda was hiding. 'I thought perhaps we might go for a walk and speak peaceably of matters whose consequences will affect the lives not only of those who reside on Isola Sombra, but of our fellow citizens far beyond these shores.'

The knight made a show of considering Estevar's offer, then shook his head. 'Sadly, you have a meeting with the Margrave of Someil and, I'm told, several legal documents to sign. These aren't necessities, you understand; we'll take the island one way or another, but a judicial decree issued by one of the King's Magistrates would smooth things along with some of our more faint-hearted generals. Also, and I say this with complete sincerity, while we're only recent acquaintances, you and I, still I feel a certain affection for you.' He looked down at the loaded weapons in his hands with a saddened expression. 'It would trouble my sleep to know that it was by my hand that you met your death.'

'In this one respect, we are in agreement.'

Sir Daven gestured with one of the pistols towards the boat. 'Good, then if you'll be so kind as to remove that rapier from your side and—'

Estevar cut him off with a raised hand and locked eyes with the young knight. He allowed his voice to deepen, ensuring there could be no doubt as to his seriousness. 'You misunderstand. I do not wish to be the death of *you*, Sir Daven Colraig, but make no mistake: if I set foot inside that boat, I swear to you on my oath as a Greatcoat that you will be dead before we reach the other side.'

The knight tilted his head quizzically. 'I honestly can't imagine what would possess you to make such a futile threat.' He broke out in a friendly laugh. 'Unless you fear your excessive weight will capsize our craft, which I admit *is* something of a danger, eh?'

Estevar took a step towards Sir Daven, causing him to point both pistols at him again. One was aimed squarely at his chest, where the bone plates *might* withstand the lead ball. The other, however, was directed at his face.

'Typically, the man *not* holding the pistol is more circumspect in his actions.'

'It is you who fails to appreciate the precariousness of your position, Sir Daven. Please, as you love life, do not force me to get in that boat with you!'

The golden-haired knight's expression darkened. 'I've tried to be civil to you, Estevar, but you're starting to irritate me. Now listen carefully: remove your sword belt and leave the rapier on the ground, then get in that boat or I will shoot you and drag you aboard. Either way, you'll be having dinner with my liege tonight. I'm told his stewards will be serving braised lamb seasoned with thyme, cinnamon and imported pomegranate seeds. It would be a terrible shame if you weren't able to enjoy the meal.'

Estevar removed his sword belt and lay it down on the rocks. He was reaching into his coat when Sir Daven coughed conspicuously. 'Ah, no,' the knight said. 'We'll have none of those wonderful Trattari tricks tonight. You'll be leaving the coat as well.'

Estevar slid his coat from his shoulders, folded it carefully and set it on a rock before placing a flat piece of driftwood over it so that the leather wouldn't get wet if it rained.

'You really are an optimist,' Sir Daven said. 'I admire that.' He motioned for Estevar to head for the boat. 'If you'll be so kind, pull it back into the water and get inside. You'll be doing the rowing, I'm afraid. Do try not to have a heart attack.'

Estevar did as he was told, observing how the wooden vessel was pitching this way and that against the currents. 'Might I ask you a question before we begin our journey, Sir Daven?'

'We'll have plenty of time for conversation later,' the knight replied, striding confidently towards the boat.

'It's only that I was wondering whether, as you rowed towards the island, you happened to see anyone with me?'

Sir Daven's eyes narrowed in suspicion, then he quickly turned and glanced behind him, swinging one of the pistols towards the rocks. 'I saw no one. Have you been hiding someone from me, Estevar? I do hope you haven't placed your faith in one of those monks. They're all mad as hatters, you know.'

He's forgotten her, Estevar noted. *Just like Strigan and Brother Agneta. When she's out of sight for a few minutes, they can't remember seeing her.*

'Come now, Eminence,' Sir Daven said, ushering Estevar into the boat. 'Greatcoats are legendary for their tricks, but without your coat, you'll have no japes left to play.'

When the two men were sitting in the boat together Estevar made one final entreaty. 'There is still time to allow reason and decency their say in these treacherous matters, Sir Daven. It is not my habit to take a man's life needlessly, so I ask again, will you relent?'

Sir Daven sighed. 'Are you going to be like this the entire way back to the mainland?'

'That depends. How long would you say it took you to row across?'

'Oh, I don't know. Twenty minutes, I suppose?'

'A short time. We'd best begin.'

'Begin what?' Sir Daven asked.

Estevar set the oars in the water and pulled hard with the muscles in his back, propelling them away from the shore. 'The interrogation. I have questions that need answering before you die.'

CHAPTER 37

CONVICTION

The half-mile-wide strait between the mainland and the island grew choppier, waves lapping higher and higher, threatening to swamp the little rowboat. Still Estevar continued to row, neither slowly nor quickly, but with the patient, steady rhythm of a sleeping man's heartbeat.

'You really are a curious fellow, you know that?' said Sir Daven, watching the Greatcoat with inquisitive amusement, the pistol in his left hand resting casually against his thigh. The other was still aimed at his captive's chest.

As a travelling magistrate, Estevar was accustomed to the way some men – often knights, but particularly those vested with a modicum of legal authority over others – liked to watch him. They would try to puzzle out from his expressions or words some insight which they believed demonstrated their own investigative talents were equal to his. Lacking his intensive, all-consuming passion for detection and a willingness to devote themselves to the study of anything and everything that might serve in its pursuit, they pretended that his reputation was, if not entirely unearned, then certainly the product of luck as much as anything else. To such individuals, the art of peering into darkness and confusion, of reaching in with both hands and wresting from those shadows the unwilling truth, emerged from nothing more than instinct hardly distinguishable from their own over-confidence.

'I really don't think you appreciate the complexity of what's going on,' Sir Daven continued, clearly frustrated by Estevar's silence. 'You're acting as if the margrave and I were villainous schemers pulled out of the pages of some old sword romance.' He waved one of the pistols towards the island slowly receding in the distance. 'As if those damnable monks were some sort of . . . well, holy brethren, I suppose.'

'You believe them to be otherwise?'

Sir Daven leaned closer. 'I know it with absolute gods-be-damned certainty.'

Estevar kept on rowing. To take the bait so soon would be to encourage the knight to embellish with extrapolation and conjecture what few pertinent facts he truly had to offer. 'If it's all the same to you, I'd as soon wait until I may pose my questions to your liege. I doubt the margrave has shared all he knows about the events transpiring on Isola Sombra with a mere . . . how did you put it earlier? A "sheriff outrider"?'

Sir Daven laughed at that, not sounding offended at all, although he couldn't quite mask the seething resentment observable in the tightening of his smile. 'Oh, Estevar, you embarrass yourself. The question is not how much his lordship imparts to me, but how much *I* choose to share with *him*.'

Estevar bent the oars back in the water. 'We're almost a quarter of the way there. If you have something to say to me, I suggest you do it soon.'

Sir Daven made a show of placing the back of one hand against his forehead as if he were about to swoon. 'Saints protect my humble soul, are we near to fulfilling your dark prophecy regarding my future?' He set his hand back down on his knee. The knight's grin was congenial, like two friends sharing a joke. 'Admit it, Estevar, that nonsense about me dying if I forced you to set foot on this boat was just a tactic meant to give lesser minds pause.' He wagged the pistol like an accusing finger. 'Even when stripped of your coats, you travelling magistrates always fall back on your little tricks and ploys, don't you?'

Estevar returned Sir Daven's smile. 'That last is not an unfair accusation, I will confess as much.' He kept the oars out of the water a moment to catch his breath. 'But allow me to return to my allegation against the margrave. Isn't this crusade he's embarked upon nothing more than a means to expand his own territory? Feigning outrage over imagined spiritual crimes to justify the illegal acquisition of the island's riches? I wonder what portion of Isola Sombra will be turned over to his trusted lieutenant in this affair once the bloodshed has ended?'

The young knight leaped on the insinuation of pursuing his own gain. 'Ah, you see? This is just like you Greatcoats! So convinced of your own moral superiority that you would impugn those fighting a just cause while defending others engaged in a plot so vile it would wither your soul to hear it.'

Estevar resumed his rowing. The boat was pushed this way and that by the rising waves. Sir Daven kept close watch on Estevar's movements, alert to any attempt he might make to use the oars as weapons.

'What I believe, my friend, is that if you knew of a crime so severe it warranted invading a holy site, you would not keep it a secret from the one person you most need to sanction the margrave's conquest of the island.'

Sir Daven sighed theatrically. 'I suggested as much to my liege. But I fear he's not one of us, Estevar.'

'And what are "we", precisely?'

'Men of the law,' Sir Daven replied, a sternness in his countenance challenging Estevar to call him otherwise. His expression softened. 'When we got word that Abbot Venia had summoned a magistrate to the island, I had no idea it would turn out to be the inscrutable Estevar Borros. Imagine my surprise, finding the King's Crucible himself riding towards the causeway on that mule of yours!'

'You make me sound far grander than I am.'

'Let's just say I'm neither ignorant of your reputation, nor do I share the margrave's disdain for the Greatcoats. It was my belief that if you were fully apprised of the horrors those mad monks sought to unleash upon this country of ours, you would be the first to take up arms alongside me.'

Estevar stopped rowing, letting the blades of the oars drift in the choppy waters. 'I cannot paddle and dance at the same time, Sir Knight. Clearly, you've been instructed not to reveal what you know. You've made plain that this injunction goes against your own judgement. Now you must either disobey those orders or, for the love of the gods, keep silent. The waters grow more treacherous with every stroke, and I haven't the time to be distracted by sly glances and unsubtle insinuations!'

Sir Daven made sure his captive took note of the pistols again. 'You have an unwise habit of denigrating your equals, Estevar.'

'Damn it, man! I'm *trying* to address you as an equal. It is for *you* to decide whether that is truth or lie – whether we are, indeed, both "men of the law"!'

Now we shall see, Estevar thought, watching the knight's reaction to his words. *I have played the penultimate card in this chancy game of ours.*

Sir Daven stared back at him, and in that moment seemed to grow taller, more dignified, as if this was what he'd wanted all along: not power over an enemy or to instil fear in his captive, but to be seen as a colleague – a peer. How strange that Caeda shared this impulse, yet always sought to *earn* that sense of camaraderie with Estevar, rather than demanding it as tribute.

Let him have this small grace, then, for whether or not we are equals in life, we are surely all brothers in death.

'What do you know about the rise of the gods in Tristia?' Sir Daven asked, now with no trace of his smug roguishness or haughty arrogance.

'What most who pursue such matters have gleaned in recent years. When the first Tristians were brought here as slaves, the ores that ran in veins beneath the mines where they were made to work proved to be awakened by faith. Thus, the gods who arose from their prayers were shaped by the desires they felt most keenly.'

'Yes, yes – but what you may not know is that Isola Sombra was the first and most potent location where this phenomenon occurred. In the prayer caves beneath what is now the abbey, masses of slaves were kept in pens before being sold to their Avarean masters on the mainland.'

Thousands upon thousands, Estevar thought, *sharing their prayers in the darkness, adding to them over the years as one group of slaves departed and another arrived.*

'Think of it, Estevar: all those men and women, slowly forging a faith together, unaware that the very rock on which they knelt contained the means to create the gods they so badly needed – Craft, to teach them how to make weapons, War to give them the courage to fight, Death to take their enemies, Coin to reward their victories. But those gods died, murdered by—'

'The Blacksmith,' Estevar interrupted. 'The first to devise a means of killing both saints and gods, releasing the esoteric forces from which they came so that he might bind them back together to create his own deity.'

'Exactly!' The pistol in Sir Daven's right hand was shaking dangerously. 'You Greatcoats stopped the Blacksmith from committing the worst act of tyranny imaginable – the whole country should be on its knees thanking you!'

'We have never been especially fond of *anyone* kneeling,' Estevar said, but he understood now where the knight was going with this. 'So you believe the factions among the monks of Isola Sombra were not fighting over which gods they believed would return to Tristia, but rather which gods to *create*?'

'Precisely.'

'Abbot Venia would nev—'

Sir Daven rose to his feet, causing the boat to list dangerously, before having the sense to settle himself back down. 'Don't you dare try to tell me about what a meek and gentle soul Venia was! The man was a superstitious lunatic, Estevar. For the past two years, every time the margrave would venture out to that island to discuss taxes or trade, Venia would dismiss such matters as incidental. "We are engaged in a matter greater than economics here," I heard him tell the margrave once. "This country enters a new age, and we must give our people new gods to meet it."'

'New gods to do what?' Estevar asked.

'Who in the name of Ebron-who-steals-breath knows? Give the clerics new speeches with which to bore the rest of us into somnambulance while they pilfer the pennies from our pockets, I'd imagine.' He slammed his fist on his thigh again, heedless of the pistols that might go off at any moment. 'Damn it, man! We might not agree on much, but surely we can agree that a few hundred monks – men and women with no authority save that they happen to occupy a ground holier than anyone realised – have no business deciding which gods should rule over the rest of us!'

The rumble of thunder punctuated Sir Daven's outrage. The next storm was coming on fast – perhaps the last one Estevar would ever see – and he still hadn't drawn from the knight the testimony needed to solve this case. 'So, rather than three factions of monks debating which gods would best serve the country, the Margrave of Someil appointed himself our new spiritual leader?'

Sir Daven didn't try to hide his discomfort with the prospect. 'I won't pretend the nobility are any more suited to making such decisions than theocrats.'

'Then who—?' But Estevar didn't need to hear the answer. He felt a loosening in his chest, the easing that came when at last the convoluted constructions of those seeking to deceive him and themselves fell apart. 'You aren't bringing me to the margrave because he's convinced he can't invade without some token legal sanction. You think you can win me to your side so that the two of us can . . . how might I put this? *Guide* your employer in his use of whatever power resides beneath Isola Sombra.'

Even as he made the accusation, Estevar sensed it was incomplete. Sir Daven, for all his pretensions of cleverly setting his will upon the world, was not unlike Brother Syme. He was a born lackey. After Abbot Venia had died, the novice had made himself an underling to Brother Agneta, even though her religious views were the mirror-opposite of Venia's. Sir Daven, though, was more cunning. He'd found his new master before the old one met with whatever fate awaited the Margrave of Someil.

They were nearing the halfway mark between the island and the mainland, which meant time was running out. 'Who is it?' Estevar asked.

Sir Daven, proving he was very nearly as clever as he thought himself, understood the question instantly. 'Those who once ruled this country, Eminence. Those who will soon rule it again.'

Those who once ruled and will soon rule again, Estevar thought. The phrasing of the question made clear the knight would reveal no more than that. *But who could he mean? The country's nine dukes called themselves princes a century ago, before Tristia was united into a single country. The Avareans ruled for two centuries before that.* Neither made sense, however; the dukes had only recently failed in a bid for power and last year the Avareans signed an armistice treaty which their sense of honour would never allow them to betray.

Sir Daven was smiling again, pleased to see his 'peer' so out of his depth. Overhead, the thunder rumbled once more. 'A storm is coming, Estevar. A tempest has been brewing for decades without anyone noticing. It comes from further away than any could foresee. In the coming years, everything you and the rest of the Greatcoats have fought for will come crashing down around you. But there's still a chance – a chance for those like you and me, who perceive the flaws in this foolish nation. We can decide the country's future, within the bounds of what its new rulers will require from it. They'll even let us choose our own gods, after a fashion.'

Estevar didn't reply at first, too consumed with the struggle to calm the anger rising inside him, especially the desperate desire to wrap his hands around the knight's throat and shake him as the waves did the boat until he yielded his secrets. But there were the two pistols in Sir Daven's hands, and the look in his eyes that said he feared his mysterious employers more than he let on.

'Think of it, Estevar,' the younger man urged, kicking the side of the boat and sending it rocking again. 'You claim to serve justice? Imagine if you and I could engineer the rise of a God of Justice for Tristia! Why should our people worship outdated gods born of antiquated values? War? Coin? *Death?*'

'Craft?' Estevar asked.

The knight chuckled. 'Craft can stay, I suppose. Love, too, if you're feeling sentimental. Hells, I don't even mind the Unnamed if people want to believe there are limits to human knowledge. But surely you and I can get behind the idea of offering a God of Justice to a nation that has known so little of it?'

'You truly believe such a thing is possible?'

'I do, I swear it. I told you, Estevar, I've seen things on that island – things that would make your soul weep. But I've *felt* the potential there, too. Venia was mad, but not deluded. The sigils he was marking on some of his monks – they can be used as a means to focus the power of faith in ways not even the ancients imagined.' He set one of the pistols down on the bench and reached out a hand. 'Let's give our people a better breed of god than they've ever known before. They can never be free – that part of their fate is settled – but even servants can prosper when the masters are just.'

Estevar looked at the hand and let the oars go slack. 'You would have me believe you could worship a God of Justice?'

Sir Daven retracted his hand. 'You think I murdered Venia, is that it?'

'I know for a fact you didn't.'

'Then what?'

Estevar gazed towards the mainland. He could see the pavilions now, the supply tents and horses, all of it. 'You were the one who contrived the poisoning of the wine in the abbey, the architect of the plan to justify the mass slaughter of its brethren.'

'I won't deny it,' Sir Daven admitted, without a trace of guilt. 'The margrave needed a pretext to ensure the support of his lesser nobles and his generals – not to mention those superstitious old biddies in armour who call themselves my fellow knights – to stop them fretting over whatever judgments will await them after they die and instead, get off their arses to do something for the living!' He jabbed a gauntleted finger back towards the island again. 'Once we've liberated the island and the toxins slowly wear off, you think the monks will care who rules Isola Sombra? Most of them *hated* Abbot Venia. Eliminate the madmen who lead the Hounds and the Trumpeters – and that lunatic old Cogneri Inquisitor, of course – and the rest will happily pray to whomever we tell them. Hell, Estevar, if it sweetens the deal, I'll put Isola Sombra under the jurisdiction of the Greatcoats!'

'So long as we never rule against your employers' interests.'

Sir Daven laughed. 'You really don't have the faintest idea what we're dealing with, do you? The forces coming for Tristia? They could hardly care less what verdicts you render in trials so insignificant they're barely worth . . .' He trailed off and shook his head. 'I'm wasting my breath, aren't I?'

Estevar responded by slipping the oars from the rowlocks and letting them drop into the water.

Sir Daven picked up his pistols from the bench. 'That was a foolish thing to do. You think I won't kick your fat arse over the side and make you retrieve them?'

'It hardly matters,' Estevar told him. To his surprise, his own sadness was genuine. 'We've had our moment, you and I. The trial is at its end.'

'The *trial*?' the knight demanded. 'You think you've been—?'

Despite the rocking of the boat, Estevar stood. It had always been his practice to rise when giving the verdict. 'Sir Daven Colraig, for the crime of conspiracy, incitement to war and treason against the people of Tristia, the most lenient sentence I can offer you is life imprisonment.'

The knight laughed, though it was a bitter, unhappy thing as he gestured to the ocean all around them. 'We appear to be a little short of prisons out here, Estevar.'

'Indeed, and for that reason, and to prevent the deaths you would surely cause if I allowed you to take my life, it is my regretful duty to consign you to the deep.'

'A pretty speech, Eminence. I'll try to get the phrasing right when I report back to the margrave and explain why I had to kill you.'

Sir Daven raised his pistol for what Estevar knew would be the last time. He watched the other man's finger on the trigger, saw the narrowing of his would-be killer's eyes as he took aim – and saw another thing, too: the mind behind those eyes trying to solve the puzzle of how his helpless opponent could possibly imagine himself fast enough to take him down unarmed. 'What are you, really, without that long leather coat you prize so highly, Estevar? A fat, ageing duellist too arrogant to know when he's beaten?'

'I was that, not long ago,' he admitted. 'I accepted the challenge of another fellow not unlike yourself. Younger than me, faster than me. In retrospect, he might even have been a superior fencer as well.' Estevar carefully lifted the hem of his borrowed shirt to reveal the wound from that fight. 'He left me this small gift as a reminder that without my coat I am, as you said, fat, ageing, and too arrogant to know when he's beaten.'

'Then listen to reason an—'

Estevar held up a finger. 'But as this unruly ocean has taught me, without my coat I am rather more . . . buoyant.'

Using that last revelation to momentarily confuse his opponent, Estevar threw himself over the side. As he dived, he reached out with his left hand and caught hold of the nearest rowlock. The tiny vessel, already barely keeping steady amid the onslaught of the waves, instantly rocked to the right. He heard the explosion from Sir Daven's first pistol, trusting that the knight wouldn't be able to resist the instinct to shift his weight in a futile attempt to keep his balance. The lead ball went wide over Estevar's shoulder.

There was no second shot, for Sir Daven had already lost his balance and was tumbling into the water. Had he not forced his captive to leave his leather greatcoat on the shore, the gambit would have been too risky, for Estevar would have been pulled under by its weight, as he had been during his previous crossing. The knight, however, was still wearing his chainmail underneath his surcoat. Against a hidden blade, or in the unlikely event that his enemy got hold of his pistol, that chainmail would probably have saved his life. Against the sea, it assured his death.

Estevar watched Sir Daven struggle against the water, grabbing for the side of the boat, but the tiny vessel had capsized, and the currents dragging him into the depths were too powerful. There was no valiant mule here to rescue the knight from his own stupidity, only Estevar to spare a last, pitying glance for the would-be chooser of gods who, as he sank ever deeper beneath the waves, raised his remaining pistol and hopefully pulled the trigger, though the faint spark that emerged couldn't hope to ignite the sodden powder.

With a heavy heart, Estevar began the arduous swim back to the sacred isle of Isola Sombra. Long before he reached the shore, he could hear the screams coming from the abbey.

CHAPTER 38

THE TRIAL SUMMONS

Shivering with cold, gasping for breath and exhausted from his battle against the frigid currents, Estevar barely had time to slide his numb arms into the sleeves of his greatcoat and slip his rapier back into its sheath before a figure darted out from the darkness of the rocks. Night had fallen over the island and the ominous shadows cast upon the beach twisted and turned as if dancing to the tune of the screams echoing down the winding road from the abbey. A wild-haired woman came running at him, and Estevar had to stop himself drawing his blade; she looked like a mad ghost coming to drown him in the depths.

'It's madness, my Cantor!' Caeda cried, grabbing hold of his arm and hauling him up the stairs towards the island gate.

'The demons have returned?' he asked.

She hadn't been in the statuary when Strigan had been tortured by the hideous creatures, but she nodded. 'Once your boat was too far away for me to help, I snuck back into the abbey.' Her fingers squeezed his arm even through the leather of his coat. 'They're even worse than you described. Demons, devils – monstrosities born of hate . . . I could never have imagined such things, had I not seen them with my own eyes! What are we going to do?'

Estevar stumbled alongside her until they reached the massive wrought-iron gate with its tall arch and the huge bell suspended beneath. Unlike his previous visit, the gate was wide open, but he didn't enter.

'What's wrong?' Caeda asked. 'Can't you hear the monks crying out for help? We must . . . my Cantor?' Her gaze was a mixture of confusion

265

and disappointment, and reflected in her storm-grey eyes he saw his own fear that the horrors awaiting them had, at last, broken his spirit.

Leaning against one of the tree-trunk-thick iron posts supporting the gate, he opened the front of his coat and confirmed that his stitches had torn again. He fumbled in a pocket to retrieve a tiny blue-glass jar that was almost entirely empty, the last of the black salve having been used up after his failed sword duel. He scraped the inside with his little finger and rubbed what little of the malodorous ointment he could find on his wound. There wasn't enough to seal it, but if he could stave off infection a little longer, that would have to do.

A few more hours, that's all I ask, he said silently to whichever gods or saints were left in the world. Grunting in pain, he stared up at the sky in search of hope, finding only the uncaring stars and an ominous full moon. *By dawn my trial will have come to an end, and should I fail, let the Margrave of Someil take whatever bitter joy he can from standing over my grave.*

'Estevar?' Caeda asked again.

He reached up to pull the rope dangling from the bell. Even that small effort felt as if a crow were using its beak to pry the skin back from his wound.

Save your strength for what awaits you, he thought.

'Here,' he said, and handed the rope to Caeda. 'I will explain the pattern to you, and then you must ring the bell precisely as I instruct.'

'To what end?' she asked. 'The gate is already open, and in case you haven't noticed the screaming, no one's in any position to prevent us from entering the monastery.'

Ritual, he wanted to tell her. *This place is no longer governed by the laws of humanity or nature, but by those of faith, devilry and ceremony.* It was on that unsteady terrain where Estevar would face his final duel. He would make one last attempt to prove that not even supernatural forces could defy the laws he'd come to worship more than any god.

Caeda watched him, longing for the answer to the mystery that had puzzled the two of them for so long, yet not ready for the terrible ending that truth would demand of them both.

He reached out and placed a palm against her cheek. Her skin was so warm, so full of—

'We ring the bell so they will all hear, my Piccolo,' he announced, forcing his unwilling back to straighten, the sagging corners of his mouth to rise into a defiant smile, and above all else, his eyes not to shed tears, but meet hers, as one Greatcoat to another. 'We ring the bell so that everything that walks upon the island of Isola Sombra will know the trial has come to an end, and that Estevar Valejan Duerisi Borros, the King's Crucible, is about to render his verdict.'

PART THE EIGHTH

THE SIGILS OF AWAKENING

Where have gone the days when prayers charged forth like knights to battle? Faithful voices go unheard, as above, so below, and now our curses hold no sway against their schemes and steel. We who serve the gods are told they are dead and well-buried. Have the strong cast aside their swords? Have the wealthy rejected their riches? Why should those of us whose only power is prayer walk quietly into oblivion while others continue to chart the course of this nation?

I have found the sigils. I have offered the sacrifice.

I have chosen our future.

Judge me without mercy, Eminence.

CHAPTER 39

THE INFERNAL ART

Years ago, Estevar had travelled his adopted country, investigating reports of a painting so horrifying to behold that even the slightest of glances plunged the unwary into the very depths of madness. Those unlucky fools clawed out their own eyes, it was said, and tore out the throats of any who tried to stop them. The accounts sounded unbelievable, and chasing down rumours of the infernal artwork's location soon became a game of cat and mouse. He found many graves of alleged victims, yet the mythical painting itself was nowhere to be found.

So Estevar sought out the blind artist believed to have painted the deadly masterpiece and was surprised not only to find the man still alive, but swearing on his soul that the tales told of his dreadful creation were true. Although he gave his age as twenty-nine, his sparse hair was grey, his skin paper-thin and covered with liver spots, and only a few of his teeth remained.

The artist told Estevar that a dying viscount had commissioned the painting. Fearing that his manifold sins in life would condemn him in death, the eccentric nobleman wished to spend his last days gazing upon an image of Hell as accurate as possible, to better prepare himself for the eternal torments to be visited upon him. The artist, intrigued by the outlandish commission, turned his hand to rendering every vision of damnation imaginable.

He spent a great deal of time and a fortune of his client's money in research, acquiring banned books of heretical theology, performing bizarre rituals and imbibing every hallucinogenic narcotic he could find. For months he gave himself over to the unholy endeavour, but never succeeded in producing anything but maudlin portraits of childish nightmares. Gallons of expensive paints were wasted, dozens of canvases tossed in the fire, until, falling into a bitter rage, he placed one of his older, most prized works upon the easel and set about ruining it, entirely out of spite. He told Estevar that his brush moved of its own accord, the new pigments mingling with the old, distorting and debasing the original work – and with each desecrating stroke, the painting took on an ever-more-hideous aspect until, at last, the artist knew his purpose had been achieved. He had painted Hell.

It was the last thing he saw before his sight failed him, never to return.

The painting disappeared from his workshop shortly thereafter, and the viscount was forced to begin his final journey without a map to his destination.

'Do you recall anything of the finished image?' Estevar had asked – and the artist had surprised him by describing every inch of the canvas in painstaking detail, his recounting so vivid and unnerving that Estevar suffered from nightmares for an entire year. He was ashamed of being so grateful he had not found the original, and after the nightmares subsided, he had reassured himself that logic dictated that the painting had never actually existed; the artist, deranged or simply duplicitous, had concocted the entire tale to add to his own notoriety.

Now, stepping beneath the stone arch into the courtyard of Isola Sombra once more, Estevar could not deny the evidence of his own eyes. The artist had spoken truthfully that day, and whether through mysticism or madness, had given Hell the most faithful of renderings.

'Saint Ethalia-who-shares-all-sorrows,' Estevar whispered, though he couldn't hear himself speak over the cries of torment.

'*The denizens of the infernal lands do not act out of rage,*' the blind artist had warned him years ago. '*The cruelty of evil lies in its perverse innocence. Vengeance and torment are trivial things to them; they desire only to . . . play.*'

As with the demons he'd seen two days before, these creatures were pale, sickly things, their leathery skin textured with subtle variations of the sigils from the *Sacrificia Purgadis*. Their gleaming eyes were the blue found on the veins of bloated corpses pulled from the water after a shipwreck. The only difference was that there were more of them now, and instead of only one victim, these were gleefully slaughtering every soul they could pull screaming from inside the abbey.

One of the monsters stood upon the roof of the cloister, dangling a monk by his ankle, while a second demon standing on distended tiptoes pushed its unnaturally long split tongue into both of the wailing man's eyes.

Another of the creatures, this one with sharp spines all over its chest and the inside of its arms, was chasing one of the brothers like a lover hungering for an affectionate embrace.

Two demons, taller than the rest, held a third with a corkscrew goat's horn protruding from the centre of its forehead upside down and were turning his body round and round as his horn burrowed into the chest of a spasming, dying monk.

Most horrifying of all was a hornless creature who could have been confused with an ordinary, pale-skinned youth, save that he was prying his own jaws apart, wide enough to encompass the head of a monk whose hands were clasped in futile prayer.

Everywhere was the stench of decay, with sewer water gushing up through the storm grates to swamp the ground. Some of the demons were splashing their feet in it, kicking foetid lumps of dung into the air, smothering the courtyard in filth. Men and women in torn robes were no longer crying to their gods for reprieve but for a quick death.

Each time one of the demons granted that wish, they would devour their victim, grunting with feral abandon, then run – on two legs or four – to the centre of the ruined statuary, there to regurgitate blood and bone onto that once-hallowed ground.

'Why are they doing that?' Caeda asked, clutching the hatchet she'd taken from a woodpile outside the gates. 'What purpose does it serve to defile the holiest part of the abbey?'

'Hell is a garden,' the artist had told him, 'with infinite variations of blooms, but a single fragrance – that of damnation.'

'They are . . . tending their garden,' Estevar told Caeda now, drawing his rapier from its scabbard.

But not all the monks were being killed outright. Those who had called themselves 'Wolves' and bore the sigils haphazardly copied by Strigan from his own, were suffering a different fate. Estevar and Caeda watched the demons playing with one of the Wolf-King's followers, first destroying the woman's robes, frayed to tatters by their talons, then setting to work on her body, tugging her arms to unnatural lengths, splaying her fingers wide. With their claws, they sculpted the bones of her head until ivory ram's horns sprouted from her temples.

'Venia tricked Strigan into imprinting the sigils of the *Sacrificia Purgadis* onto his followers,' Estevar said grimly.

The wind was picking up, the clouds gathering overhead. Her red hair whipping around her face, Caeda cried, 'But the *Purgadis* is supposed to purge the sins of a community by inscribing them onto the skin of the sacrifice, that's what Venia said!'

'Sin is not so easily banished,' Estevar replied, his hand shaking so badly his grip on his rapier was threatened. He wished he was stronger, younger, faster, but above all – and for the first time in his life – he wished he possessed more faith. 'The *Purgadis* does not expunge the sins of others, but instead transforms the victim into the embodiment of those crimes.' He forced his sword arm to rise until the tip of his blade pointed to the woman whose screams had turned to laughter as she grinned, displaying long, twisted teeth, at her demonic companions. '*That* is the result!'

Caeda only now noticed the rapier in Estevar's trembling hand. 'My Cantor, you can't mean to fight them!'

'Why not?' he asked, summoning every ounce of courage to lend his words at least the illusion of confidence. When that failed, he drew strength from a deeper well: the arrogant bluster he had long tried to purge from himself. Now it was all he had left. 'I see nothing new here,' he bellowed over the screaming, the laughter and the chaos, 'no hellish conjurations from which to cower in fear. Killing and depravity are no evidence of diabolical genius, just the base acts of cowards.'

'Estevar, don't!' Caeda cried as the demons began turning towards his discordant defiance.

He shrugged off her hand. 'Two nights ago,' he shouted, 'I rendered my verdict. That you have returned means you wish to appeal that ruling in the old way, with steel and blood.'

'Please, my Cantor,' Caeda wept, clinging to his coat, 'please don't do this.'

He hesitated a moment and smiled at her, though they both knew it was masking the despair underneath. 'Weep not for me, my Piccolo. I am under strict orders from the First Cantor not to engage in any duels unless I am certain I can win.' He glanced briefly up at the Vigilance Tower. The windows were darkened by the dozens of armed monks in yellow surcoats peering out from them. He let them see the terror in his eyes, if only for an instant. 'Though I have been known to disobey such commands.'

His hour having come, Estevar adopted a formal guard, his sword arm extended three-quarters towards the nearest of the demons, his back arm curved gracefully upwards, just as his old fencing master used to insist. To his enemies, he said, 'I will now accept your surrender.'

Many of the demons dropped their victims to join their unencumbered brethren in enthusiastically clapping his performance, before the nearest of them, clawed hands outstretched and jaws opened wide, raced towards him.

CHAPTER 40

THE CRUCIBLE OF CHAOS

At first, the demons toyed with him.

'They desire only to play,' the blind artist had told him all those years ago. *'We are no more than dolls to them, and some children love nothing more than tearing apart their dolls.'*

The diabolically transformed monks surrounded Estevar and Caeda like cheering boys at a schoolyard brawl, giving way to one of their number, allowing him the privilege of attacking first. This particular monstrosity was dragging one of his former brethren behind him, strangling the poor man with fingers so long Estevar counted seven knuckles on each. The giggling creature pranced and twirled as he approached, lifting the terrified monk up high as if intending to use him as a club to beat Estevar to death.

Estevar gave no ground. His rash boldness was clearly entertaining the creatures enough to keep them from getting bored, but at any moment, they would likely decide to join in the fun. He raised the tip of his rapier up high and back in preparation for a cut.

Some might argue that the rapier is suitable only for thrusting, claiming the narrow blade lacks the heft of weapons such as longswords, whose heavier cutting edges are the only ones capable of chopping down one's enemies. Experience had taught Estevar otherwise: with the full strength of his shoulder and arm, he slammed the edge down on the demon's wrist, hacking it off in a single blow.

The near-strangled monk flopped to the ground, gasping as Caeda tore the unnaturally long fingers from his throat until he could breathe

276

again. The pale-skinned creature stared at the stump at the end of its forearm and began to weep. The others laughed at his misfortune.

'Demons and devils do best to pursue us in our nightmares,' Estevar warned them. 'When you hunt on our soil, you are made flesh.'

'What are you doing?' Caeda whispered furiously at his side, the little hatchet with which she was threatening their enemies inducing them to paroxysms of laughter. 'You're acting like this is some kind of game.'

'Not a game – a performance.'

She glanced warily at the creatures encircling them. 'For who? These monstrosities?'

Estevar looked up towards the Vigilance Tower.

Descend from your garden, Mother of Trumpeters. What use will your army be in fending off the Margrave of Someil if the island is already overrun by even fouler invaders?

The second demon who came for Estevar was the one with the long corkscrew horn, now dripping with the blood and viscera of slain monks. Its powerful legs ended in hairless white hooves, which were currently pawing at the ground as it dropped its head low, preparing to charge him. Estevar unceremoniously shoved Caeda aside, squatted and rolled onto his back. When the monster leaped on him, Estevar planted his boot heels on its thickly muscled torso before kicking upwards with all his might. The creature flew high – then crashed back down, landing head-first on the flagstones.

The sickening crunch silenced the courtyard. Estevar had got to his feet; he turned to see the demon's horn had been driven through the back of its skull.

Two down, he thought, swallowing bile at the grizzly sight. *Luck has smiled on me more than I deserve, yet still the Trumpeters refuse to fight.*

A pair of cackling creatures rushed him, but with Caeda's help, he sent them reeling back, crying out from their wounds.

'General Leogado,' he shouted at the top of his lungs, slashing his blade wide to discourage the other monsters, praying his words would not only reach the top of the Vigilance Tower, but would pierce the armour around Leogado's conscience, 'your brethren suffer and die while you hide within the safety of your stout walls. Will you cower while others fight the only battle that mat—?'

Blood dripped into his right eye, and only then did he notice the glancing blow he'd taken in the last attack. His opponents saw it too. Laughing and jeering, one of them proudly displayed the taloned fingertip that had done the deed.

'I've taken worse from chestnuts hurled by angry squirrels offended by my napping beneath their tree on a warm summer's day,' Estevar declared, wiping the blood from his brow and flicking it at the demons.

They might be faster and stronger than any mortal he'd ever fought, their monstrous deformations as deadly as any weapons he'd ever faced, but Estevar had three advantages. First, the demons lacked his tactical expertise. Second, they were show-offs, each wanting a chance to kill him alone. Third, whatever diabolical magic had transfigured the monks had also driven them irretrievably insane.

'Estevar!' Caeda screamed in warning, and he whipped round to face an opponent even more bizarre. This one had two heads, a man's and a woman's, resting on the massive shoulders of a body easily eight feet tall. Estevar ducked under the first blow of its monstrously thick arm while slicing one tree-trunk of a leg with his rapier, although the blade failed to pierce the thick skin. Caeda made a valiant attempt to shatter its other knee with her hatchet, but the creature barely noticed, knocking her aside with such force that her feet left the ground. She landed in a heap six paces away.

Fighting back the impulse to run to her, Estevar raised the tip of his rapier and thrust it with all his might through the left eye of one monstrous head. The creature's screech of outrage and pain was cut short as Estevar drove the point further into its brain.

He tried to catch his breath as he waited for the monster to fall, but instead, gasped at the hideous squeal from the demon's second head when she began laughing uproariously at her mate's misfortune. Estevar tried to get his sword arm back up for another thrust, but he was too late; her gigantic hand had grabbed his head and shoved him to the ground, where, pinned to the flagstones, she began crushing his skull.

Smothered in that huge, leathery palm, gagging from the stench of the blood and gore of the behemoth's previous victim now splattering her, he attempted a blind thrust at where he guessed the living head would be, only to cry out as a foot stomped down on his wrist, immobilising his sword arm.

Enthusiastic clapping erupted from the other demons as the hulking beast gradually pressed down harder on Estevar's head, grinding his face into the flagstones. The pressure building between his temples was agonising. The creature was savouring his terror, almost drinking it in, until at last, she would split his skull open. Frantically, he struck out with the knuckles of his free hand, trying to catch the nerves of the demon's wrist and forearm, but to no avail.

As the last dregs of consciousness began to flee, he was left with nothing but bitter self-recrimination over his foolish gambit, arrogance conspiring with unmerited hope. He'd thought that if he could prove the demons were vulnerable to mortal weapons, Mother Leogado would bring the other surviving monks of the abbey to his aid.

His killer's breath was hot in his right ear and he felt the wetness of her tongue licking his lobe as she whispered, 'Now it is we who judge you, Tratta—'

A thunderous clacking against the flagstones interrupted the creature's triumph, growing louder as it passed through the archway and into the courtyards. The demons encircling him screeched in outrage as something barrelled through them, skidding to a stop just behind Estevar's head. He heard a roar— No, not a roar, but something else – something fuelled by an unyielding defiance and a fiery spirit that neither devilry nor the deep blue sea could douse.

A bray, Estevar had time to think as a dull thud was followed by a deafening crack. At first, he assumed it was the bones of his own skull that had given way, because the terrible pressure in his head suddenly eased. But when he managed to turn over, he was greeted by the sight of a pair of large brown testicles dangling over him, and the sorrel-haired belly of a beast no less terrifying in its fury for not, in fact, being a demon.

'Imperious!' he cried out with unrestrained joy, rolling himself out from under the mule.

Imperious whinnied agreeably, stamping one hoof on the flagstones to warn off any enemies thinking of encroaching on his territory. The demons retreated several steps to hiss and snarl at this new foe, apparently more offended – and fearful – of Imperious than they had been of Estevar. Imperious brayed a challenge right back at them, pounding his front right hoof against the flagstones as if daring them to approach.

The thumping footsteps of a hulking figure in grey robes signalled the arrival of Malezias, who ran to Caeda's side and helped her to her feet. 'You gods-be-damned fool,' he cursed Estevar. 'That idiot mule of yours broke through the wall of the stable where I was commanded to watch over him. I risked my life to try and recapture him – only to discover that you brought my Lady here, into this . . . this *madness*?'

'Cease your nagging, Malezias,' Caeda said, sounding somewhat dazed. She looked around for her hatchet. 'I'm not some waif to be fought over at the country fair,' she added, picking up her weapon.

'Forgive me,' the big man pleaded, abandoning his outrage in the face of her annoyance.

You've known all along, haven't you, Malezias? Estevar realised. You knew the truth, yet you kept it from everyone, even her, because you so badly wanted to love her a little longer.

This wasn't the time to consider the consequences of the lovelorn fool's lapse in judgement, because the demons had apparently come to the conclusion that Imperious was not some angry god come to hurl thunder and fire down upon them. One by one they grinned at each other, nodding knowingly, before all two dozen suddenly swarmed over the four belligerent mortals with ruthless efficiency. Within seconds, Estevar was being throttled by one creature while two others went for Caeda and Malezias with claws and horns, ensuring they couldn't come to his aid.

Far worse was the braying squeal that drew Estevar's horrified gaze from the demon choking him to the far larger pair who had hold of Imperious' front and back hooves. They flipped the poor mule onto his back and gleefully began to pull in opposite directions.

'No!' Estevar tried to shout, but no sound came from his lungs. The creature squeezing its hands around his neck was laughing, leaning in close to his face and repeating, '*Yes, yes, yes!*' in delighted malice at his despair. Imperious was kicking furiously at his tormentors, but they were too strong. Any second now, they would rip apart the frantic mule.

Estevar had never counted himself a praying man, but he prayed now, to any god or saint who would listen, prayed with all his heart that someone would answer the mule's cries before it was too late.

'*Please!*' he begged silently, struggling to hold onto consciousness. '*You can't let him die – he's not just a beast of burden: he's brave and he's wise, and a truer companion than I've ever known. Let there be one miracle left in this gods-forsa—*'

The voice that answered his prayers was surely not the one that either Estevar or Imperious would have chosen as their saviour.

'Leave them alone, you ugly bastards!' cried Strigan, staggering naked and dazed into the courtyard, a rapier shaking in his unsteady grip. As he looked around, bearing witness to what his vanity and greed had wrought among his followers, he bellowed, 'I am the Wolf-King! Do you hear me? I am the Sorcerer Sovereign of Isola Sombra, and I do hereby banish you all to the deepest pits of the Seven Hells!'

The outlandish rant might have failed to terrify the demons as he'd intended, but it did provide a moment's distraction. The talons around Estevar's throat slackened and the bestial creatures torturing Imperious dropped him back to the ground as they joined their eager, grinning fellows and turned on their erstwhile leader.

'Back!' Strigan shouted, frantically swinging his rapier in wide arcs that served only to reassure his encroaching enemies that his blade was no threat to them whatsoever. 'Back, damn you – I command you! *Your dread liege demands obedience!*'

While the demons flocked to Strigan like vultures on a fresh corpse, Estevar, his abused throat so raw he could scarcely draw breath, scrambled to find his own rapier.

Caeda recovered her axe and joined him in slashing and hacking at the demons, as Malezias lifted one of the smaller ones up above his head and hurled it against a colonnade. Imperious, shivering with rage as much as fear, was kicking furiously with his back hooves at a long-jawed, fork-tongued creature standing between him and the pair which had tried to rip him apart – but they had a new toy to play with.

They had taken Strigan by the ankles and wrists and to the merriment of their fellows, they lifted him up high and making of themselves an impromptu rack, started stretching him, inch by inch, until his shoulders were straining in their sockets.

Discovering somewhat too late that he was not, in fact, the Sorcerer Sovereign of Isola Sombra, the Wolf-King begged, 'End me, sweet God of Death! Take me now, I beg you!'

The thunderous discharge of a pistol broke through the cacophony of jeering laughter and panicked screams. Strigan's arms went slack as the hairless white head of the demon holding his wrists exploded. Blue-grey mush and bits of shattered bone spewed onto the courtyard. Witnessing the demise of its comrade, the creature holding Strigan's ankles dropped him – then ran to the dead demon and began gleefully dipping its claws into the open skull and painting its own grinning face with the gory remains.

A small figure in black and grey slid the still-smoking wheellock into the same pocket of her robes from which she drew a second one. 'Never thought I'd waste such a good shot on such a lousy prize,' said Brother Agneta.

Estevar, Caeda, Malezias and the near-feral Imperious fought their way to her side before the demons could rush her, but it wasn't long before the five of them were surrounded. The odds had shifted from unimaginable to merely impossible. By Estevar's count, they had dispatched a dozen of the monstrous invaders, but twice as many remained, and the weary defenders were showing their wounds.

'I imagine you conceived some brilliant plan to get us out of this mess before you chose to challenge a band of maniacal demons to a fencing match?' Agneta asked Estevar.

He whipped the tip of his rapier across the face of one of the approaching creatures to give it pause. 'I did, but I must confess, that plan has thus far failed to live up to expectations.'

The old inquisitor fired her second pistol into the gaping maw of the creature lunging at her. The ball came out the back of its horned head, bringing quite a lot of skull with it.

Three more took its place. 'Then I shall take what solace I can from the fact that it is surely as embarrassing for you to meet your death at the side of a cruel and unfeeling Cogneri as it is for me to die alongside a sentimental and suicidally idealistic Trattari.'

Estevar smiled in acknowledgment, but their gallows humour was not shared by all. Malezias grabbed Caeda by the shoulders, his deep voice quavering as he asked, 'Are we doomed, then, my Lady? Will you not save us?'

She shook him off, making space to swing the shaft of her now-headless hatchet into the outstretched fingers of the nearest demon. 'What in the Seven Hells the five of us are headed to are you talking about, Malezias? I'm doing the best I can!'

Sensing victory, the demons had resumed their playful demeanour, dancing around their soon-to-be victims, head tilted like cats watching scurrying mice in preparation for pouncing on them.

Another of the blind artist's observations about his infernal work came to Estevar then: '*We think of evil as simply a darker shade of malice. It isn't. Evil contains joy within it, ecstasy so potent that it transcends judgement, for how can we judge that which defies our comprehension?*'

He stabbed the heart of a creature with a bulbous chest and six arms so thin and curiously jointed it looked like a pregnant spider. The blow struck true, but the blade became lodged between two of the monster's ribs and snapped when Estevar tried to get it free.

'Caeda . . .' he began, the analytical part of his mind, unsilenced by even fear and despair, warning him the end was near.

'It's over, isn't it?' she asked, hurling the broken haft of her hatchet futilely at the slowly approaching horde. 'We failed.'

They had only moments before they would be overwhelmed, and Estevar could think of no better use to put those final seconds than to tell her, 'You did not fail, my Piccolo. You were as clever, as insightful as any magistrate I ever knew. In this place and at this hour do I hereby name you to the Great—'

A brassy blare broke through the din, then again, and a third time. A dozen or more misshapen heads with all their assortment of horns and fangs and spiky protrusions swivelled in the direction of the Vigilance Tower, where light from candles and torches could at last be seen through the windows. A throng of women and men in yellow and black robes, armed with longswords, spears and crossbows, raced from the open door. Leading them was a smaller figure, no less daunting in her fury.

'Her?' Agneta asked, catching Estevar's eye as the battalion of yellow Trumpeters attacked in precise formations against the demons. 'You risked everything on gods-be-damned General Leogado's heretofore undiscovered sense of decency and compassion?'

Estevar bent down to help Strigan to his feet. 'I wagered that if the monks of Isola Sombra saw that a mortal like themselves could stand against the living embodiments of malice, they might recall that this abbey was meant to be a place where men and women came together to be closer not only to their gods, but to each other as well.'

Half the Trumpeters formed a bright yellow shieldwall in front of the demons as the other half stood behind, firing arrows and bolts into the panicking ranks of the enemy. A keening whine emerged as the demons began to retreat, step by step, into the ruined statuary.

'You were wrong,' General Leogado said, coming to stand beside Estevar. 'I didn't come because of you.' Sheathing one of the twin curved shortswords she was carrying, she reached out a hand and stroked Imperious' muzzle. 'I have known and ridden some of the finest warhorses ever bred, but never met one so magnificent as this mule.'

Estevar's pride in his companion being so recognised was slightly muted by the far less glamorous reality. Leogado had spoken the truth: she would have let them all die, had not the sight of his mule's bravery and subsequent torment so shamed her followers that her own courage would have been questioned if she'd refused them the chance to fight.

'I will confess to a crisis of conscience.' Brother Agneta pointed to each of them in turn. 'Can there truly be any gods left when the General of the Trumpeters, the King of the Hounds and the Bone-Rattler's Inquisitor unite in common cause?'

Strigan laughed. He looked about to make some bold – and almost certainly lecherous – joke, but before he could, Caeda, her face as pale as a gravestone, said to Estevar, 'Something's not right.'

'What is it?' he asked.

Strigan chuckled. 'Why, is that my little Caeda? Damn, but that's good timing. I was just thinking how I never got the chance t—'

Malezias slammed his hands on Strigan's shoulders and shoved him away. 'What troubles you, my Lady?'

But Caeda was looking only at Estevar. In the night sky above, flashes of light shot through the black clouds, and a rolling thunder shook the earth beneath their feet. 'Something is happening, my Cantor.' She clutched at her stomach. 'I feel . . . hollow inside.'

No, Estevar thought, turning away from her to the statuary where the demons had assembled. Their snivelling moans were increasing in both pitch and volume, becoming hideous groans of pleasure, while the ground at their feet swelled like a pustule being squeezed.

'What's going on?' Mother Leogado demanded, but without waiting for an answer, she raced to her troops, shouting at them to continue advancing. They were looking confused and uncertain as the storm built in strength – then the site where statues of the six gods had once towered over the abbey began to blaze with an unearthly light. She had bound her followers to her with promises that a new god was coming to Tristia and it would be their duty to serve this new deity – whoever it might be.

At the centre of the ruins where the demons danced in triumph, occasionally pausing in their whirling to shudder in sudden, uncontrollable ecstasy, a hand, sickly white and skeletal, was erupting from the uneasy soil.

It reached up to the heavens.

One of the demons, taller and less ill-favoured than the others, with most of its grey robes still intact, turned towards Estevar and nodded in recognition, as if the two had been engaged in a long debate that had just been settled in the demons' favour. Brother Syme – or what was left of him after his transformation – also bore markings on his leathery white skin. He had kept them hidden – and not only from Estevar.

'*Little shit*,' Brother Agneta swore. 'I should have known anyone so flattering to an old woman was only playing the part.'

'What in every hell is happening?' Strigan asked.

As if in answer, lightning burst forth from the clouds to strike the withered hand stretching for the sky. A gaunt arm appeared, the blackened earth parting as the corpse of Abbot Venia rose from the grave for the last time.

'I cannot speak to the peculiarities of this particular phenomenon,' Estevar said, leaning against Imperious because he could no longer stand on his own. His breathing was laboured, his head felt slick and far too hot. 'Nonetheless, a rudimentary deduction of the relevant facts would suggest that Brother Syme's repeated interring of the abbot's remains was not, in fact, meant to lay him to rest, but rather to prevent the soil of Isola Sombra from rejecting this poisonous seed.'

The lightning struck again and the cadaver stepped out of his unquiet grave to stand among the crooning, admiring horde. One of its hands continued to reach upwards, but the other was pointed to the ground where tiny, glittering flecks of ore fluttered like fireflies trying to escape, only to be snatched from the air by the abbot's bony fingers. When the sky erupted in light a third time, Venia's hand grabbed hold of the bolt before it could touch the earth. The lightning writhed in his hand like a snake trying to free itself, the thunder roaring over and over, as if enraged at the indignity.

'Impossible,' Mother Leogado murmured, her military mind, so linear in its thinking, not able to conceive how such an enemy might be fought.

'What do we do know?' Strigan asked. 'How are we supposed to—?'

'Trattari!' Malezias shouted, in despair, rather than anger this time, for Caeda had collapsed at his feet.

Brother Agneta's eyes narrowed. 'What is she doing here?'

Estevar tried to speak, but his knees gave out and he collapsed over Imperious' back. He'd taken brutal blows during the battle as the demons had fought for the privilege of punishing him, but it was the older wound sapping his strength. Even through his greatcoat, he could feel the stitches had given way completely and blood was dripping down his side.

Someone hauled him upright and spun him around. 'Please,' Malezias begged, holding him upright. 'Please – you must save her!'

'Save *her*?' Strigan demanded. 'How about the rest of us?' He jabbed a finger towards the statuary where a naked figure, shaped like a man but now nearly ten feet tall, gazed up into the sky as if inspecting a piece of land about to be handed over to him. The demons were fighting each other, trying to get closer to him, shivering in delight when they touched him. 'That's our new fucking god over there, and judging by his followers, life is about to get pretty gods-be-damned miserable for the whole world!'

Malezias ignored him, pleading, 'Help her – you *must* help her.'

'He can't help anyone,' Brother Agneta said acidly, trying and failing to shove the big brute out of the way. 'Look at him. He was half dead when he came to this island and now the other half isn't long for this world.'

Estevar was hanging limply in Malezias' grip. The only thing keeping his back straight was the sturdy leather of his greatcoat, which stubbornly refused to give way, when a lesser garment would have ripped long ago. He decided to take that as a positive sign, since all the other omens were rather bleak.

'Brother Agneta is right,' he croaked, trying to find his voice; he would need it if the last gambit remaining to them all was to stand any chance. 'Strigan is right, too: none of us have long left.' He looked bleary-eyed to where Caeda was climbing unsteadily to her feet.

'Ah, Piccolo,' Estevar croaked, 'how fortuitous.' When she stared at him as if he were insane, he elaborated, 'Would you be so kind as to escort us to one of those clever secret passages of yours?'

The lightning struck again, and this time the Trumpeters abandoned their weapons and started walking towards the statuary to praise their new god alongside their demonic brethren.

'Where do you want to go?' Caeda asked. 'The causeway is still under water—'

'The prayer caves below the abbey,' Estevar replied. 'Assuming they aren't flooded, that seems an appropriate place.'

'Appropriate for *what*?' Mother Leogado asked. 'If the demons corner us down there, we'll have no means of escape.'

'Hmm?' Estevar asked, not sure if he'd heard her.

'I said, appropriate for what?'

'Ah, yes, my apologies, I thought that would be obvious. We need the prayer caves for the trial.'

'The *trial*?' Brother Agneta asked in disbelief.

Estevar gazed out towards the statuary where the man who'd once been the humble, almost bumbling Abbot Venia now looked down upon him with the wise and terrible eyes of a newly born god. Estevar knew he couldn't be heard over the thunder and the chanting and all the rest of the infernal concert praising Venia's ascension, but he was confident his old acquaintance would know what he said next.

'*Judge me without mercy, Eminence.*'

'What are you mumbling about?' Strigan asked. 'What nonsense – why would we hold a trial in the prayer caves?'

Estevar summoned the strength to stand on his own just long enough to say what both the law and his pride required of him before collapsing to the filthy flagstones. 'Mother Leogado, Brother Strigan, Inquisitor Agneta and Malezias of Isola Sombra, I regret to inform you that the four of you are under arrest.'

CHAPTER 41

OPENING ARGUMENTS

'*Is your mind clear?*' How many times had that simple question haunted Estevar during these vexatious days? How many times had he passed out and had to be dragged somewhere by the mercy of others?

Consciousness tugged at him with slow, disagreeable persistence, but he kept his eyes closed a few moments longer, determined not to abandon what few rituals he could call his own.

His aching back told him he was lying on uneven stone, and beneath the stench of the sewer, which had suffused not just his clothes but those of everyone shouting at one another nearby, he detected the sweaty, musty, wonderful scent of mule. Imperious' breathing was a low rumble that became a kind of growl every time footsteps approached his erstwhile rider – all save the light, oddly distant ones of the only visitor the mule would allow.

'Estevar?' she asked.

'Piccolo,' he said, smiling. His eyes were still closed.

A warm, callused palm came to rest against his forehead. 'Brother Agneta put salve on your wounds, but you're feverish again. Can you get up? The others are becoming . . . restless.'

A fiendish howl echoed from the abbey down through the storm grates and into the tunnels beyond the prayer room. No doubt that howl was the being which had once been Abbot Venia, displeased at the prospect of a trial being held over which anyone but himself should dare preside.

Well, perhaps you shouldn't have sent that damned letter begging me to come and arbitrate the dispute between your monks, then, Estevar thought. To Caeda he said, 'Help me to stand.'

She moved behind him and knelt down, putting her arms under his to help lever him into a seated position. She waited for a sign that he wasn't going to collapse again, and when he opened his eyes and nodded to her, she supported him while he got to his feet before handing him the broken-bladed rapier he'd abandoned in the courtyard. He slid the shortened weapon into its sheath.

His vision cleared, revealing the now-familiar slanting walls and curved ceiling hewn from the rocky prayer cavern. Someone was approaching him from the other side of the chamber, the dim light of a single flickering torch set in an iron sconce mounted to the wall making the figure appear more shadow than man. As he neared, Estevar found himself staring into the deep-set eyes of Malezias. The former monk's broad shoulders were hunched like those of a pugilist deciding which part of his opponent's face to pummel first. Though Caeda was still behind Estevar, steadying him, he could almost feel her glare.

Malezias held up his hands in submission and stepped back.

Brother Strigan, still naked, still untroubled by it, smirked at the big man's retreat. Mother Leogado, her dark skin lustrous in the reflected light of the flaming torch, couldn't hide her disgust whenever she glanced at the Wolf-King. Brother Agneta, patiently reloading her wheellock pistols, clearly viewed them both as tiresome children.

Surrounded by the crude engravings of Tristia's original six gods, Estevar speculated on his unwilling companions, and to which of those deities each might correspond.

'You would be War,' Estevar said softly to Imperious, stroking the mule's reddish-brown mane, 'for you are fierce and brave and undaunted even by demons.'

'What did you say?' Strigan asked, presuming some quietly spoken insult.

'Nothing of consequence, I can assure you,' Agneta said. 'If the Trattari's going to drone on again about trials, we may as well prepare to be eaten alive by your former followers. I for one will not be pandering to a Greatcoat's vanity.'

And yet you brought me here, didn't you, Estevar thought, *unlike our first inauspicious meeting, when you left me to bleed out in the ruined statuary. So you are not quite so convinced of my insignificance as you pretend.*

'I should be reassembling my troops,' Mother Leogado said.

'Your troops switched sides,' Strigan pointed out.

She looked untroubled, but wasn't unshakeable self-confidence the first requirement of any military commander? Stepping away from the torchlight, she approached Estevar. 'You were valiant in the courtyard, and not without tactical insight. Tell me what other weaknesses you have gleaned regarding the demons infesting my abbey, and I will do my best to see that you' – she waved at the others – 'that *all* of you survive the night.'

'*Your* abbey?' Strigan asked. 'Did you not happen to notice that Abbot-fucking-Venia isn't actually done with it yet? Besides, who elec—'

'I imagine our arrogant general elected herself dictator-for-life shortly after it turned out *your* followers were the demons all along,' Brother Agneta said, closing the powder pan and pulling out the other pistol. 'That *is* what caused all this, isn't it?' she asked Estevar. 'The idiot Wolf-King sought to garner the power of faith unto himself and his lackeys, but managed instead to transform them into demons.'

Estevar nodded. 'The rituals of the *Sacrificia Purgadis*, combined with the unique spiritual potency of this island, have made this possible. But the blame does not lie entirely with Strigan.'

'Then who *is* to blame?' Caeda asked.

'Venia, obviously,' Brother Agneta replied. 'He played the Hounds for fools – he played all of us for fools, apparently.'

Mother Leogado had other concerns. 'What good does ascribing guilt do us now? We need to be thinking strategically. Two years ago, the man calling himself the Blacksmith slaughtered the entire pantheon of gods. Surely there's a means by which we can kill a single god not yet fully formed?'

'The Blacksmith had already stolen the power of murdered saints, and he took the old gods unawares. I doubt Venia – or whatever he'll soon be demanding we call him – will be quite so easy to sneak up on.'

Estevar closed his eyes for a moment, breathing slowly and deeply to prepare himself. He winced at the sharp pain below his ribs, which felt so much like a smirking bully poking at him over and over that he almost felt like reminding the stab wound that the longer it irritated him, the more likely the two of them were to be parted – permanently.

'I believe there is a way to prevent Venia's ascension,' he said at last.

'How?' Caeda asked.

'His silly "trial", of course,' Brother Agneta replied. She held up her pistol and peered down the barrel at him. 'The Trattari's idiotic sense of justice prevents him from even *trying* to do what must be done until first he's debated every fine point of the law, and whether we have the right to kill Venia before he or his demons get to us first.'

'Whereas you Cogneri are content to dispense with the law entirely,' Estevar countered. 'But that is *not* why we must hold this particular trial.'

'Then why?' Strigan asked. 'What's the point of all this' – he waved his hands in the air – 'silly ritual?'

'I believe we have all come to see,' Estevar began, as patiently as he could manage, 'that there are some times' – he gestured to the walls inscribed with symbols of the old gods – 'and some *places* where ritual holds more power than some of us might wish.'

'What then?' Mother Leogado asked, suddenly more attentive. 'You propose to perform some sort of occult ritual? Cast some sort of magic spell?'

Estevar laughed, which proved a mistake as it awoke a number of his previously slumbering aches. 'I am neither priest nor sorcerer. I am a magistrate.'

'Well, too bad we don't have one of those,' Strigan began, 'because that would be a hell of a lot more use—'

'Enough,' Estevar said, cutting him off. 'A trial is about more than judgment. The laws that Brother Agneta scorns so casually weren't meant solely to punish the guilty. A trial is a crucible in which facts are separated from lies so that the truth can be discerned, and from that truth, a path towards justice.'

'Which truth would that be?' Malezias asked. He was sitting on his haunches in the shadows, glaring with vengeful malice at them all, even Caeda. 'What justice is left for a girl whose life was—?'

Estevar held a finger to his lips, and his eyes conveyed the promise that should Malezias tamper with what now had to unfold, he would be made to regret his presumption.

'Okay, enough of this nonsense,' Strigan said, striding to the door and heaving some nearby rocks in front to block it. 'I say we hole up here for the night and hope that whatever's happening in the courtyard will somehow draw the attention of any of the old gods who are left. Didn't your legendary First Cantor claim that at least three had returned?'

'Falcio val Mond did encounter beings whom he believed to be the embodiments of Love, Death and Valour.'

'Great,' Strigan said, clasping his hands together. 'I'll be praying for Death to come and save us, because I'm pretty sure Love and Valour are going to do shit for us at this point.'

Mother Leogado crossed the chamber and shoved Strigan out of the way. 'I'll not sit here while my flock are turned one by one into the slavish abominations yours were.'

'Nor will I submit myself to the legal whims of a Trattari,' Brother Agneta said, although it was the yellow-robed woman upon whom her pistol was now trained.

Even now they bicker, Estevar thought. *With a demonic god on one side and a margrave's army on the other, still they prefer to wage war against each other.*

A vicious, gleeful howl echoed from above, soon joined by another. It wouldn't be long now before the creatures overcame whatever uncertainty was keeping them from the caves and entered the depths in search of their prey.

Agneta spun on Estevar. 'You hear that, Trattari? You hear the living blasphemy that's been spawned on these once sacred grounds? What better "testimony" to prove that we are all of us condemned for the sins of this corrupted nation? Would you dare to place your judgment above the gods themselves?'

'As to that,' he said calmly, reaching into his coat to remove his notebook, 'I have no intention of presiding over the trial. My role is to present the case against all of you.'

'Then who do you intend to have pass judgment on us? Your mule?'

Estevar ran a hand down Imperious' neck. 'Alas, he has shown little interest in the finer points of the law, despite my many attempts to instruct him. No, as Brother Agneta rightly said, this case cannot be judged by mere mortals.'

'Then who?' Caeda asked, her voice unusually quiet as she stood against one of the rough stone walls in her thin white gown, red curls draped down her shoulders as she hugged herself like a nervous schoolgirl. 'Who has the right to judge the fate of Isola Sombra?'

Estevar tried his best to summon a smile for her. 'You, Piccolo. You must pass judgment on us all.'

'Her?' Strigan demanded. Laughing, he strutted towards her. 'Wasn't I going to bed you once?' He reached out to play with a lock of her hair. 'Since we're probably all going to die here anyway, maybe I should—' He shut up when he felt something sharp at the nape of his neck.

'You did not hear me come up behind you, did you?' Estevar asked, holding the tiny blade taken from the cuff of his coat between his thumb and forefinger. 'Perhaps then you should be more wary of baring your fangs to others, Wolf-King.'

Strigan removed his hands and Estevar removed the knife from the monk's throat. Turning to the others, he said, 'We are short of time, so before anyone challenges me again, let me point out that as of this moment, we are all as good as dead. Whatever sins brought us here, they have already prescribed a sentence from which there is no appeal. Therefore, I suggest you allow me to proceed and pray, if that is your disposition, that the truth does indeed set us all free.' He turned to Caeda. 'Will you agree to preside over the trial, my dear?'

'What . . . what do I have to do?'

'Merely listen as I lay the case before you, and when it is time, render your verdict.'

She leaned close to him, whispering so the others wouldn't hear, 'Please, my Cantor, don't ask me to do this. I just want to be a Greatcoat like you.'

'A Greatcoat presides over trials. What troubles you, Piccolo?'

'I don't know! Why must you overcomplicate everything? Why can't you just let me pretend to be your assistant and then I'll never have to . . . never have to . . .'

Her eyes met his and there was such sorrow in her that despite all that was at risk, he badly wished he could give her what she wanted.

'Am I dead, Estevar?'

He took her hands in his and raised one after the other to his lips, kissing them, before gently letting them fall. 'You feel entirely alive to me, Piccolo. One of the more sternly enforced requirements of a magistrate is that they not be dead, and this particular trial cannot proceed without you. Justice must have her song at long last. Will you assist me this final time?'

Caeda's cheeks were ashen, her expression flat as that of a corpse. Yet, acceding to this last request of her Cantor, she nodded.

In the tunnels above them, while Estevar gritted his teeth and rolled a rock to the centre of the room to serve as a magistrate's throne, demons howled and giggled as what had once been a place of sanctity and worship became one of terror and damnation in service to a holy man who had made himself their god.

'Let the trial begin,' Estevar said.

CHAPTER 42

THE TRIAL OF ISOLA SOMBRA

'The crime began two years ago, when the man known as the Blacksmith devised a scheme to murder saints and gods alike, dispersing the faith that once fuelled their existence back into the people of Tristia.'

'We know all this,' Brother Agneta said, glancing up at the prayer cave's rocky domed ceiling as if the weight of the howling demons on the levels above might bring it crashing down on their heads. 'We've been debating the nature of gods in this abbey ever since, as we awaited their return.'

'Not all of us keep wallowing in the past,' Mother Leogado interjected. 'Some of us have come to recognise the gods we once knew belonged to a different age, that our duty was to await those meant to emerge from *this* era.'

'A line of reasoning Abbot Venia found compelling,' Estevar said, taking back control of his opening argument. 'Especially when he learned that a new god *had*, in fact, come into being.'

'Rumours,' Brother Agneta objected, 'tales spun by Trattari swash-bucklers like you, who expect the rest of us to fall in line behind your preposterous notions of idealism – the heart of which could be quaintly referred to as valour. That's the name you all gave to this supposed new god, didn't you? "Valour"?'

Estevar smiled tolerantly. 'I am, I fear, somewhat less exuberant than many of my colleagues. Nonetheless, should the Greatcoats ever conspire to spread belief in a god of their choosing, I assure you that we would prefer a God of Justice to assist us in bringing the rule of law back to this country, rather than one who encourages us to risk our lives over and over again, with nothing to show for it but our wounds.'

'These pointless debates are getting us nowhere,' Malezias said, still crouched in his corner like a sulking ox. 'This is why I left the abbey in the first place.'

Strigan snorted. 'More like you left because you so badly wanted to bed the delectable Caeda, who for some inexplicable reason' – he threw his arm out towards her as if revealing her for the first time – 'now sits in judgment over us all!'

'Many a defendant has sought to undermine a presiding magistrate's authority,' Estevar noted. 'I would remind you that pleading for a different judge might result in a more . . . unorthodox sentencing.'

'And what verdict will you impose on us?' Mother Leogado asked.

Estevar waved her objection away. 'I told you before, the case is mine to present only.' He reached into his coat, removed the damp pages he'd rescued from the flooded chamber where Venia had spent his final days and spread them on the floor for the others to see.

'What is this nonsense?' Strigan asked. 'It's not even legible.'

'It's archaic Tristian,' Estevar corrected. 'One would have hoped a monk would be able to read the language in which the religious texts of his order were written.'

'The *Sacrificia Purgadis*,' Brother Agneta said, looming over the pages as if she longed to set fire to them. 'Banned by decree of the Cogneri.'

'Indeed,' Estevar agreed, 'a long-abandoned religious rite purported to imbue a single sinner with the crimes of his entire community. By giving the sacrifice over to a demon or devil, all the others are thus absolved.'

Mother Leogado, reluctant but intrigued, joined them. 'We've seen the evidence of that perverse ritual's effects. But it is one thing to invoke dark magics to transfigure a depraved and debauched monk into something approximating a demon, quite another to create a living god.'

Opening his notebook, he displayed the sketches he'd made of the sigil-covered male and female figures etched upon the walls of Venia's secret chamber. 'Sin has no more substance than holiness. But neither are they mere inclinations, to be conjured and banished like idle thoughts. Rather, both are manifestations of—'

'Faith,' Malezias said from where he crouched by the wall, hurling the word like an oath at them all. 'You speak of faith as if you understood its potency. You don't. None of you understand.'

'But Abbot Venia understood, didn't he?' Estevar asked.

Malezias sank in on himself, staring down at the floor between his feet. 'Aye, he understood,' he muttered.

'Perhaps someone could explain it to me?' Caeda said. Her voice was cold, spiritless. 'If I'm to judge this proceeding, I ought to understand the weapon used to commit the crime, shouldn't I?'

Strigan turned, his eyes widening in momentary surprise and confusion. 'Who the hell—? Oh, what shy little mouse has crept inside our hole? I have a little mouse that would dearly love to creep inside you—'

'Stop,' Estevar said, keeping a wary eye on Malezias, but the big man stayed where he was, showing no more emotion than Caeda herself. Perhaps he'd lost his faith at last.

'How did she get in here?' Mother Leogado demanded, drawing one of her two curved shortswords from the scabbard at her side. 'Speak true, girl, else I'll— Wait, I remember now.' She turned to Estevar, scowling as if her forgetfulness were his doing. 'You said you couldn't preside over the trial because you were prosecuting the case against us. We asked who else could serve as magistrate, and you chose her.'

'But she can't be here,' Brother Agneta protested, levelling her pistol at Caeda. 'She's dead. Venia killed her.'

The others stared in mute horror at the young woman sitting on a rock in the middle of the torchlit cavern. For the first time since Estevar had met her, she did indeed look like a ghost come to haunt them for their sins.

More howling erupted from the maze of tunnels outside, follow by the shrieking of iron gates being ripped from stone walls as Venia's demonic apostles made their way, slowly but surely, towards the prayer caves.

'I will not speak for anyone else,' Brother Agneta said, a tremor in her voice, the pistol shaking in her hand, 'but I find myself eager to learn how this trial is supposed to banish the devils who will soon be at our door.'

Estevar resumed his pacing, this time around the pages he'd arranged on the floor. 'Venia wondered the same thing. With his flock divided, squabbling over different interpretations of religious doctrine even as they abandoned the moral virtues upon which the abbey was founded, he deciphered the sigils of the *Purgadis* ritual, hoping to inscribe upon the flesh of a single individual the sins of the entire community, thus liberating Isola Sombra from its moral defects.'

'Me,' Caeda said quietly. 'You're talking about me. That's why he locked me up in the infirmary, strapped me to a table and dug those needles into my skin. The ink stank of blood and filth as he was drawing those awful symbols all over my—' She held up her arm, stared at the pale, unmarked flesh. 'How could it have washed away so completely after he threw me from the cliff?' Her eyes went to Malezias, who refused to meet her gaze. 'You told me the salt water washed most of them away, and you cleansed the rest from me – but you lied, didn't you?'

'Why would Abbot Venia not have spoken to the rest of us about his experiments if he was willing to go so far as to enact the *Purgadis* ritual for the first time in centuries?' Brother Agneta asked. Evidently, she had either forgotten or dismissed Caeda's presence once again. 'Strigan, Leogado and I had nearly as much support from the brethren as he did.'

Estevar retrieved the pages. 'The answer is simple enough: by the time he'd made his discovery, you'd split the brethren into factions. He tried to reconcile you all, but the Margrave of Someil's designs upon the island had become clear and Venia believed he had to prove his theories correct in order to forestall the takeover of the island.'

'As I've been saying for months!' Mother Leogado insisted. 'The margrave has long sought to conquer Isola Sombra—'

'Actually,' Estevar corrected her softly, 'Someil's generals and nobles refused to support his intended conquest, which is why he fell prey to the urgings of Sir Daven, a knight secretly working for someone else.'

'Who?' Agneta asked.

Estevar shrugged. 'Alas, I was unable to extract that testimony from Sir Daven before I killed him.'

'You *killed* a Knight of the March of Someil?' Strigan demanded, standing far too close to Estevar. 'We're the ones on trial and *our accuser* is a confessed murderer?'

'It seems to me that there is plenty of murder to go around,' Caeda observed from her rocky throne. 'Proceed, Eminence.'

'Ah, is that Caeda I see?' Strigan began, wiggling his hips. 'Have you come to—?'

'Pay attention, you idiot,' Brother Agneta said, pairing her injunction with a slap that sent the naked monk reeling. 'If you look at her every minute or so, the memory of her doesn't fade.'

Mother Leogado was staring at Caeda with the unflinching determination of a soldier wading onto a battlefield although outnumbered by the enemy a hundred to one. 'And why *do* we keep failing to remember her? Is this some consequence of the *Purgadis* ritual? Or are all ghosts so forgettable?'

Estevar looked at Caeda, saw that she wasn't ready for the answer and returned to the more mundane facts of the case. '*As* I was saying, the poisoned wine exacerbated your obsessions, leading you to retreat to your own corners of the abbey to plot against one another, even as you railed against your brethren plotting against you.'

'Not me,' Brother Agneta reminded him. 'I haven't drunk a drop in twenty years.' Her grip on her pistol was steady again. 'Nothing worse for the aim than shaking hands.'

'Alas, my dear, your particular form of paranoia is the product of your inquisitor's training and unpleasant disposition rather than any toxin.'

'I still don't understand,' Strigan complained, grabbing Estevar's notebook from his hand and staring uncomprehending at the illustrations inside. 'If Venia failed with Caeda, why did he then repeat his experiments on me?'

'Because the Trattari is wrong,' Malezias declared from his dark corner of the cavern, rising to his feet at last. 'Abbot Venia was never content with the prospect of purifying Isola Sombra so that whichever god was next reborn wouldn't be infected by our sins. He wanted to *create* a god – one who would live up to *his* expectations.

'That's why he meddled with the sigils,' Estevar explained, saddened by how easily altruism could be poisoned by pride. Venia unlocked secrets buried in the *Purgadis* texts by clerics too afraid of heresy charges to make them explicit, yet fearing that the true rites of creation might be needed to bring back the gods, should some would-be tyrant ever find the means to kill them.'

Caeda, too, rose from her seat. 'But if Venia wasn't trying to purge the brethren of their sins, then why did he—?'

But Malezias, no longer her adoring servant, walked towards her as he let his words fly like a thousand arrows to pierce her indifference towards him. 'You can't just write a few magic symbols on any idiot's skin and hope to produce a god.' He slammed a fist against his own chest. 'We are unworthy, all of us, and all of us would make unworthy gods. But Venia, he—'

The screeching howls were closer now, the approaching tide of death and devouring coming for them, but Malezias didn't appear to hear them. 'He chose a young woman from the village – she used to sneak into the abbey sometimes, stealing books to read, returning them a few days later. Venia caught her once, and rather than deny her intrusions, he allowed her to pepper him with questions about the theological inconsistencies of the holy books she'd taken. Venia told me . . .'

Malezias suddenly broke down, sobbing, his broad shoulders shaking. At last, he pulled himself together enough to continue, 'There she was, this strange, unapologetic lass who'd never even seen the inside of a schoolhouse, yet had somehow taught herself to read with more passion and curiosity than any of the religious scholars to ever come here.'

'Someone like Venia himself,' Agneta said softly, almost fondly. 'Curiosity was always his greatest sin.'

'Some would call it the greatest of virtues,' Estevar replied. 'The witness will please continue his testimony.'

Malezias clenched his fists at his sides. 'Oh, he was full of admiration for the girl – so much so that he trapped her inside the infirmary, tied her down and inscribed his perfected sigils upon her, keeping her there for days, refusing her food or water, telling her he would throw her into the sea unless she revealed herself as his goddess.'

They all turned to Caeda, who looked nothing at all like a goddess. Though it was dry in the cavern, her hair was soaked and matted to her face, her gown, which until then had always looked clean, was now drenched and filthy, clinging to a slender body that shook and shook and shook from a cold none of them could feel.

Strigan was staring at Malezias. 'How could you know all these details? Unless—'

'Venia didn't trust the rest of you,' Estevar put in. 'He feared the brethren of Isola Sombra had become so polarised in their beliefs that they would poison his experiment. So he approached a former monk who still lived in the village and convinced him there was a path to their mutual redemption.'

The fury in Malezias' eyes could have set fire to the sea itself. 'But he was *wrong*. His theories were nonsense – nothing but a fool's delusions. After his captive died of thirst and fright and loneliness, he made good on his promise and hurled her from the clifftop. But even then' – he brought up his hands, fingers curled as if he were about to claw out his own eyes, as if he, too, had seen that infamous painting of Hell – 'even then, he insisted the ritual would succeed, that she would come back, returned to us as a . . .' He left the final word unspoken.

'But you didn't believe him, did you?' Estevar asked.

There were shuffling footsteps outside the door now, the slow, tentative prowl of the predator come at last to devour its prey, yet cautious of entering its lair.

Malezias' upper lip curled. 'I took him from the abbey in broad daylight, convinced that if my intentions were wrong, someone would stop me.' He turned first to Strigan, then Agneta and finally to Leogado. 'He screamed out your names as I dragged him down into this very chamber. He screamed them over and over as I carved the very sigils with which he'd tortured Caeda into his flesh. And when I was done, I showed him the blade with which I was going to sever his head from his body. He screamed one last time, but not for mercy. All he wanted in his last moment of life was for me to bury his corpse far from Isola Sombra.'

'But you didn't,' Strigan said, gaping at him. 'You put him in the statuary.'

Malezias said grimly, 'I wanted the stench of his rotting corpse to foul the air of this place for ever. A suitable punishment for a liar and a murderer – but then . . .'

He began to weep again, shutting his eyes as if to keep the tears from escaping. 'Three days later, she walked out of the sea. At first, she didn't remember her name, or anything that had happened to her. She was so weak, but I knew – I *knew* that Venia had been right all along. I threw myself at her feet, begged forevermore to be the first and most loyal of her apostles, but she . . .'

'She thought you were a fool in love,' Estevar said gently. 'And then you wondered why she displayed no great gifts, granted no blessings, offered no redemption.'

'Why?' Malezias asked, dropping to his knees before her. 'Why wouldn't you save me, save all of us?'

'Who the hell are you talking about?' Strigan demanded. 'Who's this mysterious dead girl you keep talking about?'

Mother Leogado pointed to where Caeda stood, and when Strigan turned and noticed her again, slapped him across the face to save them all another of his lewd propositions.

Tentative, almost playful scratching came at the door, then hushed giggles from the other side. Brother Agneta raised both her pistols, determined to take at least two of the monstrosities down with her to Hell when the moment arrived.

'Before I die, Trattari,' the old inquisitor began, 'would you mind telling me why Venia's attempt to produce a god gave us a mildly irritating, inappropriately dressed, easily forgotten waif, whereas Malezias in a fit of pique seems to have created a God of Demons to devour us all?'

Estevar instinctively reached for his rapier, but stopped himself. The top third of the broken blade was probably still trapped between the upper ribs of one of the demons – not that any flourish of swordplay could hope to avert their doom this time. 'Abbot Venia's experiment had a crucial flaw. Gods were meant to be born of the faith – the aspirations – of an entire people. When the early Tristians were brought here as slaves, they shared desires so deep that the very ores that run beneath this island awoke to their needs: War to make them fierce, Craft to give them the means to fight, Death to their enemies, Coin to reward their victories, Love to give them purpose. But the monks of Isola Sombra were lost to themselves, both to the hallucinogenic toxins with which the Margrave of Someil had infected them and to their own petty theological disputes.'

'So, Venia's god was born not of faith, but of madness?' Mother Leogado asked, drawing her shortswords and taking up position next to Brother Agneta at the door, where the scratching was becoming more frantic, the giggling now howling in ecstatic anticipation. 'Why are you able to remember her so easily when the rest of us cannot?'

'She was given power, but not purpose,' Estevar answered. 'Ever since she returned to these shores, she's been unable to know herself. I alone among you remember her, for my faith is not in any god, but in seeking out the facts, no matter how dark they may be. Instinctively, she began assisting my investigation, unaware that what she was searching for was the mystery of her own being.'

'No,' Caeda said, coming to stand before him. 'I was searching for the strength to accept the truth.' That cold, emotionlessness look had fled from her face, replaced by trembling lips and streaming tears. 'I was born broken, wasn't I?'

Estevar bent down and kissed each cheek, tasting the salt water on his own lips. 'None of us is born broken, my dear, only with the burden of discovering who we might become, and what the world will demand of us.'

The door burst open, shards of wood flying through the air as the demons began to stream into the cavern, sniffing the air, convinced there was nothing for them to fear. Agneta fired her pistols, but now, perhaps armoured in the love of their new god, the demons were unharmed.

'The factions were disunited in all things,' Estevar told Caeda. 'They believed they were fighting over their faith, but their faith was gone, replaced by a singular conviction that the world was unworthy of the gods, so it must be destroyed before it could be redeemed.' He pointed to the demons. 'That is what *they* are, what Venia has become: the living embodiment of the desire to punish others for our own failings.'

The demons began to advance on them, this time marching in formation, just as Leogado's Trumpeters had attacked them.

Mother Leogado hurled one of her curved swords at them, the weapon spinning with an accuracy almost as remarkable as its complete lack of effect when it struck its target.

'What now?' Leogado asked, turning to Estevar. 'This is the outcome of your little trial? You tell us we're all to blame and then we die?'

He ignored her, speaking only to Caeda. 'I care nothing for gods or demons,' he told her. 'The facts of this case couldn't be simpler. A girl was murdered; the particularities of her death caused the crime to transcend the barriers that separate human beings from their gods. You, my dear, must now pass judgment on us all.'

Caeda stopped crying, straightened her back, smoothed her matted red hair and spoke with utmost care and heartrending regret. 'I'm sorry, my Cantor. If it is my ruling that governs this trial, then the verdict must be . . . *guilty*.'

The demons halted their advance to clap and cheer, roaring with delight, elbowing each other like drunks at a tavern sharing a rude joke.

'Ah,' said Estevar, smiling at her, 'but you see, Piccolo, when a travelling magistrate – particularly one of the legendary sword-wielding Greatcoats – renders a verdict, they must sometimes duel to enforce their ruling.'

'How?' she asked, looking towards the curved ceiling of the prayer cave as if she could see through it to the courtyard above. 'Venia's become the god. I'm just a dead girl.'

He took her by the shoulders, steadying her. 'Listen to me, Piccolo. What was once the Abbot of Isola Sombra, whatever he has now become, usurps the authority vested not in him, but *in you*. Venia's obsession turned to madness, and that madness begat mayhem and murder, but one thing I have found about this strange little country of yours?'

He waited for her eyes to return to his, and shook her gently when they didn't. The demons crept closer to listen, enthralled by Estevar's last, futile effort.

'What?' Caeda asked him, her body frail in his hands, her tone listless. 'What is so fascinating to you about this horrid country that you never returned to your own?'

Estevar grinned. 'Always, even in their worst, their clumsiest depravities, the people of this land can't help but turn failure into hope.

And Venia, for all his many failings, performed one perfect, sublime, redeeming act. He chose *you* before himself. Now, what do you think about that, *Eminence*?'

Without waiting for an answer, he let go of her, drew his broken-bladed rapier and walked past Strigan, Leogado and Agneta to face the demons. Imperious came to his side. Estevar patted the mule's head affectionately, and in return, Imperious tried to bite him.

'The trial is ended, the verdict rendered. If I am to die, if Hell shall henceforth tread the judicial circuits that were once mine to walk, I will do so with a sword in my hand, a friend at my side and a smile on my face.' He took up the narrow-footed guard he preferred when fencing in enclosed spaces. 'Come, devils; I am for you.'

At first, there was nothing. The demons performed their usual mocking antics, pretending to wipe tears from eyes that could shed none, save in the manifold joys of enacting torture and torment. Then, noting his rapier, they began tugging on each other's fingers, pulling them longer and longer until each pale, bony hand was a quintet of stilettos.

Estevar was feeling distinctly unsteady on his feet and wondered whether perhaps he would collapse from fever or fear before the demons could get to him – then he noticed a similar tremor in Imperious and realised there was a subtle, rumbling vibration coming from the stone floor, like sitting in a carriage rolling down a cobbled street. The shaking intensified and fragments of stone began tumbling from the walls and ceiling. Next came the roar of thunder – which was when he heard the gasps coming from behind him.

Estevar turned to see Mother Leogado, Strigan and Brother Agneta staring up at Caeda, who was floating above the ground, her arms outstretched, wild red hair streaming in an unseen wind.

Another crack of thunder was this time accompanied by a burst of jagged light that pierced the ceiling to wrap itself like a lover's arms around Caeda.

'The *lightning*,' Brother Agneta shouted into the deafening gale blowing through the underground tunnels, sending even the demons reeling off-balance. 'She's drawing it into herself!'

'Look!' Strigan said, pointing to the floor where tiny flakes of gleaming ore erupted from newly formed fissures in the rock, attaching themselves to Caeda, spreading out over her skin, encasing her in shimmering armour.

Estevar gazed up at her in awe, but also with trepidation, for as much as he had come to love this enigmatic, curious young woman, Caeda carried within her the torments of a troubled life and a bitterly unjust death. And through this trial that she had never wanted, he had pushed her to abandon the restraints of mortality, to take for herself a godhood shaped not by faith, but by chaos.

'She's saying something,' Brother Agneta shouted, the inquisitor's ageing eyes narrowing as if trying to read her lips. 'I can't make it out over the wind.'

Estevar stepped closer to the young woman floating above the ground. Her entire body was now covered in shimmery flecks so that she might have been a statue carved from raw metals, save that her lips were moving.

'Please,' Estevar said, 'I can't hear you, Piccolo.'

When she spoke again, it was with no greater volume, but he heard every word.

'What did she say?' Mother Leogado asked.

Lightning exploded once more, not from the skies above Isola Sombra, but from inside the prayer cave itself. The blinding eruption split apart into jagged strands of white fire that darted past Estevar and the others, striking the demons one by one, their cries of glee turning to surprised disbelief, only to be silenced by the endless booming thunder – until the thick, leathery skin and hideous bony protrusions were gone, leaving behind only the bodies of dead monks, their humanity restored at the cost of their lives.

Estevar turned back to the living and shouted at the top of his voice the words Caeda had uttered to him.

'Run!' he cried. 'Run, and do not stop until the sea has taken you!'

CHAPTER 43

THE JUDICIAL DUEL

Ignoring his injuries and exhaustion, Estevar fled alongside Imperious, racing through the tunnels and back up the slope to the door to the Venerance Tower, where Strigan had held court with his followers. That vast, circular chamber was empty now, save for the corpses of Strigan's followers strewn across the floor, the tattooed sigils now gone from their bodies.

Imperious neighed anxiously, his teeth nipping at the elbow of Estevar's greatcoat.

'Of course, you are quite right, my friend. The time for such investigations has passed us by now, however much it irks me to leave such intriguing questions unanswered.'

Man and mule ran out the doors of the tower, pounded down the steps and onto the long avenue beneath the cloister, where the colonnades were already collapsing.

'I've never seen anything like this,' Mother Leogado shouted. She had followed him, while Strigan and Brother Agneta had charted their own courses out of the tunnels.

Malezias had remained behind, insisting despite Estevar's urging that they were all condemned to die and he would do so at the side of the god he'd loved even when she was a mere mortal like himself.

The roiling black clouds gleamed like onyx as they spat lightning across the courtyard, the trails of light the jagged bars of a prison being built all around them. Torrents of rain fell upon the abbey's courtyard, turning hard ground into treacherous mud, tearing apart the flagstones.

In a sky devoid of stars, the only light came from the blue eyes of a god who looked down upon his unwilling subjects with disgust. Estevar could think of only one word to name the deity coming into being through Abbot Venia's own transgressions and those of his followers.

'Abomination,' Estevar whispered.

No one could have heard him over the hurricane winds rushing through the abbey, or the cracking of the cloister's stone roof, and yet the god smiled down at him anyway, pleased to have found his name, and when he spoke it from his own celestial lips, the bodies of dead monks began to twist and mangle themselves once more, rising up to praise their beloved god for his promise of a thousand different pleasures awaiting them: one for each cruelty they inflicted upon every sinner.

And there were so very many sinners to punish.

'Saints,' Mother Leogado swore. 'What good was that trial of yours if this is what awaits humanity?'

'You should have more faith,' Estevar told her, holding Imperious' reins tight to keep the mule from charging at the awakening demons.

'I thought you didn't worship any gods, only your laws.'

'Humanity,' he corrected her. 'The laws I serve come from mortal men and women, and it is in them that you monks ought to have more faith.'

The tremors shaking the ground worsened, and Mother Leogado pointed to the top of the Venerance Tower where massive stone blocks had begun to tumble from the ramparts. The roof gave way, and rising from it was a small, slender figure in armour fashioned of glittering fragments in a dozen different hues of silver and copper.

'There,' Estevar whispered. 'There is my faith.'

The young woman once known as Caeda Branwen came to face the entity that had been Abbot Venia, who had been responsible for both her death and her rebirth. For a moment, Estevar wondered whether perhaps the two would form the beginnings of a new pantheon to rule over the faithful of Tristia – but even among gods, it appeared, some grudges were hard to forgive. The two deities waged war upon one another, each drawing unto themselves pieces of the unnatural storms that had birthed them, neither caring that the wounds they inflicted on one another were nothing compared to the havoc being wreaked upon the island below.

'I believe I shall take my chances with the sea,' Mother Leogado said.

'On this, we are in agreement,' Estevar replied. He tugged on Imperious' reins to lead him across the treacherous terrain ahead, but the mule, braying angrily, wouldn't budge. It took a moment to realise Imperious was waiting for him to mount.

'Come,' Estevar said, extending a hand backwards to Mother Leogado as he prepared to clamber onto Imperious' back. 'Your added weight won't slow him down.'

'Alas, yours will, and that is a risk I cannot afford.'

Hearing the edge to her voice, he turned to see the pistol aimed at his chest. So Brother Agneta hadn't been the only monk hiding such weapons in the abbey, and Leogado had saved hers for the moment when it would yield the most benefit.

'Whoever survives among the brethren will need a leader to guide them,' she said without a trace of remorse. 'I won't abandon my duty to them, even if it demands the sacrifice of one whom I would have hoped to call a friend.'

'I would urge you to reconsider, Madam.'

Her finger tightened fractionally but visibly around the trigger. 'And I would urge you to step back.'

Estevar spread his hands wide and did as she bade him, saying only, 'Be kind to him, for as long as he'll have you.'

She smiled, patting Imperious' flank before leaping onto his back with the practised ease of an experienced horsewoman. 'I doubt there's a finer mount in all of Tristia. I shall never treat him as anything less.' Taking the reins in her free hand, she said, 'Farewell, Estevar Borros. I hope you make it out of this madness alive. If you do, come and find me. You'd make a fine captain.'

'May your journey be both safe and swift,' Estevar waved to her, stumbling as the abbey's foundations began to collapse beneath his feet.

Mother Leogado kicked her heels into Imperious' sides, and like the majestic steed she had praised him for being, he leapt into motion, bolting ten feet across the path before skidding to such an abrupt halt that his rider went flying head over heels to slam into the crumbling flagstones.

Estevar ran to her, being careful where he stepped to avoid trapping his heels in the widening crevices. He knelt beside her, but she was unconscious, blood matting the short grey hair at the back of her head.

'Alas, Madam, the wishes of mere magistrates rarely hold sway over the unruly natures of cantankerous mules.'

He took the general into his arms, grunting from the pain of too many untreated injuries, and lifted her onto Imperious' back before mounting up himself. 'I know, I know,' he said in response to the mule's braying snarl, 'but justice can be merciful once in a while.' He leaned over the unconscious Leogado to whisper in the mule's ear, 'Now, my friend, show the gods themselves that the Greatcoats die harder than most, and never, ever kneel, not even when Death demands it.'

With a burst of speed that forced Estevar to cling onto Mother Leoga-do's unconscious body lest she fall by the wayside, Imperious galloped madly from the cloister, twisting and leaping this way and that through the collapsing abbey.

Estevar glanced up at the blackened sky where his Piccolo, as slight as a silver flute, fought against a bloated god ten times her size. He had no conception of the mystical mechanics driving the battle or what esoteric forces infused their blows, only that she looked so terribly small, and in dire need of a friend.

Show them, my Piccolo, he told her silently, repeating the words he'd whispered to Imperious, *show the gods themselves that the Greatcoats die harder than most, and never, ever kneel.*

Onwards they rode, clouds of dust rising from the ruins in defiance of the lashing rain, blinding Estevar until he could no longer keep track of all the perils menacing their escape. He let go of the reins and closed his eyes to keep from leading Imperious astray, trusting instead to the mule's judgement of where to leap and when to turn.

Each second felt like hours, with the thunder booming all around them. Bolts of lightning left the air sizzling, filled with the stench of burnt flesh and scorched stone. He could feel the mule fighting for every pace. The dust and smoke forced him to keep his eyes closed still, but he chanced a glance when they passed through the archway and began their desperate skidding descent down the spiral road and through the abandoned village.

The mule's hooves slipped on the slick cobbles as the rains beat down upon them and all Estevar could do was cling onto the unconscious Mother Leogado and pat Imperious' neck now and then, whispering what encouragement he could, shedding tears of unbridled admiration. Of all the wonders Estevar had witnessed upon this island, none was greater than his mule's courage and daring nimbleness.

When suddenly they came to a halt, Estevar forced open his eyes once more, to behold the inevitable end of their escape. Surprisingly, even as he prepared to meet his doom, he found himself saying, 'I never thought to witness such terrible beauty.'

They had reached the edge of the rocky shore, the causeway that would have been their only avenue of escape still flooded and unpassable. The lightning that had turned the abbey to rubble was now striking the waters surrounding Isola Sombra, sizzling the ocean itself. Half a mile over the drowned causeway, Estevar could make out the flashes that were setting alight the Margrave of Someil's magnificent pavilions.

Estevar dismounted and wrapped his arms around the mule's neck, waiting for the end to come.

'By all the gods,' he heard Brother Agneta cry out, and turned to see the elderly inquisitor supporting herself against Strigan's arm, followed by dozens of those monks not slain by demons or some other calamity, who came rushing down to the shore behind them.

'Is there a chance of swimming across?' Strigan asked as they reached the water's edge.

'I do not believe so,' Estevar replied. 'Too much lightning is striking the channel – the water itself is boiling.'

'Then we're dead,' Brother Agneta said, sitting down on a rock. 'I suppose my old masters who recruited me into the Cogneri were right: the gods *do* favour vengeance over mercy.'

A voice drifted down to them from above – a voice so familiar and utterly human as to defy what she had become. 'We might think more kindly of you were you not such terrible people,' she said.

Estevar looked up, and there, borne by the wind, was the young woman who'd been known in life as Caeda, his Piccolo. The shimmering, rocky armour no longer encased her, but the flecks of sacred ore were still there, gleaming just beneath her skin. She floated thirty feet above them, her red hair swirling in the wind like a fiery halo. There was a fierce joy bursting from her, a song as yet unsung, a goddess awakening at last.

'Well?' she asked, looking down at Estevar. 'Didn't I say something to you about running for your life?'

'I took it more as suggestion than divine edict,' he replied.

'You do that a lot.'

He shrugged. 'Greatcoats make poor soldiers, I'm afraid, and even worse worshippers.' Gazing up across the cloud-covered sky, he asked, 'Need we fear the imminent return of the God of Abominations?'

She drifted in the wind and rain, then came back towards him. 'Only me, I'm afraid.'

The tremors shaking apart the island were worsening, slabs of stone breaking from the clifftop to tumble down towards the shore. The survivors were caught between an avalanche of falling rocks and a boiling sea waiting to drown them beneath its depths.

'Oh, must I do everything myself?' Caeda asked. She grinned mischievously.

The next rumbling that shook the shore came from the half-mile strait separating the island from the mainland. The surface of the water bubbled up, then sandy rock and mud broke through to form a flattened ridge. The monks, drenched by the rain, their robes in tatters, cheered with relief as they raced across the bridge Caeda had summoned to allow their escape.

Estevar handed the unconscious general into the arms of two of her yellow-robed followers, waiting with Imperious until the last of them had escaped. As a magistrate, he had one final duty to perform before the island sank into the sea.

'Thus ends the trial of Isola Sombra,' he said, and together with Imperious, set off across the causeway, the last living beings to have trod upon that once holiest of isles.

EPILOGUE

EPILOGUE

CHAPTER 44

A MAGISTRATE
AND HIS MULE

When dawn rose upon the waters near the western shores of the Duchy of Baern, the ocean was slumbering like a newborn babe. The Margrave of Someil's forces had fled, the former monks of Isola Sombra already begun the long pilgrimage back to their homes, or perhaps to some new place to seek the divine. If any had doubted the gods would return to Tristia, their belief was now restored. Their faith, however – that would be a different matter altogether.

Estevar stood at the water's edge, listening as Imperious munched on a patch of muddy grass he'd taken a liking to. He knew he should begin the journey home to Aramor, but whether because his wounds ached or because he couldn't imagine how he was going to explain to the First Cantor that he'd gone to the Abbey of Isola Sombra to settle a petty theological dispute between monks and left it sunken beneath the sea, he couldn't find the will to leave. The truth, of course, lay in neither of those conundra, but in the far simpler dilemma of not knowing how to say his goodbyes.

Venia, we were never more than acquaintances, you and I, and for the first time, I regret that oversight. We shared a fascination for the occult, but you abandoned the self-restraint demanded of magistrates and priests alike. Perhaps if I'd embraced your offers of friendship, I might have reminded you that ours is not to shape the world according to our desires, but to defend those who would be powerless against such tyrants.

Estevar unbuttoned his coat and reached inside for his notebook with the sketches of Venia's complex sequences of sigils. He tore out those pages and tossed them into the sea. Should he ever again come across a copy of the *Sacrificia Purgadis*, he might find himself hard-pressed not to violate the King's Law against the destruction of books.

As the gentle currents engulfed the pages, Estevar contemplated a small prayer. He'd never been a religious person and his days on the now-sunken island of Isola Sombra had not inclined him to piety. Yet there was one particular deity to whom he dearly wished he could be closer.

'Alas,' he said to Imperious, who had nearly finished devouring his little patch of grass, 'she will have all but forgotten us by now.'

'Who dares blaspheme so against the divine?' demanded a youthful and entirely too irreverent voice behind him.

Caeda was looking very much like a pretty, if otherwise unremark-able young woman. She'd even, he noted, found some clothes better suited to the weather and to modesty. The hem of the storm-grey coat trailed behind her, picked up by the breeze. Estevar wondered whether she'd recovered it from some abandoned tailor's shop on the island or manifested it through divine will.

'Well?' she asked. 'Will you not kneel before your god?'

'You promised never to ask that of me,' he reminded her. 'In the infirmary, remember? Besides, you should know by now that Greatcoats don't kneel to anyone.'

She shot him a cross look. 'I haven't decided how vengeful a deity I'm going to be, Estevar. Don't you think you ought to be a little more contrite when faced with a god who could strike you down at a whim?'

He walked up to her, boldly took her hand, raised it to his lips and kissed it. 'As a matter of fact, that is precisely when it's most important *not* to kneel.'

She laughed, taking her hand away. 'You are a mad devil, Estevar, and given the creatures you and I have encountered, that's saying something.'

'How do you feel?' he asked.

'Strange . . . though I'm not sure how a god is supposed to feel. When I fought the abomination that Venia had become, the blows weren't physical – not really. It was more like we were . . . tearing away from one another the faith from which we were both made. After a while, he just . . . collapsed in on himself. The forces of his creation had nowhere to return to because the island was breaking apart, obliterating the veins of mystical ore. Now what remains of all that faith is . . . in me.

She hugged herself, which Estevar found to be a most disquieting expression of anxiousness in a being imbued with the power of two gods.

'I'm ill-formed, Estevar,' she said at last. 'I should never have been brought into being. It should have been someone else. Someone more—'

'No,' he said, cutting her off, because no matter who or what she was now, Estevar Borros remained a Greatcoat, and it was not his habit to allow untruths to be spoken in his presence. 'Whatever Venia's faults and crimes, despite the madness and despair that plagued him, he made one decision for which I believe with all my heart this country will forever be grateful. He chose *you*, Caeda. Out of all the priests, monks, knights and scholars he met, some part of him sensed that the god we needed should come from the most curious, wild, free – the most *human* – person he'd ever met.'

The new god tried not to smile, but she couldn't keep the gleam of amusement from her eyes. 'You really are a soppy old romantic, aren't you?'

'Indeed.' He patted his side, where his broken rapier was sheathed. 'And I shall eagerly await any god or saint who says otherwise in the duelling circle at their pleasure.'

'Careful what you wish for,' she said. 'I can't hold onto the rest of this godly essence I took from Venia forever.' Her expression turned mischievous as she snapped her fingers and a bolt of lightning appeared out of the blue sky to strike the ground barely ten feet away from them. 'Though a most appealing – one might argue, divinely inspired – idea is coming to me as to its bequeathment.'

'I am content in my current profession, Madam.'

'Oh, I wasn't thinking about you, Estevar. You're a lovely fellow, and an outstanding teacher in the art of investigation, but you'd make a terribly boring god.'

'Well, no more storms, at least, if you please,' Estevar said, walking over to Imperious to comfort the terrified beast. 'My faithful companion has had rather a rough introduction to the life of a Greatcoat.'

'Forgive me, brave Imperious,' Caeda apologised, blowing the mule a kiss. He brayed angrily in response and she laughed again. 'How am I supposed to rule over my worshippers when I can't even get a truculent mule to genuflect before me!'

'Have you decided on your ...' Estevar fumbled for the word. 'I suppose, your dominion?'

Caeda brushed an unruly lock of red hair from her forehead. 'You mean, do I intend to be the God of Storms, or maybe Vengeance or Particularly Destructive Temper Tantrums?'

'That's one way of putting it, yes.'

'I'm not sure. Perhaps I'll meet some of those other gods you spoke about and they can help me.' She looked at him sternly. 'When you allowed me to be your partner – not at the beginning, but after you'd figured out I wasn't a ghost – did you encourage me because you'd hoped I'd become the God of Intriguing Investigations or Elusive Enigmas or something like that?'

Estevar took hold of the lapels of his leather greatcoat and gave her his most stern *harrumph*. 'Madam, I will remind you that I am a magistrate and as such judge matters as I find them. I do not stick my thumb on the scale to suit my own desires.' He winked at her. 'However, if you *did* happen to become the God of Judicial Enquiries, it would not entirely displease me.'

Her laugh came and went, quick as a gust of wind. The next thing he knew, Caeda was launching herself into his arms and reaching around him in a desperate hug. 'Why couldn't I have stayed a normal girl, Estevar? Or even a ghost, for that matter? I could have accompanied you and Imperious around the country, haunting you and dispensing enigmatic advice that never made sense until the very end when suddenly it helped you solve your cases.'

He wrapped his arms around her, aware both of how human she felt and yet of the undeniable fact that she was not and never would be again. 'Alas, I suspect you'll find more worthy subjects for your divine attention than a fat, eccentric magistrate and his ill-tempered mule.'

She pulled away from him, looking up into his eyes. 'I worry about you, Estevar. You're terribly clever, but a little clumsy – and far too reckless. Also, you insist on making speeches at inappropriate times, such as when a horde of demons is about to tear you to bits. Who's going to protect you when I'm not around?'

Estevar reached out a hand to pat Imperious' neck. 'Fear not, my dear, for I am well looked after in that regard.'

She smiled. 'I must admit, Imperious is an outstanding mule.'

'A *Great*mule,' Estevar corrected.

Caeda pushed him out of the way, then leaned over and kissed Imperious on the forehead before whispering something into his ear. The mule suddenly perked up, snorting at her.

'What did you say to him?' Estevar asked.

She stood up on her tiptoes and kissed Estevar on the cheek. 'You'll find out,' she said mysteriously.

Sensing himself dismissed, Estevar mounted on Imperious' back and nudged him towards the path that would bring them to the trade road and from there to The King's Way that led two hundred miles northeast to Aramor.

He'd almost thought they were alone again when he heard her call out to him.

'Estevar?'

He gave a gentle tug on the reins but did not turn. 'Yes?'

With a distinctly smug tone, she said, 'I may not know what kind of god am I am yet, but I do believe I've decided on a name. Would you like to know what it is?'

Estevar didn't answer at first. His gaze was drawn to the dark clouds appearing in the distance over the mainland. Sir Daven's dire insinuations of an unknown shadowy cabal preparing to wrest Tristia from its people was adding a chill to the already cool air. The storms that had brought chaos and ruin to the Abbey of Isola Sombra hadn't truly ended. Instead, they were spreading all across his adopted country. Soon, he and the rest of the Greatcoats would have to face those storms, and they would have a devil of a time doing so with naught but a sword in hand and a song of justice on their lips.

So it was with considerable bemusement that Estevar Valejan Duerisi Borros, sometimes called the King's Crucible, found himself grinning as he gave Imperious a gentle nudge and shouted at the top of his lungs, 'Piccolo!'

The mule set off at a gallop that dared the west wind itself to keep up with them.

ACKNOWLEDGEMENTS

THE RELIGIOUS ORDERS
OF TRISTIA

One of the torments afflicting fantasy authors is the need to both create a rich and detailed world into which we set our stories and then, inevitably, having to cut many of those details from the book so as not to inundate the reader with encyclopaedic trivia.

An equally tragic fate awaits the acknowledgements sections of novels because, after all, who wants to read a long list of names when they could be moving on to the book?

Readers of my novels will be familiar with my own solution to these dual dilemmas, which is to acknowledge the many wonderful people who helped bring the story to bookstore shelves inside an informal appendix detailing one aspect of the world in which it was set.

Tristia has a rather odd religious history, filled with individuals whose faith in their shifting pantheon of deities is often overshadowed by their particular church's more secular ambitions. Here, then, are the Religious Orders of Tristia – along with the names of a few individuals who would've brought greater rectitude to those roles than the characters we tend to meet in *Crucible of Chaos*.

The Venerati Magni

Preachers come in two varieties in Tristia: those who preach to the nobility and those who preach to the common folk. This long-standing duality has proved to be essential to the success of the clergy. After all, the aristocracy rarely appreciate lengthy sermons about the virtues of poverty.

There are fewer and fewer aristocrats in the publishing industry these days, but those who are can determine a book's fate as surely as that of a convict before a magistrate. That's why one should always have a good Venerati Magni preaching on one's behalf.

Jon Wood of RCW Literary, many thanks for putting this deal together. One day I promise I'll make you some actual money.

Heather Adams of HMA Literary, without whom no one would have ever heard of the Greatcoats.

Anne Perry of Quercus Books, for even high-powered publishing directors have to passionately preach about a book's virtues to get it through an acquisitions committee. Thanks for giving Estevar a home at Quercus!

The Venerati Ignobli

Some might presume the Venerati Ingobli to be of lower status than the Venerati Magni – after all, the Ingobli rarely preach inside palaces, nor do they wear expensive vestments or get invited to all the best balls and revels. But it's the Venerati Ignobli to whom the many look for guidance, and thus do these passionate preachers wield a great deal more power . . . for good or for evil.

With so many books to choose from, readers turn more and more to fans of fantasy fiction like themselves for guidance on what to read next. I'm eternally grateful to the many librarians, booksellers, book bloggers, tubers, TikTokers and all the rest who so kindly take time to share the Greatcoats with new readers.

Special thanks to:

Jade of Jadeyraereads, whom I finally met properly at ComicCon in London, and who is just as delightful in person as on her excellent YouTube channel.

Allen Walker of the Library of Allenxandria, whom I haven't yet met in person, but we shall find a way to rectify this injustice one day!

The Deators

Rarest of all the religious orders are the Deators, who claim to channel the voice of the gods themselves, which tends to get them beheaded with alarming frequency.

Every author secretly wishes they had a Deator at their side, whispering to them which chapters were divinely sanctioned by the Gods of Fiction and which ones must be hastily banished to the pits of literary hell. Fortunately for me, I've never lacked for that particular holy voice.

Jo Fletcher, my favourite literary collaborator, insightful muse and slasher of unsightly sentences. Also, the only editor I've ever met who actually claims to speak for the gods.

Christina de Castell makes no claims about speaking for the gods, but her opinions of a manuscript have the same effect on me, so she's clearly channelling some kind of mighty spirit.

The Cogneri

If secular crimes against fallible human beings are worthy of being investigated and judged by the King's Order of Travelling Magistrates, then who prosecutes crimes against the religious dictates of the gods? Are deities somehow unworthy of legal protections? Thus are the Cogneri empowered to pursue heretics and apostates whose crimes would otherwise debase the theological principles of Tristia into nonsensical gibberish.

As a frequent committer of heretical literary acts, I'm eternally grateful to the editors and proofreaders who seek out my every misspelling, my unconscionable use of commas and my propensity for word repetition.

Lauren Campbell, author assistant and hunter of blasphemous continuity errors.

Ross Jamieson, proof-reader and crime-scene investigator of the many errors that I no doubt introduced into the final draft of the novel.

The Admorteo

Contrary to the many scurrilous rumours spread by the ignorant (probably those damnable, irreligious Greatcoats), the Cogneri do not torture their suspects. This shameful and degrading task they leave to the Admorteo, who consider themselves the noblest of the holy orders, for not only do they extract the truth from lying tongues, but their agonising ministrations are well known for inducing even the most blasphemous of heathens to pray earnestly for forgiveness from the gods.

I've never read the Geneva Conventions in their entirety, but I'm fairly sure that somewhere in the fine print they must list the tearing apart of a novel by other authors to be a form of torture that should be banned by all civilised nations. If only it wasn't so damned helpful . . .

Matt Toner, Kristi Charis and Peter Darbyshire spent twelve weeks surgically poking holes in the first draft of this book, spotting incongruities and slow spots, but also identifying new areas for Estevar to explore that made the final book much, much better.

Andy Peloquin graciously took time out from writing another of his hit novels to read the manuscript and find three areas to bring more life to the story.

The Fideri

By both law and tradition, religious sects are forbidden from gathering armies. And yet, what church can long survive without champions ready to ride into battle to protect them? The Fideri, or Church Knights, as they're sometimes known, are the armoured paragons of virtue who wield sword and shield in the defence of priests, monks and other holy persons whose devotion forbids them the use of weapons.

The publication of a novel sometimes feels like sitting back and watching an entire army go into battle. Many thanks to the following paladins for fighting on behalf of this particular book.

Gaby Puleston-Vaudrey, patient and thoughtful Assistant Editor at Jo Fletcher Books, thanks for making sure this one could achieve its remarkably tight timeline!

Ella Patel, publicist extraordinaire and an excellent person to wander around London bookshops with.

Mickey Mickelson, my personal publicist, who does a lot of work but never seems to charge me very much for it. Thanks, Mickey!

Lipfon Tang, marketer magician leading the charge to make *Crucible* a hit in the UK.

Rachael Humm, James Whitacker, Amanda Harkness and Tayla Monturio for bringing the book to North American shores.

Joe Jameson, one of the truly great audiobook narrators out there. Thanks for yet again lending your talents to my books!

Jessica Leigh Clark-Bojin, Art Director for the book cover and the sigils.

Miblart, fabulous cover designers who executed marvellously on my vaguely worded brief.

Mike Shackle, without whose sage advice and kindly introduction this book might not have found such a lovely special edition hardback.

Matt of the Broken Binding, a thousand thank-yous for giving *Crucible* a gorgeous special edition hardback!

The Quaesti

With six gods to choose from, not all the faithful bind themselves to the service of a single deity so easily. The Quaesti, clad in simple grey robes and travelling the land in search of their calling, are perhaps the truest and most devout of all the orders.

Much is made of fandom these days and whether they represent faithful guardians of fictional story worlds or toxic invaders colonising one entertainment landscape after another and promptly deciding whom to exile first. For myself, I've always found more common ground with the literary wanderers: curious questi always exploring new books to read, to enjoy, to share, and then . . . to let go in search of the next.

My profound gratitude to the thousands and thousands of readers who keep finding my books and recommending them to family and friends, and in doing so, keep the Greatcoats riding off into new adventures!

COURT OF SHADOWS BOOK 1

PLAY OF SHADOWS

SEBASTIEN
DE CASTELL

Coming March 2024

Also by Sebastien de Castell

THE GREATCOATS SERIES

Traitor's Blade
Knight's Shadow
Saint's Blood
Tyrant's Throne

THE COURT OF SHADOWS SERIES

Prelude: Crucible of Chaos
Play of Shadows (March 2024)
Our Lady of Blades (March 2025)

THE SPELLSLINGER SERIES

Spellslinger
Shadowblack
Charmcaster
Soulbinder
Queenslayer
Crownbreaker
Way of the Argosi
Fall of the Argosi
Fate of the Argosi

The Malevolent Seven